THE MANY DEATHS OF
THE FIREFLY BROTHERS

Also by Thomas Mullen

The Last Town on Earth

For my parents,
brothers, and sister

It all began when they died.

No one I spoke to was entirely sure when they were first called "the Fire-fly Brothers," or why the phrase stuck. A play on the Firesons' name, or an initial mispronunciation embossed into permanence by the papers? Or perhaps a reference to how the brothers always seemed to vanish from the authorities' gaze, only to reappear so very far from their pursuers. As if they were a tiny piece of magic, an otherworldly glow, misplaced in our dark and mundane world.

But what was magic, and what mundane, in those insane times? Jobs you'd worked for two decades vanished. Factories that had stood tall for lifetimes went vacant, were scavenged for scrap, and collapsed. Life savings evaporated, sometimes in a single day. In our once fertile heartland, dry winds blew with the power and rage of untold stories accidentally left out of ancient texts, returning with a vengeance, demanding to be heard. Men disappeared, some scribbling sad notes for their wives, others leaving behind nothing, as if they'd never lived there at all. The reality we'd all believed in, so fervently and vividly, was revealed to be nothing but a trick of our imagination, or someone else's, some collective mirage whose power to entrance us had suddenly and irrevocably failed.

What the hell had happened? What had we done to ourselves? The looks I saw on people's faces. The shock of it all. Capitalism had failed; democracy was a sad joke. Our country's very way of life was at death's door, and everyone had a different theory of what would rise up to take its place. I saw the prophets on the soapboxes, spinning their own stories, trying to wring some moral lesson out of the chaos. Or the movies and pulps, hoping to distill the pain into entertainment. Or the next round of politicians, assuring us they were not afflicted by the same lack of vision as their predecessors. But I didn't believe them. Or, rather, I believed everything, because so much had changed so fast that anything seemed possible. Anything was *possible—you moved about cautiously and glanced at the sky as if expecting part of it to land on top of you.*

In the midst of it all were the Firefly Brothers.

They were already worshipped during their bank-robbing spree between the spring of '33 and July of '34. They were already celebrities—heroes or villains, depending on one's position on the ever-shifting seesaw of the times—indistinguishable in fact from the many folktales chorusing around them. But they became so much more during a two-week spell in August of 1934, starting with the night they died. The night they died for the first time.

THE FIRST DEATH
OF THE
FIREFLY BROTHERS

I.

He was a man well accustomed to waking up in unorthodox positions and in all manner of settings. He'd slept on floors, in the pillowless crevices of old couch frames, amid the nettles of haylofts, against the steering wheels of parked cars. Whether it was stationary or in motion, Jason Fireson could sleep on it: he'd snoozed on buses, phaetons, boxcars. He'd nodded off standing up, sitting down, falling over.

But this was something new.

He didn't know what he was lying on at first. He knew only that he was cold, that his skin was touching metal, and that he was naked. A thin sheet was pulled halfway up his chest.

He had suffered more than his share of automobile accidents and he was familiar with the awful feeling the following mornings. This was worse. He sat up gradually, the muscles and tendons of his neck and arms achingly stiff. He thought that it would have been difficult to imagine being any more sore without being dead.

He inhaled. He was accustomed as well to waking to all nature of scents—to animals in the barn below, or unwashed criminals sweating in a cramped room, or Darcy's occasional and disastrous breakfasts. But this was a strange, bitter vapor trying in vain to mask more human evidence of body odor, urine, and blood. The room was brightly lit, two overhead lights and desk lamps on either side casting their jaundiced glow. He looked to his left and saw cruel medical implements lying on a narrow metal table, some of them wrapped in gauze or cloth and all of them lying in a pool of dried blood. A hospital room, then. He'd never woken up in one of those before, so add that to the list. It was an unusual hospital, and his eyes took stock of the various items his physicians had left behind. On the same table as those grisly tools was a camera and its tall flash, an empty pack of cigarettes, and an overflowing ashtray.

One of the lamps flickered on and off every few seconds. Heavy footsteps followed invisible paths above the ceiling. He could taste the memory of blood in the back of his throat, and when he swallowed he nearly gagged at the dryness.

The tiled floor was filthy, as if his physicians moonlighted as hog farmers and had tracked mud throughout the sick ward. Ringing the room at waist level was a narrow counter, and in the corner a large radio was precariously balanced on it, the announcer's smooth voice earnestly recounting the latest WPA project. Most alarming was the policeman's cap hanging from a hook on the back of a door, framed photographs of unsmiling officers haunting three different walls, and, on the wall behind his bed, the portrait of what Jason figured for a governor—guys with jowls like that just had to be governors—glaring at him like a corpulent god.

He noticed that the fingertips of his left hand were blackened with ink, those five blotches the very picture of guilt, of shame, and some very unfortunate luck indeed.

At the far end of the room a similarly unclothed, half-covered man lay on a cot, pushed up against the wall as if trying to keep as far from Jason Fireson as possible.

Then Jason noticed that it wasn't a cot.

He lifted himself from elbows to palms, the sheet slipping down to his waist. His eyes widened at the grotesque marks on his chest. They looked like boils that had been lanced with dirty scalpels and had become infected, drying out crusted and black as they sank back into his flesh. Two were in his upper chest just beneath his clavicle, another was a couple of inches southeast of his left nipple, and three more were in his abdomen. Jason had always been proud of his physique, and for a moment—a brief one—his thoughts ran to profound disappointment at the way these wounds marred his well-proportioned pectorals and flat stomach. But he had been shot before—months ago, in his left forearm—and he knew the markings for what they were, even as all rational thought argued the contrary.

In a panic he tore the sheet off his body and let it collapse like a dispelled ghost onto the tiled floor. He wanted to touch the wounds but was afraid to.

"Well this is a hell of a thing."

He sat there for a moment, then forced his neck to scan the room again. Objects that before had been fuzzy declared themselves. To his right was a third cooling board, which had been obscured from view by a table between them. He thought he knew the face lying in profile upon it—how could he not?—except for the fact that he'd never seen his brother look so peaceful.

Jason stood, the tile cold on his feet, and stared wide-eyed at Whit. He reached forward and hesitantly touched his brother's stubbly left cheek. It felt cold, but everything felt cold at that moment. He grabbed the sheet that lay up to his brother's neck, waited a moment, and slowly began to pull it down. In the center of Whit's chest, like a target, was what could only be a bullet wound.

As he took in this sight he breathed slowly—yes, he was breathing, despite all the metal he must be carrying inside, clanging about like a piggy bank—and leaned forward in grief, involuntarily putting his right hand on his brother's biceps. It flexed into alertness, and Whit's head turned toward Jason. Whit's jaw was clenched and his brows quivered. Then his eyes darted down.

"You're naked," Whit said.

"That hardly seems the most noteworthy thing here." Their voices were hoarse.

Whit sat up, still staring at Jason's pockmarked chest. Eventually his eyes shifted down to his own body, and he lurched back as if shot again, nearly falling from his cooling board.

"What . . . ?" His voice trailed off.

"I don't know."

They stared at each other for a long while, each waiting for the other to explain the situation or to bust up at the practical joke.

Jason swallowed, which hurt, and said, "For the sake of discussion I'm at least going to ask if this has ever happened to you before."

"Not in my worst dreams."

"I thought you never remember your dreams."

"Well, I would think I'd remember something like *this!*"

"*Shh.* We're in a police station, for Chrissake."

Whit hopped off his cooling board. "Do you remember anything?"

"No." Jason reversed down his mental map, wildly careening through each turn and over every bump. "I remember being in Detroit, I remember driving with the money to meet with Owney. . . . But that's it. I don't remember if we even made it to the restaurant."

"Me neither. Everything's all fuzzy."

Jason felt a sudden need to look back at his own cooling board, in case he was a spirit and had left his husk behind. But no.

Whit started glancing around the room again as if searching for a perfectly rational explanation. Maybe these weren't bullet wounds but something else.

"How could we . . ." he tried to ask. "How could we have survived this?"

"I don't know. We've survived a lot so far, so why not—"

Whit pointed to his wound. "*Look* at this, Jason!"

"*Shhh.* Keep it down, goddamnit. And, no thank you, I've looked at it enough."

Whit turned around. "Where's the exit wound? Do you think it could have managed to slip out and miss the major organs?"

Jason waved him off without looking. "What about all of *mine?*"

Whit turned back around and briefly examined his brother's chest. "I don't know, maybe they . . ." Then he looked at Jason's face. "You're white as a sheet, too."

Jason lightly slapped his own face. "I'll get some color once we get out of here. C'mon, let's figure a way out."

Whit tapped at his chest. Then he closed his eyes for a moment, opened them. "I don't *feel* dead."

"Thank you for clarifying that."

"But, I mean, I'm breathing. Are you breathing? How do you feel?"

"I feel stiff but . . . normal." Indeed, Jason was feeling less sore the more he moved, as if all that his joints needed was to be released from their locked positions. "Shockingly normal. You?"

Whit nodded. "But if we've survived this and have been recovering here for a few hours, or days, shouldn't we . . . feel a little worse?"

"I don't know, maybe we're on some crazy medication. Or maybe they used some new kind of bullets. Who knows? Look, a police station isn't the place to be wondering about this. We don't have time."

Jason turned off the radio. A closer inspection of the police hat on the wall informed him that they were in Points North, Indiana. He told Whit.

"Where the hell is Points North?"

"Not far from Valparaiso," Jason said. The plan had been to pick up the girls at a motel outside Valparaiso after the cash drop-off in Detroit. So had the drop-off been successful, only to have something go wrong when they tried to get the girls?

Jason motioned to the third cooling board at the other end of the room. "Come on, let's see who our accomplice is. Maybe he has some answers."

He walked over to the body, Whit following after bunching his sheet around his waist. The man on the third board was every bit as naked under his sheet and every bit as bad off. He was big, once inflated but now sagging, and a gunshot to the left side of his neck had not only left a large wound but had torn at the loose skin, shreds hanging there. The crooked bridge of his nose boasted that he'd survived previous acts of violence before succumbing to this one.

"I don't know him," Whit said. "You?"

Jason shook his head. Something in the man's face, as well as the fact that the doctors or morticians had separated him from them, made Jason certain this was a cop.

"Hey, buddy," Jason said, a little more loudly. "You awake?" He snapped his fingers over the man's face, but nothing. Whit slapped the man's cheek.

"Have some respect," Jason chided him. He waited a moment, but the slap went unanswered. Then he placed his thumb between the man's right eye and eyebrow, pressing at the socket of his skull and pulling up to reveal the still, hazel eye beneath. This man seemed content enough in his death not to be fighting it.

"Officer," Jason greeted the cop, "we'd like to report a crime. Pants theft. We were hoping we could borrow some clothes while you investigated the crime for us."

If the cop's eyes had been wide at the surprise attack, they were wider still at the sight before him. His mouth dropped open and the color was draining from his face.

"Uh-oh," Jason said to Whit. "Better lean him against the wall here, quick."

Whit obeyed, and the cop slumped to his knees. His eyes were so wide it didn't seem possible they could widen further, but they did. Then he gagged and vomited. The brothers stepped back.

"Actually, Whit," Jason said as he viewed the mess, "he's more your size. You can have his clothes."

Whit stepped forward. He grabbed the cop's collar and pressed his back against the locker.

The cop was thin, about Whit's size minus a couple of inches. Jason relieved him of his sidearm—a Colt .38 revolver—and checked that it was loaded. He would have put it in his pocket if he'd had any.

The cop opened his eyes, keeping them aimed at the floor.

"How . . . ? How could—"

Whit dangled the scalpel into the officer's view, nearly trimming his officious mustache. "Find us some clothes."

The cop's eyes remained focused on the ground as he gingerly led the brothers to his locker, which his shaking fingers allowed him to open after two failed attempts. In the locker were a pair of trousers, a white cotton shirt, and a pair of shoes Whit could already tell were too big.

Jason took a wallet from the cop's pants pocket. A quick peek revealed a five-dollar bill and two singles, which Jason slid out. "We'll use this to fund our investigation."

Then, like a slug in the gut, Jason remembered how much money had been in their possession when they'd been driving to meet Owney Davis. *Jesus Christ,* he thought. That money was likely still in this building, but surrounded by cops, not all of whom would necessarily pass out at the mere sight of the Firefly Brothers.

"Have a seat, Officer," he said, turning the cop so his back was against the lockers. The man slid down slowly. As Whit dressed, Jason kept the revolver trained on the cop's chest, continuing to hold the scalpel in his other hand, the seven dollars wrapped around its handle.

"Look at me," Jason said, and the cop reluctantly complied. "Point me to the locker of someone my size, and be quick about it."

The cop called a number and Jason made sure there wasn't a round in the Colt's chamber before hacking at the lock with the gun handle.

"Making a racket," Whit chided him, standing above the cop with his scalpel ready.

Soon Jason was clothed, but barefoot—there were no shoes in the locker. Loudly breaking into another locker would be too risky, so he would have to go unshod.

"Give us your keys," Whit said to the cop, who reached into his pocket and obeyed. "Which is your car?"

"Green Pontiac, out back. Tag number 639578."

Whit asked where the armory was, but as the cop told them Jason shook his head—too risky. They'd have to make do with the one Colt.

"Why is it so quiet in here?" Whit asked.

"Everybody is out front with the reporters. Announcing your . . . apprehension."

"And were you a part of that apprehension, Officer?" Jason asked.

"No, no, I was away, at my in-laws'." His voice slid into a more panicked tone. "I had no idea until I showed up this afternoon. I wouldn't have gotten involved anyway—I think what you boys have been doing is just grea—"

"What exactly happened to us?" Jason cut him off.

The cop's eyes slowly drifted up to Jason. "You were shot."

"No kidding. But how, and when?"

"And who did it?" Whit added.

"And where'd they put our money?"

"You were shot," the cop repeated, his voice hollow. "You were lying there. I touched you. You were so cold. Doctor said . . . doctor said you were dead."

"It's amazing what people can get wrong these days," Jason said.

"But how did they get that wrong?" Whit asked the cop. "What did they really do to us?"

"And where'd they put our money?"

"You were both so cold." A line of sweat bulleted down his cheek. "And stiff. Chief even pretended to shake Whit's hand. But it wouldn't bend."

Whit flexed the fingers of his left hand. He made a fist and the tendons popped against one another.

The cop moaned and lowered his head.

"Oh Christ, not again," Jason said. But the cop simply slumped over, his limbs loosening like a released marionette's. Jason dropped his scalpel and bent down, putting his hand behind the man's unconscious head and gently lowering it to the floor.

The brothers stood beside each other in their stolen clothes. Something needed to be said. But neither had any idea what that might be.

Footsteps from above jarred them, and what had been a faint murmuring from the other side of the building suddenly grew louder. Laughter, or applause. They were having a hell of a time out front. And there were a lot of them. Much as it pained Jason, they would have to leave their money behind. You can't take it with you, he thought.

Jason fed a round into the Colt's chamber and stepped into the empty hallway, checking both directions. Whit followed him to the exterior door. Jason lifted the latch and slid the bolt, then nodded at his brother.

The door wasn't as heavy as it had seemed and when Jason threw it open it slammed into a brick wall. The side of the police station extended twenty yards, and before them, above the lot in which a dozen cars were huddled, the redbrick backs of storefronts rose three storys, fire escapes switchbacking past windows laid out with perfect symmetry. All the windows were dark, like the starless sky above.

Skeletal tree branches spiderwebbed overhead. Midsummer, and the tree was dead. The leafy branches of neighboring elms swayed in the breeze but this one stayed motionless, forlorn.

They scanned the tags until they found the car. Jason handed Whit the Colt and opened the driver's door.

He started the car and pulled out of the lot, headlights illuminating a badly paved road. From here they could see along the side of the station, and it was clear there was quite a gathering out front. The side street and the main avenue were choked with parked cars, and through some of the windows he could see the flashes of news cameras. The room appeared full of men, dark shoulders and hatted heads vibrating with laughter and proclamations.

"Somebody in that room," Whit said, unable to finish. He tried again. "Somebody in that room—"

"Well, congratulations to them. Poor saps can feel like heroes for a few hours at least."

He turned left, putting the station in his rearview. The street soon intersected with the town's main drag.

"Recognize anything?" he asked.

"No."

Jason tapped the top of the wheel. Driving without a git to guide them felt risky, amateurish. Main Street was dark, the theater marquee unlit and the storefronts displaying nothing but reflections of the Pontiac's headlights. He thought he'd been through Points North once—stopped for lunch, maybe, or gasoline—but he'd seen so many Main Streets in so many states that he often confused them.

They continued at a calm twenty-five miles an hour. Eventually the tightly packed buildings were replaced by the widely spaced front yards of darkened houses. Jason let his foot fall heavier on the accelerator.

"You hungry?" he asked.

"Nope."

"Thirsty?"

"Nope."

"Me neither. Christ, this is strange."

A hole tore in the cloud cover and there were the stars, informing Jason that he was headed north. He soon passed a sign for the state highway. Ordinarily they would stick to the country roads, but Jason figured there would be no roadblocks if the police thought the Firefly Brothers had already been apprehended.

"Why couldn't this have happened to Pop?" Whit asked.

Jason swallowed, driving even faster now. "I was thinking the same thing."

The highway took them through farmland so flat and featureless it was as though they were crossing a black, still sea. Jason remembered an old yegg from prison telling stories about the Florida Keys and how he'd planned to retire there after one last job, remembered the man's stories of a road cutting through long islands where the emerald ocean glittered on either side. If that was a paradise on earth, then Jason felt he was navigating its opposite. He wished it was day, wished there was something to look at, wished he had someone to talk to other than his taciturn brother, who had been struck mute since leaving Points North. He wished Darcy were here; one of the many questions throwing stones in his mind was where she was. Hell, what day was today? How long was the black hole of memory he was carrying inside him?

Jason could feel a wind chopping at the side of the Pontiac. Clouds had reclaimed the sky. He had been driving for two hours when he realized they were low on gasoline. Didn't anyone in this damned country keep his tank full? Jason had driven an untold number of stolen cars, sometimes just for a few miles and sometimes for days-long escapes, yet he could count the number of full or even half-full tanks on one hand. And then there were the cars that broke down inexplicably, or stalled out at stop signs, or dropped their fenders, or had no water in their radiators, or had their wheels loosen on rough roads and slide into ditches. If only his fellow Americans would keep better care of their automobiles.

The brothers had decided their destination was Lincoln City, Ohio, and they had many hours to go. Jason pulled off the highway after passing a hand-lettered sign for a filling station in the town of Landon, Indiana.

"Jesus," Whit said suddenly. *"Jesus Christ!"*

"What?"

"Jason! We're goddamn dead!"

"Keep yourself together."

"What the hell's going on?"

Jason pulled onto the side of the road. He turned to face his brother.

"I don't know, but I know that losing our heads isn't going to help things."

Whit opened his door and stumbled out.

"Where are you going?" Jason opened his own door, following. Whit was pacing in quick strides on the dry grass, running his hands through his hair.

"Whit. Get in the car. All I know is that until the news spreads, most cops still think we're on the prowl, so if anyone ID's us we're in for a gunfight."

"A gunfight? Who cares? What'll they do, kill us again?" Whit stopped moving, his hands on his hips. Behind him cornstalks gossiped in the wind.

"What do you think would happen if I shot myself right here?" Whit took the pistol out of his pocket and pointed it at his chest.

"I'd have to clean up one of your messes, as usual." Jason sighed. "C'mon, brother. It's late. We need to get some gasoline while we can."

Whit was on the verge of tears. "Whit," Jason said, stripping the impatience from his voice. "Put the gun in your pocket and sit down. Let's just bandage ourselves up and sit for a while. All right?"

Whit finally obeyed. Jason reached into the Pontiac and pulled the gauze and dressing out of the glove compartment, then stepped aside so his brother could sit. No cars passed.

Whit unbuttoned his shirt as Jason unwound some gauze. He dared to glance at his brother's chest; fortunately, he could barely see the bullet hole in the dark, could pretend it was just a large bruise. He placed the gauze against it. "Hold this here," he said, and after Whit's fingers replaced his he taped down its edges. "All right."

Then Jason unbuttoned his own shirt, and this time Whit taped the makeshift bandages onto his brother's chest. The wounds weren't bleeding and didn't hurt at all, so the bandages served no purpose other than to remove these monstrous questions from view.

"Good as new," Jason said, patting his brother on the shoulder.

Then he saw headlights, far away but approaching.

"C'mon, we have to get going," Jason said.

They drove another half mile to the filling station, a tiny glimmer of financial life beside a shuttered general store and a collapsed barn.

"Lean your head to the side like you're sleeping," Jason said. "I don't want you talking to anyone right now."

Whit did as he was told, grumbling something his brother couldn't hear. A moment later, a gangly teenager in overalls yawned as he walked toward the Pontiac.

"Evenin'," Jason said after shutting off the engine. "I'd like two dollars' worth, please."

"All righty." After the kid grabbed the spigot and fastened it to the Pontiac, he asked if they'd heard the news.

"What news is that?"

"They killed the Firefly Brothers, late last night."

"That right?"

"S'all over the radio. Local boys did it, not the feds. Caught 'em at some farmhouse in Points North. Shot 'em up real good. Brothers took a cop with 'em, though."

"How 'bout that." Jason looked down at the pavement. "Radio say if they killed the brothers' girls, too?"

The kid thought for a moment. "I don't remember. That'd be a shame, though," and he offered a gawky grin. "They're real lookers."

"They certainly are."

"Can't believe they killed the Firefly Brothers, though. Gonna cost me a two-dollar bet to my own brother—I said they'd never be caught."

"They're always caught eventually. Sorry to hear about your two bucks."

"Tell me about it."

They were silent as the tap clicked every few seconds. The smell of gasoline seeped through Jason's window.

"Two dollars' worth," the kid said, placing the handle back on the latch.

Jason handed the kid a five with his un-inked hand and pocketed the change. Then he looked the kid in the eye and extended his hand again. "And here's your two bucks."

"Huh?"

"For losing your bet. Pay this to your brother."

The kid looked at him strangely. "That's kind of you, sir, but I'll be all right."

"I don't like hearing about young lads already in debt. Take it and pay your brother."

The kid seemed distracted by the way the bills hung in Jason's perfectly still hand. Then he was looking at Jason again, his eyes spotlights. Jason's lips curved into the barest smile.

"Thank you, sir."

"You're welcome." Jason turned the ignition. "Night."

After they'd pulled onto the road, Whit looked up. "Did the kid look funny at all?"

"What do you mean?"

"I don't know, maybe everyone else out here is dead, too. Maybe this is the afterlife."

"That explains the hoop floating over his head."

"Go to hell."

"Maybe we're there already. Besides, I thought you didn't believe in an afterlife."

Whit scanned the horizon. "Well this is the kind of thing that shakes a man's unfaith."

Jason pulled back onto the highway and the sky flashed, light filling its vast spaces before vanishing again.

"We have to learn more about what happened," Whit said.

"We'll read the papers tomorrow."

"I'm worried about Ronnie, and little Patrick. You don't suppose . . . they might have been there, too, maybe in another room?"

Jason let himself laugh. "I don't think they have separate women-and-children morgues, Whit."

"This isn't goddamn funny!"

Jason waited a beat. "Don't think about it, all right? As soon as we get home we'll send a telegram to the girls and figure out what's what."

The window was still open and he could smell the rain before the drops started hitting the windshield. The drumming grew louder and the wipers struggled to keep up. Jason left his window rolled down, letting the water soak the sleeve of his stolen shirt, the drops wetting his hair and catching in his eyelashes. The rain was filling his side of the cabin now, the sound almost too loud to be believed.

II.

The sun rose grudgingly, as if it would have preferred to stay in hiding. Jason intermittently checked its progress over the familiar, softly sloping landscape of southern Ohio before finally admitting he was awake.

"Good morning," Whit said when he noticed his brother rustling.

Jason grunted in return. He sat up straighter. The feeling of his stolen shirt tugging slightly against the bandages on his chest told him it hadn't been a dream.

Though for the first few hours the brothers had felt charged with adrenaline and bewilderment, they had grown tired as their drive unfolded into the night. They chose to sleep in shifts, aiming to make it home as quickly as possible.

"Home" referred to the Lincoln City house they had grown up in. They hadn't lived there in years, but nothing had taken its place in terms of either permanence or significance—even though their other brother, who still lived in Lincoln City, made them feel less welcome every time they visited.

They desperately wanted to find Darcy and Veronica and let them know they were all right, or alive, or whatever they were, but that seemed too risky. If the girls thought the brothers had been caught, it would be hard to predict how they would react. Go into hiding? Surrender to the police? There was also a chance the cops had been watching the girls all along, and had somehow gleaned information from their movements that had led to the brothers' "apprehension."

With their wounds bandaged up and the scene of their ghastly awakening many miles behind them now, it was easier to tell themselves that there was some other explanation for this. The morning's clarity only heightened the previous night's dreamlike quality, and Jason and Whit both sat there in the car, hoping that this soon would make sense, hoping that God had granted them some startling favor. Or maybe the Devil had held up his end of an already forgotten bargain—that was more believable. And so they were merely trying to act the way they normally would when pursued by forces beyond their control—something with which they had considerable experience.

Over the past few months—ever since the federal government had made the elimination of "Public Enemies" a priority, like reducing unemployment and stabilizing the dollar—the brothers had been transformed from local criminals of modest repute to world-famous outlaws, as newspapers across the country printed exaggerated versions of their life stories. Jason was flattered until the drawbacks became clear: safe houses started turning the brothers away, and wary associates showed declining interest in future heists. Worse, the type of regular folk who used to put up Jason and Whit whenever breakdowns or blown tires left them stranded in the middle of farm country—the people who were grateful for the hideout money the brothers paid them and who praised their efforts against the banks—were now too tempted by the government's bounty on the Firefly Brothers' heads. Back in May, when the gang had pulled a job at the Federal Reserve in Milwaukee, Jason and Whit had barely survived when random civilians started taking potshots at them; one of their associates wasn't so lucky.

At least the bloody Federal Reserve job had been their most lucrative yet: a hundred and fifty grand, to be divided among the four surviving members of the Firefly Gang. The money, however, was easily traceable and therefore needed to be washed. Which was a problem: launderers were even more skittish around the brothers than safe houses were. *Sorry,* they all begged off, *you're too hot.* The gang split ways as Jason and Whit tried to find a reliable, less cowardly fence. There followed weeks of hiding out, of exhausting the goodwill and bad judgment of old pals, of waking to late-night police raids and sneaking through early-morning stakeouts. One fence who claimed he could help them had turned rat, setting them up for a meeting at a Toledo restaurant that was surrounded by feds. Jason had pulled off a brilliant escape that time, but barely. Finally, he and Whit had fallen so low as to live in a car, sleeping in their clothes and bathing in creeks. Jason Fireson, the silk-suit bandit, had become unwashed and unshaven. Carrying six figures of unspendable bills on his rather foul person.

The brothers' share of those unspendable bills only grew when one of their two remaining partners was gunned down by cops in a Peoria alley. Jason read about it in the paper.

Finally, they found a trustworthy guy who knew a guy who knew a guy who could pass the hot bills while on a gambling expedition to Cuba. The laundering fee would be steep; the chiseler had insisted that washing money for the Firefly Brothers was an extreme risk, as was doing business in Cuba. But it was the best Jason and Whit could do. Stomach fluttering, eyes especially vigilant after the Toledo escape, Jason had handed two very heavy suitcases to this stranger he had just met, who was boarding a flight for Havana and would supposedly be coming back to the States for a Detroit rendezvous with the Firesons two weeks later.

Miraculously, the fence did return, with seventy thousand clean bills—less than they had agreed upon, but he claimed he had run into some trouble abroad and had needed to dip into the funds for some healthy bribes. Jason shook the washer's dirty hand and took the money. Now, at long last, he and Whit could disappear and start a restaurant in California, or raise bulls in Spain, or whatever it was they had promised themselves and their girls they would do.

But they didn't make it to Spain or California. They sent coded messages to Darcy and Veronica telling them to meet at a motel outside Valparaiso, noting that they would pick them up as soon as they paid a share to Owney Davis, Jason's longtime collaborator and the lone survivor of their gang. They were supposed to meet Owney at a restaurant in Detroit, the night after getting the money washed. Neither could remember what had happened. Had they been shot while driving to the restaurant? That meant they somehow would have driven, badly injured, all the way from

Detroit to Points North, which defied credulity, but no more so than their current existence. And if they had been shot in Detroit, did that mean Owney had betrayed them? Or maybe the drop-off with Owney had gone as planned but then something had happened during their long drive through Michigan and into Indiana to meet the girls. But what, exactly? And why Points North, which was a good twenty miles from Valparaiso? What on earth had happened that night?

So now, home. Normally they called their mother before visiting, using their code phrase ("I was just checking to see if the furnace needs oil") in case the phones were tapped. But if the cops were still listening to her line, and if they were wise to the code, then calling would raise new suspicions. There was no way to tell what the Points North cop from the night before had told his colleagues, but Jason was betting on the fact that the cop would keep the bizarre encounter to himself, even after the alarm was raised about the missing bodies. For who would believe such a story? The cops had gone to the extent of announcing that the Firesons were dead, so police nationwide at least believed it to be true. That meant they would find some way to fit the fact of the brothers' escape into their pre-determined reality, and it was up to the brothers to hide in the shadows of logic that such lies cast.

"What if Ma's already heard about our . . . 'apprehension' by now?" Whit asked.

"If the gas station kid had, then she has, too. Reporters were probably calling her all night to ask for a comment."

They were off the highway now, driving through occasional farm towns that had prospered during the war but had sickened and withered years before their malaise was shared with the rest of the country. Ten miles west of Lincoln City, they were winding through a particularly desolate hamlet when Jason pointed to a general store that sat between a vacant building and a farm equipment rental-and-supply company.

Whit parked in front. The sidewalks were empty and the light felt golden, dozens of suns reflecting from store windows.

Jason reached into his pocket and handed Whit one of the cop's dollars. "Here, you're the one wearing shoes."

Whit walked into the store. Jason rolled down his window and let his arm dangle, feeling the light breeze of night's retreat. His fingertips were no longer black, as he and Whit had stopped by a closed filling station late at night to rinse their hands with a hose.

When Whit walked back out of the store, his facial expression was grim. Jason did notice that Whit looked less gray than he had the night before, and he glanced down at his own arms and saw that the same was true of him, as if their bodies were recovering from . . . recovering from what?

But they still didn't look quite right.

"We made the front page," Whit said, closing the door behind him and opening the *Lincoln City Sun* between their seats.

Before Jason could read the enormous, Armistice-sized headline, his eyes were drawn to the photograph below it. Five policemen were smiling proudly. In front of them two bodies lay prone atop cooling boards, white sheets pulled to their armpits. Jason recognized the room. The bodies' profiles were small enough in the picture for it to be possible to doubt who exactly they were.

FIREFLY BROTHERS GUNNED DOWN IN FARMHOUSE BATTLE

POINTS NORTH, Ind.—Jason and Whit Fireson, the Lincoln City natives and bank-robbing duo known as the Firefly Brothers, will terrorize no more financial institutions, murder no more officers of the law, and, one hopes, inspire no more misguided fealty among our more disaffected countrymen.

The Firefly Brothers were shot to death in a gunfight early Thursday morning that also claimed the life of Points North police officer Hugh Fenton, 42. Officers had been alerted by an anonymous tip that the brigands, who have at least seventeen bank robberies and five murders to their credit, were using an abandoned farmhouse outside the town of Points North as a temporary refuge during an attempt to flee the law and hide out in the western United States. More than a dozen Points North officers and deputies, led by County Chief Yale Mackinaw, surrounded the building under cover of darkness past midnight. After obtaining visual confirmation that the villains were in the building, Chief Mackinaw used a bullhorn to demand that they surrender. The brothers did not respond to that or to subsequent entreaties, and the intrepid officers stormed the building at approximately 1 A.M.

The Firefly Brothers, armed with Thompson submachine guns and automatic pistols, fired countless rounds from several weapons before they were vanquished. Chief Mackinaw would not divulge which of his officers fired the fatal shots, instead praising his entire force for its bravery and dedication.

Nearly $70,000 was discovered on the felons, the police reported.

"Those who choose to live outside the law will be brought to justice," Chief Mackinaw said. "We gave the brothers ample opportunity to surrender, but they chose to try shooting their way out instead."

The Department of Justice's Bureau of Investigation had declared the Firefly Brothers the nation's top Public Enemies three weeks ago, after its fatal ambush of John Dillinger eliminated him from those notorious ranks.

Jason Liam Fireson, 27, was unmarried and believed to be childless, though several young women have made claims to the contrary. Whitman Earnest Fireson, 23, was married and the father of an infant son, though the whereabouts of widow and child are unknown. The Firesons' mother continues to reside in Lincoln City, where the desperadoes were born and raised, as does a third brother.

Calls to the Fireson residence requesting comment were sternly refused.

The story continued in that vein for many paragraphs, recounting bits of the brothers' pasts, noting that they were "sons of a convicted murderer," melding fact with legend and assuming readers were unaware of such alchemy. It offered no more details about the circumstances of their apprehension.

"I don't remember *any* of this," Whit said. "And it says Veronica and Patrick's whereabouts are unknown—that can only be good, right?"

Yet neither felt celebratory. Reading the story of their death was an experience both disturbing and oddly unaffecting.

"And it says there was an anonymous tip," Whit added. "From who?"

"Seventy thousand dollars." Jason shook his head. Then he thought of something. "That means we never paid Owney his share."

Whit reread the article while Jason peered through the windshield, running different scenarios in his head.

"So today's Friday," Whit said, calmly reciting a fact, something definite. Even these were things to be questioned. He finished reading, then sighed and looked at his brother. "What are we going to tell Ma?"

Lincoln City saddened Jason. Idle men and breadlines could be found in any city, but Lincoln City was *his*—his past, his childhood, his family—and therefore it was more painful to witness all that the depression had wrought there. Better to see unfamiliar street signs standing beside evicted families on sidewalks. Better to see factories where none of his relatives had ever worked falling into disrepair. Better to see perfect strangers in some other town foraging in the dump.

Mostly, though, being in Lincoln City reminded Jason of his father.

The city was waking slowly. Jason, at the wheel now, skirted the factories and spied a few stragglers slowly making their way without apparent purpose. It was unusual to see anyone reporting to work late these days—the last thing a fellow needed to do was give his employer a reason to replace him with some other hungry bastard—and the empty expressions on the men's faces argued that they hadn't worked in weeks, or months. The boarded windows of vacant buildings displayed new inscriptions: UNION NOW, COMMUNISM NOT DEPRESSIONISM, even the weirdly out-of-date HOOVER GO TO HELL. Lawns were unmowed and sidewalks unswept, as if the inhabitants of these homes had simply vanished, which many of them had.

Upon reaching the intersection at which he would have turned right to reach their mother's house, Jason slowed down and scanned the street. He couldn't quite see the house, but he did notice several cars parked on the side of the road. He continued forward, driving another block before cutting down the parallel street. Jason pulled into the short driveway of a small two-story home that had been vacant for more than a year.

"Glad to see the neighborhood hasn't rebounded," Whit said. They had pulled in here before, an unexpected benefit of the evictions that plagued this side of town.

The city still spent its scant dollars boarding up windows with plywood to prevent derelicts from breaking into vacant buildings, but Jason had heard of evicted families who merely moved a few doors down, one household squatting in the foreclosed remains of another's. That couldn't have been done in the beginning, of course, when the banks were fixing up and reselling the properties, but now that there were so many foreclosures and so few buyers the banks weren't even bothering. Word was, if a bank hadn't foreclosed on you yet it probably wouldn't, because it couldn't afford to.

It was insane, what had befallen their world. The foundations of normalcy had been revealed as imaginary. Reality had come crashing down on top of them, buried them alive.

"Let's be quick about it," Jason said. They weren't worried about the car being traced; they had stopped in the middle of the night to exchange tags with a broken-down Ford by the side of the road.

They climbed the five steps to the front door. A stray, mangy black dog was suddenly at their heels, sniffing excitedly.

The door was locked, so Whit, as the one wearing shoes, kicked it in. The door swung awkwardly on its loose hinges, which had been busted by past Firefly entrances. Why someone kept fixing the lock was a mystery.

They closed the door behind them, though it wouldn't quite latch, and the dog gleefully nosed it open as it followed them. At least that allowed the daylight to throw a thin sliver down the long hallway, puddles offering stagnant reflections. The house smelled like piss and something dead.

Jason instinctively unpocketed his pistol. The wood floor was sticky beneath his bare feet, as if the building were sweating.

They had spent time in no small number of vacant houses and barns across the Midwest, some of which had smelled worse. They hadn't known the family who lived here, had never visited back when it had actually belonged to someone. As Jason moved, he wondered if he heard whispering from upstairs or if he was just imagining things.

The dog followed them into the kitchen, still sniffing their feet. It licked Jason's bare toes, and Jason began to fear that the tongue was only a precursor to the teeth.

He looked up at Whit. "We don't . . . *smell*, do we?"

It took Whit a second to realize what his brother meant. "Jesus, I hope not." He looked at the dog and nudged it with his shoe. "Beat it." The stray finally turned around and left the kitchen.

Whit reached over the kitchen sink and removed a loose piece of plywood where the window used to be. He could see the backyard. It was small, like the others in the neighborhood, and enclosed by a wood fence five feet high. On the other side of the fence was their mother's house.

"Curtains are drawn."

Jason crowded beside him and scanned the side yards. "There's somebody in the gray sedan there," he said. They couldn't make out the man's face, only his dark suit and tie. Just sitting there.

"I say we do it anyway," Whit said. "He probably won't see."

Jason put the gun back in his pocket while Whit opened the back door. Knee-high grass and weeds twitched, aphids leaped from strand to strand as the brothers crossed the yard. The fence sagged and threatened to topple under their weight as they pulled themselves over.

When they were kids, the back porch would have been safety in a game of tag. They both thought of this as they hurried up the steps. The guy in the sedan could be a reporter or a cop. Were the cops looking to arrest their mother for aiding and abetting? Such persistence beyond the grave seemed sacrilegious, the ungentlemanly flouting of established rules.

They climbed the back steps to the porch that their brother Weston had rebuilt the previous spring. The door was locked, so Jason knocked three times. After half a minute, he knocked again, harder this time.

The window on the top half of the door was concealed by a thin white curtain, and he saw a finger lift a corner. It pulled back as if the window were electrified. Then it returned, parting the curtain further this time. With the morning sun behind him, all Jason could see was his own reflection, his cheeks dark with stubble, his defiled hair hanging limp on his forehead. He winked.

Bolts slid from their works. Then the door pulled open, their mother's left hand holding it wide and her right hand leaning on the jamb. She was wearing her old white nightgown, and her hair fell behind her shoulders. The veins beneath her caved eyes were visible, pulsing as she stared at them.

"Jason? Whit?" Her voice tiny.

"Hi, Ma." Jason stepped forward just in time to prevent her from collapsing. She clasped her arms around him, squeezing as she uttered something that was a laugh or a cry. The sound sank into his chest. Whit slipped behind them into the house before she released Jason and transferred her embrace to her youngest son.

"I thought I told you not to believe everything you read about us," Jason said, stepping into the kitchen. The smells of home came as they always did, coffee and old wood mixed with the sulfur of extinguished matches and a certain dampness. Jason breathed them in deeply.

Ma pulled back from Whit but kept her hands on his shoulders. Her eyes were wet. "But they said . . . We've been getting these calls . . . The police . . ."

"I'm sorry, Ma," Whit said, his voice shrinking as hers had grown. "I'm sorry we scared you. We're okay."

One of her hands moved to his cheek as she stared at him, then she buried her face into his shoulder and hugged him again. Jason watched Whit's hand at Ma's back, long pale fingers kneading the thin cloth. Eventually she opened her eyes.

"Jason, you're barefoot," she said. "And your toes are black."

He laughed at how easily she'd turned maternal and scolding. But damn if she wasn't right about the toes, he noticed, hoping it was only dirt.

"Sit down, Ma," Whit said, an arm around her as he guided her into the dining room. "Take a minute." Jason scanned the room, as well as the front parlor, to make sure all the curtains were drawn.

They sat at the table and Jason handed her a dishcloth to wipe her eyes. Whenever he saw his mother after a time away, he was struck by the fact that his adulthood was pushing hers further toward senescence. He always thought she had lost weight, but maybe this was just his new awareness of how frail she always had been. Her thin dark hair was laced with gray, and she usually kept it pulled back, a reminder that she no longer had anyone to look pretty for. It amazed Jason that something as inanimate as hair could possess such sorrow.

"What happened?"

"It's a long story," Jason said. "Let's just settle in for a moment."

The telephone on the wall began to ring. None of them made a motion toward it, and there were no footsteps from above. After seven rings, it stopped.

Ma's face had been colorless when she first opened the door, but now her eyes were red and glistening. So this was what her sons did for her: put color in her face, and texture. She shook her head at them, her boys who were supposed to be dead, and her eyes moved from son to son as if wondering when one or the other might disappear.

"I could kill you," she said.

"You wouldn't be the first," Jason replied. Whit shot him a look.

The small dining room's evergreen wallpaper, dark-stained molding, and west-facing windows contributed to its customary element of morning gloom, made worse by the drawn curtains.

Then the sound of the front door opening, the key and the hinges, and footsteps.

"Ma, what's—" Jason looked up just in time to see Weston walking into the dining room, stopping midstride. "Jesus . . ."

"Boo," Jason said.

"Jesus." Weston moved back a step. He was gripping a copy of the *Sun*, rolled tight like a billy club. Jason could just make out the word BROTH-ERS in the headline, see some blurry part of the photograph shaking in Weston's tensed fingers.

"You're . . . You're supposed to be dead."

"Sorry to disappoint."

"What happened?"

Whit was already out of his chair, grabbing the paper from his shocked brother. He stepped into the kitchen and put the newspaper in the trash bin, burying it deep beneath coffee grounds and napkins. When he returned to the room, Weston was in the same spot.

"Sit down, Wes." Whit motioned to an empty chair. "I know this is kind of strange."

"Do you have any idea—"

"I'm sure I don't." Whit clapped his brother on the shoulder. "C'mon, sit."

Jason had always thought Weston looked like someone who couldn't possibly be related to him. Weston was too bookish; he seemed to have inherited the personality of an elderly man from the moment he turned twelve. And in the past few months Weston had aged at a pace that seemed almost science-fictional. He was naturally slender, closer in physique to Whit than to Jason, and the skin of Weston's face was even tighter than usual, with dark circles around the eyes. Looking at him made Jason too aware of his skull. Weston recently had started wearing glasses, and Jason wondered if that had less to do with deteriorating eyesight and more to do with a need to distinguish himself from the faces on those wanted posters.

"We wish we could have told you sooner," Jason said. "But we still don't trust the phones. Things are a bit crazy at the moment."

Weston seemed to be crumpling as Jason spoke. His head fell into his hands and then through them, hanging so low his nose grazed the table. His fingers kneaded into his hair for a moment and then stopped, but even at rest they shook. When he sat up, his eyes were wet and his muscles tense. Jason and Whit glanced at each other; they both had been so worried about how Ma would take the news of their death, they hadn't thought much about their brother, with whom neither had been terribly close the past few years.

Jason stood up and walked to his seated brother, leaning over to wrap an arm around his shoulders. "It's okay, Wes," Jason said, guilt pouring in. "I'm sorry we worried you."

Jason sat back down and Weston nodded, waiting out the tears. "We've had police outside, reporters from all over the country," he finally said. His voice was quiet. "And now everybody's reading the paper and calling us. What ... what happened?"

"Who else is here?" Jason asked.

"June and the boys are upstairs." Weston took off his glasses as if to make sure his brothers still could be seen by the naked eye. "I called a few folks this morning, so they could hear it from us and not the papers, but ... no one's been able to come by yet. I told them not to, because of ... all the ruckus out front. I wasn't sure if—"

"No, that was good. We'll need to hide out here a bit, and the fewer people to explain things to, the better."

Windows were open behind the curtains and flies clumsily patrolled the room. Jason wondered if it was just his imagination or did the insects seem to be particularly interested in him and Whit. He hoped the others hadn't noticed.

"So ..." Weston let the word drag like a broom. "The pictures in the paper ...?"

"Not us," Jason answered.

"But ... what happened?"

Whit looked to Jason, who replied, "Look, a lot gets blamed on us that we didn't do. That may not be fair, but this time it's worked out in our favor. Looks like somebody saw two fellas they thought were us, and they told the cops out in Points North. Cops ambushed the poor bastards, then got all excited and called the papers. There you go."

"Didn't they take fingerprints?" Weston asked.

"You'd be surprised how incompetent cops tend to be," Jason said.

"So . . ." Weston again took a while to get his question out. "What happened in Detroit?"

"How did you know we went there?" Whit asked.

"The radio said . . . something about an ambush?"

"Look, I know this is all pretty strange," Jason said, trying to keep a calm front while spinning his lies and taking in Weston's information. "But what matters is we're okay, and the folks chasing us are all relaxed right now because they think they got us."

"Are you boys hungry?" Ma asked, standing up, apparently anxious to conclude talk of her sons' lesser deeds. "Can I get you anything?"

"Ma, don't worry about—"

Weston's rebuke was interrupted by his brothers saying, actually, yes, they'd love a bite to eat. They surprised even themselves with this; after an evening of feeling curiously detached from physical needs, the sights and smells of the family dining room had stirred something within them.

After she had walked into the kitchen, Weston glared at them. "She didn't sleep all night, for God's sake. She certainly doesn't need to be slaving for you two right now."

Jason shrugged. "You know damn well she's happiest when she's doing something."

"I wish you two could have seen this place yesterday. I wish you could have seen *her*." Weston's shock seemed to be giving way to his normal personality at last; this was the brother Jason knew. "As if she needed a scare like that, after Pop."

"We didn't come here to get lectured, Wes," Whit said.

"What did you come back for?"

"Look," Jason said calmly, to keep Whit from escalating the matter. "The cops think we're dead. We're still trying to figure a few things out, but it seems best to lay low until the commotion dies down. The heat'll finally be off us, so we can pack up and make our way someplace, start over."

"And then you can start participating in the fabled straight life. I get it. What'll it be, law school for Whit, and maybe sales for Jason?"

"Knock it off," Whit said.

Weston shook his head. "Jesus Christ. My brothers resurrected." He studied them for a moment. "You both look kind of gray."

"It was a long night," Jason said. "So what's new, Wes?"

"Not much."

"How's the job going?"

"They're still paying me."

"That's good. How's Aunt June?"

Weston paused. "The same." As if on cue, they heard the floorboards from above. "That's probably her. Maybe I'll go up and tell her myself, ease the shock a bit."

After Weston left, Whit excused himself to the bathroom, and Jason sat there watching the flies.

Whit closed the bathroom door behind him and looked in the mirror. The light wasn't terribly good, but he did seem to look colorless, as if he hadn't been in the sun in weeks. Which was largely true, of course, as he and his brother had lived in hiding ever since the Federal Reserve job more than two months ago. He ran his fingers over his stubble. His hair was still growing. But he'd heard that happened with corpses, that undertakers needed to shave the dead, sometimes twice, so that didn't mean anything, either. He reached into the medicine cabinet for the razor he had left there weeks ago. He stared at himself again, then looked down at his left wrist, turned upward to present its veins. They still looked blue. He rolled up the left sleeve, then turned over his left arm, a few freckles showing through his dark hair. He took a breath, gritted his teeth, and sliced at his forearm with the razor, feeling the burn as it slid across. The opening in his skin seemed to widen for a moment, a yawning release. The air on the wound felt hot, as if oxygen were toxic to his insides. Then the gash flooded red. The viscous shine deepened as the tension of its molecules stood above the skin a bit. He exhaled, unsure whether he should be relieved or frightened to learn that he could still bleed, still feel pain.

He took the wound to his mouth and sucked, then removed his arm and dabbed it with toilet paper, waiting for the bleeding to stop.

Starting with Pop's arrest four years ago, Ma had taken in boarders to help with the mortgage. Her space for paying customers had shrunk eighteen months ago, when her sister June was widowed and moved in along with her three kids. June shared Ma's room, and her three young boys were crammed into a second, leaving a third bedroom for a boarder, as well as some space in the attic at an even more discounted rate. But in the past few months the attention surrounding the Firefly Brothers had persuaded Ma against allowing strangers to sleep under her roof. She wasn't used to turning away those who needed her aid, but there was no way to know whether some random person pleading for a room might in fact be a police agent come to destroy what was left of her family.

Ma walked into the dining room bearing two plates of fried eggs and toast.

"It will be nice to have everyone under one roof again," she said.

"I'm real sorry we scared you like that," Jason said between bites. "I wish things weren't this way. I'm hoping that after the attention dies down we can settle into a regular life."

He had expressed such sentiments before, and he knew she had embraced them. But each time he said them they were less believable.

She asked him again how the papers could have gotten the story so wrong. He sketched a vague tale of mistaken identity that only a woman in extreme shock would have believed. But so many unbelievable things seemed to be happening, he figured, what was one more? What about this cursed family made any kind of sense?

They chatted awhile, neither noticing how long Whit had been in the bathroom. When he finally returned, he looked at his plate of food and thanked her. Then he sat down, gripping the fork for a long moment before digging in.

Ma asked after Veronica and little Patrick, and Darcy. The brothers offered optimistic reports of their loved ones' health and happiness, failing to mention that they'd barely seen them in the past two months. Jason noticed that Whit's voice nearly broke when he mentioned his infant son, and he wondered if Ma caught it, too.

Weston finally came downstairs. "June's going to be a while. She said she'd tell the boys herself."

"They'll be fine," Jason said with a harmless shrug. "She still takes 'em to Sunday school, right? They should know all about resurrections."

"And they certainly know about their uncle Jason's God complex," Weston said.

Jason raised his coffee in a mock toast. "It's so nice to be home."

The eldest of June's boys, ten-year-old Sammy, was the next to descend the stairs. He walked into the dining room, dark hair still tousled, wearing a white undershirt and denim overalls that Jason recognized as a pair that had been his long ago.

"Wow," Sammy said. He was barefoot and the legs of the overalls dragged a bit. "It's really true."

Jason and Whit were sitting at the table alone as their mother washed the dishes. "Morning, Sammy," Jason said. He hadn't lived in town for much of the boys' young lives, though he always got on fine with them during his visits. In the past year, though, since he and Whit had become famous bank robbers, the kids had acted strangely awed in their presence.

"I didn't believe it at first," Sammy said. "About you being caught, I mean. I didn't think it could happen."

"That's 'cause it can't," Jason said. "You're a smart kid."

"Did you get in a fight with the police?"

"We don't like to fight. It was more like a chase. And we're real fast."

Sammy smiled, shifting his weight from foot to foot. Jason tried to remember what being ten had been like.

"Kids in the neighborhood are always playing Firefly Brothers. They usually fight about who gets to be the brothers and who has to be the cops."

"Do they fight about who gets to be Whit and who gets to be Jason?" Whit asked.

"Yeah, that too. Most want to be Jason."

Jason grinned, looking at his brother. "It does take a certain type to be Whit."

Then he changed his tone, leaning forward. "We need this visit to be our little secret, okay? Even more so than usual. We can't have you telling your friends about us being on the loose, no matter how badly you might want to. Can you make sure your little brothers don't say anything?"

"Yes, sir." Sammy nodded, honored to have been assigned such a task.

The stairs creaked again, too heavily to be one of Sammy's brothers. When Jason was younger, he had always figured that Aunt June had a perfectly fine appearance; she was so much younger than Ma that she had seemed more like an older sister to him. But here she was, smelling like cigarettes and looking as if she still regretted not throwing herself onto her husband's coffin those many months ago. She wore a stained blue housedress and her hair was in a graying bun.

"Sammy, go to the kitchen," she said. Her fingers grasped the back of one of the chairs, tiny muscles and cracked nails. Once the living room was free of children, she said, "I'm glad you two are okay. But I don't want you scaring the boys."

"We didn't say anything scary, June," Jason said.

"They've had enough experience with death," she continued as if she hadn't heard him. "I don't want you telling them any stories."

June's attitude toward them had changed over time. Where others saw the Firefly Brothers' acts as brazen, heroic counterpunches thrown at a broken system, June seemed to view them as just another symptom of that brokenness. Her husband, Joe, had been a war vet like Pop, but so different from straitlaced Pop in every other way. Joe had sneaked Jason his first sips of beer, tossed a baseball with him at the family gatherings Pop never attended because "someone needs to keep the shop open," even covered for Jason with a few lies to Pop when Jason started working for a local bootlegger. As a kid, Jason had loved being around Uncle Joe, and it had taken him years to understand why a guy told so many stories, why a guy so desperately needed to hear other people laugh, why the approval of a teenager could be so important to a young man.

Joe lost his factory gig four years ago, about the same time Pop was arrested, so his private battles with underemployment and the bottle had been eclipsed by Pop's trial. Joe had been more bitter and less sober every time Jason saw him, to the point that Jason wasn't surprised when he learned that Joe had died in a late-night auto wreck somewhere between Lincoln City and Cincinnati—just one more tragedy to lump in with all the others. The only mystery was whether Joe was killed coming home drunk or while trying to run away.

In the early days after Joe's death, Jason understood yet was annoyed by June's sudden lionization of her departed husband. The Joe she had once cursed for being lazy and insufficient was now a wonderful husband unfairly wronged by misfortune. Death had bestowed a kind of nobility upon him. More recently, however, her love for Joe seemed to mingle with anger at Jason and Whit, distaste for their ability to succeed in the world where her husband had failed. Joe had been "an honorable man," she noted one night when the brothers were in town. He had made some mistakes, but at least his had been legal and honest. That had not been a pleasant dinner.

Though June refused to take money directly from her bank-robbing nephews, Jason knew that she took plenty secondhand, through Ma. Poverty deprives its sufferers of the freedom to act on grudges.

"We won't be here long, June," Whit said.

She gave them a look, and for a moment Jason could see a flicker of the pain that her anger tried to snuff out. "They're good kids," she said. "I don't want them—"

"Neither do we," Jason said. "Neither do we."

An hour later, the three Fireson brothers and Ma were sitting at the table when the telephone rang. Conversation stopped and they all looked at one another, motionless, as if the telephone were a predator.

At the third ring, Jason tried to dispel the tension by telling his mother, "It's all right, you can answer it."

She picked up the receiver. "Hello? . . . Yes, this is Margaret Fireson. . . . Yes, of course, I remember you, Sergeant Higgins." Jason and Whit exchanged glances, neither of them knowing that name. Their mother was silent a long while, her expression confused. She had been staring at the floor, but now her gaze shifted to Jason and Whit. "Of course," she said suddenly, as if she hadn't realized it was her turn. "That's fine. . . . Goodbye."

"What is it?" Jason asked after she hung up.

"It was the Points North police. He said that someone has . . . stolen your bodies. Souvenir hunters—he referred to them as *morbids*. 'Some morbids must have taken them.' He assured me that he would find the . . . *bodies,* and have them shipped to the funeral home of my choice. He said he'd call again once he'd tracked them down."

"Crazy people out there," Jason said, calmly threading a finger through the handle of his coffee cup. "Poor fools got the wrong bodies."

It was decided that the Firesons—those publicly known to be alive, that is—should go about their day as they would normally be expected to. June's boys cleaned the house while June stayed upstairs, sewing and doing needlework for the Salvation Army. Playing the role of grieving mother, Margaret stayed home, too, and as more calls trickled in from friends who'd read the paper she stoically accepted their condolences. At Jason's behest, she refused their kind offers to visit, deliver food, clean the house. If she sounded somewhat less mournful than the friends had expected, perhaps they assumed she was still in shock. But after the fourth such call she found it difficult to feign sorrow, and allowed herself such comments as "Well, I'm not sure I believe all this, you know. My boys are smart, maybe there's something fishy about these stories." Her friends doubtless pitied her for being in denial.

Weston, who seemed to be living at home again, told the brothers he had been given the day off but had some errands to run. On his way out the door, he crossed paths with Jason in the front parlor.

"Listen, Wes," Jason said quietly, remembering their last conversation a few days ago. "I wanted to talk to you about something."

Weston just nodded and seemed suddenly nervous, even scared.

"I'm sorry for some of the things I said that night," Jason said. He wasn't good at this. "It was a . . . a bad time. I didn't mean all that."

Weston nodded again, as if he hoped he could nod this all away, all the bad blood between them, without having to utter a word.

"I know you've been under a lot of pressure, being the only one who's home," Jason continued, "looking after Ma and June. I know I can be a lousy brother sometimes. But what me and Whit do . . . It's a little bit easier knowing that you're here, you know?"

Weston's eyes filled again. Jason hadn't known how his judgmental brother would respond to his apology, but he hadn't expected this. It only made him feel worse.

"You're a good brother, Wes."

Weston folded his arms, hugging himself, and his neck hung down for a moment. He wiped at his eyes and looked up again.

"Thanks, Jason. I'm sorry, too."

"It's been a hard time, I know." He put a hand on Weston's shoulder, squeezed. "But we're all going to be okay, you understand? We're going to stick together."

"Yeah." Weston stared at the floor. "I know we will."

III.

———————————————————
———————————————————

New facts emerged after Darcy's third drink. The words on the newspapers danced for her now, up and to the right as if hoping to escape
her gaze. Damned words, always running from you. Always hiding things.
She stared and stared and even with her eyes wet she insisted on wrench-
ing every last bit of truth from the stories before her.

Rain splashed through the window she had shattered with a highball
glass. Thunder rolled over Lake Michigan and crashed upon the city. It
was midmorning yet the skies were dark with the wrath of an afternoon
storm, nature itself confused, nothing making sense.

She had tried to call Veronica, but there was no answer. She had even
used her own telephone, which Jason had forbidden for sensitive calls.
But would the police still be monitoring her now? She had tried other
numbers, dialing safe houses and the brothers' sundry associates, but the
few people who answered insisted they didn't know anything. She felt that
she didn't know anything, no matter how many times she read the stories.
And something akin to fear, tainted with guilt, kept her from dialing Mrs.
Fireson in Lincoln City. How could Darcy talk to the mother of two dead
sons? Would she somehow be blamed?

On her desk were discarded copies of the *Chicago Tribune,* the *Daily
Times,* the *Daily News,* and the *Herald-Examiner.* She would have scanned
the red sheets, too, if they had written about him instead of carping about

their political goals and gripes, overlooking what was truly important. *Nothing* was important but him. And they were telling her he was gone.

Two days earlier, she and Veronica had driven separately to Valparaiso, each taking a long and circuitous route to ensure that they weren't followed, checking into the tiny motel under the names they'd been assigned. By midnight the brothers were officially late. Ronny had fallen asleep at some point—after endlessly fussing around the room, unsure what to do with herself without her toddler, whom she had left with relatives—but Darcy had smoked all through the night, sitting in the room's sole chair and peering through a crack in the blinds. Few autos passed that night, and none of them stopped.

Surely the brothers would have called, unless something had happened. Or perhaps they were afraid that the girls were being watched—had they been followed after all? Did the police know about the motel? Parked cars in the lot of a nearby filling station became suspect. Maids were shooed away. By the next afternoon, she and Ronny had played cards and read the magazines they'd brought along, trying to act like friends, but without the presence of the brothers their true feelings were harder to conceal. Frayed nerves dispensed with etiquette. By the second morning they felt still more worried, and were getting hungry. Ronny missed her son and was anxious about leaving him too long. The brothers must have busted a tire, Darcy had said, trying to sound casual and unconcerned. Maybe they heard about a roadblock and needed to take a detour. They'll get back in touch. She had invited Ronny to Chicago with her, but Ronny had declined the offer. She had been cold about it, Darcy thought. As if she feared what was coming and didn't want to be in Darcy's presence when it happened.

Back in Chicago later that day, Darcy had heard the cry as she approached the first newsstand. The news was called out like a military victory, and she was the foreigner in her own town, left to mourn what others were celebrating.

The headlines she saw from twenty paces away. Competing for the largest font and most dramatic adjectives. One of them opting instead for bluntness: FIREFLY BROTHERS KILLED. The simplicity was an anvil dropping on her heart, pushing the breath from her body, doubling her over.

She didn't remember whether she had paid for her copies or just walked off with them. She didn't remember how she'd made it back to her room, but here she was. The wind picked up and rainwater darkened the pages. She lifted them to keep the ink from bleeding, to keep it from seeping into whatever mundane nonsense was printed on the back, to keep these worlds distinct. Even as the world was collapsing upon itself. Even as she was having trouble breathing. Another drink will help. Who needs a glass. Who needs something to mix it with. It's supposed to hurt on the way down.

On the running boards, it had occurred to her that she was the only one smiling.

What a beautiful day! Red and yellow leaves danced in the air before her, cartwheeling on their descent, some of them even brushing against her face as the Buick careened through the woods east of that small Indiana town. Early autumn and calm, no wind that morning, but as the car sped along, her hair was horizontal, the tips snapping at the face of the poor sap behind her. She reveled in the way the day felt against her face, the way life felt against her face, as she rushed past it, looking for what lay beyond.

This had all been very unplanned, of course. One does not plan to be a hostage in a bank robbery. It would have felt like a dream, but in a dream you can't feel pain, and her fingers did hurt; it was hardly *easy* to hold on to the side of the Buick like this, as it sped along at God only knew how many miles per hour. But my *word* this was fun.

The man across from her vomited on the roof of the Buick. That was unfortunate. There were four of them, a man and a woman on each side, positioned there by the bank robbers as a human shield. And they did their job well—the police hadn't fired a single shot. Darcy was in front on the passenger side, and she wished she could have bent down to peer inside. She wanted another glimpse of the gang leader, the man in that fabulous suit, the man who had winked at her so absurdly that she had laughed. Laughed out loud, her voice echoing off the marble walls of the very, very silent bank. She had been sitting with one of the clerks, arranging to pick up some money she'd wired from her hometown bank in

Chicago to sustain an extended visit at the home of her cousins here in the country, when the gang leader had entered with his suit and his large gun. After informing everyone of the rules and procedures, he had passed the teller stalls and was maneuvering through the various desks and chairs in search of the bank president, who was cowering behind a desk.

After she'd laughed at the leader's wink, he had smiled a bit, bemused. He hadn't expected that response. But then he had walked past her, toward the bank president. As she watched him move, she caught sight of the clerk sitting opposite her, who silently moved his mouth to ask her, quite accusingly, if she was crazy.

Yes, she wanted to answer, minutes later, as October recklessly flew through her hair. Clearly. The faces of the other three hostages were all white, their jaws as clenched as their knuckles on the roof rails, and one woman prayed, not loudly enough for Darcy to hear distinct words over the engines and the sirens and the dirt road crunching beneath the tires, but the pleading tone was still recognizable.

She had never been one to scare easily. Though her twenty years on this earth had been financially comfortable, her life story had contained enough ominous chapters and dangerous cliffhangers for her to be rather unfazed by the introduction of new threats. She had learned about the suddenness of death at a tender age, and had learned that she could survive great damage—self-inflicted and otherwise—with her sense of humor intact, though it was a bit darker than it used to be. Perhaps that was why, when she later reflected upon the bank robbery itself, she realized she had never been concerned about the possibility of her own death. She had no husband to leave behind, no children to orphan, no mother to damn into endless grief.

It had happened so quickly, she was really quite impressed. And with such subterfuge that she wasn't at all sure how many of them there were. The one who had winked, obviously. The one who stood guarding the door, holding a gun identical to the leader's. But different people kept emerging and it was difficult for her to keep up.

And about this leader. He was tall, he had a jaw sharp enough to etch diamond, and the moment she heard his voice she was convinced. Convinced of what, she wasn't sure. Just *convinced*. He could have read the most outlandish children's story and she would have believed him. He could have announced that he was here to rustle up recruits for a new communist army bent on unseating Roosevelt and she would have been convinced it was so, and convinced it was just. He could have told her that this entire, impressively choreographed, painstakingly timed, undoubtedly risky endeavor was all a ruse to win her heart, and she would have been convinced. Her only disappointment was that he spoke so little.

As the gang leader strode past the tellers, Darcy saw him notice a customer at another desk slowly pulling his hands away from a small stack of bills. The poor man looked like an old farmhand, and the expression on his face, Darcy saw, was not crestfallen but placid, as if he was so accustomed to weathering disasters that a gun-wielding bandit was well within the realm of the expected.

"You can pick that back up, sir," the leader had told the farmer as he walked past. "We're not here for your money, just the bank's. I wouldn't want to inconvenience anyone."

What else had he said? She tried to remember as the dirt road became a bit less accommodating and she tightened her grip. "I'm going to have to ask you for that combination, Mr. President." And "All righty, boys, we're down to a minute" and "I really like those shoes, did you buy them in town?" and "Get a chair for that lady over there, she looks faint" and, finally, joyously, "All righty, you and you and you and"—the finger pretending to pick her arbitrarily, even though the slight grin belied any such thing—"*you*, you'll need to step outside with us." Darcy knew the difference between fate and desire, thank you.

But that was all he'd said. How many words was that in total? Fifty? Seventy, perhaps? She wondered how many thousands of dollars they had taken with them in those Gladstone bags, how many bills each of his words had brought in. A man like that could talk in gold. She only wanted to hear him say something more.

The robbers had silently corralled the hostages in the front of the bank lobby and marched them outside, where Darcy noticed the phalanx of police officers standing helplessly on the sidewalk. This was when she first realized that she was in some modicum of danger. Not from this dapper robber and his assistants—the man positively exuded calm—but from the surely terrified police and their weapons. Her stomach tightened.

She was standing on the Buick's running board when one of the officers called upon the robbers to halt and surrender. The thieves laughed and informed him that any attempt to intervene could cost the lives of these nice hostages. Alarming words indeed, but she looked at the officers and saw their meek expressions, as if they knew there was no point in trying to stop the crooks and had spoken up only for appearance's sake.

"They're going to kill us!" the man who had vomited now screamed to his fellow hostages as they rocketed through the woods west of town. The police Fords were long gone, left behind by the speeding Buick. Given her background, Darcy knew enough about cars to be certain that this did not have a typical Buick engine beneath its hood. And she of course had noticed when one of the robbers in the backseat rolled down a window and threw what looked like tacks and roofing nails onto the road to delay their pursuers. She didn't know how long they'd been driving—one minute? ten? so hard to judge when the pace of your heart has changed—but it was long enough to exhaust the police. Initially, there had been two cars full of bank robbers (the other, also a Buick, had been similarly upholstered with four hostages); she didn't know if the second had been apprehended or if it had fled in a different direction.

The dirt road smoothed out again, and the bandits decreased their speed from reckless to very fast. They had been driving through woods— the multicolored confetti of oaks and elms showering them as acorns skittered beneath the wheels—but now the forest opened before them, revealing wide green fields interspersed with farmland. Against these colors the clear sky looked richer than usual.

"They're going to kill us!" the man repeated. His heavy beard and mustache were greasy, Darcy remembered. "We've seen their faces! They won't let us live!"

"We *all* saw their faces!" Darcy shut him up. Really. "The bank was full of people, and they didn't kill any of *them*!" Indeed, the thieves hadn't hurt anyone, hadn't pulled a trigger.

"I know how these things work!" the man insisted. "There was a bank robbery in South Bend a month ago, and they killed the two people they took with them! I say we let go now and take our chances in the woods!"

The prayer's voice had only grown louder.

"That wasn't the Firefly Brothers in South Bend!" replied the man behind Darcy. "That was some other gang! And I'm not letting go at this speed!"

As if on cue, the Buick began to slow down as it approached a crossing with another country road, where an empty car was waiting. The landscape was flat and deserted, occasional silos the only dark scratches on the horizon.

"I'm going to let go and run for it!" the man said, shifting his gaze among the three of them to enlist their participation. Then his fingers uncoiled and he was gone. Darcy turned and saw his body rolling on the ground, dirt and pebbles rising in a cloud.

The Buick parked beside the other car.

"Everybody back up three paces!" commanded a deep voice. Once the hostages had obeyed—each of them flexing tight fingers finally released from their death grips—the doors opened. One of the robbers sprinted back toward the escaped hostage, who was slowly attempting to rise, moaning.

Three other men exited the car.

"Hope that wasn't too rocky of a ride," the gang leader said to the hostages, his eyes lingering on Darcy. A long, double-handled gun dangled like an afterthought from his right hand. With his jacket open, Darcy also saw that he had a pistol in a shoulder holster. "The roads out here leave something to be desired."

"Please don't hurt us," begged the woman who'd been praying.

"Why would we do a thing like that? You've served your purpose, and did a particularly good job of it, I might add. Now, we are going to have to tie you and you"—he pointed to the other man—"to this post here, but the cops will find you soon enough. And it's a nice warm day—it'll be good to get some air."

As one of the robbers escorted the wounded escapee back to the parked cars, the rest of the gang busily moved packages, bags, weapons, and gasoline cans from the Buick into the other car, a black Pontiac. They all wore gloves, which struck Darcy as odd, considering that none of their faces were masked.

"So you're the Firefly Brothers?" Darcy asked the ringleader. "That's what they call you?"

He looked at her appraisingly, as if surprised her voice wasn't quivering. Perhaps he preferred quiverers? She didn't think so.

"They call us a lot of things. But we'll take that one over some of the others."

She had heard of them. They were making some noise in the lesser parts of the Midwest, though not in her hometown of Chicago, where the Syndicate held something of a monopoly on crime—or perhaps only an oligopoly, now that Capone was in jail. The papers must not have run any photographs, though. Surely she wouldn't have been able to blithely flip past a picture of this face.

"So why am I not being tied up with them?" she asked him as two of the robbers began tying the other hostages' wrists to the post of a collapsing fence.

"We still need some company for a bit longer, if you don't mind," the ringleader told her. "But don't worry, this time you can sit inside with us. Won't be long."

"So do you have a name, or is it just Firefly Brother Number One?"

"Better not let my brother hear you say that—he'll take offense. My name's Jason. And you are . . . ?"

"Darcy Windham."

"You aren't related to—"

"He's my father."

"My, my. An automotive heiress." He tipped his fedora. "Pleased to make your acquaintance."

"I'm afraid I'm not terribly close to my old man, so don't ask me for any free cars."

"I've never had trouble finding free cars. You aren't fond of your old man?"

"Well, he did name an axle after me, but that's about the extent of his familial affections."

Jason smiled. "It's a form of immortality."

"Yes, a rather greasy one."

The other robbers had finished tying up the hostages, and Jason motioned for her to get into the backseat of the Pontiac.

"You're just going to leave this Buick out here to rot?"

"Afraid so. The cops saw it, so the cops can have it."

"Why don't you wear masks?"

"I hope you aren't calling me ugly."

"No," and she found it impossible not to return his smile as he put a hand on her shoulder to guide her into the car. "But it does make it possible for your hostages to identify you later, doesn't it?"

The man who'd vomited screamed, "Jesus, lady, shut up!"

"Hey, watch it, buddy!" Jason snapped. But when he turned back to Darcy he was smiling again. "It's hot under a mask. Plus it's hard to breathe. And who cares if people can identify me?"

She still hadn't quite gotten into the car. "You aren't afraid of the police?"

"Are you?"

"I haven't done anything wrong."

"Never? Then why do you have that gleam in your eye, Miss Windham?"

———————

More thunder, rattling her apartment's windows. More gin, rattling her nerves. It was supposed to *settle* nerves, wasn't it? Perhaps she'd had too much, or too little. Only one way to be sure.

She hated herself as she poured. It had been years since she'd taken more than one drink in a sitting, not since emerging from the long fog precipitated by her mother's "suicide." Darcy preferred to think of it as a murder, even though there was no murder weapon for her father to leave his fingerprints on. Darcy had barely been in her teens, but her father hadn't noticed her drinking for months—or maybe he'd noticed but hadn't cared, at least not until the spectacle of herself became an embarrassment to him and his business. And then his solution had been to send her to a sanatorium—straitjackets and syringes and soft rooms.

Her father had called her a few hours ago, to see if she'd heard the news. He sounded as if he were gloating. She didn't know how he'd got her number—she had assumed this apartment was her secret. The man had tentacles; there was no limit to where they could slither. He'd asked what she was doing and she had said what does it *sound* like I'm doing, and he had told her martinis were a rather strong drink at this hour. What's wrong with strength? she'd asked. Didn't you preach the importance of strength, the necessity of strength, the primacy of strength? Sometimes a girl needs some strength in the morning.

After hanging up on him, she'd left the apartment and walked down the stairs, clutching the banister with each step.

It had stopped raining and the city glistened. Puddles like tiny mirrors lay on the roofs of parked cars. Every restaurant sign and arc light had been transformed into a leaky faucet. The city was so loud after a rain-storm, every movement shimmering with sound.

How could she be in shock like this? Did she have that right, when all along she'd known his death was a possibility? Every time he'd walked into a bank it was possible. And lately, with so many people after them, it could have happened at any time—at a filling station, in the bathroom of a supposedly safe apartment, driving down the street in a small town, buying coffee and the paper. Hiding in a farmhouse in Points North, Indiana. Why Points North? What on earth had happened these past few days? She knew something didn't make sense, but she lacked the energy to overturn these rocks and peer beneath them. All that mattered was she had been buried. He was gone. And the world was crying around her.

She walked down the street, weaving, and realized it was later than she had thought. She could smell the lake, smell it receding. Everything was pulling away from her. She'd probably never even see Ronny again, not that that was such a terrible fate. But suddenly Darcy missed her, wanted desperately to share this with someone, wanted to talk to her about Jason and Whit, breathe the brothers back to life with their stories. They could not possibly be dead.

Jason Fireson *dead*? Someone with such vibrancy, someone whose simple glance contained more energy than all the working stiffs trudging to work on the train each morning? Life was three-dimensional with him, the flatness of the mundane popped up into startling clarity, so many roads to navigate and mountains to climb. That's what it was like with Jason; he made everything possible. Except death. That was unimaginable.

The photographs, Jesus. How could they print photos like that? Gratuitous. The *swine*. Reveling in it. Was that all he was to them? All those people who had gladly hidden the brothers in their crumbling homes, lied to the police for them, sung their praises in taverns and factories. Now they were chuckling at the thought of a bunch of country officers stalking them in the night and—

A car rushed past, turning a puddle into a weapon. She was soaked from the waist down. She hollered after it, pedestrians staring at this very unladylike wraith, this banshee of madness. Goddamn you! Goddamn you *all*!

And now a police officer, Jesus, asking her to calm down. Sir, you insult me. I *am* calm. This is calmness. Wrath is calm. God, she could have slapped him, but that would have been a mistake. At least her father hadn't shared her address with any reporters; at least there were no flashbulbs recording her dazed movements. Darcy loathed pity, but she found herself telling this beat cop, this fresh-faced rookie, that her husband had been killed last night. He told her he was sorry and took her by the arm to walk her back to her building. He asked if she had reported the crime and she said, yes, yes, it's being looked into, that's not the point. Jesus, she'd told a stranger, and he was helping her to walk straight, or close enough. She was crying on his shoulder, on his uniform, already wet from the rain, so maybe he didn't mind. She wasn't sure how long he let her do that, but it must have been a while, because when they finally reached her building again and he tipped his hat to her she felt spent. Dry.

Where was she supposed to go?

They had blindfolded her for the next portion of their getaway, squeezing her between two silent men in the backseat. She instantly regretted that comment about being able to identify them.

"This is hardly the way to treat a lady," she said, hoping her strong words could compensate for her increasing alarm. A final door was shut, the engine was turned on, and they were rolling away. Where, and for how long? Maybe he hadn't been flirting; maybe he had less chivalrous ends in mind.

"Let's just say there are parts of this drive that we prefer to be secretive, and leave it at that." Jason's voice sounded the slightest bit different—not cold, exactly, but businesslike. She was a commodity, something to be held and then traded. She had felt this way before.

The men didn't talk anymore, so neither did she. She missed the exhilaration of the running boards, the wind in her hair. Already she was amazed she had felt that way—God, she *was* crazy. She was being kidnapped by gangsters and she had foolishly smiled her way into the executioner's den. The freed hostages were likely offering her description to the police even now. Somewhere an obituary was being prepared.

They drove for an hour, maybe two, stopping intermittently. A door would open and one of the shoulders beside her would depart. At least she had some room back here now.

"I'll have to ask you to lie down now, Miss Windham," Jason said after the second stop. "Wouldn't want any passersby to see your blindfold and get suspicious."

She obeyed, reluctantly. She began to wonder if she would ever see anything else again.

"So how much money did we make today?" she asked them, again hoping her own words could lighten her mood. Even when she had nothing else, like in the sanatorium, she always had herself, always had her words. She used them to calm herself, reinvent herself.

"Can't say yet—haven't had the opportunity to count it."

"Well, let's imagine. Let's imagine this was a pretty good day. What does that translate to in this line of work? Ten thousand? Forty thousand?"

"That'd be nice" was all he said, but she heard a second voice grumble, "I'll bet that's a typical day for her daddy."

Minutes later the car stopped again, though the engine was still running.

"All righty, Miss Windham, this is your stop," Jason said as two doors opened. She sat up, and then another door was opened, and she felt a hand on hers. He gentlemanly guided her out of the car, then she felt him untying the blindfold.

Her eyes needed a moment to adjust to the sun, and to him standing so close. She backed up despite herself, wishing she hadn't.

She was in a small field that looked as if it had once been a farm but had been lost to neglect. To her right was an abandoned farmhouse and a narrow pathway they had driven through. Surely this drab locale would not be her final resting place.

"Sorry to leave you here, but this is where the adventure ends. Once we've driven off, you can start knocking on doors and I'm sure someone will have a phone."

She let herself exhale. All would be well, as she had originally believed. These weren't such bad men, especially this one right here. After the period of enforced blindness, her nascent vision was fuzzy around the edges but just sharp enough in the center for her to appreciate his face. She hadn't been imagining it before—he really was this handsome.

"What a pity," she said. "I was rather enjoying myself. For a moment, I thought the famous bank robber was moving into kidnapping."

"Not my style."

"Why is that? Not dramatic enough? Not enough witnesses for your vanity?"

"Takes too long. Ransom notes, waiting for them to rustle up the money, phone calls . . ."

"You prefer immediate gratification."

"Pretty much."

"Perhaps you need to learn the benefits of patience."

"I suppose you know of a good teacher?"

"Hate to interrupt, brother," the other one said, his voice the very sound of rolling eyes. "But we're running late."

Jason was still smiling at her. He had started and never stopped. He tipped his hat.

"Been a pleasure, Miss Windham. You take care."

Twin door slams like gunshots, and the Pontiac was pulling away. She was alone now, on an abandoned farm, in an abandoned town, in some abandoned state, in the center of an abandoned country. They could have dropped her off in downtown Chicago and she would have felt the same way. After being in that man's presence, anything afterward was emptiness.

IV.

It was dark when the Firefly Brothers crept through their mother's backyard again.

They had spent much of the past two days in the garage, cleaning and organizing an area that had been their father's domain and had been collecting dust for years. There were old boxes of clothes that no longer fit June's boys, auto parts that Pop had held on to in the misguided hope that they would one day find some use, books that everyone had read and no one had liked, scraps of excess wood molding and plywood. They had done this partly to help Ma, but mostly because it gave them something to do while they stayed out of sight.

They had managed to find old clothes of Pop's that fit them well enough, and Ma had volunteered to tailor them. Jason was clad in linen slacks and a white oxford, Whit in tan corduroys and a gray work shirt. Whit carried a five-year-old issue of *Field & Stream* wrapped around his pistol.

No one seemed to be out that night, and no one had touched their stolen car, so they climbed in, Jason again at the wheel.

It was the first time Whit had left the house since their unexpected arrival, though Jason had made a brief excursion the previous night, sending coded telegrams to Darcy and Veronica at several addresses, as they couldn't be sure of the girls' locations. The message to Darcy had read:

PERFECT WEATHER FOR BIRD WATCHING / MIGRATING EARLIER
THAN PREDICTED / DON'T BELIEVE EVERYTHING YOU READ /
HAVE BINOS READY.

Jaybird was a nickname she'd given him long ago, but she used it only when they were alone.

The brothers' main fears were that the girls had already run off some-place, or were being watched by the feds, or that they would assume the telegrams were police snares. The brothers wanted to get out of Lincoln City and find the girls, but only after they had some money to escape with—and it would be easier to procure funds on their own.

It felt so strange to be wearing Pop's old clothes. Whit had gone so far as to name his son after Pop, but to Jason the subject of their father was one best left unmentioned. Yet here were these borrowed clothes, practically screaming at him.

Pop hadn't been a screamer, but he'd certainly been a preacher. All those endless sayings about the benefits of hard work, early birds getting worms, stitches in time saving nine, so hokey Jason winced to remember them. Patrick Fireson had read countless Horatio Alger novels as a young man and continued to reread them as an adult. They were stories of poor boys who worked through poverty and whose good deeds and work ethic attracted the favor of kindly rich men, who helped them up the ladder. Pop had given copies of the books to his sons, but Jason had found them deathly boring and corny; he'd been more a Huck Finn kind of boy.

But those books had rung true for Pop, who liked to joke that he himself was a character from an Alger novel brought to life. His parents had died in a fire when he was five, and his distant relatives weren't in a position to help. Pop was sent to a Catholic orphanage, and at the age of twelve he started as a clerk in a small grocery. He toiled there for many years, gradually gaining the good graces of the owner, a thrifty German named Schmidt. Pictures of the young, hardworking Patrick Fireson show a thin lad who always seems to have stopped in the middle of some activity—his hair mussed, his collar loose, his eyes impatient for the camera's shutter. Pop served in the Great War, returning to the store after nine months with some shrapnel in his right knee but his can-do attitude undiminished. Schmidt's adult son died of pneumonia in the winter of '24, and two years later Pop received an unexpected inheritance from an army buddy. By then Schmidt was tired of the store and the memories they held of his doomed legacy. Pop made him an offer, and the store was his.

"I didn't have parents," Pop would say. "My father was a broom and my mother was a mop, and they taught me all I needed to know." Maybe if Pop had grown up in a real family he would have had a better idea of how to be a father, Jason sometimes thought, instead of simply browbeating his sons with lessons about elbow grease and honesty.

By the time Jason was in high school, Pop was a ranking member of the Boosters Club, meeting with the other local businessmen to trumpet their own virtues and draft plans for the future of their city. Despite his Irish roots, he was an outspoken proponent of Prohibition—"Booze makes young people lazy," he warned his sons—and later an opponent of speakeasies, even if he himself indulged at home with the occasional glass of whiskey or scotch. He wrote letters to the editor deploring the prevalence of truants running about downtown (and pilfering from his shelves), and he happily gave money to candidates for city council who supported business (and who, unbeknownst to him, would soon become very good friends indeed with the supermarket owners who were eyeing expansion into Lincoln City).

The family store may have been what brought the Firesons out of their cramped apartment and into a modest house in a tree-lined neighborhood, but it had never interested Jason as a career. He'd always thought of it as punishment. Stacking crates, unpacking boxes, filling the shelves, taking inventory, enduring his father's constant criticism and moralizing—Jason did all these things, from a young age, just as he raked leaves or washed the family car. But he sure didn't plan on being a professional leaf raker as an adult, so why should he work at the store, either? Let his brothers take over. Whit in particular seemed the natural choice; Pop was different with him, funny and carefree. Whenever Pop imparted advice to his youngest—telling him, for example, that most men were lazy and that the hardworking man had an instant advantage over his competitors—young Whit would listen with a look of awe in his eyes, as if it was an honor to receive such guidance.

Life was a contest, according to Pop, even a battle. You needed to be strong, of course, but also upstanding and honest—a capitalist Sir Galahad—for fortune to shine on you. He worked long hours and spent much of his time at home reading various business papers and journals, ignoring the chaos of his household until he felt called upon to interrupt with lessons of struggle and success.

When Jason was eighteen, only two months away from graduation, he dared to tell his father that he wasn't sure he wanted to work at the store after he finished school.

They were sitting on the front porch, Pop's cigar burning in an ashtray between them. "And I don't really see myself being a college boy, either."

"You don't want to *work*, Jason." Pop wasn't thin anymore, his hair had gone gray, and he looked older than he was. "You want it all handed to you."

"No, sir, it's just that—"

"You want to skate by on charm for as long as you can. You got by on smiling at the teachers and getting your friends to pass you their notes, sure, congratulations. But those tricks don't work in the adult world, and suddenly all you'll have to show for yourself is laziness and a smile that won't last after you've taken a few hard knocks."

"I don't plan to be lazy, Pop. I just want to go in a different direction."

"You've had a pretty nice life, never really having to scrap for anything."

"I can scrap just fine." Jason straightened. He was an inch taller than Pop and already more muscular.

"I don't mean scrapping for girls, or for attention. I mean scrapping to get by."

God, not this again. Patrick Fireson's life had been a series of obstacles to clear. He had conjured invisible advantages from the darkness, had taken emptiness and poverty and turned them into the raw materials of a life's adventure, et cetera, et cetera. Talking to him wasn't so much having a conversation as giving him new opportunities to make old points.

"You need to keep moving if you want to stay ahead. Like what I've done at the store, expanding and moving forward."

"I'm just saying maybe there are other things."

"Such as?"

He told Pop he had some buddies from school, a few years older than him, who worked for a shipping outfit based in Cincinnati, delivering goods across the Midwest. He'd been offered a job and could move in with his friends. Even though truck driving might not sound glamorous, at least he'd get to take a step outside Lincoln City and *see* something.

"Maybe it'll only be a few months," Jason said, playing his trump. "And then I'll feel like the time's right to take over the store."

He didn't mention the illicit nature of this particular shipping outfit, or that some of these school friends were related to one Petey Killarney, the owner of Lincoln City's finest speakeasies, to which Jason had begun winning admission in the past few months. After some delicate lobbying over the next two weeks, Jason won Pop's reluctant blessing to take the job, Pop likely figuring that his headstrong kid soon would learn the hard way about the tough, cruel world.

But did he? He loved bootlegging: the late nights, the secrecy, the cool cats and code words. When you walked through that back door, you were someone special, part of the select group. The man in charge of the operation, Chance McGill, was a few years older than Pop but existed in a different realm. Chance was wise and hardworking, sure, but he didn't lord it over you. He showed Jason how to talk, how to move, whom to impress and whom to ignore. When Jason spotted a trap on the road one night and managed to elude it, Chance talked him up in the important circles, doubled his pay. Had Pop ever acknowledged anything Jason had done right? The speakeasies were loud and dark and Jason could disappear inside them or do the opposite—be the man of the show, smile at the ladies, who couldn't resist smiling back. He wasn't far from home but he felt a lifetime away from Pop's criticism.

And he was bringing in decent money, which, even then, he wasn't shy about displaying. His clothes became sharper and tailored, he wore Italian shoes and silk socks, and one night when he rolled into town for a family dinner he was behind the wheel of a shiny new Hudson.

Pop confronted him that night. He had been oddly silent during dinner, but just when Ma was about to serve dessert he finally spoke up.

"I know what you're driving back and forth across state lines. Machine parts, huh? I suppose, if Petey Killarney's booze machine is the one you're talking about."

Jason shifted in his seat and smiled awkwardly.

"That's funny to you? Why don't you tell your brothers what you've been peddling?"

Jason glanced across the table at his brothers, who were clearly oblivious.

"I haven't been *peddling* anything, Pop. I've just been driving."

Ma asked him to explain, but something in her voice betrayed the fact that she had feared this all along. Jason couldn't take the disappointment in her eyes, so he looked at his father. Pop's disappointment was more bearable; Jason had so much experience with it.

"Go ahead, impress your brothers," Pop said. "That's what this is all about, isn't it? Looking good, looking tough? It's always been about looks to you."

"Pop, everybody's still drinking it, laws or no laws. All I'm doing is . . . administering a public good. It's like being the milkman."

"So be a milkman!"

Everyone seemed waxed in place. Jason waited a beat. "It's not like what the movies and magazines make it out to be. It's all perfectly safe, and we're smart about it."

"You, smart? I find that difficult to believe."

"For God's sake, there's some in your glass right now. You can't take the Irish out of the Irishman."

Jason offered his usual disarming smile when he said that, and his uncomprehending little brothers smiled along with him, as they always did. Then Pop's fist struck the table and their glasses danced.

"I did not raise a family of criminals!"

Things got worse from there. First Pop stood and then so did Jason. His brothers' chairs slowly backed away, disappearing into the margins. He remembered pointed fingers on both sides, and then fists. He was tired of being told what to do. He was young and proud of himself and stupid, yes, he saw that now. But not then. Then he was yelling and shouting and Ma was telling them to stop, and when it ended Pop told him he was no longer welcome in their house. Fine, Jason thought, trying to convince himself that's what he'd wanted all along.

He still remembered that line, *a family of criminals*. He would think of it years later, at Pop's trial.

Another of Pop's lines: *You're better than these people.*

Jason remembered that one, too, voiced by his old man during their first conversation in a prison visiting room. At the age of twenty-one, Jason had been collared. Chance McGill paid his bail, and Jason spent most of his pretrial time with his new associates, which did not go over well at home. He had told his family that everything would be fine, it was all a mistake, but the look in his mother's eyes when he'd pleaded as McGill recommended—guilty, a plea bargain, a weaker sentence for the good of the organization—was something he would always remember. He got ten months, with a chance to be out in eight.

He had been surprised on that first Sunday to be told he had a solo visitor. He'd figured his mother would have come with his brothers, that maybe she would have been able to coax Pop as well. But when he walked into the large cinder-block room, prisoners and visitors facing off across six long wooden tables like poker players without cards, he saw, in the back corner, Patrick Fireson sitting alone.

They hadn't spoken much over the past two years. Pop had made his views clear and Jason hadn't seen why he should subject himself to such haranguing ever again. So when he saw Pop sitting there he wondered if he could tell the guard that he wasn't interested in visiting with this particular gentleman. But it was a three-hour drive for the old man—Jason had been caught and tried in Indiana—and Jason didn't want to send Pop back thinking his son didn't have the guts to look him in the eye.

He made it to the table and Pop extended a hand. They shook, which felt formal and strange, then he sat. Pop asked how he was doing.

Jason shrugged. "How are Ma and the boys?"

"They're fine. They wanted to come, too, but I thought I should come alone this one time." Jason didn't say anything as Pop looked around. "You know, I've worked awfully hard in the one life I've been given. Built a strong business, got a good house for my family. And you chose this instead."

"*This* wasn't exactly what I was choosing, Pop."

"You knew the risks."

Jason reminded himself that he would have a week, at least, until he could entertain another visitor. That meant one week to replay this conversation in his mind, so he should try, despite the difficulties and temptations, to play it well the first time.

"I guess I made some mistakes, Pop."

"Yes. I guess you did."

"I should have driven faster that one time," he said, grinning. Pop's face tightened.

"I'm so glad you have your sense of humor. That should make the months fly by."

"Did you drive all this way just to tell me how I messed up? The judge already told me that. And the prosecutor, and the cops, and half the guys in this room, to be honest."

"Yeah, what about these guys?" Pop looked around again. "I've been thinking about them, studying them a bit as I waited for you. You know, when you're a parent you can't help but look at the other kids, think of the different choices the other parents made, the different people your kids are all becoming. I thought about that at your high school graduation, looked at the caps and gowns, wondered where they were all headed. And now I look at your new cohorts here. . . . Are these your people now, Jason?"

"Pop—"

Patrick Fireson leaned forward, lowered his voice. They were still the only two at this table. "You're better than these people, Jason."

"I know that."

"You've got a head on your shoulders and you know how to succeed, you know right from wrong. I *taught* you that. You're *better* than these people."

"I *know* that," Jason said, raising his voice.

"Then what are you doing here?"

Jason stared at the wall. He would have punched it if it weren't cinder block.

They spent most of their thirty minutes that way, trying to talk casually but always forced back to these moments of reckoning. Jason couldn't tell if his father was trying to help him or torture him.

When the thirty minutes were up, they shook hands again and that was that. The conversation, as he'd expected, didn't get any better as he thought about it during the week.

The next Sunday the whole family came. Ma didn't cry, for which Jason was thankful, and Weston and Whit kept staring at the other prisoners, apparently wondering which were ax murderers and which ate children. Jason's eyes occasionally trailed his father's, to the two younger sons and back to himself, and he felt worse, not necessarily for what he had done but for what he was forcing his brothers and his mother to see. He sat up straighter that day, smiled more, did what he could to show that this wasn't so terrible. He joked with his brothers, told Ma how he was teaching some of the men to read, mentioned to Pop that he was studying the Bible a bit (failing to explain that the Good Book was the only reading material prisoners were allowed).

The Sunday after that, it was just Pop again, and Jason tensed, anticipating another browbeating. But it didn't come. They just talked—about the family, the store, Pop's real-estate plans, baseball. Eventually Jason realized that Pop was done with the lecturing. He didn't know if Pop felt he'd pointed out his son's flaws enough by then or if the old man was silently assessing what fault in this was his own. Over time, Jason learned to let his guard down.

"Tell Weston and Whit that they don't have to come if they don't like . . . seeing me like this," Jason said one of the times when they were alone. "I'd understand. I don't want them looking at me in this place and thinking, I don't know, that this is their future, too."

"They miss you, Jason."

Jason nodded, looked away.

"They don't want to talk about it, but I can tell. They missed you before, when you were out doing all *that*. But now, too."

"I'm a lousy brother."

"Brothers usually are."

"I'm a lousy son, too."

"You have your moments."

Jason let a grin pierce through his self-loathing. Then it faded. "Look, I know I haven't been . . . who you want me to be, but—"

"It's not about what I want. We are what we *do*, Jason. I've tried to show you that. I guess I failed at it. But we are what we do, the choices we make."

"I know I made some wrong decisions."

Pop seemed struck by the admission. This would have been, what, the second month? The third? How long had Jason's reserve of pride and cockiness held out?

"So when I get out of here . . . could I work at the store again? Or do you have a policy against hiring guys with records?"

Pop smiled. "That policy doesn't apply to blood relations. And I can always use the cheap labor."

And that's what Jason was after his term ended, cheap labor, the prodigal son returned. Smiles all around. The good feelings lasted a few weeks.

Eventually Jason got over his guilt at having been a lousy son and he admitted to himself how incredibly bored he was to be back at the store, performing the same tasks he'd done as a schoolboy, standing behind the same counter, making the same idle talk with the same customers. The onset of Pop's money troubles only made things worse—the stock crash and the new supermarkets undercutting his business, and the debt Pop had rung up investing in real estate just before the crash. Jason was tired of hearing about it, tired of inheriting someone else's problems. He told himself he had a right to live his own life. So finally, when Weston was working at the store full-time and Whit was in his final year of school, Jason broke the news as delicately as he could. He thanked Pop for taking him back in and told him no hard feelings this time but he was moving in with some friends to try "something new," something for himself. Pop said he understood, acting as if his son had not broken his heart again.

But "something new" wound up being something old: bootlegging again. And things didn't work out quite as Jason had hoped. He would soon do a second stretch in jail for it, but this time there would be no visits from his old man.

Years later, the resurrected Firefly Brothers were driving just north of Lincoln City to the quiet town of Karpis. Even the most devastated of cities seemed to have at least one gleaming suburb like this, the lawns watered and mowed, the Cadillacs washed and waxed. People out here had heard of the depression but didn't entirely believe the stories.

At the edge of town, where a few restaurants and taverns clung to the one narrow road leading north into emptiness, sat the safe house run by Jason's old bootlegging mentor, Chance McGill. Chance did a little of This and a little of That. He'd been jailed for This during the early twenties, but he was acquitted of That a few years back, and these days he operated his popular restaurant-nightclub, Last Best Chance, with minimal interference. There were bands three nights a week and dancing showgirls twice, and the card playing that went on in back rooms was permitted by the brass buttons as long as they got their take. A veritable House of Seven Gables of the Midwest underworld, Last Best Chance was as sprawling as its owner's many pursuits; a dance room had been added a few years back, and then an outdoor patio, and then another bar over here, and some rooms for the ladies over there, until the building was a nearly block-long labyrinth of pleasure and deception. Rumor had it that Chance had designed the floor plan to be as confusing as possible should he and his special guests ever need to elude raiding cops.

Chance and his chatty wife lived on the top floor; also on that floor were several bedrooms that hot boys could stay in, for prices ranging from five bucks to thirty, depending on exactly how much heat was on them. Dillinger had once stayed here, as well as Baby Face Nelson and even Pretty Boy Floyd, far away from his southwestern territory. But no one had doled out more hide-me money than Jason and Whit, until Chance had regretfully told them, back in May, that the volcanically hot Firefly Brothers should start bunking elsewhere.

Jason and his gang often communicated through Chance, leaving messages about when and where they should regroup. Chance knew anyone worth knowing and never seemed to have trouble locating them when the right person asked.

Jason idled in front of the building. A bottle-blond zaftig was strolling toward the entrance.

"Say, doll, do me a favor," Jason called to her. "Tell Mr. McGill that Officer Rubinsky would like a word. And to bring some smokes."

She gave him a look as empty as an alcoholic's shot glass. Then her heels clacked away. It was burlesque night, and the Firesons were treated to a blast of tarnished horns when she opened the door.

Two minutes later another brass blast, longer this time because one of the men was holding the door open. A second was beside him, and the third, Chance McGill himself, was holding a box of cigars and a level gaze aimed cautiously at the Pontiac.

Officer Rubinsky was one of the cops Chance paid protection money to; Chance could see this wasn't the cop's wheels.

"We look like a couple of Syndicate torpedoes," Whit said under his breath. "Probably scaring the hell out of him."

"Good. It'll make him easier to read."

Chance was in his early fifties but had managed to age with the grace of a silent-film star. Usually he moved with a thespian's confidence, fluidity to every gesture, but now he stepped slowly, as if under water. A thin man, his gray hair was trimmed short and his wrinkles were ironed flat in the neon light. Then his blue eyes lit red.

"Jason?" He was ten feet from the Pontiac.

"Not so loud." Jason grinned. "Tell your loogans you're okay. And get in—we have a crazy story for you."

"You weren't followed?"

"Only by the Grim Reaper—he tailed us leaving the cemetery. C'mon, get in."

Chance waved off his men and opened the back door. Jason eased off the brake and began driving the calm streets of Karpis.

"How's tricks?" Jason asked. Whit had turned halfway in his seat to keep an eye on the restaurateur.

"Not so good as they are for you two, apparently. Jesus. I even offered a prayer for your eternal souls."

"I'm sure our souls appreciate it."

"What happened?"

"Look, Chance," Jason said. "No one needs to know about the crazy hallucinations you've been having. Everyone can just go on mourning the dead Firefly Brothers, got it? They can send us all the prayers they like."

"Understood. That Houdini you pulled in Toledo was impressive, boys, but this one is by far the best."

"Thanks. And we aren't going to tell you how we did it, no offense."

"I wouldn't ask."

Jason pulled into a small park and turned around to face his passenger as Chance handed out cigars. Jason hadn't had a smoke since before the cooling boards, and just by biting off the end he saw that Chance knew how to keep his cops happy.

"Heard anything on Owney?" Jason asked.

Chance produced a lighter and that produced light. "What kind of anything?"

"We were supposed to meet him last week in Detroit." Jason left it at that. He still couldn't remember if the meeting had occurred, but the fact that the Points North cops had found the full seventy thousand dollars on the brothers meant that they'd never paid Owney his share, so either the meeting hadn't happened or it had gone very badly indeed.

"He hasn't been arrested," Chance said. "And he ain't ratted that I know of."

Even with the windows down they were consumed by delicious smoke.

"Know where he is?"

Chance didn't answer.

"We still owe him his stake," Jason explained, not mentioning that they no longer had the money.

Chance exhaled a cloud. They were like three bored dragons in a too-small cave. "There's a cottage he and his wife have used."

"In the U.P.?" Jason raised his eyebrows. Chance made an expression that was not fully a confirmation. "Jesus, then he's an idiot."

Jason had met Owney Davis in prison during his second bootlegging rap, before graduating to bank jobs. Let out two weeks after Jason, Owney became a part of the Firefly Gang from the beginning. He was a loyal friend whose life ambition was to form a new church, in the hope of spiritual as well as financial enrichment. Jason found it difficult to believe Owney would turn Judas. But he also found it difficult to believe that, with all the heat on them, Owney and his wife would run to the same Michigan lake house they'd used as a hideout months earlier, when the heat had first intensified.

"What's the word on Marriner, Brickbat, and Roberts?" Jason asked.

"Look, Jason, *if* someone did stooge on you, it coulda been anyone. Ten grand is a lot of money."

Ten grand was the most recent reward the Justice Department had posted for information leading to the Firefly Brothers' arrest. It had started at fifteen hundred, then doubled after two cops were killed during a November bank job in Calumet City, then doubled again in the early spring, when the feds belatedly realized that a fatal February bank job in Baton Rouge had actually been pulled off by the Firefly Brothers. Louisiana was far outside their usual territory, of course; after a busy autumn in the Midwest, the brothers had spent much of the winter hiding out, first in Florida and then in New Orleans. It had been a wise time to hide: the U.S. attorney general and a bureaucrat named J. Edgar Hoover from something called the Bureau of Investigation were making speeches about the need for a stronger national police force, something capable of investigating the complex cases that bumbling state squads couldn't handle. A federal crime-fighting agency would conquer gangsterism just as the New Deal would conquer the depression, Hoover claimed. When the Firesons' money grew scarce—and the exoticism of the South was overpowered by their nostalgia for home—Jason had started scouting banks in Baton Rouge, leading to the reunited gang's first endeavor in more than two months. After that, the price on the brothers' heads continued to rise as stories proliferated about their escapades, some of them accurate and some of them the falsely attributed crimes of other, less famous outlaws. Finally, the feds had rounded the price off to an even ten, causing the brothers to wonder if that number would continue to appreciate for as long as they drew breath, or if it would eventually crash like the stock market if people lost interest. Or if they simply disappeared.

"Well," Jason said now, "we're hoping to narrow the list of suspects."

"You should have too many other things on your mind to be interested in revenge, boys."

"We didn't say anything about revenge. We'd just like to know if someone did rat on us, so we can avoid that someone in the future."

"Well, if anyone did they didn't tell me."

"I never asked if they did. I just asked if you knew where our boys are."

"People haven't been using the Chance McGill line the way they used to, but—"

"Because you wouldn't let us," Whit said.

"Damn right I wouldn't let you!" He held the cigar away from his face and extended a reproachful finger. "I've worked my way up inch by inch, son, and I'm not gonna let it get torn down by a couple brothers who've managed to get ten state police forces, Pinkertons, postal cops, the National Guard, and the fucking federal government after them, no matter how goddamn charming *one* of them happens to be."

Jason put a hand on Whit's shoulder. "We're not blaming you for anything, Chance. We're just—"

"Your brother sure as hell is."

"Whit didn't mean anything by it. Anyway, back to square one. You're saying you don't know hell's first whispers about where our boys are?"

Chance managed to move his eyes from Whit to Jason. "Marriner's still living the good life, far as I know." Marriner Skelty, Jason's bank-robbing mentor with decades of endeavors to his name, had possessed the good sense to retire after the Calumet City job in November. "As for Brickbat and Roberts, nix."

"Brickbat was never my biggest fan," Jason said, to draw him out.

"I always did notice an added degree of tension in the room when he was in it. Crazy bastard. Never shoulda gotten involved with him, Jason."

"I got wise eventually."

The brothers had kicked Brickbat and Roberts out of the gang after the bloody Baton Rouge job. Brickbat was as his nickname implied, all stubborn force and no thought. He was only five-six, but his thick frame contained the coiled rage of three generations of doomed Iowa home-steaders. Still, if you were at least a few feet away from him you stood a reasonably good chance of outsmarting him before he got close enough to break your face. Unless he was packing, which he always was. Starting out as the muscle guarding cigarette shipments in St. Paul, he'd worked a few bank jobs with the Barker Gang in Minnesota. According to the po-lice, he'd rubbed three cops in the process; according to Brickbat, the body count was seven. He'd been in the opening months of a permanent holiday courtesy the state of Illinois when he was liberated during the same jailbreak that freed such now-infamous hoods as Henry Pierpont and John Makley, of the Dillinger Gang. Brickbat knew Owney through some work they'd done on a Minnesota bootlegging line, and at the time Jason needed an extra torpedo and figured the man's brand of pugilistic cockiness would make him a natural for the job. Thus was a regrettable relationship born. Jason quickly tired of the way Brickbat's palsied trigger finger made bank jobs more violent affairs than they needed to be. Jason had handed Brickbat an extra cut when he booted him from the gang, in the hope that it would constitute ending on good terms, but something in the man's demeanor had left Jason with the uncomfortable feeling that this was not yet a farewell.

Elton Roberts, Brickbat's only friend, was a heavy drinker, a trait the Firesons distrusted. A little here and there was fine, but a man who couldn't be counted on to drive straight or think straight was an unnec-essary risk. Fortyish and debonair, Roberts was a grifter who'd spent the past few years ripping off the hopeless jobless across the Midwest. Decked out in a dapper suit and possessing a smooth voice, he looked every bit the trustworthy businessman, or at least what a poor egg thought a trustworthy businessman would look like, if there were any. He would troll the breadlines and find a few suckers, preferably immigrants or farmers who had lost their property and were overwhelmed by their urban environs. He'd tell them he was the manager of a new building in town that needed four elevator operators; the job paid thirty a week— not bad at all—and all the fellows needed to do was front him fifty each for their uniforms. The fellows usually didn't have that much cash, but they'd ask for a day or two to rustle the funds from their cousins or in-laws or dying grandpas. Once Roberts had their money, he'd tell them the building's address and ask them to show at eight the next morning. When they did, they would find that Roberts wasn't there and that the building had no elevator. Roberts bounced from city to city working that grift and a few others before the cops got wise. Then, while doing time, he met a jug marker with a list of banks to hit once he got out. Like a skittering asteroid, Elton Roberts eventually came into Jason's orbit. Because Roberts looked straight and could talk his way out of trouble, Jason had taken him on as a faceman. He learned about Roberts's jobshark scams only after a few weeks of working together, when Elton got drunk and boastful. That's when Jason realized he'd never liked the man.

"Look," Chance said, "I know Brickbat's crazy, but I don't see him for a finger-louse. Last I heard he was gearing for some big job. Was trying to get the Barkers involved, but they wouldn't bite."

"What was the job?"

"He wasn't that talkative."

Jason eyed him. "You're not telling us everything."

"It'd take a week to tell you everything, and you never seem to have enough time. But I'm telling you the important parts."

Jason turned around and started the engine. "You're right—I'd love to chin with you all night, but, yeah, we've got to go."

"Where you headed?"

That was at the top of the list of questions Jason wouldn't answer, so he lied. "Very far from here."

"Any messages for me to pass on?"

"Dead men don't pass messages. This never happened."

"Got it. Except, dead men pass *lots* of messages. You can take just about any message you want off a dead man."

Jason declined the philosophical argument and drove back to Last Best Chance in silence.

"Well, if it means anything to you boys, guys are awful broken up over your alleged demise. Lotta depressed folks in my club these days. Buying plenty of drinks, though."

"That's nice. Hopefully our funerals will be well attended." Jason pulled up to the curb in front of the funhouse. Out in the parking lot, an elastic-legged drunk was supported by two prostitutes.

"Thanks for the smokes, Chance," Jason told him. "And goodbye forever."

Chance nodded at the two of them, stepping out of the Pontiac. "I've heard that one before." Then he tapped the roof and walked toward his ramshackle empire. No one was watching them as Jason hit the gas and pulled away.

"So," Jason said to his brother, "if the cops had broken up our meeting with Owney on their own initiative they would have arrested him, too, which Chance would have heard about by now."

"Or maybe they weren't just on to Owney—maybe he did rat on us," Whit said. "Maybe the feds offered him starting-out money for his new church."

Whit had never been as tight with Owney, perplexed by the many contradictions between the man's deeds and his proclaimed holiness. A recent convert to revolutionary politics, Whit proudly proclaimed himself an atheist, but to Jason that was just a front for the fact that Whit hadn't forgiven God for what He did to Pop. Regardless, anyone who claimed a special relationship with the Man Upstairs was someone Whit could not understand.

"I just can't see Owney rolling on us," Jason said.

"If we assume there even was a rat and that there isn't some other explanation, then if it wasn't Owney, that leaves Brickbat and Roberts."

"I wasn't interested in getting mixed up with them anyway. All I wanted to know was whether it was safe to try to find Owney and get him in on the next endeavor. My take is maybe, but maybe not. So let's avoid the risk and lure Marriner out of retirement instead."

"You act like all you're interested in is doing another endeavor. Like you couldn't care less about finding out what happened to us."

"It's what I told Chance: I'm not interested in revenge. I just want to know who to avoid so we can make a score and cash out of this once and for all."

Whit looked at Jason incredulously. "You're saying you don't want to figure out *what the hell happened to us?*"

Jason sighed. As usual, it would be his job to keep them focused. "We can look into it once we get back on our feet, okay?"

Whit held his hands in front of his face for a moment, staring at them. He'd been doing that a lot lately, Jason had noticed. "We can still bleed, you know, if we cut ourselves."

"That's fascinating."

"It hurts, too."

The stars were still out but they faded as Jason drove back into Lincoln City. He hadn't driven with so little fear in weeks—but he did check the rearview every few minutes, out of habit.

"No one's following us," he told his brother. "Being dead has its advantages."

V.

———————————————

Darcy woke amid newspapers, smudges on her cheek. Her head was a desert scoured by a sandstorm, and she had no memory of the event or whatever had preceded it, no memory of anything since that policeman had helped her back to her building. She was in bed, the sun rudely shouting through the windows, and the first thing she saw when she opened her eyes was a headline about some FDR speech, and another about the Nazis' latest grab for power, and another about . . . Yes, of course. That.

Darcy rose, and was reminded that she should move more slowly. Oh, my. She had forgotten about hangovers. If she drank in the face of death, what should she do after she'd stopped drinking? Death didn't stop, so neither should the drinking. Sad how easily she slipped into past routines; this was how she had responded to her mother's death, and now death was again chasing her to the bottle. Jason had always been so controlled, never overdoing anything, and she thought it had rubbed off on her. How sudden and irrevocable death was.

She rose from the bed and poured herself a gin. Then the bathroom, her penance, and next a long shower, holding the walls. Everything was vibrating, pulsating. She scrubbed the ink from her face and hands; she opened her mouth and drank hot mouthfuls from the shower. She wanted to clean her tongue, clean the insides of her skull. The worst part was knowing she would feel this way for so, so long.

Leaving the bathroom, she gathered up the newspapers, crushing the awful reality into a great crackling mass, and stuffed them into a wastebasket. The basket wasn't big enough. She gathered the remainder and carried it into the kitchen, threw it into the bin. Her hands were filthy again. She walked back to the bathroom, willing herself not to cry, scrubbing at her fingers with soap, watching the dark remains of spiteful text swirl down the drain.

Minutes later, she was sipping ice water when the buzzer sounded. Western Union, the tired voice said. She buzzed him in before thinking that no one was supposed to know she lived here.

A knock on the door, a man in uniform sweating from the summer heat.

"Came by yesterday, ma'am, but there was no answer."

She signed for the telegram without making eye contact. When he was gone, she tore it open. She read it once without understanding. She read it again. Images revealed themselves, sounds. Again. Voices now, textures. His laugh, the silk sleeve reaching out to touch her face.

PERFECT WEATHER FOR BIRD WATCHING / MIGRATING EARLIER THAN PREDICTED / DON'T BELIEVE EVERYTHING YOU READ / HAVE BINOS READY.

She crumpled to her knees. *What?*

"Don't believe everything you read." That's what he always said, or some variation: don't believe everything you hear, or everything they say, or everything you see, or everything you feel. His mantra—that life was a big trick, that the gullible were secretly guillotined while only those who doubted everything had a chance to escape. She had believed, for a day, and it had nearly killed her.

She was down the stairs and out the door in seconds. It was midday and the sidewalk was scalding on her bare feet. The Western Union truck's engine had just started but she banged on the door before he could pull away. *Who sent this?! When?! How?!* The poor man didn't know anything, shaking his head at her. There were no other messages, no other clues. Only this. A whisper in a graveyard. He drove off, left her standing there in her bathrobe, receiving looks.

Back inside, she tried Veronica again. Woman would *not* answer her phone. Did she know? Was she with them even now? Darcy *hated* her; she *burned*, envy lighting her aflame. She emptied the wastebasket, tore through the newspapers, and found the photographs. Well, they *were* grainy. She *had* thought that he looked so . . . *different* in them, but had assumed that was how it was in death. And now? She was crazy. Surely.

Could this be happening? She would kill him. If he were really alive, she would kill him when he came for her, for doing this to her. But, Lord, please let it be so.

She sat on the bed. She was crying again.

And, despite it all, there was pride. She knew it couldn't possibly have ended this way, knew he wouldn't have let that happen.

She remembered the time he first came for her, waiting on the sidewalk in front of his shiny new Ford. Here in Chicago, where an unconnected hoodlum like him was not welcome. Just standing there, as if absolutely certain that this was where he was meant to be.

She was off balance, amazed. The world was tipped from its axis, compasses swirling. But she did regain her composure enough to speak first, thank you.

"I'm afraid there's no bank in my building, and my purse only holds so much," she said.

It had been two weeks since her day on the running boards. After the brothers had left her at that farm, she had called the police, but mainly because she needed a ride home. She had found, when the cops questioned her, that she wasn't all that interested in feeding them information; she had been vague in her answers, playing the role of flustered young lass until the cops pocketed their notebooks. Once back in Chicago, she'd read everything she could find about Jason at the library. He and his gang already had robbed another bank, or three, or seven, depending on which rumors were to be believed. Reporters couldn't keep up: the Firefly Brothers were allegedly responsible for a train robbery in Utah, had orchestrated prison breaks in Missouri and Minnesota, robbed National Guard armories across the Midwest, and even made off with three fighter planes from a factory in western Pennsylvania, all in the past two weeks. They were suspected of being communist insurgents, or Nazi agents, or Confederate loyalists in the mold of Jesse James. They were committing crimes in Republican counties to help local Democrats in the upcoming election, or maybe the opposite. Mostly lies and conjecture, Darcy figured. But what fun it would be to try to find the truth hiding beneath it all.

She had seen an approximation of Jason's face on a wanted poster outside the post office and had let her nails linger over the badly drawn cheek. Surely the police artist had never seen Jason Fireson with his own eyes, felt his presence.

"Could have sworn First National used to be here." Jason's suit might have been dark blue, but in the night it was black. "City's changing so fast these days."

"Or are you here because you've reconsidered kidnapping?"

It was cold and she could see her breath. They both could: he watched her breath hanging there and the moment felt even more intimate than when his eyes were on hers.

"I'm still not a fan of it, I have to admit. I had a feeling you might come willingly."

"With a known desperado? What do you take me for?"

"A fascinating woman who hasn't been fascinated enough."

She stepped closer. She thought of that wanted poster, and she wanted her fingers on that cheek. "You're offering me fascination?"

"I'm offering you an evening. For starters."

She smiled. Except she'd been smiling the whole time. He made her put smiles on top of her smiles.

That had been barely ten months ago. Despite what she'd told that officer, they were not married. But a ring seemed trivial to her, as it must to him. She had no need for rings or necklaces, brooches or earrings, rocks or stones. Just him. Whether Jason had understood it or not, the money had never mattered to her.

He had wooed her for the better part of three weeks, like the carefree man of means he was. Each day, after she returned from her achingly dull job as a typist—her father had objected to her even having an occupation, as such servitude did not reflect well on the family name, but she refused to take another cent from him—Jason's car would sidle up to the sidewalk. He took her to the sorts of nightclubs proper suitors would have been scandalized to set foot in, dancing her through the steps he knew and allowing her to show off the latest crazes; he escorted her to the World's Fair, winning marksman contests and surveying his domain from the top of the Ferris wheel; he drove her through the countryside, gunning the V8 engine of his new coupe, testing the truthfulness of the salesman's boasts; he bought tickets to air shows, the two of them lying beside each other on picnic blankets, their lazy fingers reaching up to trace the daredevils' paths through the heavens.

Darcy had avoided alcohol ever since her initial troubles with it, but with Jason she found she was able to partake of a drink here and there. He always ordered but never had a second. She commented on this, and he said something about the need for control. Such calmness, so different from her. She wanted to sample all of life, and although she sensed this craving in him as well, it didn't gnaw at him as it did her. He seemed to know he would get around to everything eventually, that there was no need to rush. It *had* to be an act, didn't it? But my, such a good one.

On the tenth night of her whirlwind courtship, her father called her, asking who was this man she had been seen with. Seen by whom? Outraged, she had switched apartments the next day, moving to a different neighborhood, changing her telephone number, not leaving a forwarding address. It exhausted her meager funds, but Jason happily paid for the next three months' rent; he had been spending the past few nights with her anyway.

What a strange new life, and so sudden. Darcy had returned to Chicago from boarding school a year earlier, having turned down her father's invitations to be sent away to some girls' college. She was sick of being sent away, imprisoned by others' expectations. Wasn't that what had finally driven her mother to despair? Marilyn Windham had been trapped by expectations that she couldn't fulfill: being a kindly mother, the petite and smiling trophy for her tycoon husband, producing a male heir for his legacy. So she had broken free the only way she knew how. Darcy refused to let such onerous and limiting expectations be placed upon her. She had no interest in playing the society princess, the debutante, the prize for the next generation of financial barons.

In truth, she hadn't known what *did* interest her, until the day Jason Fireson winked at her. It was tiresome, she had realized that day, to define

yourself against things. So refreshing to find something you didn't want
to rebel against, something you wanted to wrap yourself inside.

———————

After reading the telegram, Darcy hurriedly put on a white-flowered dress
and light sweater and ran down the stairs. Her heart was frantic, and her
stomach was reminding her that she hadn't eaten in twenty-four hours.
Life had returned, and she needed sustenance. She clasped the telegram in
her right hand, folded in half.

"Excuse me, Miss Windham?"

A voice she did not recognize. You never knew how Jason would contact you, and she turned to face the man. But he wasn't there.

She was about to turn again when she felt a hand clamping on her
right forearm. A car had pulled up on her left, by a hydrant. There was another man, and a hand pushed her head down before she could see his
face.

The men were moving toward the car and her feet did their part to
keep up. Then she was in the backseat and someone pushed her head
down again, and another set of hands was riffling through her hair. A
tightness was pulled over her head, stopping at the eyes. Goggles? She felt
them sucking at her skull. In front they were stuffed with dark cloth. Like
the blindfold from that other time, but far less gentlemanly.

"*Go!*" someone hissed.

The car was moving when she asked if they were with Jason.

"Keep quiet and everything'll be fine," said a voice beside her.

"She say Jason?" someone asked from the front. "Doesn't she know?"

"Know what?" Darcy asked.

Something jabbed her ribs. "You know what this is, doll? Keep talking
and you'll be as dead as your boyfriend."

Darcy was very still even as the car took a sharp right. Jason had not
sent these people.

She pressed her palms into each other, the fingers pulling on their op-
posites' knuckles. The world around her was mad but she tried to be its
calm center.

She felt very alone, and she had dropped the telegram.

VI.

———————————
———————————

Weston Fireson's brothers haunted him long before they were dead. As their adventures had filled newspapers the previous spring, twice Weston was arrested by police officers exuberant at their luck—*I nabbed Whit Fireson buying a coffee at the Doughnut Stop! I caught Jason Fireson myself, walking down Garfield Drive, alone and unarmed!* Twice Weston had guns pointed at him, their barrels lean and sinister. Twice he had been frisked, shackled, hauled in, and fingerprinted, his pleas ignored. At least he'd been alone, with no friends or pretty date to see his face go white and his raised hands shake with fear.

Those two disasters had occurred during errands to Cincinnati and Dayton—at least the Lincoln City police seemed to know who Weston was—so he soon concluded that travel outside of town was no longer advisable, at least not until his brothers were arrested. Or killed.

The haunting had intensified four months before his brothers' deadly shootout in Points North.

When Weston showed up at the office that Monday, minutes before his usual eight o'clock, he was unexpectedly called into his boss's inner sanctum.

Henrik Douglasson, Esq., occupied a tastefully decorated, not too large office on a prime corner of the downtown building's fourth floor. At that hour in April, the air was cool, yet the wide, east-facing window baked a generous swath of ovenlike warmth across half the room. Douglasson motioned for Weston to take one of the leather chairs, both of which were glowing in the sunlight.

"How was your weekend?"

"Fine, sir. Helped my mother around her house, mostly. Getting the yard in shape and fixing the porch."

"Good, good." Douglasson was in his late forties, gray-haired, heavy enough to appear sufficiently well-off but not so slovenly as to scare away a prospective client. Much of the politically connected real-estate attorney's current work involved foreclosures and searching the titles of vacant or disputed property. Even bad times resulted in windfalls if you were standing on the right hilltop.

Douglasson's decades-long assistant had passed away in '30, a few months after the conviction of Patrick Fireson and the foreclosure of the last family store, which Weston and Whit had been desperately trying to keep afloat. Douglasson had been tangentially involved in Pop's horribly timed real-estate gambit, and had met Weston at a few meetings, where he was impressed by the young man's quiet perseverance and seriousness. After Pop's trial, Douglasson offered Weston a job as a legal assistant, which Weston happily accepted, as he'd been without work for weeks. Weston saw the offer as a sign of the man's decency, whereas Whit took it as a sign that Douglasson had something to feel guilty about. *How can you work for him?* Whit had accused his brother. *He's just another rich man who helped Pop get into trouble and then didn't lift a finger once it all blew up.* But what choice did Weston have? At the time, Jason was still in jail on his second rum-running conviction, Uncle Joe was drinking himself into oblivion, and Weston and Whit had barely earned a cent since the store closed.

"How is your mother doing?"

"Fine, sir. Looking forward to spring, like the rest of us."

Douglasson quickly listed new assignments for Weston, who carefully took notes, wondering why his boss had felt the need to do this in his private office; usually he boomed such orders over the intercom.

"There's one more thing I wanted to mention, Weston."

"Yes?" His stomach tensed. To save money, he was forgoing breakfast, apart from a cup of coffee. This worked well enough on days that produced little stress, but any time his quiet routine was disrupted his insides would feel stabbing pains like the ones he'd endured during Pop's ordeal.

"I'm afraid I need to talk to you about your brothers."

Weston sat up straighter and folded his hands on his lap, letting the pen lie still atop his pad. He tended to remember, with perfect clarity, whatever people said about his brothers.

"Yes, sir?"

"I'm sure this is difficult for you. . . . I've been very satisfied with the work you've done for me these last—what is it, now, three years?"

"Yes, sir, three and a half years now." Jesus, was he being fired? He was completely, completely still, as if Douglasson were one of those nervous cops aiming a revolver at him. What was the difference between being fired and being fired upon?

"Well, then, I knew it was a bit of a risk hiring you, given your lack of experience, but it turns out it was the right decision all along. I don't regret it. And I knew, of course, about Jason's brushes with the law, the bootlegging and whatnot. It's a shame so many people were sent the wrong way by that foolish Prohibition business, so I was willing to give him the benefit of the doubt on that. Bank robbing, however, is another matter. As is murder."

"Sir, I—" Weston stammered for a moment. "You know I have nothing, absolutely nothing, to do with any of—"

"Yes, yes, of course. I realize you're an innocent man caught in an awkward position. But what I need you to understand, Weston, is that this awkward position is beginning to ensnare others."

Weston practiced breathing.

"As I'm sure you know, police in numerous states are trying to find your brothers, as is the federal Department of Justice. They are leaving no stone unturned, and that means they're investigating everything they can not only about your brothers but also about their associates, past and present. Including their relatives. And those who employ their relatives."

From the fourth floor, the sound of street traffic was eerily nonexistent. Weston reached up to prevent his glasses from sliding down his sweaty nose.

"The police have . . . contacted you?"

"Now, Weston, a good deal of my business comes from state and local government, or from banks that are pointed my way by various officials. It has been brought to my attention that employing the brother of two famous outlaws is not the wisest thing for one in my position. That my past—albeit brief and entirely legal—association with your father is a black mark made worse by your presence here."

The walls of Weston's throat were two pieces of sandpaper.

"Now, I'm not such a helpless codger, Weston, and I can hold my own against a little friendly pressure. I've been here a long time, as has my family, and my business is strong. But I am hoping, quite fervently, that this matter will pass soon. Perhaps your brothers will . . . turn themselves in, and justice will be done as, er, as *painlessly* as possible. Otherwise, the pressures on my firm may mount."

"I'm very, very sorry if I've caused you any trouble at all, sir. And I want—"

"Now, now, it's no trouble at all." He waved his hand. "But, Weston, I want you to think very carefully about what I've asked you this morning. And perhaps we can do what we can to make things right."

"I'm, I'm sorry, sir—um, what exactly have you asked me?"

Douglasson placed his hands on the large ash table, which that morning was immaculate, as it was cleaned to a shine each Friday evening by Weston himself. Then he took a business card from the top drawer of his desk and handed it to Weston.

"It would be in everyone's best interests for you to get in touch with this gentleman."

The card belonged to one Cary Delaney. Below the name was a phone number and a Chicago address, and above it was the crest for the Justice Department's Bureau of Investigation.

Weston placed the card in his shirt pocket. "Of course, sir."

The shirt was old and thin—it had been his father's—and he could feel the card's corners poking at his chest the rest of the day.

He wondered if this Agent Delaney had been one of the men he had seen leaving his mother's house two weeks earlier. Weston had stopped by after work to have supper with Ma and Aunt June, and when he saw how bare the pantry was he had run out to buy groceries. That task still seemed odd, after growing up in a shop-owning family. One of the new supermarkets had opened up a few blocks away, but whenever he went there he felt ill. Weston remembered the first time his father had allowed him to run the register, remembered the bad days when they'd had to accept scrip from tire workers whose factory had run out of cash for their pay. He loathed buying groceries—maybe this was why he'd grown so thin— and the only reason he did it for Ma was to spare her the same pain.

He had been walking back to her house that night, a cold one, late March, when he heard his mother yelling.

"Do you have sons, Detective?! Do you know what it's like to worry about your children?!"

Twenty yards away, two men in dark suits and snap-brim hats were standing at the edge of the Firesons' front lawn, shoulders turned as if they had been leaving but were now reconsidering. Weston's mother was on the porch, the door open. She wasn't wearing a coat, but that's not why her fists were clenched.

At the risk of dropping the groceries, Weston jogged past the last two houses and onto his mother's lawn.

"Some of the people that they've killed had sons, ma'am," one of the men was saying, his voice accented like a cowboy from the Westerns. "Have you considered that? I don't think they have."

"What's going on?" Weston asked.

The hats turned to face him. One of the men shared Weston's lanky build and probably his age, give or take, but the other was of more powerful stuff, forged to a certain hardness, perhaps by the war. He was the one who had spoken, and his eyes seemed to glint with pleasure.

"Well, well," the big one said. "It's a Firefly Brother. In the dark it's kinda hard to make out which one he is. Maybe we should take him in, just in case?"

"You leave him alone," Ma said before Weston could react.

He felt himself shrinking in the men's eyes. "What do you want?"

They told him their names, but he instantly forgot them when they added that they were Justice agents; this bit of information burned into his memory and obliterated whatever had come before.

"My brothers aren't here. We haven't seen them in months. You should know that."

"We do know a lot. And we're learnin' more every day." He touched his brim mockingly. "You have a good night now."

Weston watched as they opened the doors of a dark Chevy, the silent young one taking the wheel. He felt like a fool standing there clutching groceries, one of the bags almost slipping from his grasp. He only hoped they would drive away before eggs and bread spilled all over the walkway.

The older agent, riding shotgun, kept his eyes trained on Weston as they drove past. Weston looked at the younger one, whose expression seemed to convey something akin to pity for the shattered family standing in the cold. But maybe that was only in contrast to his partner. Even indifference can feel like empathy when you've grown used to so much hostility.

"What was that about?" Weston asked.

"Just asking after them."

"I figured they would have stopped that by now."

Ever since the previous fall, when the Firesons realized that an undercover state cop had been boarding in Ma's house, they knew they were being watched. Ever since, Ma had noticed an unusual number of cars driving past each day and early evening, always driven by two men, their eyes slowly scanning the modest property with a mix of boredom and predation. As far as Weston knew, though, no one in the family had been questioned in weeks.

"Are you all right?" he asked.

"They told me they'd put me in jail if I ever did anything to 'abet' your brothers. If I ever helped them. Fed or 'sheltered' them." She was still staring at the street, either in shock or in a calm rage. "My *sons.*"

The other son put a hand on her shoulder. "C'mon in, Ma. It's cold."

Sammy, June's eldest, was in the parlor reading one of his pulp magazines, *Black Mask* or *Dime Detective,* beside a dim light. The marine warfare of June giving her other sons a bath echoed down the steps. On the cover of Sammy's magazine a buxom brunette was tied to a chair, luscious mouth frozen in a silent scream as a fedora-topped shadow crawled the wall behind her. Weston had flipped through one of Sammy's pulps the other day and had found a wanted ad for Jason and Whit printed between two stories, fact nestled where one fiction ended and the next began.

Weston wondered how much Sammy had heard of the conversation outside, whether he had been the one to answer the door. He remembered the time he himself had opened the door to the police late one night, three years ago.

Ma sat in the dining room and was silent as Weston unpacked the groceries.

He had lied to the Justice agents, and he wondered if that, too, was something that would haunt him. It had not been "months" since he'd seen his outlaw brothers; Jason and Whit had stopped by just over a week ago. They had called ahead to alert Ma and then sneaked in through the back, late at night. They stayed one night and gave Ma some cash; she rarely discussed this, but Weston always knew from her sudden silence about money. Each visit from Jason was a financial relief, for a while at least.

Weston couldn't deny that it was more than that. Ma's mood would brighten, rendering her almost unrecognizable. Her prodigal sons, returned! Safe and healthy, and making jokes, and laughing at hers, and playing with the kids! Weston knew she didn't approve of their lifestyle, but those battles had been fought between Jason and Pop years ago, and Ma's lifelong role as peacemaker continued despite the fact that one warring party was now gone. In truth, Pop's absence seemed to make her less disapproving of Jason than she might otherwise have been; robbery was wrong, sure, but so was what had happened to her falsely accused husband.

Ma's good mood at her sons' reappearances would continue after their equally sudden departures, but after a couple of days she would descend again, the landing always worse than the one before it, so much so that Weston began to wish his brothers wouldn't visit anymore, wouldn't tease her this way. He hated himself for it, but sometimes he wanted them to dispense with the running and chasing, the long and torturous prologue, and get on with the obvious conclusion, allow their mother to grieve in peace. Grieving over people who weren't even dead yet—this was cruelty, and he hated his brothers for forcing her into such a position.

He knew that his brothers would die, and badly, and soon. The ending was inevitable, just as it had been for past hoodlums like Jesse James and Billy the Kid. The only question was whether it would be at the hands of the police, jealous associates, or court-ordered executioners.

After unpacking the groceries, Weston walked into the dining room, where his mother was still sitting at the bare table, the gas lamp too dim.

"That should set you for the week." He told her he needed to head home and kissed her on the forehead.

"Thank you," she said, but her eyes seemed to be on something else.

If he were Jason, he would have known a joke to brighten her face. But mirth tasted funny on his lips, like bad moonshine that skipped the buzz and went straight to the headache.

The steps creaked as he walked upstairs to say good night to June and the boys. He noticed that the banister was coming loose from some of its posts, another repair for the list. He knocked on the bathroom door, which wasn't quite shut, and walked into the warm air as June was violently towel-drying Mikey's hair. The tub was draining, toy boats capsized in the vortex.

June asked if Uncle Weston would like to read the boys bedtime stories and the kids cheered. Weston had been hoping merely to say good night and make his escape, but he saw that June was even more tired than he was, so he played along.

After reading to them about trains and heroes and happy endings, he walked downstairs and saw June sitting at the dining-room table, sipping what looked like bourbon. Her graying hair was in a bun, and patches of her red cardigan were still wet from the bath. It was barely eight, but she told him that Ma had excused herself for the night, saying she wasn't feeling well. Weston wondered if June knew about the federal visitors.

"Have you heard from them?" she asked.

"Who?"

"Your brothers."

"No."

She stared at her glass. "Sometimes I wish . . . they'd just turn themselves in."

He had overheard her arguing with Ma about them, not infrequently. She'd even told him she suspected that her late husband's past applications for state aid had been denied because of Jason's run-ins with the law, as if the state of Ohio had blacklisted the family. To Weston it was insane to believe a few bureaucrats in the aid office had any clue that Joe's nephew had been a bootlegger, but now that Weston had Douglasson's warning ringing in his ears he wondered if June could have been right.

"They're doing what they can to help the family," Weston said.

"I get the dirtiest looks from people on the street. What they think of us."

"I get some, too, but I get just as many people telling me how they're rooting for them. More, actually."

She rolled her eyes. "Male fantasies, all of it. Women know better. They're tearing your mother's heart out, you know. Bit by bit, day by day."

He needed to change the subject. "The boys seem to be doing fairly well."

"Mikey still cries for Joe at night, sometimes."

He didn't know what to say. He made a short frown.

"It wakes up the other two."

She looked at him as if she expected that he, as someone who'd lost his own father, would have some advice for her. But Weston had been twenty-two when Pop died, three years ago. Compared with little Mikey and Pete and Sammy, he'd been an old man. Then why had he felt like such a kid?

They forced themselves to chat about mundane matters and soon they were both yawning, so he bade her good night. With his hand on the doorknob he turned for a last glance. June was still sitting there, staring at her glass like she wished she'd poured herself more.

* * *

After his talk with Mr. Douglasson, Weston felt as haunted as ever. Now it wasn't only his brothers haunting him but this Agent Delaney. Surely Mr. Douglasson wasn't threatening to fire him. Surely the conversation was just meant as a well-intentioned reminder of the seriousness of the Fireson family's plight, Douglasson feeling the need to dispense paternal advice to the fatherless. Surely Weston's fate—and his brothers'—was not resting in his shirt pocket.

He often imagined the many ways in which things would be different, if not for the hard times, if not for the curse of his family. He would have a better job than that of an office assistant, certainly, and would be in a more lucrative field. Still, he knew he was fortunate to have this job; at a time when so many were out of work, most employers would never consider hiring a Fireson. Though Jason's irregular contributions had temporarily saved the house from foreclosure, that specter was always hovering around the corner. One day, surely, the brothers' payments would end, leaving Weston as the bachelor breadwinner supporting a sprawling family.

That bachelor part was one of the things that rankled most, when he allowed himself to think selfishly. He had dated a few girls, but getting close to anyone was out of the question; he had too many obligations as it was. And so his romantic life had taken on a distressing pattern. He would meet a pretty girl and ask her out, or, more typically, he'd call a girl he had known in school, someone whose parents knew him and (hopefully) hadn't warned their daughter to stay away from that no-good Fireson family. But of course the girl would know about his brothers—perhaps she would be attracted to the sense of adventure, or doom, that the Fireson name evoked. He would take her to dinner at a carefully chosen, inexpensive restaurant, and perhaps see a movie. But after a few dates it would be obvious he wasn't in a position to take things further. Some of the girls had stuck with him for a few months, maybe had even fallen in love with him. But as time passed and they saw that no proposal was forthcoming, that indeed Weston never spoke of the future at all, they would break things off. Which always came as equal parts disappointment and relief.

At least he wasn't the only one deferring his dreams for some fabled, future moment of prosperity. None of his old school friends—few of whom he saw much of anymore—were married, as everyone seemed to be putting off important decisions. But that didn't make it any easier. He ached to touch someone, but that was a luxury he couldn't afford. He didn't want to get a girl in a jam, both for her sake and his. Somewhere out there, Jason and Whit were carousing with their tawdry fans, women they probably had met in Jason's speakeasy days, molls enamored of the brothers' myth and money. Weston's dates, when he was lucky enough to have any, ended with a chaste kiss at best.

He was lucky enough to have a date on the Friday after Douglasson's warning. At six o'clock he took the streetcar uptown to the Buckeye Theater, where he was to meet the secretary of a real-estate company whom he'd chatted up while running an errand for Douglasson. He was early and no line had formed, but dusk was settling and the marquee's lights glowed. Then he noticed the title displayed above.

"Excuse me," he asked the girl at the booth, "wasn't *The Invisible Man* supposed to start showing today?"

"Yes, but we're holding *Scarface* over an extra week because it's doing so well. We'll open *The Invisible Man* next Friday."

Weston's heart sank. His knuckles tapped the edge of the booth.

"I really do recommend *Scarface*," the girl said. "It's rather risky, I'd say, but very thought-provoking. And exciting, of course."

He smiled thinly at her. The gangster movie had been playing all month; he hadn't seen it yet, nor would he. "Let me guess: he dies in the end."

She didn't know what to make of him. "Well, er, you'll have to see it to find out."

He backed up and stepped aside. Why all this fascination with criminals? His date was running late, which he was thankful for. He needed to come up with some other idea, maybe dinner first, maybe dancing instead of the movie. He needed to devise an escape, some miraculous evasion, something worthy of a true Firefly Brother.

Within minutes, the line was twenty deep. So many people, so happy to watch tales of others' bloodletting and sorrow.

VII.

The depression was making people disappear.

They vanished from factories and warehouses and workshops, the number of toilers halving, then halving again, until finally all were gone, the doors closed and padlocked, the buildings like tombs. They vanished from the lunchtime spots where they used to congregate, the diners and deli counters where they would grab coffee on the way in or a slice of pie on the way out. They disappeared from the streets. They were whisked from the apartments whose rents they couldn't meet and carted out of the homes whose mortgages they couldn't keep pace with, lending once thriving neighborhoods a desolate air, broken windows on porches and trash strewn across overgrown yards. They disappeared from the buses and streetcars, choosing to wear out their shoe leather rather than drop another dime down the driver's metal bucket. They disappeared from shops and markets, because if you yourself could spend a few hours to build it, sew it, repair it, reline it, reshod it, reclod it, or reinvent it for some other purpose, you sure as hell weren't going to buy a new one. They disappeared from bedrooms, seeking solace where they could: a speakeasy, or, once the mistake of Prohibition had been corrected, a reopened tavern, or another woman's arms—someone who might not have known their name and certainly didn't know their faults well enough to judge them, someone who needed a laugh as badly as they did. They disappeared, but never before your eyes; they never had that magic. It was like a shadow when the sun has set; you don't notice the shadow's absence because you expect it. But the next morning the sun rises, and the shadow's still gone.

Jason Fireson himself disappeared whenever he needed to, which was quite often.

Indeed, for all the glorified stories of his prowess at shooting his way out of dragnets, his fabled ability to slide his wrists out of handcuffs or simply vanish after a job, Jason knew that much of his success was due, quite simply, to his tolerance for long drives. When you robbed a bank in southern Illinois, cops wouldn't expect you to be hiding in St. Paul the next day. When you knocked over a bank in Akron, the heat wouldn't even be simmering in the Ozarks. All it usually took was a good ten to twenty hours of driving and he'd not only be safely beyond the authorities' reach but beyond their comprehension. The bulls assumed that hoods were lazy, and maybe most were; good, old-fashioned work ethic was what separated Jason from the others. Maybe Pop would have been proud after all.

The sun had barely risen when Jason and Whit set out for Cleveland, the morning after their visit with Chance. Jason had borrowed money from Ma—money that he had paid her after an endeavor, but money he now needed back; he couldn't travel north to gather a gang without cash for food and gasoline. But he was deeply ashamed to take the cash and was worried about what it might mean for her. He vowed to get her more within the week.

What bothered him the most wasn't the bullet wounds in his chest, which seemed to be fading rather rapidly, but his empty pockets.

Their telegrams to Darcy and Veronica had gone unanswered. In desperation Jason had risked being overheard and called Darcy from a downtown pay phone the previous night. But she never picked up. He'd tried again that morning after leaving Ma's, with the same result. Whit's luck hadn't been much better. He'd called Veronica's mother's place in Milwaukee—for which he had occasionally paid the rent, not that they treated him any better for it—but the suspicious old lady wouldn't put Veronica on or even confirm whether she was there.

Jason's mind had trailed every conceivable path for Darcy, and none of them were a pleasant ride. Had she been arrested for aiding and abetting but the press hadn't reported it yet? Had she received his message but was under heavy surveillance and couldn't respond? Was she convinced he was dead and had descended into hysterics, or something worse? She was an impulsive girl, prone to brazen acts and startling shifts in temper. He regretted that he and Whit were driving to Cleveland and not straight to Chicago, but the brothers had agreed that they needed to get a gang together before making any other moves.

It always seemed to come back to this. The need for money, and the only means for obtaining it.

Jason Fireson had started bank robbing a few months after his release from Indiana State Prison for his second bootlegging rap. During that second stretch, the visits from his mother and brothers had been far less frequent than the first time; they were busy trying to keep the family business afloat while Pop was in Lincoln City jail awaiting trial, and then, after Pop was convicted and sent to prison in Columbus, the remaining Firesons had only so much time to divide between their two imprisoned family members.

Pop in jail? None of this seemed real. It was impossible. *Pop* arrested for murder? For killing a business partner and bank man who reneged on an agreement? Patrick Fireson, mild-mannered, hardworking, churchgoing, tithe-paying, Hoover-supporting, flag-waving civic Booster extraordinaire? It was a sick joke, a horrible mistake, a vicious frame, one more symptom of a world gone not only mad but cruel.

All the bad news had hit while Jason was waiting for his release: he learned by telegram that Pop had been convicted of second-degree murder, and then, less than six months later, Weston had visited Jason alone, his face still white even after that long drive, to tell him that Pop's heart had given out the night before.

Jason had petitioned his warden to be allowed to attend his father's funeral under guard, but he'd been refused. The last time he ever laid eyes on Pop was when he took the stand months earlier, offering futile corroboration of Pop's alibi.

After Jason's release, the brothers went their separate ways. Weston disappeared to his law office and his newly rented room—even the good son needed distance from the remnants of their broken family—Whit to his factory gig and the tiny flat he shared with three other working stiffs, and Jason to his itinerant band of ex-cons and ne'er-do-wells. He had always liked guys like these, men who didn't want to fit into society's staid categories. But the rising tide against Prohibition—it would be repealed by summer, people were saying—and Jason's bitterness over his two stints in jail had made him think differently. These men seemed so much less than he remembered. With bootlegging jobs on the verge of extinction, their new ideas seemed either juvenile (petty thefts) or hopelessly grandiose (train robbery). Their skills were nominal, their views of the world badly blurred. Would he continue to link his fate with men like these? Maybe this was growing up: realizing that you're better than the situation you've landed in.

He told himself the straight life wasn't all bad and he tried to find a job, but he barely understood this world, let alone the vast changes that had befallen it during the past few years. Hat in hand, Jason walked into countless offices, his self-esteem shrinking each day. With Pop and his business gone, he didn't even have that to fall back on anymore. Whit's factory was laying men off; Weston's lawyer boss wouldn't even meet with Jason. And, Jesus, the looks he received, full of either pity or outright scorn. He was used to being greeted with smiles, fresh drinks, pretty ladies, and all the other signs of respect. Now the tone of his voice was unrecognizable to himself.

The closest he came to finding honest work in that cold and constricting winter of '32–'33 was with a small shipping outfit. The owner needed another driver, so Jason explained his qualifications, lying about the exact kind of freight he had experience shipping, and even provided references. Two days after that meeting he walked back into the man's office, and the references had been checked. The job was about to be his.

The office was a single long room at the front of a warehouse, with drivers and other lackeys hustling in and out, grabbing keys, checking clipboards, telling jokes. He could do this. It was so busy that he hadn't noticed another man walk in behind him.

"You ain't doing business with this guy, are you, Larry?"

Jason turned around. It was a cop. Jason was fairly sure he'd never exchanged words with this cop, but he looked familiar. Hell, they were all alike—same clown suit, big feet, sunburned noses.

"Was thinking about hiring him," the manager said. "Why?"

"You don't know who this is?" The cop had a good fifteen years on Jason but even without his gun and his club and the weight of society behind him he would be a tough one in a brawl. "You're looking at a two-time convict here."

Jason tried to sound polite. "We're conducting some private business here, Officer, and I think—"

"What's the idea?" Larry said. "You didn't say nothing about doing time."

"Well, you didn't ask about—"

"Don't you come into my place of business pulling some con!"

"It's not a con. I just want a—"

"The son of a murderer, too," the cop added. "Probably be a murderer himself soon, if he ain't already. Be a real addition to your workforce, Larry."

Jason glared at the cop.

"No thanks, son." Larry shook his head.

The cop chuckled. "Hit the road, Fireson."

Crushing the brim of his hat, Jason turned and walked out. He paced the sidewalk, too enraged to give up and head home. He'd been there less than a minute when the cop joined him.

"You have no right to run me like this," Jason said. "I was a kid and I made some mistakes—and they're about to change those laws anyway! I have a right to try and make good."

"You did make some mistakes, I'll give you that. That cop you beat on in Indiana? That was my cousin—and *those* laws ain't about to change."

Jason had resisted arrest the second time he'd been taken in, had gotten a few licks in before they paid him back tenfold. "I did my time for it! I paid my debt!"

"Everybody's got debts right now, and I couldn't give a damn about yours."

"I'm trying to do the right thing here!"

"You wouldn't know the right thing if it hit you on the head." The cop's right hand dangled onto his billy club. "Now shut your mouth and go make your living someplace else. Someplace very far from here."

It took a second to register. "You can't run me out of my own town. I got family here, I got—"

"I can't? You're lucky I'm being so polite about it. I ain't always in this good a mood."

They stared each other down. Jason could feel some of the truckers from inside the office and others out on the sidewalk watching them. He searched for some angle to play, but there was none. He turned and walked away.

The next day he inquired about a few more jobs, but halfheartedly. The straight life was revealing itself to be nothing more than a mirage, and Jason cursed himself for being so gullible. Pop had always believed in playing by the rules, working hard and following the law, the American dream, and look where it had gotten *him*. Jason burned with shame at the way he had lost face in front of that cop. He was better than this. If the cop was so sure that Jason's Fireson blood doomed him to being a murderous outlaw, then Jason would do him one better: he would be the best goddamn outlaw anyone had seen.

His thoughts returned to Marriner Skelty, an old yegg he had befriended during his second stint in jail. Marriner wasn't like the Lincoln City small-timers Jason had walked out on; he was smart and professional. Marriner had other friends, particularly skilled friends, some of whom Jason also had met behind bars. Marriner's jail term was nearing its end, as were some of the others'. Jason started visiting Marriner at the same visiting room where his brothers had very infrequently visited him. The view's nicer over here, he told Marriner the first time, smiling.

"I imagine it is," the old yegg said. "Can't wait to see it."

"What else can't you wait to do?"

"The only thing I was ever good at, if I ain't too old."

"You can always borrow youth. I myself am looking to borrow expertise. Perhaps we can arrange a trade."

"A trade," Marriner mused. "I always have likened myself to a tradesman."

Plans were laid, releases were won, and the first Firefly Gang was assembled.

Marriner picked the spots, showing Jason what to look for. Outside Indianapolis, they used an old barn that belonged to one of Marriner's dead relatives as their staging ground, laid out like the interior of their targeted bank. They went through the routine countless times; they knew how many steps to take and how quickly to move, what to say and what not to do. It was like a movie set, with Marriner the director, his once and future accomplices the stars. But Jason knew *he* was the leading man, and the others picked up on this eventually. He wasn't nervous, he wasn't a fumbler—bootlegging had been all about timing and numbers, knowing the route and following it, and being able to improvise when the situation warranted. This was much the same, only he wasn't stuck behind a wheel. All that begging and groveling for admission into the straight life, *that* had been the movie set—*that* had been the acting. This was who he really was.

As Jason drove the stolen Pontiac, Whit was asleep in the passenger seat, loudly snoring as usual. Ever since his nose had been broken by Lincoln City cops the previous summer, Whit's nights had become noisy affairs. Jason had knocked him for it many a time, especially when they were stealing sleep in haylofts or parked cars. Dillinger was plugged leaving a theater with his girl, Machine Gun Kelly was nabbed in his underwear— it would be too fitting for Whit's snoring to one day be their undoing. Hell, maybe it had been that fateful night; they still couldn't remember.

The road stretched on with a central Ohioan lack of elevation, as if God had carefully wielded a level while building this part of the state. Jarred from the monotony by a pothole, Jason glanced at the face that stirred briefly beside him. As bad as Whit had looked on his cooling board with that bullet wound square in the center of his chest, Jason had once seen him looking even worse. In fact, Jason remembered as he drove north, it was not the first time he had mistakenly thought, *My brother is dead.*

The first time had been the previous June, in the Hooverville that grew along the southern hill of Lincoln City. By then, Jason and Marriner had successfully spearheaded four of what Marriner called "endeavors." They would live in an apartment or a rented house in a respectable neighborhood and quietly survey each new target; after each endeavor, they'd run off to a new hideout in a new state for a few weeks. The scores had allowed Jason to buy fine clothes, a decent car, and even to fill and crown his teeth—which was a hell of a lot better than most men could say. They also afforded him the idle time to catch shows in town and see the movies, eat in decent restaurants; nor did he have to worry about there being a roof over his head. But after dividing each take and allowing for laundering fees, and losing out a bigger chunk whenever they had to pass Liberty Bonds or other complex transactions, and then paying off whoever had supplied the autos and other equipment they needed to abandon during each endeavor, the resulting green in his pocket was never quite as thick as he'd hoped. Jason periodically stopped by Lincoln City to check on his mother and slip her some bills, first saving her house from foreclosure and then supporting her and June's family, but it was hardly enough to set them up for life. There would always be more banks, and bigger ones.

Each time Jason visited, Ma took the opportunity to inform him of Whit's various problems: those of Whit's making and otherwise. The latest was that Whit had lost his job at the plant.

Had he and Whit been such fierce rivals growing up, or was that only the way he remembered it? Whit had always seemed to resent Jason's successes, the way his smile and bravado won him easy pleasures. Whit was four years younger, so why hadn't he just accepted Jason's superiority and learned from it? Maybe all brothers had their problems, and the only thing that made Jason and Whit different from any others was what had happened to their father. The seismic blow that should have drawn them closer together but instead only pushed them apart.

Now Ma hadn't heard from Whit in a couple of weeks, she'd said; his latest apartment had no phone and she'd been unable to reach him. A new crop of stiffs was in Whit's apartment when Jason came knocking. Jason tracked down Whit's old friends, but they weren't much help, either. They all mentioned various fights: Whit had said something, or done something, or borrowed something, or stolen something—was there a difference anymore?—and his friends were no longer his friends. Jason picked up a few stories placing Whit at the Hooverville, but he didn't want

to believe them; surely Whit would have gone back to Ma's before allowing that to happen. People pick which stories to believe, Jason knew, and
the best you could do was hope you'd made the right call.

Jason had pulled off bank jobs in Indiana, Illinois, and Michigan, so
he was not yet wanted by the Ohio police in that July of '33. Still, past history with the Lincoln City cops suggested his stay in town should be brief.
After a few days, he was ready to reconnect with his gang—one of the
guys had a tip on a bank near Toledo—but then the mental blackjacks got
him, twice. First, on what was supposed to be his last night in town, he
heard that Whit's most recent roommates had been arrested the previous
month for some harebrained red plot to sabotage their factory. The cops
wanted Whit, too, but he'd lammed it in time. Jason did seem to remember Whit dropping odd words like *proletariat* and *revolution* the past few
times they'd spoken.

The second blackjack got him the next morning, reading the *Lincoln
City Sun* in Ma's dining room: cops and Legionnaires had raided the
Hooverville the night before. The mayor had decided that the ramshackle
collective had grown too vast, declaring it a public hazard. The article
stated that although the hordes of unfortunates had not been mistreated,
a few malcontents and agitators had resisted, and were subdued. The
Hooverville was more than two years old at that point, so Jason figured
the real reason it had been raided was that the owners of the tire plants
were leaning on the mayor; the tire workers were unionizing behind the
auspices of the NRA, as the Wagner Act gave them the right to collectively
bargain for better wages. Law or no law, plant owners still fired unionists,
but those unionists would only wind up at the Hooverville, rallying others to their cause.

It was a Tuesday morning. Jason read the rest of the paper and considered the matter for longer than he cared to admit. Then he got into his
car.

Before heading to the Hooverville, he allowed himself a short detour. He
drove slowly through neighborhoods where he'd once played stickball,
past his old high school. He turned a few more corners, skirting the
mostly dormant industrial heart of the city, four stories of brick looming

above his royal-blue Packard, as if he were a soldier riding along the stone walls of his fortressed town.

There it was, on the corner, still derelict. It once had been a prime location for a grocery, within easy walking distance of three factories and just outside a densely packed neighborhood of tire workers. Its modest success had even spurred their father into opening two others, in equally ill-fated sections of town. No one had moved in since the bank had taken it, and foot traffic was nonexistent now that the nearest factories had closed.

Jason stared at the front door as if he could set it aflame with his eyes.

He drove on to Grover Cleveland Park, the official name of the patch of land that had become home to the dispossessed. The southern tip of the park was only two blocks from the last train station before downtown, making it a perfect jump-off point for hoboes and others hoping to avoid the rail yard bulls. He had driven past the park many times—whenever he returned to Lincoln City, he saw that the unofficial township had grown larger—but this was his first time entering it.

Twin stone lions rendered meek in their paralysis flanked the entrance gate, helplessly watching as Jason parked before them. People were sprawled all around, on blankets and newspapers and one another. With their slow movements and heavy eyes, they seemed to have borrowed the mannerisms of the strays that had patrolled this territory during Jason's childhood. There were so many of them.

"Spare a dime, brother?" a man no older than twenty asked before Jason had taken two steps out of the Packard. He was thin and his cap was too large and askew. He was flanked by two others, tatterdemalions of wool and dirt.

"What's your name, friend?" Jason asked.

"Ben'dict." Teeth yellow and stumpy as grubs.

"Well, Benedict, I'll spare you and your buddies two bucks if you make sure no one lays a hand on this Packard."

Benedict nodded. The shoulders of the other two sprang into military alertness.

"You know of a Whit Fireson in here someplace?" Jason asked. Two of them shook their heads and the other just stared vacantly. Jason described his brother, to no avail.

He walked into the park and up the hill, which soon crested and began its long downward slope. The trees protected him from the sun, but still it was that devious kind of Ohio weather that tricks you into thinking it isn't that hot, until you've walked five minutes and your shirt is sticking to you. I *am* that hot, the weather laughs, and don't you forget it.

Jason was wearing a light-blue serge suit he'd bought before rolling into town, the jacket concealing his gun. He hadn't yet learned the importance of conservative attire in his line of work. And he had in his gait a certain confidence that had become all the more noticeable as so many other men had lost theirs. As he walked through the Hooverville, people gazed at him suspiciously. Jason tried not to return the stare but he couldn't help himself.

Women held thin blankets cinched around their bodies like squaws, their feet bare and black. Children sat on the ground, weirdly motionless. He'd never seen so many men without hats before. And the smell, rank and farmlike, reminding him that people are merely animals with words. Trapped in the heavy air with that bestial thickness was fatback grease and the scent of burned cornbread, all of it held down by the oaks' heavy boughs and the cruel humidity.

He saw shanties made from fruit crates, saw the heads of family members poking out of rusted auto bodies like prairie dogs. On a small promontory, a hollow train car lay on its side like the detritus of a flood. How the hell it had been transported out here, he had no idea, but there it was, with dozens of people inside. He'd read a few days ago that three derelict families had been killed by lightning; such news had been startling, but now he was surprised that more hadn't met similar fates, with all the tin and corrugated iron roofs lying about like convenient targets for God's wrath. A very Old Testament God. He was angry and cruel and people wore glazed looks, as if they had long internalized their victimhood and knew there was nothing they could do to get on the old bastard's good side.

Jason walked along the main path asking people if they knew of Whit, and some nodded. He'd worked at the tire plant, one said. Yeah, I know him. An angry sort. The cops dealt with him yesterday. Did they arrest him? Jason asked. The cops weren't interested in making arrests, one said. Just sending a message. Yeah, replied someone with a shiner and an empty laugh, they were messengers, and their message was pain. Jason trudged on.

Beads of sweat ran down his face. He came to an oak tree on whose low branches someone had tied pieces of string; at the ends dangled shards of colored glass, metal nuts and bolts, acorns, beads. Jason parted the makeshift curtains as he approached a long tent of gray flannel set up in the oak's shade. Six bodies lay prostrate on the ground, wounds covered with wet clumps of cloth, blood hardened into ferrous armor.

"Jesus," he said.

A young woman was pouring water from a kettle into a man's mouth. The mouth was the only part of his face that was visible; the rest was covered with a filthy cloth. Jason would have assumed the man was dead if not for the way his mollusk tongue lapped at the water she was pouring. On the periphery of the tent stood an older woman and two thin men, their faces guarded.

The young woman looked at Jason. "Yes?" She might have been eighteen. She wore a loose-fitting man's cotton shirt with the sleeves torn off and brown dungarees rolled up at the ankle. Her shoulders were sunburned and her brown hair was tied back with what looked like a man's handkerchief.

"I'm looking for Whit Fireson."

"Don't know him," she said, too quickly. Her eyes were hard.

"I'm not a cop. I'm his brother Jason."

Someone's knee twitched and one of the bodies was moaning, but Jason couldn't tell which one.

He swallowed. "Please. Do you know where I can find my brother?"

She watched him for a moment, then relaxed slightly and pointed to the body on the far right. "There."

Jason had seen men beaten unrecognizable before, but never someone he cared about. Despite all the distance that had opened up between himself and Whit, he realized how immutable was the fact that this was his brother. He bent down beside a face covered in blood dark as charcoal, with eyes swollen shut and a gruesomely misaligned nose, one of the nostrils flat against his cheek and the other bubbling with a stew of snot and blood. The bubbles were the only indication that Whit wasn't dead yet.

"Oh, Jesus." He reached into his pocket for his new silk handkerchief and mopped at his brother's face. Very little of the blood came off. "How long has he been like this?!"

"They came night before last," she said. So the paper had taken its time to report it. "Just tellin' us all to git and knockin' down shanties, arrestin' some folks. He fought back, so they just beat on him instead."

"They told us they'd send an ambulance," an older woman said from behind Jason.

He noticed then that they were near the side entrance to the park, that someone had set the tent up as if it were a triage area to facilitate evacuations to the hospital. They'd actually believed the cops.

He unbuttoned Whit's shirt. "They shoot him?"

"No. Just used their clubs."

Whit's stomach was a pile of eggplants, swollen and purple. Jason lifted himself to a crouch and slid a hand beneath his brother's head.

"What're you doing?" the woman asked.

"Taking him to the hospital, what do you think?"

"You have an auto?"

"Parked out front."

"These others are bad off, too," someone said.

Jason slowly lifted Whit's body. "I can't carry more'n one," he said through gritted teeth.

Someone said they could rally people to carry the others, and Jason stood there with his brother heavy and broken in his arms. "I'm not waiting around. I'll take whoever you can fit in my car if you get 'em there *now*."

Whit had always been thin, but that didn't make him an easy burden. Jason walked as quickly as he could. He could hear people behind him struggling with the other wounded but he didn't stop or turn to check on them. Nor did he ask anyone to help him carry his brother. His only thought was, *Don't drop him, don't drop him, don't you goddamn drop him.*

Benedict and his companions were scattered about the shrinking patches of shade by the Packard. They saw Jason coming and snapped to attention, opening the passenger door. Jason gingerly slid Whit into the seat, and then the human stretchers appeared, wearily carrying their freight. Jason sighed and opened the back doors, hoping that the guns lying in canvas bags on the floorboards weren't loaded. Twelve people were carrying six more bodies by the armpits and ankles. Trailing this bedraggled parade were a few others, including the girl who'd been in the tent. It was the first time Jason had seen her standing, and now he noticed that her baggy shirt had previously concealed that she was with child.

They loaded the bodies. It was difficult to get the doors shut without closing them on something. The fifth body, a young man with a blood-soaked cloth around his head, wouldn't fit in the back with the others. Jason relented and let them put him in the front, gently nudging Whit into the middle.

"I'm coming with you," said the pregnant girl. She was standing on the running board.

He leaned out the window to face her. "I can't let you do that. It's not safe."

"I need to see him off. He may be a brother to you but that don't mean he's nothin' to me."

"Sister, in your condition, I—"

"This'll only take longer you keep arguin' about it." Then she looked away from him, gazing forward. Jason leaned back into the seat and turned the wheel.

The others backed away from the Packard, all save Benedict. "Buddy, about our deal?"

Jason hurriedly took the clip from his pocket and slid out two singles. Benedict bowed his head in thanks and his two friends were pulled to his sides as if he'd turned magnetic.

Jason headed out of the park, driving more slowly than he'd wanted on account of the woman, whose shirt ruffled in his rearview. He hoped he wouldn't pass any cops.

Later he would reflect on the strange fact that, at the time, it was not panic or fear that flooded him so much as anger. Anger that this had befallen Whit, anger to be amid such suffering. *We are better than this, brother. This is not our fate.*

"We can't take these people," a doctor said when Jason approached the hospital carrying his brother in his arms. "There's a free clinic on the South Side. You'll have to bring them—"

"I've got money, goddamnit! Now get me some stretchers before I drop him on top of you!"

One was soon produced and various medical underlings were unleashed onto the Packard, whisking away its human contents like hoodlums stripping auto parts.

There were no chairs outside the operating room, so Jason dragged one from the other end of the hallway. The hospital was at least as hot as the world outside, the open windows useless. Jason had loosened his tie so hurriedly that the top button of his new shirt had popped off. In his discomfort and fury he considered taking off his bloody jacket, for relief and to inform the medical staff that he was armed, but he decided against it.

"What's the story?" he asked a young nurse leaving the room.

Her white uniform was no longer white. It took a moment for anything human to register on her rigid face.

"There is no story yet. I'm sorry, but it'll be a while. And you really shouldn't be sitting here."

"And my brother really shouldn't be having the hell beaten out of him and left to die. Crazy things are happening, huh?"

She didn't know what to do with that comment, so she dropped it onto the floor and they both looked at it for a moment. Then she continued with her errand.

Minutes later, the pregnant girl from the Hooverville found Jason. She had tucked her men's shirt into her pants, as if doing so would make her presentable. The effort struck Jason as hopelessly sad; it only enhanced the bulge of her baby and revealed the old length of rope she used for a belt. It would have taken more than primping to clear the dirt from her arms and clothes, the peeling skin from her shoulders, the grime and sweat from her face. And her hair was the deadest thing Jason had ever seen.

He stood and offered her the chair.

"So, how long have you known my brother?"

Her eyes followed his to her belly, and she blushed.

"I didn't mean it like that." He realized he was looming over her, so he sat on the floor, leaning against the opposite wall. "It's just, he and I have lost touch. I don't know much of what he's been up to."

"He used to stop by now and again, to see some folks he knew," she said. "Then he lost his job and started to stay with us. He says they fired him because he was trying to get people to organize. Sent the Pinkertons after him, but he hid well enough. Till the cops came."

The long white corridor was silent.

"You have family out there?" Jason asked.

"Some."

"You from Lincoln City?"

"Since I was twelve. Lived in Pottsville before then, but my father lost the farm. He worked at the factory, too, for a time, but that was before your brother worked there. Whit was lucky to get a job when he did."

"But not so lucky to get fired. Though I suppose if he was organizing he brought it on himself."

She opened her mouth to say something, then seemed to think better of it. Then seemed to think that there was nothing better after all. "He wouldn't agree with that."

"I'm sure he wouldn't. So what's your name, miss?"

"Veronica Hazel." He introduced himself again and said it was good to meet her, circumstances notwithstanding. He was not yet famous or infamous, just a man who happened to be born to the same parents as Whit, so such introductions were not as fraught as they would one day become.

They barely spoke for the next two hours, until the surgeon emerged from the room, looking scornfully down at Jason on the floor.

"How is he?" Jason asked as he pulled himself up.

"Look, I don't want to get involved in anything here, but I need to know who you are. If you're some union guy rounding up everyone who's—"

"That man is my brother." Jason pointed into the room. "My actual *brother*, not like some comrade or worker. Now, how is he?"

The doctor explained that much of Whit was broken—his clavicle; his left arm; his jaw, which would be temporarily wired shut; and several ribs—but they didn't suspect any organ damage. "He'll be eating through a straw for a while." Whit had lost a good amount of blood and had a serious concussion. "He's not going to feel normal for a good long time. But he should eventually."

"Good," Jason said, trying to convince himself. "Good."

"To tell you the truth, I'm a bit amazed. He took a hell of a beating. But he came to and seemed alert, which is a downright miracle. We have him sedated—he'll need that for a while. But his brain seems to be working."

"That's an improvement, then."

Months later, as Jason drove north to Cleveland, he thought of the

doctor's choice of the word *miracle*. He was tempted to wake his obnox-
iously snoring brother with a question: Had Whit seen anything during
his long unconsciousness—if that's what it had really been—at the
Hooverville? Angels, some celestial light, an echoing voice? Jason wondered what he himself had missed while he'd lain on his cooling board,
whether some important earthly instructions had been imparted to his
soul, only to have his waking self completely forget.

Jason had stayed in Lincoln City after Whit's release from the hospital,
helping Ma care for him. Also helping was Veronica, whom Jason ferried
back and forth each day until he slipped her enough money to get a cheap
apartment for a few weeks. Ma had, of course, been struck by Veronica's
obvious physical condition upon first meeting her, and she had lectured
Whit the moment Veronica left the house that night. No son of hers was
going to abandon a baby like that. From then on, she practically force-fed
Veronica rich meals.

Withdrawal from the morphine left Whit an insomniac for a few
nights, so Jason would sit beside his bed and talk through the evening.
Whit's metal-rimmed jaw, hardened eyes, and dented nose imbued with
permanence the hostile look he had been wearing for so long.

"My associates and I are going to do a certain endeavor, probably in a
couple weeks," Jason told him late one night. "Our first jobs were small,
but we know what we're doing now. In a couple weeks, I'll have more
money. You and Veronica can get your own place."

"I want to help," Whit said.

"No." For years Jason had been circumspect about keeping Whit un-
involved in his crimes, and he wasn't going to change that now. "You're
about to have a family to watch over."

"All the more reason. I can do a lot better by—"

"*No.* End of discussion." He paused for a moment, staring his brother
down. "So, how far along is she?"

Whit looked down at his feet. "I'm not sure."

"Looks pretty far to me. You've got your own work to do now."

"I don't know a damned thing about being a dad."

"I didn't know a damn thing about being a bank robber," Jason said.
"But necessity can teach you a lot."

Whit squinted at his brother. Pop had always used that line, and Jason had always made fun of it behind the old man's back. They sat there silently for a while, remembering this.

Three months later, Jason learned that Whit had joined the ranks of the disappeared.

"He left Veronica and the baby three weeks ago," Ma told him at the breakfast table the morning after one of his brief returns home.

"Jesus. He leave a note or anything?"

"A short one. It said, 'I'm sorry.' "

Jason shook his head. After Whit had recovered enough to move around, he and Veronica had quietly gone to a justice of the peace and married. Jason had not been in attendance, as he'd been hiding out after a lucrative bank job in Toledo. But late one night he had delivered his wedding gift in the form of a bundle of bills, enough for them to rent an apartment for a few months and buy some furniture and baby clothes. The happy if overwhelmed couple was living in Dayton, an hour from Lincoln City, just in case the cops were still interested in pursuing Whit for whatever shenanigans had put him on their list in the first place. Patrick was born in early July, and Whit had tried unsuccessfully to find work.

"How's Veronica?" Jason asked.

"She's all right. If you ask me, she's the toughest person in this family."

"I can't believe he ran out on her. And the baby."

"He's had a hard time," Ma defended her youngest.

"Who hasn't?"

She ignored him, moved on. "Veronica's family moved to Milwaukee last month, and she said she might have to follow them. I told her she's welcome to live here, too. I'd probably have to stop taking in boarders, but I'd manage somehow."

It was not yet six and the sky was dark; his mother had woken him up at five so they could eat breakfast together.

Marriner always preached the importance of lying low between jobs, so visiting home was a risk. Most of Jason's bank jobs had been miles away, but his escapades were beginning to receive press, particularly a recent job in Kalamazoo, in which a young cop had given chase but had lost

control of his vehicle, ramming into a tree and severely injuring himself.
And Jason's most recent heist not only had been in his home state but was
the biggest in Ohio history: they had liberated some fifty-seven thousand
dollars from Toledo Consumers Union and Trust. Marriner had objected
to Jason's plans to visit family so soon afterward, but Jason figured he
was being cautious enough by wearing a disguise (clear eyeglasses, a dull
charcoal-gray suit that fit a bit too snugly, an old cap, and a thin mustache), by slipping into Ma's place late at night and sleeping on the couch
downstairs so he could rise before the boarders. And by carrying a loaded
gun beneath his jacket.

"How are you?" he asked Ma. "You working too hard? You don't have
to take boarders in anymore—I can get you what you need."

"I don't want to rely on that, Jason. You know that."

He glanced at his empty coffee cup. "The Wilsons' old place is still
empty, I see."

"It is. Their yard has certainly gone to seed, which doesn't help the
neighborhood."

"It also makes it easier for hoboes to sneak to your back door and beg
for food. I know your heart's in the right place, but it might not be the
best idea."

"What might not be?"

"Ma. It's good of you, but at the same time it's a risk. You never know
if it might be . . . someone who isn't who he says he is."

"You don't give your mother much credit, do you? I managed to raise
you, don't forget."

"You have a reputation now; this place does. Didn't you see the chalk
marks of a cat on the front fence? That's hobo code for 'a kindhearted
woman lives here.' "

She was thrown for a moment. "I just thought some neighborhood
boys had done that."

"It's why every time one of those trains comes by, the bums know
where to look for free food."

"You don't like knowing that some of your money is feeding them."

He scowled. "That's not what I mean at all."

"I expected better of you, Jason."

"Ma, that is not . . ." How had he let himself get talked into this corner?
He should have just erased the damn drawing himself.

After a painful silence she said, "Find your brother, Jason. Bring him back to his wife and son."

Footsteps overhead told Jason that one of the boarders was up. He frowned—Ma had said they usually didn't wake until six-thirty. Ma took his plate into the kitchen, and Jason grabbed his bag without another word. He quietly opened the back door and slipped through the darkness into the garage. It was freezing inside, but at least he'd thrown some blankets into the car the night before. He would have to hide there for an hour or so, until the boarders had left for work.

First he stood at the small window on the side of the garage. He could see into the bright dining room from there, see the young man at the table, one chair over from where Jason had been sitting. Jason still wasn't used to seeing strange men in the house, even though Ma had been taking them in for months now. The boarder was thin and blond as a stalk of wheat, and he barely looked old enough to shave. Ma said he was a former accountant, laid off, who had recently got a job planting trees for the CCC; he was so scrawny it was hard to imagine him lasting more than a couple of weeks on such a job.

Jason stood there for a while, watching the man yawn and stare off into space. Then Ma slid a plate of eggs in front of him and the man smiled and nodded. Jason crept into the backseat and pulled the blankets around himself, waiting until it was safe to be in his mother's house.

With the exception of quick, late-night drives to deliver cash to his family, Jason had been away from Lincoln City for three months at that point. Upon driving into town he had noticed that the Hooverville seemed larger, like some unnatural weed that flourished despite the dipping temperatures. The cardboard and plywood walls of the lean-tos were double-layered as protection against the cool wind, or adorned with carpeting scavenged from derelict buildings. Clothes that didn't fit were nailed to the shacks, as were strips of hay and anything else that could serve as insulation. At night Jason had seen the fires on the hill, the glowing trash barrels and stolen heaps of coal. How did they decide which of their meager possessions to burn? The yellow lights glowed on the black hill like the signal fires of some invading tribe.

The summer's hesitant hope for Roosevelt's New Deal and National

Recovery Administration had soured in the past few weeks as things seemed only to backslide. Governments could change and policies could be enacted and banks could temporarily close and then reopen, but the disease was still festering. When the depression had first hit, everyone talked about it as if it were a hurricane or tornado or flood—another horrible act of God that simply needed to be endured. They were resigned villagers bucketing out the floodwaters or sawing the felled trees, expected to trudge patiently through the aftermath. But now people weren't so sure. Maybe depressions weren't God-made but man-made, bound to all the messiness and contradictions and barely concealed flaws that plagued us all. But if the depression was the result of human nature, how could you escape it? Preachers on the radio told listeners to repent, socialists and communists tried to recruit the dispossessed to their revitalized creeds, and people in the vast middle wondered whom to blame—God or themselves or someone else. Blame had become the only thing more precious than money.

Little Patrick was asleep in his mother's arms. The last time Jason had seen his nephew, he looked like a bald-headed monster. Now he was kind of cute.

Veronica was living in a tiny apartment on the third floor of a dilapidated building in a Dayton neighborhood where Jason wouldn't have wanted a pet dog to roam, let alone his wife and child. He silently cursed his brother—Jason had handed him a healthy amount of dough, and this was the place Whit rented?

Jason had managed a glance into the small pantry and saw that its shelves were sagging from age and poor craftsmanship but not from the weight they were carrying: two sacks of cornmeal, half a dozen cans of beans and vegetables. At least Whit had bought his new wife some decent clothes; she was wearing a pretty yellow dress, though from the look of it she'd been wearing it for a few days now. Her hair was messily pulled back and unwashed. The pouches beneath her eyes were the color of used tea bags and looked just as heavy.

Whit's disappearance had not been precipitated by a particularly bad fight, Veronica claimed, but Jason wasn't sure he believed her. Even in her current state, she wasn't the type to admit pain or reveal weakness.

"Any idea where he might have gone?"

"No. I don't know. Maybe. Few days before he left, one of your uncle's old war buddies stopped by and they went out drinking. An Italian. Name was Gustavo something-that-rhymed-with-Confetti. Whit told me the guy lives in Columbus and was goin' on about him knowing a guy who knew a guy who had jobs."

It was as good a hunch as Jason was likely to stumble upon. Columbus was no more than four hours' drive, so he was relieved to hear that his expedition would be a short one. Still, there was something particularly sad about running out on your family and making it through only a few counties. Part of him had wanted to believe Whit was staking out for the bounty and risks of California, or testing himself against the anonymous lottery of greater cities like Chicago or New York. The thought of Whit trying to reinvent himself in goddamn Columbus only made Jason shake his head.

"Did he say he was going there to work a job and send money home?"

She shook her head. "I just woke up one morning thinking he was out looking for work. I thought he'd be back for supper, but he never came back."

Jason slipped her money for rent—enough for at least three months, he figured, plus food. She protested the charity only halfheartedly before accepting.

"I'm sorry he did that to you, Veronica. I'll talk some sense into him."

"He's having trouble growing up," she said.

"I guess I haven't been the best example for him."

"He'd yell and scream one night and cry the next. Not unlike this one." As if insulted, the baby uttered a little yelp.

"You know you're welcome to stay at Ma's. We don't want you to be alone."

"I don't want to be a burden on her. She has enough on her hands with June's kids."

"You're not a burden, you're family."

"What's the difference?"

The baby cried again, and this time his eyes opened. The cries were short but constant; Jason had never heard anything more grating. He could imagine how it must have sounded to Whit.

"I should feed him," Veronica said.

"I'll talk some sense into Whit," he repeated as he stood, grateful for the excuse to make his exit. He told himself he was doing the right thing as he walked out of her apartment, down the creaking steps, past the bum in the first-floor hallway, and out the front door with the broken lock.

Despite Marriner's advice about lying low, after Jason's uncomfortable talk with Ma he'd felt the only way he could salvage her opinion of him was by doing as she had asked. So here he was, poking into this Columbus bar and that, checking in at a veterans' office for the mysterious friend of his dead uncle, walking up and down breadlines in the hope of spotting Whit. At the eighth bar Jason checked, the barkeep said a guy who sounded like Whit had been by a few days ago, drinking with a Gustavo Colletti, who lived around the corner. When the barkeep mentioned that Whit had skipped out without paying his tab, Jason paid the amount, plus a fat tip. The barkeep's eyes froze on Jason's thick billfold.

Colletti's neighborhood was a modest block, tree-lined but lacking shade, as the maples were spindly things that had been planted recently, probably in '29, before every municipal budget had zeroed out. Long shadows sprawled on the sidewalks beneath the late-afternoon sun. Though it was barely five o'clock, Jason saw a dispiriting number of men smoking on porches or watching him from behind windows.

"Gustavo Colletti?" Jason asked when a man in an undershirt and patched trousers answered the door. He was Jason's height, and though his arms and chest were thick, they seemed to sag a bit from fat that had once been muscle.

"Who's asking?"

"I'm looking for Whit Fireson."

"He ain't here anymore." The man had curly dark hair that had lost an inch or two of real estate to his forehead.

"You two had a spat?"

Colletti folded his arms. They were not insignificant arms. "I said, who's asking?"

"I'm family of his. He left his wife and kid high and dry, and I want to talk some sense into him."

"All I tried to do was help out the nephew of an old buddy who's down on his luck. He overstayed his welcome, and I told him as much."

"He doesn't have a job in town?"

Colletti laughed as if he had long ago stopped seeing real humor in the world.

"Where's he staying now?"

"Got me."

"He alone? Or does he have a frail in town?"

"Last couple times I saw him he was chatting up a girl named Alice Simmons, but he can't be staying with her, since she lives in a girls' dorm."

"Buddy, if you have any idea where I might find him, I'd appreciate it. As would his two-month-old son."

Colletti unfolded his arms and let his heavy hands fall into his pockets. "Know where I'd look? Greater Columbus Presbyterian—the school, not the church. He and Alice were talking about going out for the dance marathon."

"You mean, to watch it?"

"I mean to win it. Two-hundred-dollar pot."

Colletti invited Jason into his tiny kitchen to check his copy of the *Dispatch*. Jason found the story in the front section, on page 3 no less, under the headline WALKATHON DOWN TO 12 LUCKY COUPLES. They were officially called walkathons for propriety's sake, when in fact dancing was what the contestants did until they collapsed. Jason skimmed the story, which noted that the contest was in its twelfth day now, and though there was no mention of a Whit Fireson, he saw one couple identified as Alice Simmons and Will Franklin—the name Whit had used when signing for his Dayton apartment.

"I know who you are, by the way," Colletti said. He had lit a cigarette while Jason read the story, and he spoke with it dangling from his lips.

"That so?"

"Your brother can be quite a talker after a few drinks."

"And quite a liar. Don't believe everything a guy says."

"Oh, I don't. But I believe enough." He removed the cigarette from his mouth and tipped it into a dark-red ashtray. "Last April, bank threw me and my wife out of a house we'd bought five years ago. Had never been late on a payment before, and they didn't care that I had that army bonus due me eventually."

"That's too bad. I'm sorry to hear."

"Was three times as big as this rathole. And now we got another kid coming. Anyway, I'd just like to shake your hand."

It was the third or fourth such overture Jason had received, and during the next few months it would be followed by many more. He always told his well-wishers they had the wrong guy, denying his identity while secretly being warmed by them. But he also found these gestures puzzling—the way people thought of him, how they attached their hopes and grievances and fears to his every movement. They placed great meaning on his acts, which they didn't understand. He felt undeserving of their praise but also somehow above them and their flailing despondency, both unworthy and superior.

"Tell me," Colletti said as Jason released his hand and tried to make his exit. "It true what they say about you tearing up mortgages when you're in the banks? You really do that for folks?"

Jason's shoulder had already forced the door open. He could hear a bus trawl by, kids insulting one another.

"Like I said, don't believe everything a guy says." He donned his hat and turned out the doorway in one fluid motion, wondering how Colletti might color the encounter when retelling it to friends.

Jason's stomach was begging for food, but he felt close to finding Whit and didn't want to let supper cost him his chance. He drove to the school, a long, two-story gray box beside which was a smaller structure with the tall windows of a gymnasium. In front of the school building, a sign announced COLUMBUS FIRST ANNUAL WALKATHON! $250 PRIZE! NIGHTLY CONTEST EVENTS! LIVE MUSIC! NOW IN TWELFTH DAY! SPONSORED BY VFW. ADMISSION 25¢.

He was surprised the promoter had been able to land a church's school gym, as most preachers strongly opposed the contests, given the licentious dancing, the depraved crowds, and the announcer's lewd jokes. The promoter must have offered the church a cut of the take.

Jason parked at the spot closest to the exit behind the building, backing in, always prepared for a hasty escape. He could hear the music when he was halfway to the door. In the small entryway hung banners boasting of football and basketball championships. Below them a dimpled blond girl sitting at a collapsible desk and cash register charged him a quarter. From the gym a waltz faded, followed by the sound of a needle scratching on the phonograph. Next up was another waltz, sleepier.

"Things will really get moving again at six o'clock," the girl told him. He thanked her and walked through the doors.

Two dozen spectators were scattered on bleachers on one side of the gym. The tall windows provided little light at that hour, yet only half the lamps above the main floor were lit. The markings of a basketball court lay beneath the feet of eleven dancing couples—apparently the twelfth had been disqualified since that morning. Before taking a seat, Jason scanned the faces of the dancers. Calling them dancers was inaccurate. Their slight movements may have been enough to pass muster with the judge, who darted among them with birdlike inquisitiveness, but it certainly wasn't dancing. Many of the contestants were leaning on their partners, faces wan, arms hanging loose like corpses. Some of their wrists were bound with rope, and knotted kerchiefs connected a few slumbering necks to their more responsive mates. The waking partners gingerly nudged the feet of their dozing companions, keeping in accordance with the rules. The balding floor judge carried a white yardstick, and he flicked it at the calves of a short woman who was nearly crumpling beneath the weight of her partner. She moved faster after the strike, and began shaking her man's shoulders.

"Allllllrighty, people!" The announcer's energetic voice was in such contrast to the torpor on the floor. It sounded inhuman, a sinister force. "After this song it will be five o'clock! That means the live band will be setting up, that means the tempo will be picking up, and, most important, that means—"

The thin but lively audience, mostly female, chimed in: "No breaks!"

Jason spotted the pin-striped announcer, standing at a desk at the far end, beneath one of the retracted basketball hoops. Beside him two headphoned men sat among consoles of electronics, wires spilling in every direction. Local radio, of course, set to broadcast the night's events. Jason had never attended one of these, but he'd once talked up a traveling promoter for such events. The man had been soused and bragged about his lucrative calling, how he would skip from town to town, putting on the events only at locations that had never hosted them before, so the crowds would be enthusiastic and the local hosts wouldn't realize that he was likely to disappear without paying their take. He talked about how he rigged the contest with his small legion of professional dancers, whom he referred to as "horses": ex–vaudeville players who needed the work and had the endurance to outlast even the most desperate of participants. He described the ridiculous nightly games and wind sprints, the insults they lobbed at the contestants, the ice baths they dunked them into if they fell too deeply asleep on their cots during the hourly fifteen-minute breaks backstage. The promoter had been with a circus in his youth, he'd explained, until he decided that torturing animals wasn't enough of a challenge.

Finally, Jason spotted his brother. Whit was one of the sleepers, and at first Jason hadn't recognized him, since his face was pressed into the padded shoulder of a green dress. Whit's dance partner was a tall redhead. She was wobbling in a clockwise slumber, and now Jason could see only the back of Whit's head, the pale right ear sticking out like a crumpled white flag. Pinned to both of their backs were yellow pieces of paper displaying the number 37.

Jason clambered over the bleachers and sat in the back row. He considered the flask of bourbon in his pocket but decided to hold off. Then he weighed the scene that would be created by wandering onto the floor and pulling Whit aside. The way that drunken promoter had described it, these operations were tightly controlled, and there were probably some security toughs scattered about. Jason didn't want to attract attention, so, for now, he sat and watched.

More people were filing through the entrance. Jason had forgotten it was Friday night, which likely meant that an array of especially outlandish events were in store. As if on cue, the emcee announced that wrist attachments, leg irons, and other contraptions must be removed for the next twelve hours.

Jason glanced at the program. Apparently there had been one hundred couples at the beginning. He felt a glimmer of something that wasn't quite pride that Whit was among the final eleven. A pop vendor started climbing his way, but Jason shook the kid off. Other teenagers were hawking hot dogs and chips as if this were a ball game. Baseball had always bored Jason—all those fat men standing around in pajamas, moving once every three minutes—but this was even worse.

"It's been more than eleven days, ladies and gentlemen!" the emcee hollered. "Two hundred and seventy-one hours these crazy folks have been keeping in motion for you! Two hundred seventy-one hours of right foot, left foot! I've been checking up on them during the backstage breaks, folks, and I've seen blisters big as half-dollars! I've seen bunions that could split a metal-tipped boot! I've seen blood, sweat, and tears! And that's just one couple I'm talking about!"

Now the band launched into a shag, choosing to start the proceedings with the most frenetic number possible. The couples whirled into insane variations on the Charleston. They clutched each other violently and their moves were jerky. They were wrestling, with each other and with gravity and whatever unnamed forces had conspired to put them there. They didn't seem fully cognizant of where they were or why; they were dancing merely because it was all they could remember to do, like men on assembly lines.

Next was a black bottom and then a couple of fox-trots at a faster tempo than normal. The pianist might as well have been firing a pistol at the dancers' feet.

"Barbara and Glen met in the first grade at this very school," the emcee announced. "So wouldn't it be sweet for them to win on their home floor? Danny and Donna will be celebrating their second anniversary tomorrow—but will they still be dancing? Otis and Lindsey have five pretty daughters at home and need that prize money for food and school clothes! Lou-Lou's hubby, Francis, has three medals for fighting in France, but our trophy is the only prize he cares about now!"

Jason couldn't fathom the combination of willpower, self-delusion, and masochism necessary to compete in such an event, and after sixty minutes of sitting there he'd reached his own limit. He made his way down the bleachers, winding through the thickening ranks of jovial spectators. Skirting the periphery of the floor, he approached a man whose blue shirtsleeves advertised triceps that couldn't possibly have been earned by standing around dance floors.

"Say, buddy," Jason said. The man had to lean close to hear Jason above the racket from the band, which was only twenty yards away. "How many horses you guys got out there?"

"Excuse me?" But he'd heard Jason just fine.

"What would you say are the odds couple number thirty-seven is going to finish as high as the top three?" The program had promised two hundred and fifty dollars to the winning couple, seventy-five for second place, thirty for third.

"I don't care for your line of questioning."

"No offense to you or your associates meant, but I have business with the taller half of number thirty-seven."

"He owe you money?"

"He owes me time, and I'm tired of spending it watching him dance. He's a lousy dancer."

"They all are after twelve days."

"What I'm saying is, I wonder if you might be able to get them disqualified so I can conduct my business with him and get out of here. But I'd feel kind of bad if doing that would keep him from winning."

The gorilla folded his arms. People seemed to be doing that to Jason today. "Why would I want to get him disqualified?"

Jason reached into his pocket and discreetly took out the billfold, slipping out two singles. "My time is worth money to me."

"Nuts to you."

"Christ, pal, we both know you're going to disqualify them eventually. If you want to get something extra for it, great. If not, I'll go take my seat and grab a nap."

He made to return the bills to his pocket, but the gorilla extended his hand. They shook, and the money was in the man's pocket. "Dangle a minute," he said.

Jason walked back to the bleachers, sitting in the front row this time. From here he could smell the dancers' perfume and cologne, as it had likely been slathered on during breaks to cover up body odor. He leaned forward, elbows on knees, and watched as the gorilla wandered through the careening dancers, finally tapping the judge on the shoulder. The two retreated to a corner and exchanged words, then the gorilla returned to his station. He briefly made eye contact with Jason, looking away without a nod.

And then it happened, just as whirling Charlestons were devolving into what might have been Lindy hops as a new song began: the judge tore the number from Alice's back. It was the first disqualification Jason had witnessed, and even though he was the only spectator who had known it was coming, it was still shocking. He was willing to bet the judge always tore off the woman's number; the thin sheet of paper was all that came off, but the suddenness and the violence of the act must have felt tantamount to having her dress ripped off. The girl froze in place, even as Whit, oblivious Whit, continued to move. The connection between the two was severed. Whit had finally begun to show some recognition of their new reality when she collapsed.

Spectators were laughing and cheering. Jason heard someone say, "I *knew* she'd faint when it happened. She had that look."

Jason turned back to the crowd for a moment and saw people exchanging coins.

Whit was arguing with the judge; Jason could make out only a few words. But the judge moved on to assess the other dancers now, and Whit's burst of panic and fury fled instantly, as if he were waking from a dream. He slowly turned back to his fallen companion and reached for her. She was conscious after all, clasping his hands as she staggered to her feet.

"Let's hear it for couple number thirty-seven, William and Alice!" The emcee was downright ebullient. "They did a great job these two hundred and seventy-two hours! We'll especially miss Alice's performances in the wind sprints, won't we, folks?"

Cheering, jeering—it was hard to tell the difference, and Jason had been there for only an hour. He couldn't imagine how it must sound to Whit and Alice. The other dancers continued their spastic movements, opening a wide circle around the newest losers. But they betrayed little awareness of the fact that their odds had just improved. They barely blinked.

Couple No. 37 had made it a few paces toward the backstage curtain when she started hitting him. Her hands weren't closed into fists, but it clearly didn't take much to harm a man who'd been dancing for twelve days. Whit raised his arms into a protective position. The cheering intensified.

For a moment Jason worried that Whit would fight back, take a swing at her. It wasn't like his brother to just take a beating like this, and it broke Jason's heart to see Whit meekly endure the assault. Then Alice collapsed again. Whit caught her and whispered something into her ear.

Jason moved before they could disappear backstage. A young man, thin as a hiccup, was parting the curtain for doomed couple No. 37 as Jason approached.

"Whit," Jason said. The sound made Whit jump.

"Oh. Hello." He sounded very, very tired.

"Tough break. I was just starting to think you might pull it off, too."

"How—" Whit took a breath. The two of them smelled even worse up close. "How long have you been here?"

Alice gazed in Jason's direction with what he first thought was hostility but was probably just exhaustion, and now she shifted her gaze to Whit, whom she was still leaning against. "Who's he?"

"I'm his old pal Sonny. And you must be The Other Woman."

She had the type of pale skin that probably yielded freckles in the summer but was now waxy from her days indoors. And surely her hair wasn't supposed to look like that.

"What?"

Whit eyed him. "Can this wait, Jason?"

The use of his real name galled him. "No, it can't." He reached into his pocket and slipped something from the billfold. He reached out to Alice. "Here, sweetness, buy yourself some new feet."

Her lips curled for the better hurling of insults until she noticed the denomination. She swallowed her curse and took the money.

"Now grab hold of something solid, miss. I need to borrow your partner for a bit." Jason took his brother by the arm and pulled. Whit looked displeased yet came along so freely that it was clear there was no longer any connection between his mind and his body. Let alone any connection between him and Alice, who had collapsed into a metal chair, her head slumped.

It was dark outside and small packs of young people were scattered in the parking lot, smoking and telling jokes. Jason spied a flask being passed around, which reminded him that he wanted a sip from his own, but not while he was dragging Whit across the now crowded lot. Someone had even parked a sedan on a narrow strip of grass between Jason's car and the exit, but it wasn't quite blocking his way out.

"Lovely girl," Jason remarked. "She always smell like that?"

Whit shook off Jason's hand and stopped a few paces in front of the latest in Jason's long line of automobiles, a black Plymouth. "What do you want?"

"Call me crazy, but I think Veronica's more of a looker than that one."

"Alice isn't my girl." Whit exhaled deeply with each phrase, like a panting dog trying to master speech. "We just thought . . . the dance thing might work. But we're not that way."

"Still, you removed your wedding band, I see. Or did you ever have one?"

"Hocked it weeks ago." He had no doubt bought the thing with money Jason had given him. "Ronny knew about it. You can't eat gold."

"Speaking of which, how do you eat if you're dancing all day? I've been wondering."

"They feed you. Eight times a day. Eggs, oatmeal. Oranges. Set up little tables next to you. So you can keep your feet moving. Haven't eaten that well in months." He looked down at himself, then back at Jason. "Now." Pant. "What do you want?"

"This isn't about wanting, Whit. I did not want to spend my time looking for a deadbeat that left his family high and dry."

"Don't lecture me about leaving town, Jason. I haven't seen you around much lately."

Jason poked a finger in Whit's chest. Any harder and Whit would have fallen on his back. "You're talking to the guy who just paid for the roof over your kid's head for the next three months."

"So I'm supposed to thank you, that it? Or just admire you from a distance, like everyone else?"

Jason didn't reply.

"You have your way of helping family," Whit said, "and I have mine."

"Explain to me how this is helping."

"I was going to send them money." Pant. "Once I made some."

"That's not how it looks to Veronica."

Whit stared at him for a moment, then let his eyes wander over to the packs of parking-lot hooligans. "You don't get it, do you? That's some world you live in. But you can't even see."

"What can't I see?"

"They're better off without me."

"They didn't look so well off this morning."

Whit opened his arms. "Do you know what I made in the last three months before I left? *Nothing.* At least without me around they have a better shot at getting on the government rolls."

"So hide in the closet if the government people come by to check."

"Old buddy of Uncle Joe's said I could get a job here. But it didn't work out. Think I'll try Detroit next."

"Why do you even need to bum around for work after I gave you that money?"

"Your money doesn't stretch forever."

"Well, it should have stretched enough for you to put your family someplace better than that rathole of an apartment. What did you do, drink the money away? Gamble it?"

Whit scowled. "I don't do that stuff."

"Then help me with the math."

"Times are tough, Jason. I had some buddies in worse shape than me, some guys I used to work with—"

Jason shook his head and took a moment to contain his rage. "That dough was for *you*, Whit, you and your family. Not for some other stiff or a friend of a friend or some fellow traveler."

"We're all in this together."

"Jesus Christ, I'm not here to support all of Ohio. Give your red slogans a rest."

"I had no right to hold on to that money and not help folks who were hungry. My obligation is to my fellow man, Jason, even if you don't like to—"

"Your obligation is to your own family. You're a father and a husband now. Things change."

"Yeah. Everything's changed, all right."

They stood silently for a moment.

"You *really* want to help me?" Whit asked. "And my baby, and Ronny? Let me join your gang. I'm a good shot, and I can drive as well as—"

Jason slapped him. He had held back, but even that slap was enough to knock a dance marathoner to the ground. Conversations around the lot stopped.

Though Jason was more powerfully built than his brother, Whit had always let sheer desire make up for any physical shortcoming when the time came to fight. But the litany of his lost months, let alone the past twelve days, had softened his muscles and stripped him of his will. Whoever said what doesn't kill you makes you stronger, Jason thought, was a very wishful thinker indeed.

"Sorry," he said as he helped his brother up. "But I told you about that."

"You don't understand." Whit wasn't bleeding, but only because all his blood was in his feet. "You have no idea."

"*You* have no idea." Jason struggled to keep his voice down. "You haven't boxed yourself into a corner like I have. You still have options, Whit, possibilities. I'm not going to have you making the same mistakes I did, especially when you've got a wife and a kid to look after." He stopped himself and pointed to the Plymouth. "I don't have time to explain this to you. Now get in before I hog-tie you to the roof."

Jason saw that his brother's eyes were wet.

Whit looked away, ashamed. "You saw them today?"

"Yeah."

"How . . . How are they?"

"You've got a cute kid. Don't know how you managed it. And a fine wife, in a lot of ways, and I definitely don't know how you managed that. But they miss you, Whit."

"I can't." He shook his head. It wobbled awkwardly, his skull loose on its perch. "Just let me go. Tell them you couldn't find me. Tell them I'm dead. Tell them—"

Jason put a hand on his shoulder. "C'mon, brother. We'll make it."

He nudged Whit forward. That got Whit's feet moving toward the Plymouth, and, as on the dance floor, he appeared unable to fight the momentum. Jason walked a step behind him and took a snort from his flask. He was about to tap Whit on the shoulder and ask if he wanted any when he heard a man's voice.

"Jason Fireson?"

To his left, from the direction of the street, three men approached. They stopped ten, fifteen paces away. The speaker was in front, a gruff, portly type, a square crammed into a circle. He wore a snap-brim hat and a gray suit. Behind him were two other men, one in a suit and the other, younger, wearing the newest-looking cop uniform Jason had ever seen.

"Excuse me?" Jason said. The Firesons stopped and turned, Jason's right hand hidden behind Whit's back. His shoulders were squared and his feet firmly planted.

"State police. You're under arrest." There was a badge, then a gun. Behind the men a bus moaned its way down the street. The headlights didn't reveal any other figures in the background.

"You've got the wrong guy," Jason said, shaking his head. He still held the flask before him with his left hand. An arc light glinted off the steel.

The men began moving toward them.

"Jesus, Jason," Whit croaked.

A sudden burst of applause from within the gym. Whit and Alice were no longer the most recent losers. Two of the cops' heads tilted and Jason dropped his flask from his left hand. Before it had even hit the ground he'd unholstered his gun with his right and fired three shots.

The crowd was still laughing and jeering, the gunshots only so many taps of a snare drum in their delirious little world. Jason put his other hand on Whit's shoulder and pulled him down as the shots multiplied.

His fake eyeglasses fell from his nose as he and his brother ducked behind the sedan parked on the grass. The guns paused for breath. He dared to lift his head again and fired twice more. He ducked and glanced at Whit, who despite his red eyes now looked very awake indeed. Another burst of gunfire from the cops, and the shattering of glass, then silence.

Jason opened the car door and motioned for Whit to crawl in. He followed, crouching out of view, and popped open the glove compartment. It took Whit a second to realize he was expected to reach in and grab the revolver. Jason shifted his gun to his left hand so he could fish out his keys with his right. Then he sat up, blindly fired two rounds out the window, and started the Plymouth with his other hand. Gravel sprayed as he pulled out as fast as he could. The teenagers' glowing cigarette butts had vanished like fireflies and the lot behind him might as well have been a black wall.

A shot to his left. People were screaming now; the secret was out. He fired in return.

Jason hadn't turned on his headlights and he almost missed the body as he was pulling out. But there it was, to his left, faceup. He slowed down just enough to look at it, see the young face. He knew him. From where? Jesus, from Ma's kitchen. The tree planter, the skinny former accountant, who could not possibly have been a cop. A badge helplessly dangled out of his jacket pocket.

And as Jason's mind raced through his mother's boarding house, he noticed, too late, more movement to his right. Whit fired twice, the shots echoing mercilessly in the tiny car. Jason hit the accelerator just as the cop was falling down.

"I got him!" Whit cried. "Oh Jesus, I got him!"

Jason couldn't tell if Whit's voice was panicked or thrilled, but he didn't have time to ask. The Plymouth's speed kicked in once it made it to the asphalt. Jason turned his neck like a crazy man to scan in all directions, but there was nothing to see. No roadblock? No backup? He raced through unusually calm Friday-night streets, uttering silent prayers as he ran reds.

An hour later, they were racing through the kinds of country roads Jason had lived on during his bootlegging days. But he'd never run any routes around here, so he didn't know these particular roads. It was cloudy, too, so he could only hope he was headed west, toward the border.

"You're going to have to move your family," Jason said to Whit after a long silence. His adrenaline had faded by then and he spoke calmly. Whit was not nearly so placid; though his dance-marathon experience had him on the verge of narcolepsy, each time his eyes shut he was immediately awakened by the encroaching and nightmarish realization that he had just killed someone. "It won't be safe for Veronica to stay in Ohio."

"Jason," Whit said, choosing his words carefully, remembering the slap in the face. "There's no way around it now. I'm in this with you."

Jason just kept driving. The night had turned cold but he kept the windows down because Whit smelled so terrible. After another minute Whit said his name again, and Jason abruptly pulled over. He killed the headlights and there was nothing beyond the windshield, no world at all except what the brothers were carrying with them.

"Just tell me we won't be arguing the whole time," Jason said, staring straight ahead. "I swear to God, I can't take your grumbling much longer."

"I won't argue. I'll be the model accomplice."

"Model *apprentice.*"

"Whatever you say."

Jason turned and finally looked at his brother. He felt a heaviness in his stomach, pulling at him. It was fairly easy to make risky, even dangerous decisions when he was on his own, but it would be so much harder with a brother to protect. Worse, inviting family into the gang would mean inviting introspection, forcing him to take the kind of look at himself that he had studiously avoided. He wished for the hundredth time that Whit had been able to live a quiet, stable life managing Pop's store, the way Jason had always envisioned. Things had turned out so differently than he'd expected. He didn't want to think about how much of the blame was his.

"I've tried to protect you from all this," Jason said. "But I suppose you've made it clear that, if left to your own devices, you'll get yourself killed any day now. So I might as well let it happen on my watch. That way I'll at least be able to explain to Ma exactly how you got killed, instead of, I don't know, just stumbling upon your corpse in an alley someplace."

"That might be the nicest thing you've ever said to me."

"Don't get used to the sentimental stuff," Jason said. "I can be a hard boss. There's a way to do things, and we'll show you how, and you'll do it exactly that way. I'll need to teach you a lot, and you'll need to listen a lot. A lot more than you've ever demonstrated the capacity for, to be quite frank. Sound like you can handle that? Once you get a couple days' sleep and shave off your blisters?"

There were other reasons for Jason's relenting, one of them being a mistaken belief that Whit's recent near-death experiences—that night, and at the hands of the Lincoln City cops—would have purged him of his rage at the banks, at the cops and the judge who'd put their father away, at anyone who wielded an ounce more power than he did. But Jason would soon learn that Whit's rage was not something that could be beaten out of him. Or even killed out of him.

"Can the next endeavor be Third National of Lincoln City?" Whit asked.

"No, it cannot."

"Why not?" Already Whit was demonstrating a reluctance to follow orders.

"For one, it's local, and we'd have cops on our tail anytime we came back to town."

"That problem seems to have presented itself anyway."

"And, second of all, it's too personal."

"What's wrong with personal? What's wrong with really goddamn wanting to rob that bank?"

What's wrong, indeed? For here they were, months and many crimes later, driving north to find Marriner and cobble together what they could of the broken bricks and crumbling mortar that had once constituted their gang. With a newly unified group, they would plan one last endeavor. And this time, since they were believed to be dead, since the police could not possibly be on the alert for them, they were setting their sights on that familiar, formerly untouchable foe.

The bank that Whit believed killed their old man was going to be robbed by the dead Firefly Brothers.

VIII.

The goggles no longer chafed at the skin above Darcy's ears. She wondered if that meant they had slackened with time or if her skin had toughened to the pressure. Her eyelids, however, did not react so agreeably: they itched as though the cloth stuffed inside the goggles were infested with mites.

"I really would like to scratch at my eyes, please," she said again.

"No dice. And if you ask again I'll scratch them myself with sandpaper."

She had heard a number of voices, her invisible guards in this mystery room, and had privately assigned them names. She recognized this voice as belonging to The Particularly Mean One.

Darcy had finished her breakfast, bitter coffee and toast that should have been rescued from its hell thirty seconds earlier. This was the second full day, meaning the third since they'd taken her.

They had driven her through the city and then on a highway for possibly an hour. Then they had brought her into a house where their footsteps echoed too loudly in her ears. She had been given a hard chair to sit on and was told not to touch her goggles, that someone would always be beside her, watching. It was true; even when she heard voices in another room, there was still breathing nearby. Someone had eventually brought her a cheese sandwich, and guided her to the bathroom. She was given some degree of privacy in those moments but was always told to "be quick about it," and warned that they would be able to tell from her hair if she dared to adjust the goggles.

Then it was back into a car for a longer drive. She guessed it was night, when they would be less conspicuous escorting a hostage. Time was unknowable for her—the goggles were not only stuffed with dark cloth but also, she suspected, painted black. By the time the car stopped, she would have believed it was eleven P.M. or four in the morning, would have believed they were in a Chicago suburb or in Oklahoma or Saskatchewan.

Darcy felt half drunk and queasy, her head pounded by the dueling drummers of fear and confusion. Jason was alive, but she had been kidnapped, and these men believed him to be dead. She had been given a glimpse of a long, lonely, desolate life, then rescued from it for approximately ten glorious minutes before being confined to darkness of a more tangible sort. Memories of the day she'd met Jason kept flashing through her mind in cruel contrast to this very different abduction; the men's voices were hushed, full of aggression and alarm, lacking Jason's sunny chivalry. She told herself that the telegram from Jason changed everything, that his being out there somewhere rendered this episode a mere inconvenience, but she didn't entirely believe that.

Her mood darkened as time passed. Based on the way the voices ricocheted off the walls, she knew only that she was in a small, mostly unfurnished room. She was seated for hours each day in a wooden chair, her ankles tied to its legs, her calves and buttocks deadened into numbness. She never would have imagined the sheer torture that came simply from being unable to cross her legs or twitch her feet. At night—she knew it from the different calls of the birds, and the humming crickets, and the cool breeze from some half-open window—her feet were untied and she was guided to an upholstered chaise that they brought in from another room. Her legs again were fastened, as well as her arms, and she was given a thin sheet. They assured her that she was being watched as she lay, which did not make sleep come any easier.

When you first close your eyes, the screen before them seems to glimmer and glow, the vanishing colors leaving an aura of their past selves, like light from a dying star. But as time passes and your eyes stay shut a brute darkness takes hold. Darcy saw the blackest black she could have imagined, a permanent winter.

This was her world now. The seclusion and deprivation made her too conscious of the rope on her ankles, of the goggles on her eyelids, of her swollen legs. By day her right arm was free, thank God, and she scratched obsessively at her other arm and side. She chided the men for submitting her to this infestation of mosquitoes—couldn't you at least put me in a room with a screen on the window?—but they insisted there were no bugs, that the itching was imaginary.

And so, today. She heard a plane overhead. It occurred to her that she had heard one such plane each day. She asked what time it was.

"About noon."

This was a different voice, not The Particularly Mean One but the one she thought of as The Lovable Thug. He had a deep and slow voice, and from the way he spoke to her she could tell that he felt uncomfortable with the way they were treating a lady. The others were tight-lipped and borderline abusive, but she could work on this one.

"I suppose that means my peanut-butter-and-jelly sandwich is on the way."

What bothered her was that she hadn't noticed The Particularly Mean One leave and The Lovable Thug enter. Were they really that quiet? Had she fallen asleep? Or was her mind allowing different scenes to blur together, forcing one character to become another, like an amateur play with too few actors for so many roles, the slain Mercutio rising to play Paris and die again?

"You don't like peanut butter and jelly?"

She had insulted him. "I love it. I deeply admire the interplay of complex flavors. Sometimes I serve it for dinner."

"You're joshing me now."

"Well, a girl needs to have *some* fun. Regardless of the situation."

"That's the right attitude to have, miss. Just keep your spirits up and this'll be over soon."

"Does that mean things are progressing?"

"I think so."

"They don't tell you much, do they?"

"I know enough." Again he seemed insulted, and she smiled.

The first night, they had handed her a pen and a pad of paper and dictated a message to her father. She didn't remember what it said, and she hadn't the faintest idea how legible it wound up being. But the basic message was that they had her and she was safe but these men "meant business" (she remembered that phrase, the cliché almost comical) and that her father should do whatever they asked.

"I'm not exactly close to my old man," she had dared to interject.

"Well, you'd better hope this brings you closer to him, dearie." A voice disguised by a rasp, which she thereafter identified as The Threatening One. *"Or it'll spell big trouble for you."*

She paused, the pen rigid between her fingers. "And how exactly do you spell big trouble? It starts with a *B*, right?"

"Hilarious." The man had continued with his dictation.

"How much are you asking him for?" she inquired when they'd finished.

"Enough questions, dearie."

"Don't I deserve to know what I'm worth to him? Or to you?"

"You're worth nothing to me. You need to understand that." She knew there were others in the room, but this man, the ringleader of her invisible circus, seemed to enjoy employing the first-person singular. *"But, like I said, you'd better hope you're worth a lot to your old man."*

"All right, but my advice is to ask him for cold hard cash, and no cars." She knew she sounded flippant; it was an act, of course, but if she could convince herself maybe her nerves would calm down. "His cars are designed to fall apart after four years. Insider information."

"Thanks for the tip. Any other wisdom you'd like to impart?"

"Wisdom, no, but a criticism: I think it's rotten that you stole my idea."

Indeed, this had been *her* plan for embezzling money from her crooked old man. The Firefly Brothers would kidnap her, demand a steep ransom, and, after they received it, she and Jason would disappear together. She would eventually write her father a letter explaining that she was all right, that the nameless crooks had released her and she had decided that it would be best for her and her father to go their separate ways. She had never been able to persuade Jason to act on this plan—too complicated, he always said—but now these strangers had the audacity to do so. It was as if they had stolen not only her physical person but also something from inside her.

Darcy sighed as she sat, on the third day, in the room with The Lovable

Thug. She liked him. He had apologized whenever he swore in her presence—gallantly but unnecessarily, as she herself had cursed a number of times in his without reciprocating. He had even procured some aspirin and water when she confessed to being hungover that first night. He sounded to be in his early thirties, uneducated, likely an ex-convict.

"I assume by this point my father has agreed to your request? Payment and delivery are being arranged?"

"Don't worry about all that," he said, not unkindly. "We're on top of it."

"So what's your name, anyway?"

"Can't tell you our names, miss."

"Well, I can't very well go on calling you *you*."

"Why not?"

"Because then how do I tell you apart from the others?"

He thought about this. "I don't think you're supposed to."

"At least *make up* a name."

"Can't do that, either."

"Whyever not?"

"Boss told us that if we made up any names we might accidentally reveal some part of our identity'r something."

"Very well, *I'll* make up a name for you. I'll call you Rufus."

"Why Rufus?"

"Would you prefer something else?"

"I told you, I'm not allowed to ma—"

"And do you always follow orders, Rufus?"

"When it'll result in a big paycheck, you better believe I follow orders."

"How big of a paycheck?"

"Let's see. . . . Split seven ways, it should bring me about thirty or so. Minus the laundering fees. Bastards bleed it out of you, pardon my cuss."

So there were seven of them. "That really is an awful lot of money. I should be flattered."

But what she felt was worried. Two hundred thousand dollars? Jasper Windham was hardly Henry Ford, even in the best of times. And, from what she had surmised, Windham Automotive had not glimpsed such times in a long while. As the rest of the industry consolidated in Detroit, her old man had stubbornly held out in Chicago, clinging to the gangland connections that kept his workers from causing trouble. But such connections carried their own price, and Windham Automotive was slipping behind the pack. Greed was blinding Darcy's kidnappers to a certain unfortunate truth: there was no way her father could pay two hundred thousand.

She opened her mouth but realized, as the first syllable made its mad escape, that telling them this would be a mistake. So she ended the sentence before it began.

Hoping to distract herself from this new fear, she started over. "Tell me about yourself, Rufus. Something interesting."

"Can't do that, miss."

"Very well, tell me something about yourself that no one else knows."

"Why do you think that's any different?"

"The reason your boss doesn't want you to tell me your name or your vital statistics, presumably, is because that way I could later give the information to the authorities, who would use it to discover your identity, correct? If you told me you were a former longshoreman from Baltimore, for example, and they have a list somewhere of underworld characters who in their youth packed crates out of Baltimore, you'd be finished. But if you tell me something about yourself that no one knows but you, then it can't be connected to you. You see?"

He seemed to puzzle over this, wanting to trust her but frightened of the snares she had surely hidden somewhere.

She sighed. "Oh, just make something up."

"No, it's okay. I'll tell ya something no one else knows. Once I robbed a dead man."

"Now, *this* sounds good."

"It was in Chicago. I didn't even know about the crash until a while after it happened, 'cause it's not like I owned stocks'r nothing. But when I got to Chicago I started hearing more and more people talking about it, worrying about it, comparing what all they'd lost. It was weird to hear that, all these people who'd had so much more'n me, and now they're all panicked that they don't have quite as much more'n me than they used to. I started hearing how people were jumping out of windows. Stockbrokers or people who had all their money tied up in things they didn't even own, and now they couldn't pay back what they'd never had in the first place, and they owed more'n they could get their heads around. Talk about real crooks—and now they couldn't handle it, so out the windows they went. You heard the stories. My God, it was—"

"Yes, I'm familiar with the stories, Rufus." She was angry now, but it was her fault for getting him started. She could stop him, but then he might hear the pain in her voice.

"Well, I'd just been bumming around that day, checking in on some old friends, you know, back in town and hoping to find a lead on work or something, anything. I'd been inside the Loop most of the day and now I'm on Wacker Drive, maybe about four o'clock. It was early autumn, I think, one of those days that was colder'n you thought it'd be. But the sun was out and I remember the shadows, how long they are when you're surrounded by the downtown buildings like that. And, just as I'm thinking that, I look up.

"I see this guy—and it's not like it took me a second to figure it out, it's not like him being in midair confused my mind'r anything like that. I knew exactly what it was, right away. I'd always figured they'd fall limp, you know, as if they were dead already. Resigned to it. But this guy, his legs were cycling, like he was hoping to ride away, and his arms were flailing. Like maybe he'd actually thought he *could* fly and was only now realizing his mistake."

Darcy was thinking of her mother. It had been five years ago, before death by skyscraper was considered a business decision. *Emotional problems,* her father had tried to explain to her. Hysteria, then depression. *Surely you, too, had noticed.* But Jasper Windham had not known of the letter his wife had posted to their daughter only moments before opening that window. She had written to Darcy about her father's affairs, cataloguing his various sins and even naming some of his conquests. She had failed to produce a male heir, had suffered all those miscarriages after the birth of their daughter, and couldn't take his blame or hostility any longer. She had written Darcy the letter and posted it from her husband's tenth-story office while he was away in some strumpet's bed. And then she had transformed herself into a bird, and then an anvil, and then a corpse.

"At first it looked like there were two of him," Rufus said, "because his shadow was right there next to him, flat against the building. But then when he got low enough other buildings were blocking the sun and his shadow vanished. I remember that. Like, suddenly at that moment, he was fully alone. For half a second. Then he landed on the sidewalk."

She had visualized it before, of course. But never had someone explained it to her.

"There were ladies screaming, and some cars and buses swerved into the wrong lane. I ran over and there were about four other people standing near him, but not too near. He was flat on his stomach, with his right arm underneath him so you couldn't see it. His left arm was out and it was sporting an awful nice watch, and I remember it was still ticking. That's a heckuva watch. Nice suit, too—navy with pinstripes—and shoes with brand-new heels, I saw, 'cause they were facing up. He didn't have a hat, but it might have landed somewhere else."

"Lovely." Her mother had been beautiful. Several portraits in the Windham manor reminded visitors of this fact, at least for a few months, until Jasper abruptly had them removed. That strategic redecorating, occurring hours before some soirée he was throwing, had precipitated the first of what he considered his daughter's "scenes." Accusations were thrown, then a glass. Inflamed by her drinking, the scenes continued. They were the only times her father seemed to notice her. So he sent her to the sanatorium, as the mother's emotional problems clearly had been passed on to the daughter. Emotional problems—*Yes, Father, the problem is that I have emotions.* Treatments were forcefully administered; solutions were injected; stern judgments were issued. For months. By the time the doctors conceded that Darcy was sane enough to be released, her father had remarried. Darcy was sent to boarding school, staying over for the summers, straight through to graduation. By the time she returned to Chicago, she had two adorable half brothers whom she never wanted to see again.

"I'll spare you the gore, ma'am, but I'll mention he was facing my way. His eyes were shut, which surprised me. He musta been scared to see the end. Anyways, the other people were all shaking their heads and calling out for the police, but none of 'em were really doing anything. I stood there with 'em and after maybe a minute I decided, hey, we should at least find out his name. There was a bulge in his back pocket that was probably a wallet, so I stepped forward and looked for his ID. Maybe it was crazy that I had the stomach for it, but I seen some things in my time."

"No one tried to stop you?"

"Seemed the decent thing to do, you know? I just figured we should know his name. But also, hey, I admit it, a wallet's a wallet. So maybe it wasn't the decent thing to do. Or maybe it was both, you know, maybe I was pushed by good things and bad things at the same time."

"We all are."

"So I took out his ID and read his name out loud, *George Sampson*, to see if anyone knew him, but no one said. And when I could tell wasn't no one looking at me I slipped the bills into my pocket. I stood there for another minute maybe, but with me and the Chicago cops having a history, I figured I needed to git. So I handed the wallet to an older bird and told him to give that to the coppers, and off I went. After I rounded a corner I walked into a coffeeshop to buy a doughnut and count my score. And here's the thing: Mr. George Sampson, thirty-six, of Oak Park, Illinois, killed himself with *two hundred and seventy-eight bucks* in his pocket. You believe that?"

"Maybe he owed someone two hundred and eighty."

"Huh. Hadn't thought of that."

"Or maybe money had nothing to do with it, Rufus. Maybe someone had broken his heart the night before."

"Nah, I don't buy that. If a suit takes a dive out of a skyscraper, it's 'cause of money."

So like a man to say that.

"So I went to a steakhouse, even though the maître d' took one look at me and suggested maybe I might want to try the diner round the corner. I showed him my bills'n he changed his mind. But I was thinking about ol' George Sampson and his life not worth living 'cause all he had to his name was about two hundred times what I had to mine. Let's just say that I didn't enjoy that steak much. Hadn't had steak in ages, but it didn't sit right. It felt—this is weird—like I wasn't eating a cow, I was eating another man. Only I wasn't thinking about the dead stockbroker, I was thinking of myself. Like, *I* shoulda been the one who jumped outta the window and George should be the one sitting here in a steakhouse. He was the one who could afford it, you know? I even went into the men's room just to look in the mirror, to make sure I was really me and not George.

"Now, I ain't the type to think crazy things like that. I don't do that Ouija board nonsense, I don't let Gypsies play with my hands. But the whole rest of the day I was worried. I walked around the city all day and all night, just thinking about it." He paused, exhaled. "I've never told anybody about that."

Just as she had never told anyone about how her father treated her mother. Until Jason.

"I'm honored, Rufus. Or whoever you are."

"Yeah. I wonder sometimes."

Darcy didn't have a change of clothes, and her keepers were uninterested in providing her with any. Doubtless, a man walking into a clothing store to buy ladies' undergarments might have looked a tad strange, perhaps suspicious. She was allowed to wash her still goggled face twice daily—an odd sensation—and had been given a toothbrush and some powder, but such were the limits of her hygiene. Her summer sweater was hardly necessary in that hot room, but she kept it on over her somewhat low-cut dress, buttoned to the neck.

The house was secluded; the only times she heard a motor was when one of the men left or returned to the premises. They apparently had more than one car, for there were times when she heard a second one depart before the first had returned. Unless she had dozed in between, or her mind was playing tricks on her. What else could a mind do under such conditions?

Eventually night showed up for its shift. The silence was even more complete in the early evening; the crickets wouldn't begin their drone for another hour.

Wondering what your old man is up to right about now? a voice asked Darcy.

"Actually, he's the furthest thing from my mind."

An interesting phrase, isn't it? The furthest thing from one's mind. As if anything can be inherently near to or far from a mind. That's not true, really. We can imagine anything, imagine a boring afternoon like this one or a fantastical universe of bending physical laws, and neither of these things is any further from our mind than the other. Every thought is equally possible.

"A metaphysicist. Fascinating. And here I was thinking the conversations in this room were a bit dull."

You have to do your part, too.

"So, which one are you?"

I'm the voice in your head.

"Wonderful."

You don't believe me?

"How odd that the voice in my head is only present when I'm kidnapped and tied up in a small room in—what town is this again?"

How would I know? I only know what you know. I wish I knew more, that's for sure. Since you don't know very much.

"An *insulting* voice in my head. Divine. A voice that bears an uncanny resemblance to that of one of the kidnappers."

True, but your own imagination is what put it there. I suppose you could have given me your father's voice, or an old schoolteacher's voice, or the voice of some movie narrator. But you chose one of the kidnappers' voices—the one you call The Threatening One.

She hadn't told them she thought of them by those names, had she? She tried to remember the various snippets of conversation she'd been granted over these dull three days. Then her memory stretched back even further, and she felt very cold.

Enough about me. Let's talk about you. How does it really feel knowing your lover is stiff as a board? You don't seem to be pondering those feelings the way you should be.

"Ah," and she tried to stifle the worry she felt in the depths of her gut. "The supposed voice in my head reveals itself as the fraud it truly is."

And why is that?

"Because if it was truly in my head it would know what I know about Jason."

That he's still alive? I do know that. Or, I should say, I know that you think so. I'm just not as gullible as you are.

"Meaning what, exactly?"

Perfect weather for bird watching. Migrating earlier than predicted. Then the voice laughed, and Darcy shivered.

No, there must be a rational explanation for this. It was indeed The Threatening One sitting in the room with her, she told herself. When she'd dropped the telegram during her capture, one of them must have retrieved it. Or, she realized, and felt colder still: *they* had sent the telegram. It had been a snare, used to draw her outside, where they were waiting.

Or there really was a voice in her head. Which perhaps was not so unimaginable. She tried not to think of her time at the sanatorium, the drugs and the nightmares. And the voices. It had been the doctors' or nurses' voices, she had assumed, but she'd never been sure. The judgments and chiding, syllables like spades trying to unearth the grave of her mind. She had forgotten somehow, but now the memories rose up.

"Look, I know you aren't a disembodied voice." She was trying to convince herself, and she feared that it showed. "I know you're a man sitting in this room. I can hear you breathing, for God's sake."

Can you? Listen again. That's yourself breathing.

She listened in silence for a long while.

See?

"You held your breath."

The voice laughed again. Like the last laugh, it was short and quick, the jab of a dagger. A laugh without exhaling, if such a thing were possible. She thought about that, and concluded that it was not.

You really believed he was alive, didn't you?

"He *is* alive." She was gritting her teeth.

So sad, what people in love will believe. What people in desperate straits will believe. When we're weak, we become the most fervent believers. All those Bible thumpers starving on their farms, all those hymn-singing Negroes in their slave chains before and in their chain gangs now. Life collapses on us yet we believe, even more than before. The last shall be first, the meek shall inherit, the dead shall rise up. Ridiculous stories, yet they give us such hope, such sad and misguided hope. And then, when we finally hit that bottom that we didn't think could possibly exist, that's when even the most devout of us lose that belief. Not only in God but in everything. We become the unbelievers, empty and vacant. That hasn't happened to you yet. But it will. And it will be terrible.

"I'd like you to leave now, please."

We'd all like the voices in our heads to leave. But it doesn't quite work like that.

"For God's sake, stop! As if kidnapping me isn't enough, you like to engage in psychological torture, too?"

I wouldn't torture you. You're my vessel, after all. My hull in these rough waters. I need you to stay more or less afloat. But I also need you to confront reality, or at least accept reality, rather than retreating from it. Retreating to your bottles like before, or to those poems and stories you write, or to your memories of Jason, your dreams never realized. This is the world, and you need to see it for what it is.

She was shaking. "Leave me alone. Send in one of the others. Just go."

Suddenly the crickets rose up midsong.

Darcy was wet with sweat. She realized she was lying on the chaise, though she didn't remember being transferred from the chair, didn't remember being granted her nightly ablutions. No, they had happened, surely, but her lack of vision was rendering each memory oily, difficult to grasp.

She so desperately wanted to open her eyes, to see something. She pulled with her bound wrists as hard as she could, panting as the bonds held, trying again despite the tearing skin.

"Hey in there!" A voice, a different one, from farther away. "I hear you doing that. Cut it out or I'll sit right next to you all night."

Slowly her eyes began to soak the goggled cloth.

IX.

Even with the windows up and fans blaring it was hot and smelly in Elmo's Diner, a nondescript joint nestled between the industrial maze of southern Cleveland and the asphalt flatlands of Parma. Jason had never been here before, but it was close to where Marriner Skelty was hiding out, and because he'd already left the note for Marriner he couldn't switch locations. At least he had given the gun to Whit, which meant he could remove his jacket in public. He gulped ice water between brutal sips of coffee, and he could feel the plastic stool beneath him melting.

The morning *Plain Dealer* ran a brief piece remarking on the odd fact that the Fireson clan had not yet scheduled a funeral or a memorial service. There was nothing about any missing bodies. Jason had asked Ma to keep quiet about the call she'd received from the Points North cops, and so far the press hadn't been tipped off.

A front-page exposé noted that large dogs in the Cleveland animal shelter received more food per day than did adult residents on relief. Skeletal budgets were blamed. In another article, merchants petitioned the welfare agencies to increase their doles to the needy, as local stores were being plagued by desperate shoplifters. Jason piled the paper beside him.

He was seated at the counter, on a corner stool so as to afford a view of Whit, who was sitting in the Pontiac across the street as lookout. It felt so odd—after weeks of living in hiding, Jason was sitting in public, facing the entrance, even making eye contact with a few of the customers who walked in. No one lingered on his face, no one stopped midstride to take a second look; with his tiny mustache and eyeglasses, his appearance was just different enough, and the reports of his death just persuasive enough, to make him comfortable he wouldn't be recognized. (The previous spring he'd even walked through police stakeouts two separate times, as the officers assigned to catch Jason Fireson never seemed to be sure they had seen him.) He still was deeply confused by whatever had happened to them in Points North, but, as he'd told Whit, he was trying his damnedest not to worry about it. All he wanted to do was revel in this feeling of being restored, of being himself again.

The brothers' skin was looking less gray, and Jason's dark toes had returned to normal. He had showered that morning, and even the wounds on his chest were less ghastly than before, the skin seeming to close upon itself.

Two stools from Jason a sharply dressed man motioned toward the discarded newspaper.

"Anything interesting in there?"

"Afraid not, but help yourself."

"Thanks," the fellow said. He was quite the jellybean, wearing a Panama hat and an expensive tan suit complete with white handkerchief spilling from the jacket pocket. As he flipped the pages his eyes darted quickly from corner to corner, as if he weren't so much reading the headlines as making sure they were where they were supposed to be. His hat was pushed back a bit, whereas Jason had placed his father's old duster beside him on the bar. Jason had used so much pomade in his unevenly shorn hair that his head was probably bulletproof, though he wasn't sure if bullets were something he needed to fear any longer.

"And how do you pass your days, sir?" the jellybean asked after ordering steak and potatoes, the most expensive option on the menu.

"I'm in sales," Jason said. "Based out in Des Moines."

"A fellow warrior." The gentleman smiled. "What do you sell?"

"Typewriters." Sometimes he claimed to sell farm supplies, or adding machines, or cash registers, or kitchen equipment, or whatever object he happened to glance at when he was asked.

"Well, hang in there, buddy. You get through the next quarter or two, things will get better. Assuming that nut FDR doesn't keep tinkering with the natural order of things."

Jason nodded and offered the same slight, infinitely interpretable smile he offered any stranger who brought up politics.

"That old coot is such a con man," the jellybean continued. "And the worst thing about it is that people are starting to believe in his fairy tales. He's taking advantage of all those misguided souls." He shook his head sadly. "The point, my friend, is that, yes, people are being tight with their purse strings, but that'll soon pass. See, this depression, if they really want to call it that, it's just a psychological condition."

"How's that?"

"Well, the economy's still producing plenty, understand, the factories have the means and the workers have the know-how and the farms have plenty of seeds and cows and hogs—my God, you saw how they had to go and kill those surplus pigs? So we can churn out whatever people could want to buy. We aren't lacking for anything. The reason for the depression is public confidence, national mood, et cetera." He pointed to his head and smiled. "It's all in our minds."

The waitress delivered the man's plate. He speedily sliced his steak into strips, as if it might still be alive and in need of a death stroke.

"So tomorrow all I need to do is wake up in a better mood and, presto, things are fine?"

"Well, no," the man said with his mouth full, too exuberant to yield to decorum. "You need to get everyone in the country to wake up in a better mood. It's a psychological condition, but I didn't say it was *your* psychological condition. It's someone else's. Everyone else's."

"So my circumstances are a victim of someone else's mood."

He winked and pointed at Jason with his knife. "Exactly."

"If I really wanted to make things better, all I would need to do is cheer everyone up."

"Now you've got it."

Jason extended one hand magnanimously. "What we need is a clown on every street corner, and all will be well."

"Clowns. Interesting. Hadn't thought of that. But I like where you're going."

Jason watched the man for a moment of contained rage, either from the heat or from impatience at Marriner for not showing up yet or from this man's staggering naïveté. *All in our minds?* His father had shared such boundless optimism, once. There were so many things Jason would have liked to say to this guy.

But he steadied himself with another sip of coffee and pressed those feelings down, as straight and neat as the crease of his slacks. What he said, he said with a smile.

"You seem like a good man, but I'm afraid you might be a little bit crazy."

The guy laughed with his mouth full. Jason saw white teeth in a universe of pink, pink gums and pink cheeks and pink flesh gnawed into a new shade of pinkness. "Okay, maybe I am. But there you have the same problem." Again the knife was employed as an eleventh finger. "Someone else's mind. Your circumstances are being held hostage by the conditions in someone else's mind. How do you break free of that? Used to be a fellow was his own man, his own person, had his destiny in his own hands. Now everything's so interconnected, he's trapped in other people's brains. And as a salesman, sir, your job is to liberate him from the minds of others. Get him to think for himself, *be* himself. Once you and every other drummer can do that, then we'll snap out of this."

"So the fate of the nation is in my hands."

The man thought for a moment, as if he hadn't realized the awesome responsibility he was imparting while devouring his steak. "Afraid so."

Jason's eyes were drawn across the street as Whit, baking alive in the Pontiac, took off his hat. The brothers made eye contact and Whit put his hat back on. Seconds later, the bell at the diner's entrance was jostled into music.

Marriner Skelty had the sort of mug that did not convey shock easily; his rubbery skin deadened the impulse from brain to face. It bore the marks of his fifty-plus years: a knife scar across his chin, an eyebrow whose leftmost inch had been burned off in a chemical accident (of which he had endured many), old smallpox scars, shaving wounds, and the sudden smoothness of past cauterizations. For many years he had understandably hidden his cheeks beneath a dense beard, until images of his scruffy face had appeared on enough wanted posters for him to take up shaving.

But all those wrinkles and crevasses were nearly immobile as Marriner made like he was scanning the diner for an available seat. His gray eyes rested on Jason for an almost imperceptible moment before he turned and sought out an empty booth on the other side of the diner.

Jason dropped change on the counter and excused himself, picking up his hat and jacket and strolling over to Marriner's booth. The old man was facing away from him, so Jason took the side that faced the entrance.

"Jesus Christ."

"No," Jason corrected. "But I do a great impersonation, don't I?"

"They said you were dead."

"They've said a lot of things."

Marriner stared for a long moment, and Jason finally broke the silence. "You certainly are ugly without the beard."

"So they tell me." Only a guy who'd known him as long as Jason had could have seen how shocked those eyes were. "How in hell—"

"Do you really think some farm cops could take us like that?"

"I'm waiting for your explanation."

"Mistaken identity, police desperate for good publicity, gullible press—you know."

Marriner nodded, clearly aware that Jason's story was fiction but unsure how much of it was veiled autobiography. "You are one hell of a lucky bastard."

"So you've always said."

Marriner Skelty was an old yegg from St. Paul, an expert safecracker whose adolescent glee at mixing chemicals proved quite lucrative when it was applied to shattering hinges and melting locks. He'd been robbing banks since the days when it was a nocturnal activity conducted by those with an affinity for liquid nitrogen and other silent destroyers. By the time Jason met him—in Indiana State Prison, during Jason's second bootlegging rap—Marriner's chosen profession had changed dramatically. The advent of faster cars, the expansion of state highways, the invention and easy accessibility of submachine guns and other automatic weapons, and the inadequacy of local police forces—most of which still hand-cranked their Model A's, if they could even afford automobiles— had turned bank theft into a speedier, daylight affair. Years earlier, after serving a different stretch for a moonlit job that turned foul when his chemicals froze on an unexpectedly cold September night in Rochester,

Marriner had taken up with the various St. Paul crews that had turned that town into a haven of criminal minds. At underworld taverns and cooling-off joints where wanted men circulated in and out, ideas were bandied, hot tips traded, hands lent and borrowed. For a time, Marriner had run with the Barker Gang, until one of the Barkers' lesser witted associates was arrested and rolled on him. So another jail term, this time in Indiana, where Marriner met a charismatic young man determined to succeed where others had failed.

Marriner spent nearly seven months robbing banks with Jason before retiring. After the Firefly Gang's lucrative Calumet City job in November, Marriner persuaded Jason and Whit to hide out until spring, as Midwestern country roads became too unpredictable for getaways in midwinter. But while the brothers vacationed first in Florida and then in New Orleans, Marriner heard the noise coming from J. Edgar Hoover and his band of upstart agents and decided that the time had come for him to walk away. *These are the last days of bank robbing,* Marriner had said, with an apocalyptic tone. Jason had come to realize the old yegg was right.

"When I saw your note," Marriner said, "I figured it was the cops."

"I was afraid you would. I'm glad you came, though."

Having decided the cops were getting too close back in Indianapolis, Marriner had moved to a nondescript neighborhood in Cleveland Heights. *You disappear best by not disappearing at all,* he'd always said. Jason had made a point of memorizing the address should he ever need it. This morning, as was their old method, Jason had left a copy of the *Plain Dealer* on Marriner's doorstep, and on the bottom of the twelfth page (for twelve o'clock) he had scribbled the name of the diner.

"So how are those ice cubes coming?" Jason asked.

"I'm damn close." Marriner's life project was to invent ice cubes that would not melt. He spent countless hours dabbling with new chemicals, compounds, and colloids. He would come agonizingly close to achieving his goal, but every time he found one with a high enough melting point it proved too toxic. He had poisoned himself dozens of times, occasionally requiring hospitalization, though usually he just treated himself with restorative swigs of whiskey.

"Well, I look forward to my first scotch with Marriner Cubes dancing in the glass," Jason said.

A young waitress whose red hair matched her apron smiled at them.

They both ordered ham and eggs, and coffee. She finished scribbling into her notepad and had started to walk away when she turned back, eyeing Jason. He looked back with eyes as innocent as he could make them.

"Anyone ever tell you you look like Jason Fireson?"

He smiled. "I get that from time to time. But he's a lot deader than I am."

She shook her head. "It's amazing. The spitting image. Lucky no one's shot you by mistake."

"He is a lucky man at that," Marriner monotoned.

Jason glanced out the window at the Pontiac, where Whit was pretending to read the newspaper and likely plotting some savage payback for being assigned lookout duty on a ninety-degree day.

"So I guess congratulations are in order for you being alive—and for that last job of yours, too. Hear you boys set the all-time record. You here to get my thoughts on retirement?"

"Not yet. Whit and I are planning an endeavor, and we need your help."

Again, the old man's face was unreadable, like a pile of discarded typesetting keys in a junkyard. But his voice was a billboard. "After that last job you did?"

"We're no longer in possession of those funds."

"You buy an island or something?"

"Yes, but it flooded. Never go into real estate, Marriner—those people are crooks." The waitress brought coffee. Marriner spent a solid ten seconds adding sugar to his mug—he could barely taste anything owing to the potpourri of nonpotable substances he had scoured his tongue and palate with.

After he took his first sip, Marriner lowered his voice. "What happened to the money? Washing problems?"

"Yes, sort of. I don't want to go into it." Jason shifted in his seat. "Bottom line is that we're cash-low. We're doing an endeavor, and we have it all planned. We need you and at least two other guys."

"What about the guys you been with lately?"

"As you probably know from reading the papers, they've developed the bad habit of being arrested, or dying. The ones who are alive have already disappeared, if they're smart."

"You aren't doing such a swell job of selling me on this."

The waitress returned and slid plates before them, the eggs shiny, the ham thin, the toast damp with butter. Even thin pig smelled delicious, and Jason saw the way Marriner looked at his own plate.

"I'm betting that your impressive devotion to the ice-cube task is beginning to drain on your resources. Don't tell me you couldn't use this."

Marriner liberally salted his food. "I didn't say that. And yes, I know of a couple guys could be helpful."

"They ever done an endeavor before?"

"No. But they're eager, and smart enough." He took a bite. "You seem awfully sure I want to do this."

Jason cut into his ham. Since his awakening, food did not necessarily taste better than it had before, but ham was still ham, which was something you did not take for granted. "I know how much fun I am to be around."

"Your brother more than makes up for that. That why you made him wait in the car?"

"One of many reasons."

"Why do you even need to do an endeavor? What about that heiress of yours?"

He put his fork down and spoke with barely contained fury. "I'm not with her for some payout, goddamnit, I'm with her because I'm with her."

Jason was surprised by his own outburst. He was worried about Darcy.

"So," the old man asked after a pause, "when are you thinking?"

"Four days from now. We do two in one day."

Finally, surprise registered on Marriner's face.

"The heat's vanished," Jason explained. "But once they realize we aren't dead it'll get uncomfortable again. We want to take what we can, then disappear."

Marriner finished his ham. Then he reached into his glass and his fingers emerged with an ice cube. He held it as if he had excavated a priceless gem. The air was thick and hot and the cube seemed to visibly diminish as tiny rivulets ran down his wrist, wetting his sleeve.

"We all do, Jason. Most of us just aren't as good at it as you are."

X.

—————————————
—————————————

Their numbers were dwindling, as if each time one of the Public Enemies died so did ten reporters. But there were still enough of them
camped out in the hallway between the elevator and the office door to
make Cary Delaney's arrival at work—not to mention trips to the bathroom—exasperating.

The reporters shouted a few questions as he walked toward the door
for the Chicago field office of the Department of Justice's Bureau of Investigation. Queries about the various remnants of the now-headless
Dillinger and Firefly Gangs were tossed out, and Cary's expression was
stoic until one threw him.

"The Firefly Brothers were spotted in Cleveland yesterday—what's the
Bureau's take?"

Cary rolled his eyes and cracked a grin. "We only arrest live criminals—dead ones are beyond our jurisdiction. Cathedral's two blocks
south if you want to get their take on it." Then he opened the door.

Cary nodded hello to the secretary and found his place with the rest of
the agents in the bullpen, a room consisting of desks so crushed together
that it looked as if it had once been a much larger room until the walls
had closed in by twenty feet. Off the bullpen were doors leading to the
impenetrable file room, which no one but the secretary was allowed in; a
conference room, also used for particularly delicate phone calls or inter-

rogations; and one decent office for the SAC, the special agent in charge. The headquarters were on the twentieth floor of the Bankers Building, in the financial district, a block away from the Chicago Federal Reserve, which had been robbed a year earlier by the Barker Gang in a speedy, silent, but nonetheless botched job: the five bags the crew made off with were actually filled with mail, not cash. The Barkers had crashed their armored Hudson a few blocks away, killing two flatfoots as they switched cars. Cary often wondered how many sad stories or checks or money orders had disappeared in those mailbags, which the escaped crooks likely burned.

This morning it was hot, again. The windows were all along the same wall, and fresh air refused to enter the workspace, as if it had been warned off by an armed guard.

"The Firesons were seen driving through Lincoln City yesterday morning," said the agent two desks over from Cary, his head obscured by an open *Tribune*.

"There, too?" Cary smirked. "I was told Cleveland. Those are some busy corpses."

For weeks Cary had rotated between the Bureau's special Dillinger Squad and its Fireson Squad, both of which were now focused on apprehending the dead men's few at-large associates. Most were small-time in comparison with their fallen ringleaders, troglodyte misfits who eluded capture only because they likely hid away in tiny apartments or abandoned farmhouses, where they would remain until they grew too hungry or bored. The highest-profile Public Enemies still breathing were Baby Face Nelson and Brickbat Sanders: diminutive, hot-tempered gunmen from the Dillinger and Firefly Gangs, respectively. Cary was following up on various leads, reading wire reports, and calling many an overexcited small-town cop who insisted that the petty thief sitting in his dusty jail was in fact a notorious outlaw. There were days Cary never left the office.

Which was perfectly fine with him. Cary Delaney was not a police officer, after all; he was an agent of the Bureau of Investigation. Although the two occupations were becoming more similar, that certainly had not been the case two years ago, when Cary joined the Bureau fresh out of Georgetown Law. He had hoped to procure a job at a prominent firm, but the depression was in full-throated howl when his graduation date arrived. Many of his silver-spoon classmates had appointments lined up, of course—their places had been secured the moment their mothers mailed their gilded birth announcements—but to a scholarship boy like Cary life came free of guarantees. He had decided to stay in Washington and look for a government job, something that could pay for a roof over his head. What little he had known about the Bureau of Investigation made it seem like any other legal-research office, with just a splash of intrigue due to its focus on crime.

How things had changed in two years. He had started by investigating interstate auto-theft cases, looking into crimes of passion on Indian reservations, and pursuing seditious rabble-rousers. When Cary joined the Bureau, agents weren't even allowed to carry firearms. But that unwritten law was reversed after the Kansas City Massacre in June of '33, when three police officers and a federal agent were gunned down at K.C.'s Union Station while escorting a bank robber to prison. Cary and his fellow agents had watched in amazement as Mr. Hoover used that case to lobby for a strong federal police force, nominating his Bureau for the job. This would be a War on Crime, the Director declared, and suddenly Cary and his stunned colleagues were thrust into the role of upholding civic order, restoring public faith in a strong central government, and chasing down vicious, homicidal maniacs.

The Bureau had suffered many embarrassments in Cary's time: suspects walking away from stakeouts; dreadful performances in shootouts; and, worst of all, the disaster at Little Bohemia. The Bureau had cornered Dillinger, Nelson, and others in a small lake resort in Wisconsin, surrounding the building, only to discover, after the passage of a frigid night, that the criminals had escaped hours ago via an unknown path along the frozen beach—and had managed to kill an agent along the way. Mr. Hoover's prized young Ivy Leaguers were out of their league, and only when he began recruiting more "cowboys," as he called them—toughened cops from the Southwest—did the successes mount: Machine Gun Kelly and his kidnapping crew had been nabbed, Dillinger was ambushed, Clyde Barrow and his poet girlfriend were gunned down along a rural Louisiana road, and now the Firefly Brothers were dead. Suddenly every kid in America was reading comic books about heroic G-men, and Mr. Hoover was consulting with Hollywood on forthcoming pictures about the Bureau. There was no end to the ironic grumbling among the real, flesh-and-blood, overtired, underpaid, caffeine-riddled, stakeout-sunburned agents.

There were always more leads for the agents to explore, but fewer now that the Firesons were dead. That was the thing with death: it could leave the old mysteries unsolved. The stories could go on telling themselves, altering with the passage of time. And there were plenty of mysteries about the Firesons, such as how they managed to get money to their relatives when the family was so carefully watched, how they eluded so many ambushes. Most perplexing was a stakeout in which Cary had taken part. Two months ago the Chicago cops had arrested a grifter who had laundered money for the Barker Gang, and upon questioning he claimed he could cough up the Firefly Brothers. The launderer said the Firesons were desperately trying to wash their score from the recent Federal Reserve job in Milwaukee; he was to meet them three days later at a restaurant in Toledo. The Bureau mobilized a huge squad, studying the building's floor plan and staking out men at every possible exit. At eight o'clock on a rainy evening, Cary—who had been requisitioned by the understaffed Cleveland field office—had sat in a closed deli across the street from the restaurant when a taxi pulled up in front of the building and deposited Jason Fireson, carrying a briefcase. There he was, a living, breathing man entering the restaurant. His dark-gray fedora was turned low and his lapels were pulled up, but Cary recognized the eyes. Smart and watchful, and something else, indefinable. The SAC put out the curious order not to storm the building until the second Fireson showed up: they would wait as long as thirty minutes for Whit to appear. Two agents were already stationed inside the restaurant. Time passed.

Cary's heart had been loud in his chest—it was one of the few times he had needed to wear his sidearm, in a shoulder holster beneath his jacket. He had spent hours practicing with the thing, especially over the preceding few weeks, as more and more agents suddenly had use for them. He tried not to think about his mother back in Pennsylvania, and how panicked she had been since realizing that her son's job consisted of more than just poring over legal books on the distinction between theft and grand larceny.

Time passed as the agents waited for Whit, but he didn't show. The SAC finally gave the order to signal the men inside and storm the building. But the men inside couldn't be signaled because the curtains were drawn, which had not been the case when they'd studied the place the previous evening. Still, storm the building they did. Inside they found three or four tables' worth of terrified customers raising their hands as armed agents and cops ran in jagged lines in search of Jason Fireson. In the men's room they found the two agents who had supposedly been watching him, unconscious and handcuffed to each other. The launderer, too, had disappeared. The Bureau frisked and questioned every busboy, waiter, cook, and customer while they searched for hidden nooks, looked beneath planks in the attic, and combed through the cellar, opening boxes of pasta and crates of onions. The agents outside swore that Fireson and the launderer hadn't left the building, but they weren't inside, either. They had simply vanished. The launderer turned up a week later in Joplin, but he wouldn't talk. How on earth Jason Fireson had escaped was something Cary had spent far too much energy on. It couldn't have happened, yet it did. Reporters loved that story.

Earlier this month, right before their death, Cary himself had received the tip he'd been waiting for: the Firesons had finally laundered their money and were due to pay off their old partner, Owney Davis, at a restaurant in Detroit. Again a building was surrounded, and surely past mistakes would not be repeated. New ones were made instead: somehow the Firesons sniffed out the trap, driving past the restaurant without stopping, speeding onto the highway, and escaping after a short chase.

Still, they would meet their maker that night. Meaning that the mysteries of those impossible escapes no longer mattered. Mythmakers could invent whatever explanations they wished. Had the brothers really sent death threats to President Roosevelt and half his cabinet? Who knows. Did they really operate a pirate radio station based in the southern Midwest, broadcasting secret intelligence to their legions of fellow hoodlums? Who cares. Was Jason really a mystic who could pass through walls and read the thoughts of his pursuers? Cary thought, *Let the people think what they want.*

He wasn't surprised the press was now reporting on all the crazy Fireson spottings—they'd done the same after Dillinger was killed. Like the other agents, he laughed at the stories and did his best to focus on facts as they searched for the remaining Public Enemies.

Still, the stories served as a good reminder that he should call the

Points North police and check on the recovery of the missing bodies. After a two-minute delay, he was connected to an officer who claimed that several leads were being pursued. The man's explanations withered under further questioning.

"Honestly, Agent Delaney," the officer said, yawning, "we don't feel too good about our chances. They're probably at some freak sideshow in the Yucatán by now, in which case it's kinder out of our jurisdiction, y'know? We'd love to have those bodies back, maybe do some more photo shoots if they haven't gotten too decomposed yet. But I doubt that whoever took 'em stuck around inside county lines. So it's a state job now, or maybe federal. You boys interested in taking over the search party?"

Cary tried to imagine a more thankless task than tracking corpse thieves. "I think we have other priorities at the moment, but thanks for the offer."

"Oh, that reminds me. Chief Mackinaw wanted me to ask you when we should expect that reward check."

Cary tapped his pencil on the desk. "Exactly three days after you find those bodies."

He hung up before the officer could object. He tried not to walk over to the other agent's desk and read the *Tribune* story about the Fireson sightings, tried to focus on real facts. But he couldn't resist. He grabbed the paper and sped through the article, shaking his head at it all.

People believed the damnedest things.

XI.

Stories of the Firefly Brothers, John Dillinger, and Pretty Boy Floyd had inspired a litany of misguided and maladroit imitators across the land. A handful were successful, their hijinks mistakenly attributed to one of the more famous outlaws, but most tended to be as spectacularly unsuccessful as their earlier efforts to find honest work.

In Chillicothe, Ohio, an evicted farmer drove a stolen tractor through the front entrance of the bank that had foreclosed on his property. He succeeded in ramming the door down, but in doing so he trapped the vehicle between the brick walls. He rustled a few hundred from a teller before climbing over his tractor and sprinting down the street, where he was shot dead by the local sheriff, a Great War veteran and an expert marksman.

In Dalesville, Illinois, an unemployed accountant who had been conned by a huckster into buying a "bulletproof" vest made of tin and iron marched into his local bank, which had been put on alert after the Dillinger Gang robbed a nearby institution. The overconfident robber had taken his time looting the vault and, upon exiting, was shot to pieces. Witnesses claimed the sound of bullets piercing the man's metallic harness was almost musical, like coins plinking a pond's surface as they're transformed into wishes.

In Flint, Michigan, two laid-off assembly liners from the nearby Pontiac plant ignited smoke bombs inside a bank as they made their entrance. It had been a hot but breezy day, and the smoke funneled in circles around the men, a miniature smoke devil. One had coughed until he collapsed, and the other, frantic from blindness and from the sound of his accomplice gagging, ran headlong into a stone wall and fell unconscious.

Countless getaway drivers shut their engines off during the job, only to find that they wouldn't restart; or they decided to parallel park, and afterward wasted precious seconds freeing their vehicle as the police surrounded them. Other robbers panicked at the sight of oblivious officers strolling the sidewalks outside and announced themselves by firing unnecessary shots through the bank's windows.

In Liberty, Missouri, four ex-convicts actually would have accomplished their heist were it not for inconvenient timing: they emerged from the bank only to find their escape route being closed off for the town's annual policemen's parade. They were enthusiastically apprehended.

A former, excommunicated communist in St. Cloud, Minnesota, was killed by his own dramatic entrance, firing a shotgun into a bank's ceiling, whereupon a five-foot-wide chunk of ornately inscribed plaster dropped twenty feet and crushed his skull.

And, of course, there were the robbers who succeeded only in locking themselves in bank vaults. This always brought a smile to Jason's lips. He liked knowing that his skill was so extraordinary.

He was left to reflect on this as he sat with Marriner in the stolen Pontiac, reading a story in the morning edition of the *Sun* about an Estonian immigrant who had tried to rob a bank the previous day in Lexington, Kentucky, armed with an antique musket he had stolen from a Civil War museum. The bank manager had calmly explained that the weapon would not fire, but the thief's grasp of English had proved less adept than his grip on the musket, which he butted into the manager's forehead after its trigger indeed refused to budge. The immigrant had been overtaken by heroic bank customers and was being held on charges of assault, attempted robbery, and desecration of a historic site.

Jason put down his paper and checked the pocket watch he'd borrowed from Marriner. It was not yet nine o'clock and they were parked across the street and a few storefronts down from Third National of Lincoln City. It was the third morning Jason had studied the bank's opening procedures, the habits of its staff and the security guard. The previous day, wearing fake eyeglasses and a thin beard, Jason had taken a closer look at the interior by opening an account with a ten-dollar bill and false identification, both of which Marriner had provided—the old man was an expert forger. Jason had been in Third National before, of course, as had Whit, to make deposits for Pop when they were kids, but that had been years ago. The tellers were new and Jason didn't recognize anyone.

"Guard's older than you," Jason commented as they watched the codger enter the bank.

"Imagine that," Marriner replied. "Miracle he's still alive."

"Morning, Mr. President," Jason narrated as the staff entered the building. "And those are the two assistant managers. A maximum of three tellers."

The nearest police station was twelve blocks away. Third National sat in the middle of Taft Street, a wide avenue that cut through the north end of downtown. Whit and the two rookies Marriner had recruited had spent the past two days timing various paths out of town.

"So tell me about this bank," Marriner said.

"Restaurants from Taft and the busier side streets make their deposits every morning around ten and again in the afternoon before closing. Bank is flush every other Thursday to cash paychecks for the tire plant on Fourth; other factories in town do Fridays, so they're unusual. Big baseball series this week means the local places are doing decent business. It's a sweet pea: there's only one guard, the cops don't—"

"That's not what I meant. Tell me about this bank."

A pause. "They backed a bunch of loans to my old man when he started buying up property in '28. After he opened a second and third grocery, he was starting to buy up lots in the factory district to build new apartment buildings, on account of the workers seemed to be making more bread." He shook his head. "My old man's delusions of grandeur were based on the idea that other people wouldn't be failures."

A car started idling behind Jason's, waiting for him to leave the spot. Jason waved it on.

"Crash hits, factory cuts its hours, its wages, its men. New supermarkets open nearby and undercut the family stores. Then the cash-poor factories start paying in scrip, meaning the stores have to accept scrip and cross their fingers that the factory gets its money soon so it can pay 'em back. Weeks roll by, my old man's pulling his hair out. Thought I'd told you all this."

"I'm remembering."

"My old man can't meet the mortgages for all this worthless property, can't meet the mortgage for his own home, can't even buy new inventory for his stores. Asks his suppliers to stretch him. Begs the banks to let the mortgages float for a bit, or take the scrip, but they won't budge on either score. Knocks on the factory owners' doors, raises hell. Goes to one of his real-estate partners, Garrett Jones, begs him for a loan. Jones was a retired bank man, lived well and liked to dabble, and somehow he and Pop had met a few years back. They'd—"

"This Jones have a relation to Third National by any chance?"

Jason nodded. "Used to run it, yes. Anyway, Jones was retired by then, but he and my old man had gone in on most of the real-estate moves together, Pop borrowing like crazy, Jones throwing in, too, but it wasn't such a hard shake for him since he was loaded anyway. When things got tough, Pop thought Jones would come through for him, help him with some payments, or maybe twist some arms at the bank. But Jones wasn't inclined to throw good money after bad, and he said so. One night Pop stops by Jones's place, and maybe Pop had had a few drinks, and after he'd begged and pleaded again, maybe he made some threats that Mrs. Jones overheard. The next night, while Mrs. Jones is out playing bridge, her husband either shoots himself in the head or gets murdered in his den, depending on your view of human nature."

"And this is all the bank's fault?"

Jason breathed. "I didn't say that."

"But you aren't not saying it."

"True. I'm not not saying it."

"And Whit believes it."

"With every fiber of his being. Whit was the baby of the family, so for some reason Pop didn't ride him like he did me and Wes. Whit idolized him, so he took things the hardest. We'll have to keep an eye on him tomorrow. He'll be tempted to blow up the building on the way out."

"You remember I wanted to put blanks in his gun the first time?"

"I remember."

"You remember I was right?"

"Did I ever fail to listen to you again?"

The old-timer smiled. "I'll say this for you, Jason Fireson: you never make the same mistake twice."

"That's because there are so many others to get around to."

Customers started entering the bank at nine o'clock.

With the little money Marriner had left to his name, he had rented two rooms in a motel across the river, a base of operations for these few days of planning. The Firefly Brothers would hit Third National tomorrow morning, escape, regroup, then hit a smaller but equally attractive bank in Hudson Heights, a short drive south, near the Kentucky and Indiana borders. It was the best way to make a big score before the cops caught on that the Firefly Brothers were still out there. With the combined take and just a small crew to split it with, Jason had told his brother, they could find the girls and cash out of this increasingly dangerous career, head west and figure out a way to reinvent themselves one last time.

Jason had never pulled two endeavors in one day, but hell, he could use a challenge.

They sat there watching the bank, counting foot traffic.

"We were just a working family trying to move up, whatever that means. And then trying to get higher still. Like I said, delusions of grandeur."

"American dream."

"Same thing."

Across the street, a portly beat cop walked past the bank at 9:25, exactly when he had the past two days. Ten more minutes and they'd seen all they needed to.

"One thing I always wanted to ask you. About your old man."

"Go ahead." He knew what was coming.

"Do you think he did it?"

"No." He dead-eyed Marriner. "You ask Whit that question, he's likely to shoot you."

The next morning they woke at sunrise. The blinds on the motel windows were just beginning to glow as they dressed and donned their bulletproof vests. They methodically rechecked their weapons, half listening to Mar-riner's radio for news of a downtown accident or anything that might affect their plans. One last time, they had the rookies recite their instruc-tions. By the time the Firefly Brothers stepped outside, the sun was above the trees and so hot it seemed to be aimed directly at them.

THE SECOND DEATH
OF THE
FIREFLY BROTHERS

Already the stories were coming to life.

When news got around that the Fireson family had not yet held a funeral or a memorial service, that set ablaze the public's appetite for fantastic stories. More people claimed to have spotted the brothers, despite their alleged demise. They were seen robbing banks, holding up gas stations, saving the elderly from burning buildings. They were impregnating ex-lovers, coaxing kittens from flimsy branches, delivering impromptu sermons at Congregationalist services. They'd sent death threats to Republican governors and donated food to Hoovervilles. They were beating communist insurgents, wooing widows, helping crippled war veterans carry their groceries.

It was Dillinger all over again. He'd been sighted in all forty-eight states, Canada, Mexico, Cuba, England, and even Sicily, all since the day he was shot dead by federal agents while leaving a Chicago movie house. Dillinger's sister, after viewing the somewhat unfamiliar body in a police morgue (her brother had recently undergone plastic surgery, bad dye jobs, and other degradations), insisted that it wasn't the Johnnie she knew and loved, sparking a fury of conspiracy theories and tall tales. The authorities had quickly arranged for a second viewing, and only after she had been shown certain scars and birthmarks did she recant. By then it was too late; the stories were out.

People were equally suspicious about the reports of the Firefly Brothers' deaths. Everywhere I went, people were questioning reality. You really think some country cops could just stumble upon the great Firefly Brothers that way? the elevator operator in my building said with a laugh. If the Firesons had escaped from so many stakeouts and ambushes before, why would this one be any different? the shoeshine boy asked. Soon people were saying that the Points North cops had lost the bodies; it was never in the papers, but the rumor was everywhere, whispered and then shouted. There was speculation that those dead guys in the photograph weren't really Jason and Whit but some bums that J. Edgar Hoover had rounded up, nothing but a government ploy to convince us that Washington was still in control. "What should you believe anymore?" people would say to me with a shrug.

The stories only grew stronger after the dead Firefly Brothers were spotted robbing a bank in their hometown.

XII.

Whit felt buried alive. His arms were useless and some immovable weight was pinning him down, making breathing impossible. He couldn't see. Jesus, what had happened? Memories rushed at him. The job at Third National—no, the *second* job, that's right, hadn't they tried two in one day? Did that explain why he was lying here like . . . hell, where was he?

The memories were winning the fight, handily, and he felt all the more buried, each regret another thug and every mistake another goon leaping atop the pile, pinning him down. The cop with the Thompson. The crowd on the street. Each face from this long litany of crimes, each body flinging itself upon him. He needed to breathe.

He screamed as he pushed his arms out, and whatever was on top of him rolled off. Panting, he sat up and leaned against something. He felt behind him: metal, and a tire. A car, then. He stood and reached into the open window, found the steering wheel, heard the keys clink as his clumsy fingers brushed against them, then turned the switch for the headlights.

He was inside a garage, but not one he recognized. It was exceptionally clean and free of clutter, except for the body on the ground.

Whit was fairly certain who it was. He took a breath, steadying himself, then bent down, grabbed it by the shoulder, and rolled it over. Even though he'd been expecting it, he still gasped. Jason's eyes were shut, blood-stained dirt caking his left temple and jaw. Just above his temple, a shiny tangle of hair was thick with a combination of pomade, dried sweat, blood, and worse. Whit stepped back, turned around, and gagged. But nothing came out—he'd probably emptied himself already. When *he* had died.

There didn't seem to be any way to deny it this time. Whit turned around and saw that the ground he had been lying on was nearly black. He inspected himself. He wasn't wearing his jacket anymore, and his bulletproof vest was stiff with blood. When he moved it made crinkling sounds, bits flaking off. The material was a shredded mess.

Good God. It really happened. We really died before. And now we've died again.

Whit looked in the car and saw that its backseat was even bloodier than the ground, so much so that he wondered if a third or fourth person had died back there, too. *How much of the stuff do we have in us?* he wondered. *And how many times can we bleed it all out?*

He gripped some of the shreds and pulled off his vest and the shirt beneath it, his clothing disintegrating around him. What in the hell point was there in wearing a twenty-five-pound bulletproof vest if you could still get gunned to death? Apparently these things weren't designed to stop submachine guns, particularly at such close range. And since when did cops in nowhere towns like Hudson Heights carry Thompsons? The Firefly Brothers had scouted not only the bank itself but the local police force, making note of their automobiles—number, type, condition, estimated maximum speed—and their weaponry. Apparently they had missed the fact that the tiny Hudson Heights police force had access to an armory. Whit had heard that the hoopla over Public Enemies had inspired towns to vote more money for their police forces, so that even small-town outfits could strap themselves like fascist militias, but he hadn't quite believed it until he saw that overweight cop aiming the Thompson at him.

With his shirt and vest off, the sight of his own chest was repulsive to him. Everything was deep scarlet. Tattooed across his chest and abdomen were purple welts; he stopped counting after six. The cop had riddled him good. His pants, too, were stained with blood, but they were untorn, so at least his wounds were above the belt.

He noticed that a few feet from Jason's body was a small burlap sack labeled LYE. Of course. Marriner was planning to erase their faces so the bodies, when found, couldn't be identified. They would have done the same thing to one of their dead accomplices, if it had come to that. Thank God he'd woken up before the old man had poured the acid onto his face.

He sat on the ground and his head lolled into his hands, his fingers tacky with blood. So were his jaw and neck, and his lips were coated with the stuff. He couldn't believe this, yet he could. They hadn't somehow survived the still forgotten shootout in Points North—they really had died there. They had been granted a second chance, and they had chosen to devote that extra life to the same misguided pursuits as the first. It had happened again.

It was probably some mystical payback for all the harm they'd done, he thought to himself. He didn't normally aim such downcast thoughts at himself—*I'm fighting back against the crooked bankers, damn it, I'm doing good*—but he knew that he and Jason had wrought more than their share of damage. All summer long, Jason's plan had been to run out west someplace and start over once they had their Federal Reserve money washed, and they still could have done that after their awakening in Points North. But they had woken up penniless, so Jason had altered the plan, and the seduction of his unassailable confidence had been all Whit needed. *Sure, we need money if we want to start over and live quietly someplace. And yes, these two banks have money, and yes, we are particularly skilled at obtaining money from such banks. Sure, let's risk our lives again. Yeah, we'll put one of the rookies in charge of cleaning the street—great idea.*

That's how it was with Jason—he gave you reason to expect better, despite the long odds and misery surrounding you. The man truly believed he was meant for grander things, and anyone in his orbit was equally blessed. *We are not meant to wallow in poverty. We cannot be stopped by idiot cops and malevolent bankers. We shall revel in our rightness, in our superiority. Until it kills us. Twice.*

And of course Whit had been happy to walk into Third National of Lincoln City and rob the same bastards that had pushed their father into his impossible position. How different might things have been if the bank had held off on the foreclosure notices and waited for the factories to back up their scrip? Pop's dreams of real-estate prosperity might not have been realized, no, but neither would this nightmare have come to pass.

There would have been no late-night confrontation with Garrett Jones, no threats that could be used against Pop later, at the trial for Jones's death—Jones, who so obviously had shot himself in despair over his own lost fortune. Pop's confrontation with him the night before had been a bad idea, certainly, and perhaps the stress of that conflict had been part of what had led Jones to take his own life, but that didn't make it Pop's fault.

Jason still wasn't moving. Whit dragged his brother over to the car and sat him up against it. Hmm, Jason had been the first to wake the last time, and he'd had his hand on Whit's arm when Whit awoke. Had Jason muttered some incantation, blown into Whit's mouth, donated a rib? What was Whit supposed to do to bring his brother back?

On the right side of the garage was a narrow door, and Whit opened it. He needed to escape his brother's presence for a moment, needed to be spared the horrible and unknowable responsibility of being a living person in the company of the dead. Outside it was calm, a faintness of dawn on the right side of the sky. He was in the ample backyard of a two-floor, white clapboard house that he didn't recognize. In keeping with Marriner's preferred methods, this appeared to be a well-off neighborhood. Every house was dark except this one—there were lights on downstairs, though the blinds were drawn, those tiny slivers of yellow evidence of what was probably frantic activity: counting the money, or mapping a new escape, or trying to get the two rookies to relax about the fact that their famous ringleaders had died in the backseat.

Whit let himself remember. The Lincoln City job had been a success, and they'd driven two cars along different routes to the predetermined rendezvous point, where they had two other cars waiting. They had stuffed the Gladstone bags and assorted sacks into the trunk of the new vehicles and driven down to Hudson Heights for the second endeavor. They walked in right as the bank was closing, a time when, they had learned from observing, the place tended to be nearly as empty as other banks were at their nine o'clock openings (the usual time for endeavors). Yet, for some reason the place had been packed.

That didn't check out—maybe some factory's payday had been changed, or perhaps the bank was having problems that afternoon, too few tellers to handle the crowd. Regardless, the gang should have decided right then to call off the endeavor, but cockiness had taken hold. Jason wanted the second job, insisted that the extra money was what they needed to finally escape, to offer the better lives that Darcy and Veronica and little Patrick deserved.

Hell, who was Whit kidding? He'd wanted the money, too.

He'd always suspected that he didn't get the same joy out of doing endeavors that Jason did, but then again Jason seemed to enjoy *everything* more than most people. And Whit less. He worried about himself sometimes. Why he carried so much spite, so much vindictiveness. He didn't *want* to be this way, did he? Wouldn't it be easier to be like Jason—laughing, carefree, exuding such freedom? How had Whit been thrust into the role of the angry one?

Funny how people can live through the same events and turn out so differently. How family can react to the same disasters in such varied ways. He was who he was, and if death couldn't change that, then surely nothing would.

The air outside was warm, the humidity not letting up even in night's hidden moments. Whit's head ached. He'd been plagued by intermittent migraines ever since the beating he took at the Hooverville, and he felt the familiar throb as the blood flowed through his brain once again. It was dark out, but the birds were doing their part to get the day started. They seemed unusually frantic, as if trying to warn the neighborhood of its unlawful, unnatural inhabitants.

Whit screamed. It wasn't premeditated but had simply risen in him like a primal urge. His head tipped back and he hollered at the vanishing night, at his past, at whatever forces were keeping him bound to a life he had long tired of. He fell to his knees and for a moment wondered if he could possibly make himself stop inhaling, finally undo whatever it was that his body kept redoing. But no—after kneeling there for a long moment his lungs expanded again, and he slumped forward.

He was huddled up in a ball, his blood-encrusted fingers wrapped around the back of his head, when he heard the familiar voice.

"You screaming to wake the dead?"

Whit turned and stood in one motion. Jason was standing outside the open garage door and scrutinizing Whit's raw chest. Even in the dark they were close enough to see each other's wounds.

"Guess I was," Whit said.

They stared at each other.

"So . . ." Jason's voice trailed off. "This is really happening."

"Yeah."

That was all they could muster for a good while. Jason began to finger the hole in the side of his head, but he stopped when he saw the expression on Whit's face.

"Sorry," Jason said. "I was hoping all this blood was just from a nasty cut, but—"

"I took a good look at it," Whit said. "It's not a cut, it's a bullet hole. Plus, I saw it when it happened."

"What did happen? I remember robbing the second bank and being about to walk out, but nothing after that."

"Sniper from across the street. Got you soon as you stepped outside."

Jason shook his head. "At least it was quick."

Whit had not been so lucky. He remembered the force of the cop's Thompson, like someone punching through him, so many times in too quick an instant. He remembered seeing his own gun in midair as his arms spasmed. He remembered the claustrophobia of his face in someone's armpit as he was stuffed into the backseat; remembered the choking and coughing, like he was drowning, his senses at war with one another; and finally he remembered painting the upholstery red whenever he tried to speak, or tried to ask someone where Jason was, or tried to ask God for a favor. Apparently he had been granted one.

"Jason, what the hell is happening?" Whit whispered this, as if it was all he could do to admit it out loud.

"I don't know."

"This can't be a dream. It's too . . . too long, for one thing. I don't know, all it could be is . . . a miracle. A goddamn *miracle*."

"Or a curse."

"We can't die," Whit said in disbelief. "We . . . we just can't die."

"No, we seem to be pretty good at dying. But something's not letting us stay dead."

"Jesus, you'd think the second time would be easier to deal with, but—"

"At least this time we got to keep our pants on," Jason said, looking at himself. "So I guess two jobs in one day was a bad idea."

"Yes. You could say that."

"Did I get anyone else killed?"

"I don't know. I was kind of focused on myself, tell you the truth. And on you."

Lying faceup on the Hudson Heights sidewalk after being blasted, he had seen Jason step outside. Suddenly there was a shot and Jason's head had lunged impossibly to the side, his right ear touching his shoulder. After wobbling awkwardly, Jason's head had returned to a normal position, which was when the blood began to cascade, in rhythmic, pumping bursts, as if his heart were in his skull. Then Whit shut his eyes, and Jason fell on top of him.

"Let's get inside before they start dividing the money and leave us out," Jason said.

"But . . . what do we say? How do we do this?"

"I don't know, but people are starting to turn on their lights. We don't have a choice—c'mon."

The plan, assuming the survivors were still following it, had been to hide out at a place in Gary, Indiana, before splitting up. Jason had chosen Gary because it was a healthy distance away—and on the other side of a state line—from the banks in Lincoln City and Hudson Heights, and because they knew it from a past cooling-off period. Two days ago, Marriner had rented the new place from an elderly landlady.

The back door opened into a mudroom. Apparently their bodies had been laid here at some point, as the floor and the lower inches of a wall were stained red. Jason shook his head at the sloppiness. Past the mudroom was the kitchen, and they could hear the sizzle of bacon and eggs cooking.

"Make some extra for us," Jason said to the cook. "We're starving."

The cook turned around, and added to the chorus of frying and popping was the clack of his spatula landing on the floor. Young, red-haired, and freckled, he was one of the two rookies Marriner had brought in for the job. He had the face of a fat man but not the body; maybe his extra weight had been leached by the hard times. His name was Randy, Whit remembered, and the other recruit was named Clarence. Both were of limited intelligence and were too fond of alcohol, but the brothers had been forgiving in their desperation to recruit a gang. Besides, the brothers reasoned, as long as the rookies didn't do anything stupid to get them all caught their drinking might prove beneficial: once they parted ways, no one would believe two drunks who claimed to have pulled a job with the deceased Firefly Brothers.

Randy's eyes were wide. "You . . . you . . ."

"Yeah, we know," Jason said. "It's pretty goddamn strange. We're still kind of working through it ourselves."

In the kitchen was a small wooden table and three chairs, one of which Whit pulled out. "Sit down. I'll take over." As Randy sank into his seat, Whit picked up the spatula from the tiled floor, rinsed it in the sink, and flipped the eggs. There were only two, but Whit figured he and his brother could eat them, as Randy was doubtless losing his appetite.

"You . . . you . . ."

"Just breathe, Randy," Jason said. "We'd be lying if we told you we had any kind of explanation for it. You can close your eyes and try to sleep it off if you'd like."

Jason's neck was reddish black, as was his shirt collar. He was still wearing his jacket, which apparently was dark enough to absorb the blood without changing color, though it did seem to shine differently in the light, and hang unnaturally on his frame, the coagulation binding the cotton to him.

Whit plated the food and rinsed his mouth at the sink, then daubed as much of the blood from his lips as he could before sitting down. Randy's head was on the table now, his laced fingers pressing down on his scalp. He moaned quietly while Jason and Whit ate their breakfast.

"Where are Marriner and your buddy?" Jason asked when he was finished.

Randy made no reply, so Whit pulled at the man's collar until he sat up. Randy's eyes slowly arced in their sockets.

"Marriner's looking for a place to ditch the car." He spoke very softly. "Clarence is out looking for, uh, looking for . . ."

"A place to bury us?" Jason guessed.

Randy nodded.

"Looks like he's wasting his time." Jason smiled, and Randy tried to return the smile. He looked as if he was about to scream.

The rookie's eyes focused a bit to the left of Jason's, where the bank robber's pomaded hair was leaping out in a grisly cascade. Jason touched it self-consciously.

"I need a comb, huh?" He excused himself and went to shower.

Randy leaned so far back in his chair that Whit was afraid he'd tip over. "Um, I think I need to go lie down," he said.

"Go ahead," Whit said, releasing him. "Let me know if you have any crazy dreams."

Whit envied not only crazy dreams but boring ones, even dreams about waking up and making breakfast and reporting to work, at a factory where you did the same thing over and over. Even a dream about assembling a Ford would have fascinated him, because Whit Fireson hadn't had a dream in years.

He wasn't sure when the dreams had stopped, though he had his suspicions. At a certain point, his hours of sleep simply had been rendered blank. Perhaps he didn't dream because his waking life had become so dreamlike. A long hallucination, in which even coming back to life was only slightly more unusual than the other inexplicable events. He had robbed banks, he had been shot at, he had suffered auto wrecks. He had watched a drunk, back-alley surgeon sew up a gunshot wound on his brother's arm. He had seen his own father handcuffed and carted away to prison, had watched as a prosecutor described his hardworking, moralizing, decent Pop as a deranged killer, had sat motionless beside Ma as the foreman read the verdict. Whit had spoken with Pop in the cement visiting room thirty minutes at a time, once a week; he had written Pop letters and received some in return, various phrases blacked out by hidden censors. What could his father possibly have written that was considered so unlawful or dangerous? Maybe he had written about his dreams, his jailed visions of escape, and the warden or some other watchman had forbidden such delusions, just as Whit's subconscious had forbidden his.

Whit had seen long marches of the unemployed petitioning City Hall in Lincoln City for more jobs, for controls on landlords and banks; he had seen cops on horseback stampeding into the mob of unemployed, swinging their clubs. He had seen horses scurry and sway, their legs buckling atop marbles that the savvier marchers had thrown. Weren't these moments as dreamlike, as surreal, as any fool's twilight imaginings?

Whit had seen people gunned down, seen men beaten to death, seen men without jobs fight and kick and dig their teeth into their rivals for employment. He hadn't just seen it; he had been one of them. He was there when Lincoln City Tire announced that it needed more men for its factory. It hadn't even made an official announcement, had merely allowed word to get out, tiny crumbs of information multiplying among the masses like so many Biblical fishes and loaves. Only they didn't feed anyone. Whit had shown up outside the factory gate at five the next morning, along with at least four hundred other bastards. They stood there in the cold and wet of late February, the men gathered too tightly, but at least each mangy body protected the other from the wind, from the rain that changed into sleet and back again as if Mother Nature hadn't yet decided which torture to inflict. So many men, driven by that odd combination of desperation and exceptionalism, of fear and faith, each of them somehow believing that *I* would get the job, that things would work out for *me,* that despondency and starvation could not possibly be in *my* future. Whit was one of them. He hadn't earned a cent in weeks. His hands were buried in his pockets, narrow shoulders sliding between and past his competitors until he was nearly at the front of the crowd.

A suit appeared on the other end of the heavy gate flanked by four cops. The suit didn't even have a bullhorn, so what he said went unheard by the vast majority. What he said was: Lincoln City Tire needed two men for its line. The men in the front few rows immediately descended upon one another, everyone trying to fit himself through the gate that the cops had barely opened. There were more cops higher up, standing with rifles on the walls in case the crowd threatened the factory's property, but Whit wouldn't notice them until later. For at that moment he was consumed by the scrum. There were no discernible blows, just the weight of so much desperation and so many men. Whit couldn't see; his face was pressed into someone's back or chest or neck. Suddenly his knees gave way—too much pressure, something added to it, maybe an unconscious body slipping down and hitting the soft spot of his legs, and now he, too, was on his way down. If he hit bottom, he knew, he'd be trampled. They'd find him hours later imprinted in the earth like a symbol, like the mere outline of a man. He wrapped his arms around something and squeezed. Somehow he found himself rising. He would never know whom he was holding or why this person was rising higher, whether from supernatural strength or some strange entropic force, the proximity and number of these bodies creating new physical laws. He felt almost airborne, and he let go of what he'd been holding and fell forward, bouncing atop bodies and riding shoulders until he fell forward, in front of the gate. It was nearly within reach.

One man had already slipped inside and a second was just behind him. Whit stood up and reached so far forward he nearly lost his balance, his left hand clamping upon the second man's shoulder. The man turned—not much but enough—and Whit slugged him in the face. Never even saw the man's eyes, just put his fist where the nose would have been. The man bounced against the wrought iron and hadn't hit the ground yet when Whit slipped through the gate. The sound of it closing and latching behind him was one of the greatest things he'd ever heard— the finality of it, the heaviness.

He cradled his right fist in his left, the pain so sharp it was as if he'd broken not just the knuckles but his forearm, too. It would hurt more later, after ten hours on a new and uncomfortable job. But when the suit asked him why he was holding himself that way he said he was only cracking his knuckles. The job required two good hands, the suit said, so Whit banished any look of pain from his face, then reached out and shook the suit's hand. The suit had looked at Whit's filthy fingers and palm for a distasteful instant before daring to touch them, as if he and not Whit were the one who felt sparks and explosions and even a surge of nausea when their hands clasped.

The suit led Whit and the other lucky winner toward the factory, the martial percussion of gunshots echoing behind them. Whit never dreamed about that day, though doubtless many other men did.

Most dreamlike of all, though, was when Whit had killed people.

The first time Jason took him along on an endeavor there had been seven men, Jason and Marriner, two wheelmen, and Whit and two other torpedoes. Only later would Whit look back on that job and reflect that it had been executed with perfection—up to a point. He and another man had been the first to enter the bank, at five minutes after nine o'clock. Despite the morning sun, they had been wearing long raincoats to conceal the Thompsons nestled in their specially tailored inner pockets. Whit had carried two Red Cross posters rolled tight like batons. Without making eye contact with any of the tellers, he had affixed the two posters to the bank's front-facing windows, concealing the tellers from the outside. Before any bank employee could think to ask who had given him permission to post here, Jason and Marriner walked in. All the men were clad in dark suits, fedoras, and grim faces; witnesses later described them as looking like pallbearers. Except Jason carried a black trombone case. He laid it on the counter before one of the teller cages and calmly, deliberately, opened it like any salesman displaying his wares. Then he removed his submachine gun and explained to the teller how this would work, by which time the others had unholstered their weapons.

Jason and Marriner escorted the bank president into the vault and emerged with several bags, the old yegg having some trouble carrying his share of the loot. While one torpedo stood outside the entrance to keep the streets clean and another corralled the hostages in the center of the lobby, Whit stood in the back, watching in case anyone—

"Hey!" he yelled at one of the bank managers, a thin man with a toupee. The manager had leaned forward onto his desk, his hands hidden behind stacks of receipts.

The manager's head snapped up, his toupee migrating south an inch, while Whit leveled the heavy Thompson at his chest. Whit had practiced with the monster all week, marveling at how powerfully it kicked back. He pressed the handle between his right elbow and hip, determined not to be knocked off balance if he needed to pull the trigger.

"Get away from that desk."

The man slowly lifted his hands and took a step back.

"What's going on?" the other torpedo asked. Jason and Marriner were in the vault.

"He was hiding his hands there."

Whit walked to the desk, glancing at the disheveled mounds of paperwork. How many lives were being destroyed in those pages? he wondered.

"I wasn't—"

"Shut up," Whit said. "There an alarm button here?"

"He hit the alarm?" the other torpedo asked.

"No, no, I didn't! I was just feeling dizzy and I—"

Whit hit him in the face with the barrel of the gun. But he'd never wielded one like a club before and the motion was awkward, more of a slap across the man's nose. It merely made Whit look like a fool, as he'd nearly lost his grip on the handle.

"Please," the manager said, pointing. "The button's underneath the desk, right there. If I'd touched it, it would be depressed, but it's still sticking out. See?"

Jason and Marriner emerged from the vault, Jason shooting Whit a look that said, *Whatever you're doing, stop it, for God's sake, because it's probably a bad idea.* Whit backed away from the manager. He had seen the button, and it did seem to be sticking out, but did that mean anything? What if a message had been sent to the police station five blocks away?

The two cars were weighted down with the spoils of victory, and four hostages had been enlisted for each. Jason and Whit were the last two in the building. Whit walked backward, scanning the room for movement. A woman lay on the floor, her legs twitching as she cried. A ticker printed bad news from Wall Street. Whit smelled burned coffee, and someone was wearing too much aftershave.

He was nearly out the door when the same bank manager leaned forward again, his fingers disappearing from view. Whit took a step forward and Jason uttered a syllable that escaped into the vacuum that preceded Whit's pulling the trigger. That sensation again, as if someone were drumming on his rib cage. Feeling the vibrations even in his toes. Then Jason's hand on his shoulder as his voice returned from the vacuum, yelling at Whit to stop.

Whit didn't see the manager anymore. He had been so concerned about blowback that he apparently had shut his eyes while firing. The manager had vanished, not with a poof of smoke but with a long, thin trail of it, spiraling from the tommy's barrel. The wall behind the desk was newly ventilated, thick masses of red clinging there.

Outside, Jason and Marriner yelled at Whit, but he barely heard them, his ears ringing. Gunsmoke in his nose as they sped off with the windows down. For what seemed like hours, he sat in the backseat, behind Jason and Marriner and beside all those Gladstone bags and canvas sacks and typewriter covers whose contents he could only imagine. Jason drove them past farms and fields and streams and clouds and dust, the world passing as Whit sat in a daze.

This wasn't his first killing—there was that cop outside the dance marathon, true, but that had been lost in a blur of exhaustion. It was as if someone else had pulled the trigger that time, and Whit had only been watching from very deep inside his jellied mind. This experience was altogether different.

By nightfall the roads were even emptier than before and the bright stars seemed to mock them, shining with neither clouds to conceal them nor moonglow to overpower them.

"I'm hungry," Whit finally said.

"We don't eat," Jason said. When Whit protested, Jason snapped, "I told you the plan. I didn't say anything about eating supper."

"I figured it was included in there somewhere. You didn't say anything about taking a piss, either, but I assume it won't wreck your careful planning if I were to do that at some point?"

"We don't stop to eat. We lay low. Low means not showing up somewhere to buy food."

"How about breathing? You never mentioned that. Can I breathe tonight?"

Marriner spoke first. "I'd rather you didn't, son."

They parked at a secluded house in the woods, property that belonged to one of the men's girls. Southern Minnesota, and the black flies careened through the air. Whit pulled his collar more tightly around his neck. He stood by the garage in which Jason had parked the car, and within minutes the second car arrived, everyone exchanging triumphant handshakes. They began filing into the house, but Jason grabbed Whit by the arm and held him there until they were alone.

"You mind explaining your line of thought back there?" Jason asked.

Whit shook off his brother's hand. "What, the bank manager? He was going for an alarm, you saw him."

"I saw him fainting is what I saw. Too bad you didn't faint, too. Though I would have had a hard time deciding whether to carry you out or leave you there."

"What's the problem? Some banker gets shot up and you're in mourning?"

"Robbery is one thing, and murder is another. Look, we didn't have any choice with those cops in Columbus—we did what we had to do that night. But more bodies will only make them come after us harder. Which I explained to you, not that you were listening." He shook his head. "Marriner wanted to fill your gun with blanks, but I thought I could trust you."

"Jesus Christ, Jason, we're robbing a bank. Don't tell me you didn't think it was possible somebody might get shot."

"*Possible,* sure. That doesn't mean we go out of our way to make it happen. Whit, if whatever crazy agenda you have in that head of yours threatens to ruin everything I've built, then you can go back to Lincoln City."

"I don't have an 'agenda.' "

"The hell you don't. I do these jobs so I can get by—because they're there to be done, and the cops are too inept to stop me, and because I'm good at it. I'm not doing this to fight back against bankers or the law or capitalism or whoever it is you like to blame for things, understand? Don't fool yourself about what we're doing, or why."

"You have your reasons, and I have mine."

Jason stared at him. Whit had left his jacket and gun in the car, and he felt weirdly uncomfortable about the fact that Jason still had an automatic in his armpit.

"Whit, if you want to be some rebel, do it without me. You can go rally up an army of the hungry and pathetic and storm the Capitol, but I'll have no part in it."

"Because it's only about you, right? You're the star of the show. The center of the universe. Whatever's happening to everyone else doesn't interest you. Let 'em starve. Jason Fireson can handle himself, and to hell with the rest."

Jason shook his head.

Whit continued, "The hell with your own family."

"*What?* I paid off Pop's debts and saved the goddamn house, while you were fighting cops and messing around with your red pals. And I'll be getting more to Ma soon as I can."

"Yeah, Jason to the rescue. Just in time, too."

Jason stepped closer. Whit had grown to Jason's height years ago, but Jason still seemed to think he was taller. "What are you trying to say?"

Nearly a year later, Whit still wasn't sure whether it had been the gun in Jason's holster or something less tangible that dissuaded him from taking a swing. Why he had kept silent despite all the things he wanted to say.

Although, he realized now, sitting in this kitchen in Indiana and staring at his hideous wounds, if he had said anything, then maybe he and Jason would only have skipped over the past few months and proceeded to where they were now. Dead, and haunting each other eternally.

Jason reappeared in the kitchen, glistening with such cleanliness he seemed of a different species than Whit. A white towel gone pinkish in places was bunched around his muscular waist, and his hair was combed well enough to conceal the bullet's entry and exit points.

"Damn," Jason said, reassessing his unwashed brother. "You do look terrible."

"Do you think . . ." Whit asked, "this is going to keep happening . . . forever?"

"I thought you didn't believe in forever."

"I'm wondering if someone is trying to tell me I've been wrong about that."

"Whit Fireson admitting he's wrong." Jason searched the cabinet, his hands emerging with two cups. "Death is an illuminating experience indeed."

"This isn't *funny*," Whit said. "We need to figure this out."

Jason poured coffee, handed a cup to Whit, and sat down. "I'm focusing my energy on solvable problems," he said, voicing another of Pop's old maxims. It was like hearing a ghost, one dead man speaking in place of another. "Like getting a new car and finding the girls."

"But why is this happening to us?" Whit held out his hands. His brother offered no explanation. "Maybe we should talk to a priest."

Jason nearly spilled his coffee. "What about your whole God-is-an-invention-of-the-ruling-class bull?"

"I just figured a priest might be able to, I don't know, offer some guidance on this."

"He'll throw holy water on you and call you a heretic."

"Then I'll show him my bullet wounds."

"Why would this have anything to do with God?"

"That's blasphemy."

Jason loudly lowered his cup onto the table. "Whitman Fireson, you are going crazy."

"That much is obvious, thanks."

"Look, if God did feel like saving somebody, it would not be us."

"Well, why anyone other than us? Has to start with someone."

"Look, after we find the girls you can join a monastery if you like. But until then, please, save your conversion story for someone else. I might be able to handle . . . whatever the hell this is, but I don't think I can handle you being saved."

They sat in silence while they finished their coffee. Dawn was sliding its delicate fingers through the blinds, the planet still circling, the birds singing their clockwork ditties. There were still a few things in this world, Whit figured, that worked the way they were supposed to.

XIII.

_____

_____

Cary wore his usual no-comment expression with the hallway reporters that morning.

"The Firefly Brothers robbed two banks in Ohio yesterday—what's
the Bureau's take?"

"With Jesse James and the Headless Horseman as accomplices, right?"
he said. "C'mon, guys, have facts really gotten so boring for you to write
about?"

The reporters responded with more questions—what about the numerous eyewitnesses, the grainy photograph?—but Cary just shook his
head as he escaped through the office door.

One of the agents near Cary's desk was flipping through telexed copies
of stories from the _Lincoln City Sun_ and the _Dayton Daily News._

"So I hear the Firesons have risen from the dead to rob more banks?"
Cary said.

"Apparently so." The agent laughed. "Two of the robbers were shot by
police at the second bank—one in the head, supposedly—but they still
managed to escape."

Cary yawned. "I suppose we should start telling banks to stock up on
silver bullets and garlic?"

He spent his morning returning calls from small-town Minnesota officers and citizens who claimed to know the whereabouts of Homer Van

Meter, one of Dillinger's cronies. After two hours of debunking their false sightings, he was interrupted by the office secretary.

"Mr. Hoover is on line two."

Although he was one of the youngest agents, Cary had grown accustomed to receiving orders from the Director, who had lost confidence in the local SAC and was taking charge of the Chicago office from afar. Usually it was requests for follow-up calls or criticisms for incomplete paperwork. Still, Cary's stomach was already fluttering as he picked up the receiver.

"Good morning, Mr. Hoover, this is Cary Delaney."

"Delaney, I trust you've heard the latest Fireson stories." Dispensing with greetings, the Director always made Cary feel as though he himself had joined the conversation one minute late.

"Yes, sir. Unfortunately, people love stories like that."

"I want you to look into the Lincoln City job immediately."

"Sir, the Lincoln City police said there was no reason to think anyone linked to—"

"Of course *I* don't believe the Fireson Brothers were involved." Never Fire*fly* with Mr. Hoover. "But I want these stories silenced immediately. We need to keep public perception in mind."

"I agree completely, sir. I just, ah, didn't realize it would be the best use of resources for me to—"

"I'm told one of the Lincoln City bank managers is being particularly vehement about having seen the actual brothers at the bank. I want him informed in no uncertain terms that his insisting on such nonsense will only bring damage to the good name of law enforcement and the U.S. government. Furthermore, I want him to know that solving the robbery of his bank will hardly be a priority for the Bureau if he can't manage to bring himself into line."

"Yes, sir."

After hanging up, Cary scurried through the office in search of the reports. There had been two bank jobs yesterday, the first in Lincoln City and the second in the rural town of Hudson Heights. The Firesons had never robbed a bank in their hometown, and neither had anyone else. The first job was described as professional, neat, and quick; the second job had begun that way but was nearly thwarted by the speedy arrival of local police after a clerk tripped a silent alarm. Usually cops assumed those were false alarms and sent only their oldest, fattest officers to check on the bank and receive a free basket of pastries as an apology, but news of the first job that morning had put the authorities on edge.

Though legend had it that the Firefly Brothers had occasionally robbed multiple banks in a single day, Bureau records said otherwise. As Cary had come to know the outlaws' habits and personalities, he had found them too circumspect for such moves.

Nonetheless, he had to admit that the jobs' MO was startlingly similar to the Firesons': a getaway driver at the wheel of an idling car, one Thompson-armed torpedo standing watch in the back or side alley and a second in front of the bank, one man to manage the staff and the hostages, and one to enter the vault. (The Firesons initially had used a second car and an additional torpedo, but records showed that their final jobs had been attempted with fewer men, evidence of the gang's dwindling numbers.) Unlike that lunatic Brickbat Sanders and so many copycat criminals, yesterday's crooks hadn't fired a single round until the Hudson Heights police fired on them: there had been no bombastic "warning shots" into the ceiling or at startled pedestrians outside. The Lincoln City job had occurred at nine o'clock. An attractive man in a dark fedora had appeared at the bank's entrance precisely when the teller unlocked it. The man chatted with her about the weather as they walked toward the teller cage, during which time two other men followed. He then revealed an automatic pistol, and the two others brandished submachine guns. One of these men was thin and "angry-looking"; the other was much older. Only the handsome man in the fedora spoke, calmly instructing the tellers to sit on the floor, then ferrying the bank manager into the vault. After it was over, the bank manager checked his watch as the men hustled into a nondescript black car, possibly a Plymouth. The entire procedure had taken seven minutes, the police had never been alerted, and the thieves had escaped without the need for hostages. The Hudson Heights job had occurred later that afternoon, minutes before closing time, and though the robbers had managed to escape with a sizable, still undetermined score, two of them had been shot, perhaps lethally, while running into their car. They had been chased as far as the Indiana state line.

Cary noticed that eyewitness descriptions of one of the robbers were a possible match for Marriner Skelty, a longtime Fireson associate who had disappeared a few months ago.

He dialed Third National of Lincoln City and questioned Ronald Schooner, the assistant manager.

"I understand you've been saying the Firefly Brothers are the ones who robbed your bank."

"Yes, sir. That's because they did."

"It's my understanding, Mr. Schooner, and the understanding of most of this country, that the Firefly Brothers were apprehended and killed earlier this month."

"I read the papers, too, Agent Delaney." Schooner's voice was a wide Midwestern hammock of politeness and flexible consonants. "But I'm telling you that, God as my witness, the Firefly Brothers are the ones who robbed this bank yesterday. Them and three other fellows."

"Could you tell me what you're basing that identification on, sir?"

"On the fact that I went to school with them."

Cary sat up straighter. "I'm sorry?"

"I was in the same class as Jason, through high school. I crossed paths with him a few times after that—before he became a real outlaw, of course. I know his face, and his brother's."

This information wasn't in either of the newspapers, but somehow Mr. Hoover had known.

"Mr. Schooner, Jason Fireson was twenty-seven when he died last week," Cary said. "If you knew him from school days, that's going back, what, ten years? People change over a decade—particularly when they've done time, and have been in hiding."

"I understand that, which is why I doubted myself at first. To be honest with you, there were quite a few things going through my mind at the time, what with armed gunmen ordering me into my own vault."

"Of course."

"But after I'd showed him to the stacks—it was Jason leading the way, with Whit and the older fellow waiting back by the entrance—I'd calmed down just a bit and had a moment to get a close look at him. He'd grown a mustache, but I could see it was Jason, and he seemed to notice me noticing him. See, everyone knew Jason—even back in school, he was a popular one."

"I understand, Mr. Schooner. I also understand you were undoubtedly under quite a lot of stress, as you say, and what with all the recent attention the Firefly Brothers had been receiving, the pictures in the paper and whatnot, it's perfectly understandable for you to have felt that way. But now that the dust has cleared I need you to understand that it couldn't possibly have been Jason or Whitman Fireson. I think the investigation will proceed much more smoothly if you refrain from making such . . . incendiary comments to the newspapers."

"Look, I'm being as clear as I can possibly be. It was them. And, as I was saying, he was about to leave the vault when we looked at each other and I said to him, 'If I didn't know better, I'd say you were Jason Fireson.' He smiled, like I'd given him a compliment, and said, 'You don't say. So would I.' So then I said something about how he's supposed to be dead, and he said, still smiling, 'Yeah, that's what the people who killed us said.' You believe that?"

"No."

Unfazed, Schooner continued. "Then he started backing away again, and he said, 'You can tell the cops if you'd like, but I doubt they'll believe you. Have a good day.' " Cary heard a loud exhalation. "Looks like he was right."

"Mr. Schooner, even if we wanted to pretend the Firesons were still alive, they never would have robbed a bank where they knew someone. They were very careful, they spent days researching their targets, and they wouldn't have—"

"I was out sick for over a week. Yesterday was my first day back, so they wouldn't have known I worked there."

They continued to parry with decreasing gentleness. Finally, Cary repeated his warning and assured the assistant manager that the Firefly Brothers would be robbing no more banks. He hung up.

Cary had not seen the Fireson's bodies. He and the Chicago SAC had been pursuing a lead on one of Dillinger's associates in Davenport when they received word of the farmhouse shootout. The Points North police had failed to alert the Bureau during the lengthy stakeout, calling only when the bodies were cooling. Cary and his superior had tried to fly to the nearest airstrip, in Gary, but a thunderstorm forced their plane to land in Springfield. By the time they'd made it to Points North, the bodies had been stolen—before any member of the Bureau could view them.

Though Cary and the SAC had been willing to shrug off the missing bodies as a strange footnote to an otherwise triumphant chapter in their War on Crime, Mr. Hoover was outraged. Part of the Bureau's job, the Director had always explained, was to dictate reality—to investigate reality, fully understand it, and then, under the aegis of Mr. Hoover's vigilant public persona, explain that reality to a public cowed by the depression and frightened by stories of gangsters and increasing lawlessness. It was the Bureau's job to reassure people that these shockingly hard times were merely speed bumps along the shared path to prosperity, and not a sign that the nation was spiraling into anarchy and madness.

Still, there were other reasons to doubt the bank manager, weren't there? Cary tried to suppose, for the sake of argument, that the Points North police really had killed the wrong men. If Jason Fireson was alive but knew that he was believed to be dead, why would he so cavalierly rob a bank in his hometown? Why would he make those comments to Schooner? He should have used the smoke screen of his purported death to help him disappear forever. On the other hand, Cary knew that Jason was brash and confident, playful and vain. He may have felt a need to let people know he was alive, a need—inadvisable but irresistible—to demonstrate his superiority, smirking all the while.

Cary allowed himself to consider the impossible for a moment. Then he dug out the report from Points North and read it through, looking for the holes and not liking how many he found.

He dialed the Points North police and got the same officer as the last time. He wondered how many cops they even had out there.

"Any progress on those corpses?" he asked, less friendly than before.

"I thought you said you'd be taking that over for us?"

"That seems to be happening by default, doesn't it? Let me talk to whoever identified the Fireson bodies that night."

"I'm sorry?"

"I'm looking at your report here," Cary said. "What of it you've filed thus far, that is. I just want to make sure there's no chance you might have shot up two crooks who were not the Firefly Brothers."

The officer started to say something, then stopped. "Agent Delaney," he said, starting again, "I was there that night. We'd been told they were in the building, so after we surrounded it we warned them on the bullhorn to come out and surrender. They ignored us—didn't fire at us, didn't call out, didn't make a peep. We shot in tear gas, still nothing. We waited a few hours, then we decided to go in. That's when they started firing. If there was any chance that we had the wrong guys hemmed in there, wouldn't they have yelled out at some point and said so?"

This was all wrong. What Cary was asking the officer was insane, after all—of *course* it had been the Firefly Brothers; how could it not have been? Cary would have preferred it if the cop had simply laughed, but instead he was responding with extreme care.

"Thank you, Officer. I'd just like to speak to whoever identified the bodies."

He was put on hold again before being connected to a sergeant who also served as the county coroner.

"Sorry to trouble you with this, Sergeant, but I wanted to ask you a few questions about the Fireson Brothers. The bodies were identified as those of Jason and Whit Fireson based on—?"

"Fingerprints and mug shots."

"But we don't have any record of your having sent the prints to our Washington office for verification."

"Well, I guess we've been a bit slow on the paperwork aspect. Figured it was just a formality, since we never really had any doubt it was the Fireflies."

"We're pretty strict on formalities here, Sergeant. What about scars? Jason had been shot on his left arm a few months back—did you confirm that the body had a scar there?"

"I honestly don't recall whether we bothered to check that, because, as I say, we really had no doubt. There was all the money we found on them, for one, and the guns they had . . ."

Still Cary found himself dragging the reluctant sergeant down the checklist of police procedurals. "No known associates were able to ID them, because the bodies were stolen before that could be arranged, correct?"

"Unfortunately, yes. But—"

"Now, these prints that you haven't shared yet—how certain are you that they match the Fireson Brothers' on file?"

"Ninety-nine percent."

Cary put down his pencil. "Why not a hundred?"

"Fingerprinting is not an exact science, as you surely know. Matches are never perfect. We all have these whorls and—"

"Mr. Hoover makes it my job to look for perfection, Sergeant. I don't mean to be rude, but we'd like to get those prints sent to Washington so—"

"Look, I'll do that, but in the meantime I say the fingerprints matched. Plus, for goodness' sake, the men looked just like their mug shots, and they had seventy thousand dollars and a dozen weapons on them! Are you actually worried that we killed two men, one of whom happened to look just like Jason and the other happened to look just like Whit? The odds of that are microscopic."

Unlikely things seem to be happening lately, Cary thought. Dillinger's escape at Little Bohemia, and his wooden-gun jailbreak from Crown Point before that. Jason's vanishing act in Toledo, and now the flawlessly executed copycat crime in Lincoln City. Breadlines, dust storms, men jumping from skyscrapers.

"I understand, Sergeant. I'm only saying that if it's my job to look for certainties, for concrete facts, then the fact is, you're saying that there's at least a chance it wasn't them."

Cary could visualize the man shaking his head. "Agent Delaney, I don't think I should continue this conversation."

"Excuse me?"

"I think you should be speaking with Chief Mackinaw." Cary leaned back in his chair as the sergeant explained that Chief Mackinaw was away until the day after tomorrow.

Jesus Christ, Cary thought as he hung up the receiver. *They* are *hiding something. What the hell happened at that farmhouse?*

XIV.

First Darcy lost track of hours, then days. She feared weeks would be next, and that eventually her entire life would slip past her. She would not be able to grasp it because her hands were bound, would not see it because her eyes were covered. She would only hear it: Crows berating one another. Wind through heavy boughs. Bottles clinking, glass breaking. The echoing scrape of a coal shovel in the oven's bin and scuttle. Floorboards creaking beneath the pacing of kidnappers losing their patience. A single, daily airplane, so many miles above, its engine humming and fading out in such an accursedly linear pattern that it certainly wasn't circling in search of her.

She couldn't remember how many notes they'd had her sign. Her captors didn't dictate them anymore, only forced her to sign them to prove to her father that she was still alive. Which she herself was beginning to doubt. Was this life? No freedom, no vision, no food, save the same sandwich for lunch and a crumbling baked potato for dinner, sometimes offered with scraps of dry meat.

At least she could walk—after the fourth day they had untied her from her chair and fitted her into handcuffs that were chained to some anchor around which she was afforded five feet of wandering space. She could reach the room's perimeter and had traced her cell with her fingertips. Wood paneling on the walls, cracked in places. Heavily repainted windowsills. Nailheads protruding from the old, talkative floor. Surely she would be able to identify this room if the police ever found it once she was released. *If* she was released.

For the first few years after the sanatorium, she had been plagued by nightmares. Those nightly terrors were returning. Even while awake, she feared she was in some semiconscious state, combining her memory of that long-ago internment with her sorrow over Jason. Ever since that mysterious voice had mocked her that night—how long ago had it been?—she had been terrified that it was right, that Jason was indeed dead. That doubt had been exacerbated by fear and boredom, but she tried to fight it. She conjured Jason into life, visiting with him in the dusty rooms of her shuttered mind.

He had tried to protect her from something like this. One night in Chicago, during their whirlwind courtship, Jason was unusually silent during the drive back to the apartment. He had pulled to the curb and made no motion to turn off the engine and get out. Instead, he'd looked at her with a grave face and told her that they shouldn't see each other any longer.

"Excuse me?" She had known he was between jobs, so to speak, and he had made allusions to future engagements, but she had not expected a brush-off. "I'm not some precious vase, Jason. I know what I'm getting myself involved in."

"No. You don't."

"Oh, you have girls in other cities? Is that what you're saying?" Darcy Windham was not vindictive, except where rivals were concerned—those she would mash beneath her bare feet.

"No, I don't have anyone else. I don't have anyone. That's what I'm telling you." Quickly he looked her up and down as if he were committing her to memory. She felt crumpled, stuffed in a pocket. "It was a mistake to come looking for you—"

"You've made your share of mistakes, Jason Fireson, but I am not one of them."

"—and I need to correct it. For your sake. If you steer yourself right, you'll have a nice and prosperous life."

"Oh, don't give me any paternalistic—"

"Then for *my* sake. Darcy, please get out. Please go back to your life."

"My life is sitting right here, looking at me," she said, trying not to let her voice break. "Being a tad impetuous, perhaps, and not thinking very clearly beneath his persecution complex, but he's—"

"Sweetheart, please. Before I have to do something regrettable. Get out of my sight."

Her eyes had burned and finally it was her determination that he not see her crying that propelled her out the car door. She didn't even close it, just clasped at her shawl with both hands as she walked into her building. She heard him close the door, then pull away, engine revving as if he were afraid of being pursued.

But how afraid? It took her only three days to find him, after all. He had dropped enough hints that she had deduced where he was headed: Springfield, the home of one of his confederates, a so-called jug marker blessed with the gift of determining which banks would make the easiest victims. Refusing to pout, she drove to Springfield the next day, rented a room downtown, and methodically visited every tavern, nightclub, and bar that seemed even remotely like a venue Jason and his mates might frequent. At every one she asked the bartender if he knew Jason Fireson, receiving responses varying from nonplussed to paralytic. She was blowing his cover to the extent that his gang would have to cancel the Springfield job, surely, but she didn't care. He could find another bank, but he would not find another girl.

And what fun it was, slinking about, quizzing the sorts of men that a respectable girl was supposed to steer clear of. If the choice was between this and resuming her life as a typist at a downtown law firm, between this and becoming the smiling bride of some Miracle Mile financier, then there *was* no choice.

The third afternoon a bartender told her where she could find Jason at six o'clock. And there he was, sitting with his brother at a booth in a dimly lit Italian restaurant. Only blocks from the State Capitol, where powerful men stared at their hands and wondered if they were indeed powerful anymore or if the times had swung the balance elsewhere. Whit shook his head at this woman who had already foiled a perfectly good plan, then stood and walked away. Jason was wearing a black double-breasted silk suit with a red-and-white striped tie and a red spillover handkerchief. She matched him, in a red velvet dress he had paid for two weeks earlier. It was too fine a dress for a place like this, but she didn't mind. People would look at her regardless.

"I hope the cops aren't as smart as you," he said. He tried to appear emotionless, but his eyes betrayed him.

"Surely they aren't as single-minded." She slid beside him.

"You're taking a chance."

"Less of one than you seem to think."

He kissed her and neither seemed to care if people watched. He told her he was glad she had come. And that he was sorry.

"Yes, you are rather sorry, sometimes." She grinned. "But the rest of the time you're *exceptional.*"

She didn't have any moral qualms about his chosen profession—stealing from the sorts of privileged bankers she'd met through her father hardly seemed a sin—but she did warn him once that money wouldn't solve all his problems, whatever they were.

"Spoken like someone who's never suffered from want," he said.

She half-smiled. "I want plenty of things."

"I meant need."

"Yes, we confuse the two, wanting and needing. But my point is that money can be surprisingly insufficient at delivering contentment." She knew how men treated money, how they judged one another by it, valued and devalued their foes and friends alike.

"That may be true," he said, "but it does dispel fear. Fear that you're going to lose your house, that you're going to go hungry, that your loved ones will be cold and sick. Folks with money don't have to think about that, and they don't realize how light their shoulders are because of it."

She looked away for a moment, then back at him. "I suppose I've never really worried about my loved ones. I don't think I've ever had one before." She traced his jaw with a fingernail.

"Sorry to add complication to your life," he said.

"I suppose I'll manage." She kissed him, then asked how many banks he had robbed. He answered. It was a decidedly lower number than the newspapers claimed, but impressive all the same.

"And how many do you want to rob?"

"Exactly as many as I need to."

"Need, or want?"

"Need."

"Need, for what?"

"To never need again."

"That sounds like an awful lot of banks."

"I have an awful lot of needs."

She didn't remember doing any more talking that night.

Of course, the lifestyle she had chosen was not without its downside. Jason was away quite a bit, always scouting his next location, running dress rehearsals with his fellow actors in crime. And the constant relocations quickly grew monotonous. Their excursions to Florida and New Orleans had been fun; the work trips to Peoria and Toledo and Cedar Rapids, decidedly less so. Darcy did play a few roles; her accursed finishing school had included seamstress lessons, which she put to good use by sewing secret pockets into the men's jackets and pants, and the admittedly limited information she had picked up from her father on the automotive arts helped Jason devise new places to stash extra license plates or pistols. She was frequently employed as errand runner, since someone as attractive and doe-eyed as she was beyond suspicion. And her voracious appetite for information—she bought as many newspapers as she could—kept the brothers well informed about current events in their various haunts.

She often wrote in her journals when alone, describing the gang's activities and even her private moments with Jason. It was fun to record the various escapes and close calls, to remember the warts of this money launderer or the cabbage ear of that bouncer. One day she would publish them, under a pseudonym, of course, and changing the brothers' names and key characteristics. The country was so interested in crime these days. Prohibition had forced nearly everyone to become a criminal, and so the moralizing of previous ages had faded as people realized how tenuous the lines between crooks and commoners were.

Jason had never read her journals, but she knew that he would not have approved of the vast amount of evidence those books contained. Still, they had never gotten the gang into trouble. Her scrapbooks, however, nearly had.

She saved every article she could find about the brothers—a task that became more and more time-consuming, and required her to expand her reading habits, as you never knew what trashy pulp or high-minded political leaflet might include a few words about the notorious Firefly Brothers. Whit loved to flip through the scrapbooks—it was the only time he had complimented Darcy for anything—but Jason seemed disinterested.

In late April, the gang had spread out in a few small houses in a quiet Davenport neighborhood, from which they scouted banks in town and across the river in Moline. Veronica and her baby were with family then, so Darcy was often alone or with Bea, the wife of Owney Davis, Jason's oddly religious compatriot. When she wasn't running errands or writing, she and Bea would spend the days shopping, having lunch, walking along the Mississippi, or indulging in the occasional steamboat ride when the weather was good. One afternoon she took the bus back to the house— Jason and the men were using the cars to time escape routes, and Bea was seeing a matinee—and she saw two sedans parked on the street. As she approached them, she noticed a pair of hatted heads in each car.

She thought about walking away, but where would she go? Quickly she took a mental inventory of the house. She wasn't the neatest of ladies, but she was certain no contraband had been lying about when she left that morning.

Darcy turned up the walkway and began reaching into her purse for the keys. She heard the car doors opening behind her. She concentrated on keeping her hand from shaking as she slid the key in.

"Mrs. Tenley?"

She turned to offer them a polite if surprised smile. "Yes?"

They were Davenport police. The one in front showed a badge, introduced himself as Detective Collins, and asked if they could come in.

"Of course, of c—" Then she stopped, theatrically, but hoping she wasn't overdoing it. "Has something happened to my husband?"

"We'd like to talk to you about him, actually," Collins said. Behind him, one of the others smiled. She noticed from the corner of her eye that a squad car was slowly driving down the street.

The best way to conceal her nerves, she decided, was to keep acting. But she had barely taken a step into the living room before she realized that all was not as she had left it. She could see into the kitchen and noticed that many of the cabinet doors were still open, and two half-empty glasses of water were sitting on the coffee table, beside her scrapbooks, which she had not left there.

"Oh my," she said. "Someone's been *in* here. Is that why you've come? Have I been robbed?"

"We took the liberty of looking around the place, Mrs. Tenley. Your landlord, Mr. Gleeson, did us the honor of letting us in this morning."

"But whatever for?"

"Take a seat, please, Mrs. Tenley." Detective Collins was calm and seemed quite proud of himself. She sat on the sofa, in front of the scrapbooks, and the other two detectives sat in chairs opposite her.

She tried to think what could have gone wrong. If Jason or any of the other men had been detained while doing their reconnaissance work, they would have arrested her by now. These local cops haven't been hunting for the Firefly Brothers, she told herself. They just think they've stumbled onto world-class criminals, and thousands of dollars in reward money.

"Why don't you tell us where your husband is, Mrs. 'Tenley'?"

She ignored his emphasis on her alias. "He's up in St. Paul today, then Rochester for a few days, but he should be back at the end of the week. His sales job takes him away from home rather longer than I would like, but one can't complain about one's employment these days. Now, could you explain why—"

"Your landlord's received a few calls from one of your neighbors complaining about men coming and going at strange hours, ma'am. He did some poking around this morning and called us after he found what he did."

"And what did he find?"

He smiled at her innocence. "It's right in front of you."

"My Firefly Brothers scrapbooks?" Her journal, thank goodness, was in her purse, which she'd been carrying with her that day. "I'm rather confused, Detective Collins."

The cops exchanged glances. Apart from Collins, they remained mute.

"Are you saying you don't know where we can find Jason and Whit Fireson?"

She was beginning to worry that her uncomprehending expression would wear thin.

"Your husband's name is Charles Tenley?"

"Yes, of course. And I'm Darcy Windham Tenley, of Chicago." Jason had signed for the place using the names Mr. and Mrs. Charles Tenley—Marriner had doctored an ID for him a few weeks ago—but Darcy decided on the spot to include her real name as a maiden name. She amplified the patrician accent in which she'd been trained as a young lady. "We moved here just a few weeks ago after our wedding. Charlie was put in charge of this region for Daddy's company, and it's true that some of the other salesmen do stay with us when they're passing through, as the company is trying to save money on hotel costs these days, and sometimes they do get in quite late, though I'm rather annoyed the neighbors chose to bother you with it instead of doing me the courtesy. But I still don't quite understand. . . ."

She watched the gears turn behind Collins's eyes. "You're related to Jasper Windham?"

"Of course, he's my father." Darcy's name had not yet been linked with the Firesons (her father knew about her dalliance with Jason, but he certainly wasn't going to publicize it, as it didn't quite go with the aura of hardworking know-how he'd put forth in his recent, briskly selling autobiography). Jason had always figured word would get out eventually, but Darcy was betting these Iowa cops weren't wise to it. They had been expecting to find some low-class hussy in the Firesons' lair, a foul-mouthed working girl or prostitute.

"It's true, I did marry a bit beneath my station," she continued. "But what can I say—we find love in mysterious places. Daddy gave Charlie a bottom-rung sales job rather than placing him up high right away, you know—force him to learn the business, that sort of thing, which I quite agree with. I wouldn't want anything just *handed* to us. I believe in hard work as much as the next person."

Their morning search would have turned up some of Jason's clothes but no photographs, as he owned none, and no incriminating papers, as he always kept his escape routes and other important notes on his person. Most of his cash he also kept on him, or hidden at some other location; he had learned his lesson from past experiences with unexpected police raids, when he'd had to abandon hideouts and many thousands of dollars.

Jason usually stored his extra guns in the toolshed in the backyard. She hoped they hadn't thought to look there. There was no sign that they'd checked for fingerprints, either.

"Ma'am, I'm sorry to trouble you, but could I see some identification?"

"Of course." She reached into her purse and removed the ID, apologizing for the fact that she hadn't yet changed her old Illinois one for an Iowa one with her married name. Collins read it slowly and handed it back.

One of the other cops finally spoke, motioning to her scrapbooks. "So what's with all this Firefly Brothers stuff, Mrs. Tenley?"

"I'm rather interested in them, I must say. I'm a Chicago girl, you know, so I must confess that I've grown perhaps too . . . *accustomed* to the existence of crime. And these Firefly characters intrigue me. I've been compiling all I can find on them, as I was thinking I might like to write a book about them. After they're caught, of course. It would be better for me if they were taken in alive, so I might be able to interview them in jail, but I suppose if they're killed it will only increase the interest. That is how it tends to work in our society, sad as it is." She went on like this for a bit, even flipping through the pages to point out some of her favorite pieces. The cops who had been sitting stood up and shot Collins angry glances. One of them went over to the window and waved the squad car off.

She let her voice trail off and looked at Collins as if noticing him for the first time. "Wait, you don't mean that you . . . that you thought *my husband* might be Whit Fireson?"

"Ah, um, no. Jason Fireson, actually."

Darcy laughed. "Oh my, I can't *wait* to tell him. Honestly, he looks a bit more like Whit, I think—he's not quite so handsome as Jason, but *don't* tell him I said that. Oh my, that's funny. My husband, a Firefly Brother. I'll have to tell Daddy that; he thinks I married poorly enough, but at least I didn't marry a dangerous *criminal!*"

She kept the banter going even though she could tell they were dying to leave. Then the phone rang, and she excused herself to the kitchen.

"Tenley residence," she said.

"How are you, sweetness?" Jason asked.

"Oh, Sally, *so* good to hear from you."

It took him a second. "Who's over there?"

"Yes, yes, I'll be there. I'm actually entertaining at the moment, but I believe they're on their way out. Anyway, I'm *so* looking forward to it, and I'll bring the cakes."

"Local cops? Feds?"

"Oh, the first, of course. Nothing to worry about—I was afraid I was going to burn them, but everything came out just fine."

"Did you just get home? Were they waiting for you there?"

"Yes, exactly."

"Then don't leave yet—no matter how good you are, they'll probably still watch you. Make it two hours. Take the bus to the diner where we ate on Wednesday. Leave the clothes and whatever you can't stuff into a small bag. We'll drive to the front of the restaurant ten minutes after you get there. Order something and leave money for the waiter and walk out without explaining why." He hung up.

She had been watching the cops exchange accusatory whispers the whole time. When she walked back into the parlor, Collins offered her a smile so forced that it seemed to pain him.

"I'm sorry to have troubled you, Mrs. Tenley. Please wish your husband good luck from us. When did you say he'd be back in town?" She repeated her lie, and she didn't skip a beat when he asked for the name of the hotel where he'd be staying in St. Paul.

"Well, again, he'll be staying with the local sales director while in St. Paul to save on costs. I believe the man's name is Mr. Johannsen? Something Nordic like that."

She started packing a small bag as soon as they had driven away. She would have to leave most of her things behind, but no matter. She packed the scrapbooks, of course, all those reports and exaggerations and flat-out falsehoods. They had almost caused the brothers' capture, but she preferred to think that they instead had made possible her ingenious escape.

XV.

WINDHAM DAUGHTER KIDNAPPED
Ransom Demanded from Stunned Auto Magnate

CHICAGO—Darcy Windham, daughter of Jasper P. Windham, President and CEO of Windham Automotive Manufacturing, was abducted from the streets of Chicago one week ago by an unknown ring of gangsters.

Mr. Windham has received notes believed to be written by his daughter along with typewritten instructions from the perpetrators instructing him to pay a steep ransom to prevent harm from befalling his eldest child. Although Chicago law enforcement and the federal Department of Justice immediately offered their services to Mr. Windham, the magnate wishes to make clear that he is not working with the authorities, in accordance with the kidnappers' wishes.

"We are following the instructions laid out by the people in question," Windham explained.

It is believed that the kidnappers are demanding a ransom of $200,000.

Witnesses claim that last Friday afternoon Miss Windham, 20, was on the sidewalk outside a downtown apartment building where she allegedly had been renting a flat under an assumed name. An unknown number of men wearing dark hats spirited her into a waiting automobile, identified only as a black sedan with dirt-covered tags. Some witnesses claim to have seen firearms, including submachine guns, brandished by the captors.

Miss Windham has been rumored to be a past associate of the Firefly Brothers, though she and her father have repeatedly denied such allegations. Police would not say whether they suspect any connection between this crime and the remaining, at-large members of the Firefly Gang.

In what police believe to be an unrelated matter, Third National Bank of Lincoln City, Ohio—the hometown of the deceased desperadoes—was robbed yesterday morning by armed bandits who apparently modeled their appearance on the Firefly Brothers (*see story, page 5*).

Mr. Windham would offer no further comment on his daughter's kidnapping and is said to be . . .

The article jumped to a back page and Jason read it twice without making a sound. Finally, he dropped it on the motel bed.

They had left the hideout an hour earlier, while Marriner was still out. Randy had locked himself in one of the bedrooms, terrified. The brothers had dressed in spare outfits that weren't bullet-riddled and counted the loot. It wasn't as fabulous a take as they'd been hoping, since they'd rushed the Hudson Heights job—though obviously they hadn't rushed enough—but they cleared twenty-five thousand dollars. After Marriner's expenses for the cars and the guns, and figuring in the lesser percentages the brothers had imposed on the two rookies, Jason and Whit were left with a total of twelve grand. Jason had stacked their share in a beige suitcase, and in a second case he had stuffed assorted weapons and, after some hesitation, two bulletproof vests that had emerged unscathed.

After mopping their blood out of the car—which they would soon need to exchange for another one, assuming it had been spotted by the cops after the second job—they had checked into a motel across town to clear their heads. Then Whit had gone out to buy the paper.

"I'm sorry, Jason," Whit said as his brother scanned the article again.

Jason stood with arms folded tight as he pondered various angles and arranged the events into the best timeline he could figure.

"Think it's a real job?" Whit asked.

"I don't know." Thinking, *I was off planning a goddamn endeavor while this was happening to her.*

"She might not have gotten the telegram," Whit said. "She still thinks we're dead, so she figures this is her only chance to make a score off the old man. That makes sense. . . ."

"Which is what I don't like about it. Nothing else has been making sense lately."

After letting his brother think for a bit, Whit asked Jason what he wanted to do.

"I want to know what her father knows."

"But he's probably surrounded by police right now."

"And he never much liked me anyway." Jason shook his head. "Let's make a call."

At an earlier point in his career, it had occurred to Jason that bands of criminals rarely stick together for long periods of time for the same reasons that bands of musicians don't. Robbing banks was similar to the musician's craft, in that it involved taking the wild ideas flying through your mind and transmuting them into reality. A jazz or ragtime band was formed because the seven or so guys were possessed by similar spirits, but as time passed they would come to realize that their inner visions were no longer concentric. Either the band would dissolve or, worse, they'd take the stage while their minds were set to different rhythms and tempos. The result would be unsyncopated disaster at best, drunken fistfights at worst. Gangs of bank robbers were much the same, Jason realized, only they carried firearms.

In his months of pulling endeavors, Jason had taken on and jettisoned nearly a dozen associates. If Darcy had been kidnapped by any of their former allies, then Jason and Whit had a long list of suspects.

It would have been even longer if not for the fact that, as Jason had told Marriner, so many of their cohorts were now in jail or dead. The Firesons' associates liked to joke that the brothers had become folk heroes, but the end result of such notoriety was not good. Hiding in obscurity was far more difficult when your cartoon-colored face was all over *National Detective* magazine and your mug shot ran in dozens of midwestern rags. Running across state lines made little difference now that the feds were knitting the nation's various municipalities, cities, and states into a cohesive whole. Officers in towns Jason had never heard of had studied his MO, memorized his height and weight. Despite the fact that many people embraced their Robin Hood aura, others were tempted by the reward money.

And thus the Firefly Gang was picked off, piece by piece. During the Federal Reserve job in Milwaukee, a brawny high schooler had tackled the street torpedo, and an old tax lawyer had shot at them from his second-story window, killing Jake Dimes, a former racecar driver and the best wheelman Jason had ever known. Dimes had steered nearly every Firefly heist, but that damned lawyer had taken some ancient revolver from a wall display and lodged one behind Jake's left ear, from across the street. When Jason emerged from the bank, Jake's body was slumped on the dash, blood and gray matter strewn across the inside of the windshield. Jason's only option had been to pull Jake's body onto the road, wipe at the windshield with his handkerchief, and steer the Buick himself.

There had been a time when you could show up at a fellow's funeral; funeral-home directors never wanted to disrupt a service by calling the cops, and usually the families in whichever small town were happy to have a famous outlaw pay his respects. But, with the wanted posters and the steep rewards, observing such rituals was unthinkable. Jake facedown on the Milwaukee pavement was the last image Jason had of his trusty wheelman.

Only days later, Gordy McGeorge, an old school chum Jason had known since his first bootlegging rap, had been ambushed by two plainclothes in Peoria, where his twist had an apartment. Gordy had been pining after his girl and had swung by for a visit despite Jason's advice to hold off. Feds had been staking out her apartment and spotted Gordy his second day in town; they followed him as he walked her to the local bowling lanes. Gordy had felt their presence and run off, but they gave chase and cornered him in an alley. He got off four shots, hitting brick walls and the windshield of a parked car, but the cops' rounds were more numerous and better placed. He'd been gone three days when Jason saw the story in the paper.

Which was why the twice-resurrected Firefly Brothers needed to figure whether this was a real kidnapping or something Darcy herself was orchestrating. Darcy had once floated that idea, but Jason had vetoed it. For days Owney and the others had needled him to reconsider, arguing that it would be safer than an endeavor. Maybe Owney had gone forward with it as a strange favor to Darcy—with Jason and Whit dead and their money vanished, Darcy and Veronica had been left with nothing. Owney would help her stage a kidnapping as a way of assuring the dead men's girls of a comfortable widowhood, a criminal variation on laborers at a wake slipping twenties to the lady in black.

If it wasn't Owney, then it wasn't a fake kidnapping at all. In which case the top candidates would be Brickbat Sanders and his shady sidekick Elton Roberts, who also had been present when Darcy proposed her idea. Brickbat and Roberts could have turned rat, somehow causing the brothers' initial apprehension. Or they might have been lying in wait all this time for the moment they could grab Darcy. Or maybe both: first they point the feds in the right direction so the Firefly Brothers can be vanquished, and then, with Darcy's protective shield removed, they move to score a ransom.

Still debating the angles, Jason and Whit walked to the outdoor pay phone that hid in the far corner of the motel lot. Jason shouldered the booth open, dropped a nickel, and gave the operator a number he had committed to memory but hoped never to use.

Two rings later, a young secretary informed him with a tone bordering on joy that he had reached the office of Windham Automotive Manufacturing. He asked for the boss, and in turn was asked what this was regarding.

"His daughter."

"Sir, Mr. Windham thanks everyone for their concern and good wishes, but he must—"

"Sweetheart, I'm not a well-wisher, and I'm not some bounty hunter or clairvoyant wasting his time. He'll want to take this call, and he'll blame you if he doesn't get it, so go get him, please."

A pause, and then Jason was asked to hold. He looked at Whit, who was carefully eyeing the drivers of the few cars that passed.

A new voice, gruff and already annoyed. "Who is this?"

"Someone who wants to find your daughter a lot more than you probably do, you crooked bastard."

"Excuse me?"

"We've never had the pleasure of meeting face-to-face, though we've shared words a couple times. But never mind past history. Usually someone in your position doesn't get the cops involved, but because you never really cared about Darcy I'm betting you're letting them monitor this. Since you're willing to share information with them, share it with me: what have the kidnappers told you so far?"

"This . . . this can't be who I think it is."

"Of course not. That would be ludicrous."

"Then . . . to whom am I speaking?"

"The archangel Gabriel. I want to find Darcy before the kidnappers get impatient with your hedging on them. Which I'll bet you've been doing. I'll bet you even tried to bargain them down, you crooked bastard."

"This is . . . most unusual."

"You don't know the half of it. But here's all you need to be concerning yourself with: I'm a guy that can help you out. And it won't cost you a cent, because I don't want your crooked money. I just want to find Darcy. So tell me whatever they've told you so far."

Jason heard voices whispering on the line. He visualized half a dozen cops and maybe even reporters scribbling away in their notebooks. Windows open, fans blaring, pages fluttering in the wind.

"They want two hundred thousand, in tens and fives. They don't—"

"I don't care what they *want* from you. Of course, you'd start with the money. Tell me what they've said, what they've hinted, how they've communicated—pen or type, postmarks, carrier mail or people showing up at your door, that sort of thing."

Windham stuttered for a moment. He was the kind of person who dictated the dimensions of his universe, not the type who gazed heavenward to interpret some greater power. He was having difficulty adjusting to his new position in the spinning infinity.

"I, er, I received a phone call when they first took her. I didn't even know it had . . . *occurred* until they informed me, so I sent a man to her apartment to look for her." So he'd already known about her Chicago apartment. "The police confirmed that—well, that there had been a scene at—"

"What'd the caller sound like?"

"He was whispering, raspy. It was a short conversation. I didn't—I didn't quite understand at first. He might have been an Italian."

Wealthy victims of extortion always thought the kidnappers were Italian or German. Any hick kidnapper knew enough to fake an accent to throw them off.

"Any other calls?"

"None. They instructed me to choose an intermediary, and I picked my business partner, Septimus Grant. He's been receiving the notes: once by post, with a Chicago postmark, and the other two were left on his doorstep."

"Which is why you've been going about business as usual while waiting for word, you crooked bastard."

"I am not accustomed to being spoken to this way, Gabriel."

"Yeah, I'm sure the kidnappers have been real polite."

The titillated operator interrupted to request more coins from Jason, who fed the machine.

"Who are the cops looking for?" Jason asked.

"I, er, I have not involved myself in all of the detecting details. I don't feel I sh—"

"Of course not; you don't care." Already he was looking forward to the satisfaction of hanging up on the old man, but not until he learned more from him. "Read me the first ransom note. Have whichever dumb cop is standing next to you go fetch it."

Jasper Windham had once telephoned Jason, months ago, to warn him against using Darcy for any moneymaking gambits. The old man had startled and impressed the bank robber with his ability to procure the number of one of Jason's hideouts; Darcy had mentioned that her father had Mob connections. Windham wasn't calling out of love but self-interest. "She's been cut out of the will already," the auto baron had informed him then, "so marrying her will yield nothing. And if you or anyone you know is considering kidnapping or some other con, don't bother, because I won't pay a dime for that hussy. I'm telling you now only because I'd rather not have my good name dragged into the papers by such foolishness. Do with her as you please, but don't expect to involve me in any of it."

Jason hadn't told Darcy about that conversation, but of course he was thinking of it as Windham consulted with whichever underlings were gathered at his office. Finally, Windham read the ransom note, a badly written mash of threats and instructions about when and how to pay up.

Jason had hoped for some obvious tip-off—an accidental use of a catchphrase or a lapse into familiar slang—but nothing registered.

"So you're getting the money for them?"

Silence for a beat. "I don't see how that's any of your business."

"Listen to me: I don't have anything to do with this, Windham. Whoever's doing this is someone I can't control. If you hedge on them and they lay a finger on her because of it—"

"Whoever you are, Gabriel"—Windham laid on the aggrieved father act—"you should know that I am following orders and anxiously awaiting their instructions so that I can get my beloved daughter back home as soon as poss—"

Hanging up on him wasn't as satisfying as Jason had hoped.

"He's not going to pay them," he told Whit after taking a moment to exhale. "He's a stubborn old son of a bitch who doesn't understand he isn't holding the cards here, and he doesn't care enough about her to be nervous about calling their bluff. If it's a real job, they're going to get impatient. They're going to get angry."

He walked back to their motel room, Whit following, and started to load the car.

"Where to?" Whit asked.

"Up north. To Owney's."

"Even though he might have tipped off the cops in Detroit?"

"Yeah, but I don't think he did—we'd have heard he was arrested by now."

"Then who did?"

Jason stopped. "Look, I didn't say I had everything figured out. I'm still working on a few things. Anyway, where should I drop you off?"

"What are you talking about? I'm coming, too."

"You should take your share and find Ronny and Patrick. This isn't your problem."

"I'll make it my problem. They can wait—at least no one's kidnapped them."

Jason was surprised that Whit would take the chance—he and Darcy had never been close.

Once they were on the road, Jason headed for the highway. He drove exactly the speed limit. "Since when did you become such a saint?" he asked.

"Maybe I'm not so saintly. Maybe I have a weird feeling that whatever's been happening to us won't keep happening if we were to split up. Maybe I don't want you to walk into something you can't walk out of unless I'm there, too."

That's exactly the reason I took you into this gang, Jason thought, *and look where it's gotten us.*

XVI.

It was a long, dull drive to Michigan's Upper Peninsula, the sun growing bored and slipping off to sleep somewhere in Wisconsin. The headlights cut a narrow path through the thickening woods and finally illuminated the small sign for Cedar Grove. Jason remembered the name of the town where Owney and his wife had a hideaway, but that was the extent of what he knew. He drove down a winding road and found a small general store, which likely doubled as the post office. Whit waited in their newly stolen Chevy as Jason walked in and smiled at the portly shopkeeper, asking her assistance in locating his "cousin." Jason used Owney's alias and offered descriptions of the couple, noting that they had a place nearby. It was a risk, he knew, to show himself like this, and to bring such attention to Owney. As the woman mentioned that the couple did sound familiar and were probably renting from the Marshalls at 32 Tamarack Lane, Jason knew this busybody would remember him, and that if one day the police did drag their rake of suspicions through the U.P. beaches her memory would be the precious gold watch lying in the dunes. He thanked her and left.

Tamarack Lane was nothing but a pair of narrow ruts worn into the impressionable earth, winding a trail between a marsh to the left and the lakefront homes to the right. Beyond the marsh was a forest of cedar and black ash and maple, filling the air with a spicy richness unlike anything

Jason had smelled in his recent weeks in the dry, lower Midwest. The cottages were modest one-story structures, and although cars were parked in every drive there was no activity. All the brothers could hear was the thrumming of frogs, low and ominously loud.

Jason killed his lights as he approached No. 32. The half-moon and its reflection in the lake provided a surprising amount of light. Neither he nor Whit recognized either of the two cars in the sandy driveway, but of course they shouldn't have, if Owney was smart. The front lot was not large and through the partially drawn curtains they had a view of the parlor. They could see only the blond back of a head. Jason drove on. The road soon dead-ended, and Jason turned around. There was no sign of cops or any other kind of stakeout.

"Let's wait a bit," Jason said. He parked on the side of the trail, the Chevy half obscured by two dogwoods and spiny explosions of sea grass. Already mosquitoes were gleefully entering the Chevy's cabin, overjoyed at the scent of new blood.

Jason thought he recognized a face through one of the windows. Before he could say anything, Whit had thrown open his door. So much for caution.

By the time Jason had walked into the house, Whit was standing in the middle of a sparsely decorated room surrounded by silence and by Owney, his plump wife, Beatrice, Veronica, and, wobbling a bit but undeniably standing on his tiny, one-year-old feet, little Patrick.

Jason's entry into the room seemed to unfreeze the moment, the presence of a second living dead man somehow making the first less stunning.

Veronica, who had nursed Whit as he recovered from his near-fatal beating, was perhaps accustomed to the miraculous. She looked less stunned than surprised, as though she hadn't been expecting Whit to rise from the dead until next Tuesday or so.

She walked toward Whit and he met her halfway in a silent embrace. Jason watched them for a moment, then took two steps toward Owney. His longtime accomplice wore an undershirt and tan summer slacks and a look that, in Jason's opinion, could not have been hiding guilt or fear because it was so perfectly transparent.

Jason smiled and extended his hand.

It took Owney a moment to reciprocate. "Howdy, Lazarus. Nice to see you again."

Absences, both planned and impulsive, were a typical part of Whit and Veronica's relationship, and so, therefore, were reunions. In addition to those required by bank jobs, Whit and Veronica always devised other reasons for separating. He never outright abandoned her and the baby again after the dance-marathon incident, but still, their love was marked by accusations, both petty and severe; fights, both tame and explosive; and threats, both offhand and deeply, deeply serious. Whit wasn't always sure how they started or why they escalated; sometimes he said the wrong thing by mistake, sometimes on purpose. Sometimes it was the stress of a recently completed endeavor, or maybe he'd been thinking too much about that bank manager he shot or one of the cops he'd gunned down, and maybe she wasn't showing enough sympathy for his sacrifices. Sometimes he was tired of the baby waking him in the middle of the night, tired of the responsibilities placed on his shoulders. Sometimes he thought he never should have gotten involved with someone as strong-willed as himself.

Regardless, there had been plenty of times they had fought and parted ways, though usually the absences were brief. He might go out driving that night and not return until morning. On the more tempestuous occasions, she would take the baby to her parents' apartment in Milwaukee—the Hazel family had been able to leave the Lincoln City Hooverville, and Veronica's father had finally found work at a reopened brewery, thanks to some starting-out money that Whit had provided. But Veronica's anger at Whit would cool in the presence of her parents' greater dislike of him. Despite Whit's largesse, they had never been shy about voicing their disapproval of this man who had gotten their daughter in a jam before finding the decency to marry her; that would have been enough to alienate him from her clan even if he hadn't become a famous outlaw. Every time Veronica ran home to them with her baby, their complaints about Whit only rallied her to his defense, and off she'd go once more to find her misunderstood, heroic man.

And so this lakehouse reunion was not as terribly strange as it should have been. Veronica was probably surprised he hadn't used death as an excuse for disappearing on her before.

"You didn't believe what they said, did you?" Whit asked.

"No. But everyone else did, so, after a while—"

"You didn't get any of my telegrams? I sent one to your folks'."

"I was only there for a day—can't stand them anymore. Mostly I was with my aunt's people, in Iowa."

"We've been looking for you. Driven a thousand miles. Through hell and back."

"Apparently."

She stepped back to look at him. He worried he might look different, that his skin might have retained the deathly hue it had seemed to possess that morning. But the light in the cottage was dim, and she didn't say anything.

As Jason palled around with Owney in the background, Whit turned to face his son. The boy swayed a bit, gazing at Whit in wonder. Could a child's eyes discern what adults' could not? Did he know?

"Look at him." Whit had never seen Patrick stand—his posture seemed no less a miracle than Whit's own presence here. "Is he walking?"

As if he understood the question, Patrick took two quick steps, then a hesitant third, still looking up at his father with impossibly big eyes. His white shorts were sequined with sand from his day at the beach.

For a moment, Whit was afraid to pick Patrick up. When he did, Patrick felt heavier than before. The toddler's smile spread to Whit's stubbly face.

"I'm glad he isn't old enough to ask questions," Veronica said. "I don't know how I would've explained."

A surge of guilt belted Whit in the chest. "You won't have to explain that to him, ever. I promise."

She gave him the smile of one who had been promised too many things to believe this one.

Owney had read the news about Darcy, he told Jason an hour later as the two sat in the kitchen. Over leftover chicken and potatoes, Jason explained what little he'd learned from Mr. Windham.

"I was kind of hoping you were behind it," Jason said.

"No, sir. And I'll try not to be insulted by that." With his sandy hair, wide cheeks, and blue eyes, Owney's face was full of corn-fed cheerfulness.

"So what happened in Detroit?" Jason asked, hiding the fact that he still had no memory of that evening.

"Somebody was on to us. I'm sitting there waiting for you in the restaurant, then I see you two drive by without stopping. Then you do it again, and I worry you've seen something I missed. Then I figure, hell, there *are* a lot of guys on the sidewalk. So now I'm panicking. I head back for the men's room and somebody up front says my name."

Jason tried not to show how carefully he was watching Owney.

"I drew on him and fired a few. Ran into the men's room, someone's hollering, 'Police, stop,' and I jumped out the back window. Lost 'em in an alley, but it was darn close. I hid out north of the city and got word to Bea to leave the lake house for a few days. Then I came up here and poked around, but it didn't look like anybody'd found the place."

"So you don't know how they were on to us."

"Couldn't have been on my end, or they would've come up here, too." Owney said he figured they would need to leave the cabin eventually, and he had some acquaintances scouting towns in California where they might relocate and start his church.

It sounded believable. Even if Owney had ratted, he likely wouldn't be a free man, not with all he'd done. And the fact that he had taken in Veronica and little Patrick argued against his culpability. Still, Jason was haunted by the possibility that Owney had betrayed them. This was what life had been like the past few months, Jason thought: haunted by possibility.

"Surprised to see Veronica here. The plan had been for her and Darcy to wait for us outside Valparaiso."

"After you and Whit didn't show, they split up and she hid with family in Iowa. When she heard the news about you, she got scared—said she figured the feds would be after her, too, and that she'd be safer with us than with her family."

Now it was Owney's turn to toss questions. He asked Jason to explain Points North and all the headlines. And what happened to the money

Jason had been carrying, a third of which was technically his? Jason fed him the same badly cooked hash of half-truths he'd fed Marriner: that they'd been robbed that night but didn't know who had done it. The expression on Owney's face showed he didn't trust the taste.

"So . . . it's all gone?"

Jason nodded. "Have you heard anything from Brickbat and Roberts?"

"I haven't heard anything from *anyone* up here—that's the point. But especially them."

Jason took a last bite of chicken, giving Owney time to linger on the question.

"But you're thinking they could be behind it." Owney thought for a moment. "I wouldn't have thought Brickbat capable of yaffling anyone— too long a job for him. He's more the shoot-and-grab type. I can see him *wanting* to do it, sure. Maybe Roberts is masterminding it, with Brickbat the muscle to keep the other guys in line?"

"It's a theory. Best one I have at the moment. And since you're the one who did the honor of introducing me to that sorry son of a bitch—"

"You're going to take that grudge to the grave, aren't you?"

"And beyond. The grudge isn't the point, though. You know him better than I do, so I want to hear about his family, old friends, where they live, everything."

They tried to recall every comment Brickbat or Roberts had made about their pasts, Jason scribbling a long list of possible locations spread throughout the Midwest. Many of the sites he rejected immediately—if they'd kidnapped Darcy, they were unlikely to be hiding out in Chicago or Detroit. They'd need a big place to fit their gang, plus a room or two where Darcy could be hidden without any neighbors spying her. Or even overhearing—that ruled out apartments. It would be a house, probably a farmhouse, of the type the Firefly Brothers and their gang had often hidden in during their early days.

Jason looked at the list and tried not to panic. It could take a week to visit all the possibilities, and there was no guarantee Darcy was being held at any of them.

Owney's mind had already drifted. "You know, Jason, I got a thought. Could be some money in it. A *lot* of money. Assuming you stay underground and people still think you're dead and all, once I've started my church I could resurrect you. I'd give a sermon on the healing power of penitence and forgiveness, and you'd walk in from the back door, a no-good criminal risen from the dead, come to apologize to the Lord and be rebaptized by my hand."

Jason tried not to look horror-struck.

"I mean, golly, what a scene! I could time it with one of the retreats I'm planning, a big powwow under tents and all, when attendance is at its peak. This would be the big showstopper. Telling you, the money would *pour* in. You'd get a cut, of course."

"I'll have to think about it."

Jason could never tell whether the church idea was a con or Owney felt that the profit motive was just one facet of a legitimate religious experience. The man did read from the Bible quite often, and prayed before every endeavor, and there had been many an afternoon when Jason was subjected to that damned Father Coughlin on the radio, excoriating the evils of gamblers and international bankers and Orientals. But the recited passages and the nods toward piousness never got in the way of Owney's pulling the trigger or swinging a club when needed. Jason had met him in prison, where Owney had beaten men beyond recognition at least twice.

Jason stood. "Thank Bea for the food, Owney."

"You're leaving *now?*"

"Guess that means I'm leaving Whit with you. Sorry about that."

"Jason, it's ten o'clock. Spend the night. You'll only fall asleep and drive into a ditch if you leave now—you aren't doing Darcy any favors that way."

He waited a moment, then grudgingly sat back down.

"I don't think I've ever seen you so worried before."

"I usually hide it better."

Owney clapped Jason's shoulder. "C'mon, buck up, there. She might not be enjoying herself, but she'll be all right. Folks always come out of these snatch jobs okay. They want the old man's money, so they won't touch her."

Jason nodded, although he didn't agree.

"You know Darcy," Owney said. "She's probably ordering the sons of guns around, telling 'em what to cook her. . . ." Finally, he changed the subject. "Hey, I forgot to mention: congratulations. Some town near Urbana voted you constable. Read about it a few days ago. You were a write-in candidate. Beat a real cop by fifty votes."

"Well, I guess if you can be a minister I can be a constable. Was the election before or after I supposedly died?"

"After. A posthumous honor, the paper called it. They gave the job to the cop on a technicality."

"He can have it." Jason pondered the word *posthumous*.

"How's your mother?"

"Thinner. Grayer. I think she's wasting away worrying about us. Thought we were dead for a day." Jason shook his head, hating himself. "If you run fast enough, you can avoid thinking about things. I've always been good at running."

"From where I'm standing, you've always been pretty good at thinking, too."

"Sure. From where *you're* standing, because you're about the only fellow I know who I haven't gotten killed or arrested."

"That ain't on you, Jason. Guys make their own decisions—you haven't put anyone anyplace he wouldn't already be. You aren't as all-powerful as you like to think."

Jason stared at his hands, remembering the ink that had been on his fingertips the night he'd woken up. "Maybe that's been my problem all along."

Whit sat on the bed silently while Veronica rocked the baby to sleep. The process was quick; Patrick's short lifetime of apartments crowded with men had taught him to be a hard sleeper indeed. Then she sat on the bed beside Whit, the two of them leaning shoulders against the wall and staring at the other's silhouette.

"I waited at the motel for over a day. Me and Darcy. Was ready to wring her neck by the time we gave up."

"I'm sorry we had to leave you like that. Things got . . . complicated. We ran back to Lincoln City for a couple days, tried to telegram you."

"I'm not gonna lie and say I haven't thought about what it'd be like if you died. I'm not gonna lie and say I'm not prepared for it."

Jesus, she was a tough egg. He wondered for a moment if she had even been sad to hear the news, but it wouldn't be her style to admit it.

"We've got some money," he told her. "Jason and I lost our share of the Reserve job, but we just got a bit more. Once we track down Darcy, we can head out somewhere."

Even in the dark he could see her frowning. "You're going to leave your girl again so you can help Jason find his?"

"I know you don't like her, but . . . I have to help him."

"You have your own family now, remember? Over there, with a teddy bear."

She was right that he didn't think about the kid as much as he should. He wasn't entirely sure what his role was supposed to be, not merely as a father but as one in a uniquely dangerous profession. He'd always told her that eventually he'd have enough money for them to run off someplace and start over, but he found it impossible to imagine such a scenario. A life of comfort and bliss—could he really have that? With no one to lash out at? Even if he could carve out his own place in this world, that wouldn't change the fact that everything was so crooked and broken and wrong. He feared he would only be left to lash out at her and Patrick. Better to live this way, to surround himself with the enemies he was accustomed to hating. He knew she had tired of this lifestyle, but what she didn't realize was that it insulated her from so much of him.

"Did you have Patrick with you at the motel?"

"I'd left him with my aunt. I had a bad feeling about things and didn't want him there till I knew things were right. Figured we'd pick him up on the way out west."

"That was smart. And it's good that you're here. It's safe, for a time at least. I'll be back soon as I can, no more than a few days." His eyes had adjusted to the dark, and he saw that hers were angry. "I know it's strange, but I . . . have this feeling that if Jason and I were to split up, something bad would happen. Something that we couldn't walk away from."

"He doesn't make you as invincible as you think he does."

"I never said that."

Eventually they lay down beside each other, and she told him of their son's latest accomplishments. Then silence, and he kissed her. She slid a finger between two of his buttons, the nail scraping the undershirt. "So I only get the one night with you?"

He explained that he'd like to keep his undershirt on if it was all the same to her—he had a nasty scar there.

"Not like you to be so vain. Your brother's rubbing off on you."

You have no idea, he thought, then tried to submerge that thought in the amnesia of a long kiss.

The living-room floor was no more or less comfortable than any of the other floors Jason had slept on. He woke early the next morning to a rustling sound, and when he opened his eyes he saw Patrick, clad only in a diaper, playing with the zipper of one of the brothers' suitcases.

"Jesus! Get away from that, son." A thin layer of canvas was all that separated half a dozen firearms from the baby's fingers. Jason stood and hoisted his gleeful nephew into his arms, then walked into the kitchen.

"I don't approve of your son's sleep schedule," he told Veronica, who was heating milk on the stove. The sun hadn't yet risen over the lake, but a faint glow suggested that it planned on making an appearance. No one else seemed to be awake, in this house or in the entire time zone.

"You aren't the only one," she said.

Patrick started to clap his hands and babble at the sight of the bottle she'd prepared.

"How do you understand what he's saying?" Jason asked as he handed her his nephew.

"It's not too hard to figure out—either he wants food or milk or a change. No different from any other male."

"We are a predictable lot, aren't we?"

She sat on a chair as she fed Patrick the bottle, his tiny feet kicking the bottom of the table. "I'm sorry to hear about Darcy. Didn't get a chance to say that last night."

"Thank you."

"You be careful looking for her."

"You know I'm a careful man."

"What I'm asking, of course, is you make sure Whit is careful. Because he isn't." She continued, "After you find her, you're done, right? No more 'endeavors'?"

"That's the idea. We don't have as much as we'd hoped, but it's enough to disappear and start over someplace. Once we find her."

"You and Whit talk about disappearing more'n a magician does. Like you believe those stories about you. But you two aren't the disappearing type. You especially."

"Well, maybe we'll split up and Whit'll be better off without my untoward influence." Then Jason thought of something. "When you two were waiting in the motel, she didn't say anything . . . ?"

"About what?"

"Planning a fake snatch if something happened to me? Or maybe mentioning she was scared something might happen to her?"

"Of course she was scared something might happen to her." She gave him a look he didn't appreciate. "But you know she's never been one to admit it."

"You two get along all right while you waited for us?"

"She and I are different, is all."

"Like me and Whit."

She laughed. "No, not like that. C'mon, Jason. You're lucky she and I didn't kill each other, cooped up there. And, for the record, you and Whit aren't so different. You like to think you are—you both do—but you're fooling yourselves."

He let her comment dangle as they watched the sun rise.

At a more forgiving hour, they ate breakfast on the beach, twin dogwoods providing long slivers of shade. They balanced plates of eggs on their laps and watched Patrick crawl in the sand, throw sand, eat sand, and stare very intently at the sand sticking between his fingers. The lake was so calm Jason figured he could walk across it.

"I'm dusting in an hour," he told Whit when the others were back in the house.

"I'm ready when you are."

"Just stay, Whit. Take your family and lam it, before we're hit with something we can't wake up from."

"I just think we have to stick together while all this is happening. I have this feeling—"

Jason nodded before Whit could finish. "Yeah, I do, too." His voice was quieter. "It's weird, isn't it?"

"Yeah. And the second time hurt like hell, by the way. You're lucky you got it in the head."

The little boy raced toward the water and Whit gave chase as Owney walked outside. Jason told him he was leaving, and Owney wished him luck.

"You should go west *now*, Owney. This place feels secluded and far away, but it isn't. They only need one tip and they'll have twenty men here in an hour."

"Not like you to be so fretful."

"Let's just say I've suffered a few eye-opening experiences lately."

"I ain't stupid, Jason. I'll go when I need to."

Jason wondered how he could possibly be clearer to Owney, short of pulling at his own hair to reveal the bullet wounds that were slowly closing on his scalp. *You are stupid,* he wanted to say. *We all are.*

XVII.

———————————

W eston Fireson was afraid of losing things. He knew exactly how many formal shirts he owned (four, three of them Pop's hand-me-downs), how many pens (four, including the two he kept at his desk at work), how many pairs of shoes (two, one formal and one everyday), and how many socks and underclothes (seven pairs and five pairs, respectively). He brought his laundry home for his mother to wash each weekend, and before packing the clean garments in his bag he counted them to make sure he hadn't misplaced anything. The books on his leaning shelf were alphabetized by author, and his various periodicals (the *Saturday Evening Post*, *Time*, and *Commonweal*) were neatly filed in stacks according to date. He kept them until he'd read every last syllable, including the letters to the editor. No word wasted.

His room, located one floor above a squalid coffeeshop, was small and dank and smelled of cooked lard no matter how often he cleaned it. He cleaned it often. Many mornings he rose to find someone sleeping in the hallway outside his door, or at the bottom of the stairwell, as the locks had been broken more times than he could remember and the landlord had tired of buying new ones. He kept his hands in his pockets, one of them clamped on his thin wallet and the other clasped around whichever coins might otherwise jingle there, as he sneaked past the less fortunate.

It was late April, before his brothers had been killed. The card for

Agent Delaney had sat in his dresser for two weeks, and he'd heard no further warnings from Mr. Douglasson.

Sunrise was coming earlier, and, despite the thick curtains at his room's lone window, Weston had been waking earlier, too, as if the sun were as loud as it was bright. That morning, a Tuesday, he finally rose at six and trudged down the hall to the shared bathroom, the lack of a line his one reward for insomnia.

He decided to walk to work, an hour's journey. He would save money on streetcar fare, and he had skipped his morning coffee in the hope that the exercise would serve the same invigorating purpose.

He was afraid of losing things because everyone seemed to be losing things. You walked a few blocks and passed a table or a chair lacking legs and sitting there like a war amputee. Or you passed a car whose windshield wipers clung to such a bursting notebook of parking tickets that you knew it was abandoned, its owner having decided it was too expensive to maintain. In certain neighborhoods the police weren't towing cars anymore, so the heaps simply sat there unmolested. Scavengers didn't even strip their parts, because whom could they sell them to?

Weston had already lost enough, his mother having sold, given away, or discarded whatever he couldn't take with him to his tiny apartment, to clear enough space in her house for boarders. Now she couldn't even do that, thanks to Jason's suspicions, so her house was hollowed by empty space, like guilt or regret.

What else had he lost? His youthfulness. His energy. He was losing his hope and sometimes, at night, when he imagined what might be around the corner, he feared he was losing his sanity. And worst of all he had lost his father.

It was not yet seven-thirty when Weston approached a street corner crowded with furniture. None of the items were on their sides or broken; they seemed to have been carefully arranged. As Weston drew closer, two men emerged from the building, a four-story redbrick apartment whose cornice window was regally painted with the name THE HAMPSHIRE. The men each picked up wooden chairs and carried them into the building. Before the door could close behind them, two other men emerged and grabbed either end of a chaise longue.

Weston waded through the furniture. As he turned the corner, he saw a family standing there. The mother had thick dark hair cut in an awkward pageboy; many women had short hair these days, if not for style then for the money that hair could bring. Two boys stood by her feet, one of them barely old enough to walk, clinging to the tail of her housedress. The other might have been three or four, and his eyes were puffed and red. Ten feet behind them, standing at the base of an arc light and looking in the opposite direction, was a young, balding man who Weston supposed was the father. The man looked as if he were trying very hard to become invisible.

When you bump into an old acquaintance on the street, you ask him how he's doing. He tells you a story and then you tell him your story, and both of you are trying to see where you fit within the other's. Your story says: This is the way the world is, and I'm the center, over here. But if the other guy tells a different story, with the world like *this,* where the center's actually over *here,* then you realize that you're way off to the side.

This man did not need to be told he was off to the side. He clearly realized it.

Weston recognized him. It took him a moment—it had been a few years, and the poor fellow was losing his hair already. His name was Ryan, and they had graduated from high school together, two of the brighter kids in class, both somewhat shy. Ryan managed to lift his eyes from the pavement and see Weston, then look away, then look back again. Weston had been about to walk past but now he couldn't. He needed to say something, but what? He greeted Ryan by name and tried not to look at the furniture.

Weston realized that all the furniture movers had pinned to their shirts or jackets yellow paper cut into the shape of badges proclaiming their wearers members of Unemployed Council No. 7. A small crowd was gathering to watch. Weston heard both criticism and praise from the onlookers: the council folk were do-gooders or troublemakers, fools or saints.

Whit had heard about the Unemployed Councils, ragtag groups of citizens who had decided to fight back. When they learned of an eviction, they descended upon the scene and performed a reverse eviction, moving the displaced family back into their home and thus sending a message to the landlords. It was a magic trick, a refutation of the natural order of things. But the recipients of this good deed were not smiling. Ryan's un-introduced wife had now picked up their youngest, and her spine curved as his tiny legs straddled her side. Something in Ryan's eyes made Weston feel that his own presence here was torturing the man.

Weston asked if he was okay. In a quiet, deliberate tone, Ryan explained that he was close to landing an office gig set up by the WPA. He had been in accounting, he said, but had chosen a bad time to quit a firm and hang his own shingle, and his few clients had disappeared. The WPA thing wouldn't be bad, he said. He would find out any day now. He had tried to explain to the landlord.

They were standing beside a maple desk. It looked like an antique, the wood marked in places but well cared for. Weston wondered when the eviction had occurred. At six in the morning? Or the night before? Had they slept out here?

It was a good writing desk, he thought. His own mother had sold the one he'd grown up with, the one at which he'd written his stories of heroes and villains, fierce cowboys and African explorers, naval expeditions delayed by leviathans and typhoons. His new room had no desk, and these days he did his reading in his lap. He hadn't written a story in years.

One of the Unemployed Council men emerged from the Hampshire and assessed the desk. It looked very heavy indeed.

Weston rested his fingers on one end of it. "I'll help," he offered.

Ryan's family lived—or had lived, or would live again—on the third floor. Even with no inhabitants, it was a crowded two-room apartment. They wedged the writing table between the dining table and a dresser, by the window, where the morning sun laid its hands upon the smooth maple surface. They didn't know if this was where it had been before, but it seemed right.

On the way out, he saw that the men had affixed to the apartment door a piece of yellow paper declaring "This Home Reinstated By Unemployed Council No. 7."

Outside, the sidewalk was now devoid of furniture but teeming with witnesses. Ryan was standing by the building's entrance, talking with a trio of perspiring Council men.

"I didn't ask for this." His eyes were blank, as if he was having trouble focusing.

"You didn't have to," one of the Council men said.

"But . . . they'll only come back and do it again."

"Then we'll come back and do this again. We'll let 'em know they can't treat folks like this."

"What I mean is . . ."

Weston picked up his briefcase. The people on the sidewalk were already losing interest, as the event had unfolded peaceably, no sirens approaching. There was nothing to see but one of the sad stops on the ever-spinning circle of the times. Weston stole another glance at Ryan and then at Ryan's wife, who was crouching on the sidewalk to look into her older child's eyes. Then he hurried to work.

Before entering the building, Weston heard the newspaper vendor crying out headlines. He had walked so long through the city it was surprising he hadn't heard them yet.

"Firefly Brothers kill two lawmen in latest bank robbery! Firefly Brothers strike again!"

Weston felt something inside him die. Hope for a pleasant day. The lingering goodwill from having helped the Unemployed Council. The adrenaline of a long walk. So many things could be killed by the mere mention of his brothers.

With extreme reluctance he bought a *Sun* from the newsboy. It wasn't a boy at all but a short dark-haired man at least Weston's age, his skin toughened by hours in the sun. Weston remembered trying to buy a *Sun* from him a few months ago, during FDR's bank holiday. People had been bewildered that week, no one sure whether their money would exist when the banks reopened, whether the country would still exist or be subsumed by scattered outbreaks of panic and rebellion. During the bank holiday, he had handed his fifteen cents to the man and had been told that his money was no good. "What's money, anymore?" the suddenly philosophical vendor had scoffed. Then he'd thrown Weston's coins into the street, two disks glinting in the light, devaluing in midair. People were insane, Weston realized. The next week, when some modicum of normalcy was restored, Weston had successfully purchased a *Sun* from the same man, who never offered to reimburse him.

On this beautiful spring morning, Weston handed over fifteen more cents that he shouldn't have been wasting on his brothers' exploits. The article said his brothers had struck a bank in Iowa, near the Illinois border. Police had arrived on the scene more quickly than usual, and the two sides had exchanged fire. The reporter did not claim to know which members of the Firefly Gang had fired the fatal shots, yet he penned his tale in such a way that blame fell on the ringleaders, Jason and Whit. The stories always managed to portray Whit as particularly bloodthirsty, Weston noticed.

Should he believe this one? He'd lost track of the number of bank robberies attributed to his brothers—sometimes multiple banks on the same day, on opposite sides of the country. He was surprised that law enforcement hadn't found a way to pin the Lindbergh kidnapping on them, or maybe even the stock-market crash, or the depression itself. People seemed to believe his brothers possessed special gifts—that they could journey across space, multiply themselves, predict the future. They weren't men but ghosts, trickster spooks who disobeyed not only man's laws but God's as well.

Weston stuffed the paper into the nearest trash bin and walked into the building, the sounds of the street hushed and then silenced by the thick revolving doors.

"So what's it like?" Weston had asked Jason the last time he'd seen him, a month earlier. It was almost midnight—Jason and Whit had sneaked in hours earlier—and they were alone in their mother's dining room, Whit and Ma asleep upstairs.

"Like anything else. You do your work and make your money."

"I didn't mean the robbing part."

"Then what did you mean?"

"The killing part."

Jason had been about to take a sip of his drink when Weston said that. His hand paused the slightest amount, but still he took the sip. "What makes you think I've done that?"

"Papers say you've done quite a bit."

"I told you not to believe everything you read."

"Okay. So the *Sun* said the number's somewhere around seven. Let's say it's really only two. Or even one."

Jason tapped at the table with a tensed finger.

"I've never shot at anyone unless I had no choice."

"Meaning . . . ?"

"Meaning it was a situation where it was them or me."

"In which case, you win."

"Do you disagree with that?"

Weston bought himself time with a slow sip. "I guess I wouldn't know. I haven't been in that situation."

"Be thankful for it."

Weston laughed.

"What?" Jason had been cool and composed, but now he seemed insulted.

"You act as if you were *put* in that situation. Those situations. Did someone put a gun to your head and force you to hold up those banks?"

Jason eyed him for a long silence. Then he smiled as if this had all been a game. As if they were still kids.

"You're funny, Wes." Then Jason had stood and walked up to what had once been, and would certainly always be remembered as, his bedroom.

———————————

———————

Weston had been sitting at his desk for less than five minutes when his phone rang.

"Douglasson Law Offices, Weston speaking."

"Is this Weston Fireson?" A young man's voice. The confident kind of young man's voice that made Weston realize that he himself was no longer as young as he thought he was.

"Yes?"

"Mr. Fireson, my name is Cary Delaney. I'm an agent with the Department of Justice's Bureau of Investigation. I've been trying to reach you."

"Oh. Uh, hello." He looked around furtively, then leaned forward in his seat. Luckily, the office was still nearly empty.

"You're a difficult man to reach."

"I, uh, I don't own a phone."

"Yes, I've left several messages with different people at your building. I guess they aren't inclined to pass on messages."

"It's, uh, it's not such a friendly building."

"Sorry to bother you at work, but there seemed no other way."

He felt his hands shaking. How had this Agent Delaney known that Weston showed up at work early?

"I'm very sorry, but I'm not allowed to take personal calls here."

"Well, name the time and place and we'll talk then. We have a lot to discuss."

"Look, sir, I just read the paper myself and I only know what I read. I have nothing, absolutely nothing, to do with any of that."

"I'm not saying I don't believe you, Mr. Fireson. But that still leaves us with much to discuss." Weston heard voices in the lobby—the secretary and one of the attorneys were walking in.

"Mr. Fireson," Delaney continued, "I believe it's been explained to you what could happen if you don't cooperate. I'd like to talk to you about that, but also about what could happen *for* you if you did. I'm sure this is a difficult time for you, but—"

"You have a good day, too, sir," Weston interrupted as one of the attorneys walked past. Then he hung up.

Weston was fired the following day.

"I'm sorry, Weston," Douglasson said as Weston sat across from him. It had been only a few seconds ago that Douglasson broke the news and already Weston couldn't remember exactly how he'd phrased it. The shock had erased his memory of the act itself, leaving only the ramifications.

"I deeply admire the way you've conducted yourself through this difficult time," Douglasson went on. "I do feel that you deserve better, but unfortunately right now a lot of people deserve better, and there's only so much I can do."

Douglasson noted the recent downtick in government business and the moribund real-estate market, as if Weston's firing were a normal business decision.

"Sir, if this is about the, uh, the man from Chicago, I was hoping to give him a call—"

"As I said, there's only so much I can do. I do wish your brothers were as upstanding as you, Weston. But they are not, and though I very much want to help you and your family, I'm afraid I've reached the limit of what I can reasonably offer. I can't put my own livelihood at stake. I have a family, too."

"Yes, sir, of course. But isn't—"

"I'm very sorry, but my decision is final. Now, I know you had a bonus promised to you come December, and due to your hard work so far this year I've arranged to pay you a prorated bonus as a sort of severance. Didn't have to do that, of course, but I wanted to be fair." The old attorney stood up and walked toward Weston, one arm extended toward the door.

In the lobby, the office secretary offered him a white envelope without making eye contact.

Weston waited a second, as if he was being offered poison. Then he took the envelope.

"Thank you, sir." Was his voice always this quiet? "And thank you again for hiring me."

Douglasson nodded without speaking and did not offer to shake Weston's hand. Weston looked at him a final time before walking out.

Inside an empty elevator, he opened the envelope, which contained a check for just under a week's pay. Also nestled inside was a business card. It was another of Agent Delaney's.

Outside, because apparently nothing of interest had transpired in the past twenty-four hours, the news seller was still hollering about Weston's brothers.

XVIII.

Darcy had noticed clinking glasses and the smell of booze over the past few days. The men were arguing, worse than before. So many voices down there. Perhaps that meant . . .

She reached for her goggles, but Rufus scolded her. "Don't, miss."

She was still under surveillance. His voice echoed oddly—he must have been watching her room from the hallway. She wondered if they even bothered to turn her light out at night.

An exterior door slammed, a car stuttered into alertness.

"Rufus, what's happening?"

"Nothing's wrong, miss. Go back to sleep."

"Don't lie, Rufus, it doesn't become you. I haven't been asleep—I heard all that."

The floor informed her of Rufus's entrance into the room.

"What's happening? Why hasn't this ended yet?"

"Just go to sleep."

"Your voice is dry and you sound like you've seen a ghost. Tell me why you sound even more worried than me."

He was so close now that she could practically feel him, his presence a palpable thing, the air around her growing thick.

"I'm gonna ask you a question now, miss, and you gotta tell me the truth."

"I haven't lied to you yet, Rufus, and I don't see any reason to start now."

The whispering of a shirt collar, as if he was looking behind him to ensure that they were alone. He was crouching before her. "Are the Firefly Brothers still alive?"

Her lips quivered in anticipation of her answer, but her throat grew too thick.

"Guys are concerned," he continued, "because, uh, there's some rumors that the Firefly Brothers aren't dead after all."

She was breathing more loudly than she meant to, her throat tighter and tighter still.

"We didn't believe it at first, figured it was just stories and all, but now there's word they might be . . . looking for us. I mean, for you."

Tears were seeping through her clamped eyelids.

"So I need to know," Rufus said. "Is it true? Are they really alive?"

Her windpipe was a champagne bottle. Pure joy, combined with the compressed tension of too many days and too many bad dreams, finally opened it so her voice could escape. *"Yes, they're alive."*

She wanted to say something more but couldn't, not yet. She gave a half laugh of euphoria and relief, her voice and her face seeming to crumple upon themselves.

"How?" he asked. "I saw the pictures in the paper. For Chrissake, there's no way that could've been bogus. What'd they do, pay off the reporters?"

"I can't explain it all to you, Rufus." Her throat still hurt, her voice hoarse. "Even I don't understand everything."

"Goddamnit!" His voice grew softer as he paced into the corner of the room, then boomeranged as he returned. "Goddamnit. Knew this was a bad idea. Never shoulda played the snatch game."

"Talk to *me*, Rufus, not to yourself. Why does this matter to you?"

"Well, miss, I don't mind a bunch of cops looking for me. I can handle cops—been handling 'em all my life. But Jason and Whit Fireson—well, that's something else."

Darcy was familiar with the brothers' aura. The fact that someone as gentle and kind as Jason could elicit such fear in others was a source of wonder for her, though she was never shy about using it to her advantage. And she sensed an advantage.

"How did they fake their death?" Rufus whined.

"It seems you don't know as much about the Firesons as I thought you did, Rufus."

"What do you mean?"

"All right." She sighed dramatically, her emotions cooling as she played her new hand. "You've been good enough to open up to me, so I'll tell you a secret of my own. I'd be lying if I said I understood it, but . . . the Firesons aren't regular men. They have these . . . *abilities.*"

She could almost hear him swallow. "I heard about this."

"Yes, you know the time they were surrounded at some restaurant in Toledo? What was it, a dozen federal agents, watching the building for two days? They see Jason walk in, they storm the place . . . and he's gone. How do you explain that?"

"I don't know, I don't know."

"He knows what's coming before anyone else does. He's driving with a target in mind, then he sees a message in the clouds and he realizes his destination is being watched, so he turns around, hits a different bank instead."

"How? How can he do all that?"

"He walks through walls. He can change faces, slip through stakeouts." She knew she was pushing it now, but she couldn't resist. "Bullets pass through him, Rufus. I wash the man's clothes, and there have been times, after he's robbed a bank, when I've noticed *bullet holes in his jacket,* in his shirt. Bullet holes, but no blood. How do you explain that?"

"Jesus . . ."

"I may share a bed with the man, but I can't say I fully understand him. I don't think anyone *can.*" She was speaking quietly now, as if frightened herself. "Rufus, there are times when he's read my mind. Where he tracked me down without my knowing how. The Chicago police took me in for questioning once"—a lie, but she was rolling now—"and they were grilling me in some dark room; *I* didn't even know where I was. It wasn't even a police station, just some warehouse where crooked cops drag witnesses they need to break. They'd been interrogating me, *threatening* me, when suddenly Jason and Whit showed up, spraying the room with bullets."

"Jesus."

"Jason hadn't tailed anyone, hadn't any clues to go on. He just *knew* where I was. And that gunfight—my God, I was terrified. It's a miracle I wasn't shot in the middle of it. But it *wasn't* a miracle, Rufus, it was *him*."

"How come I never heard about that?"

"The Chicago police do have their pride. They didn't tell a soul. Why do you think I've lived in Chicago all this time without being bothered again? The police may have their hands full with the likes of Frank Nitti, but Jason Fireson they *fear*. And Jason only causes trouble for bankers and the law, crooked folks. But now, Rufus, you and your associates have made the mistake of crossing him. And I'm sure he's watching over me now just as he was then. I'm sure he's driving here, with all his men, and planning the most ruthless way to—"

"I don't want to hear about this."

She waited a moment for his fear to steep. "I like you, Rufus. You've shown yourself to be several steps above these Neanderthals you surround yourself with. But you need to understand that once the Firesons get here, once the shooting starts, there's no way I'll be able to stop it. Jason can become quite bloodthirsty, particularly when my safety is involved. He's rather chivalrous that way," and she smiled, enjoying the feel of these fictions on her lips. Then she pursed the smile away. "But also rather frightening. The only way to save yourself is to—"

"Stop, stop. I just gotta think. Lie back down, miss. I gotta think."

"Rufus—"

Her entreaties for him to return went unanswered as his footsteps whispered themselves silent. How could she be expected to sleep after this revelation about Jason's being alive? Or re-revelation, perhaps. What do you call it when a truth is covered in lies but then shines through them?

She made a move to reach for her goggles, as Rufus didn't seem to be watching her anymore.

Don't. It was back.

Darcy waited a beat, refusing to wither again. "My, this gang is rather efficient at relieving one another. One of you wanders off and the next one immediately—"

Do we have to keep going over this? Rufus may wander off, but I don't. Never can. I may lie low from time to time, but I'm always here.

She still didn't want to admit that there was a voice in her head. She'd had them before, but she was so much better now, wasn't she? She hoped again that it was one of the kidnappers, that she could jibe him into confessing his ruse.

"Whatever makes you happy, sir. So, isn't it interesting that these kidnappers seem so terrified of the allegedly deceased Firefly Brothers? They certainly don't seem the bravest of criminals, do they?"

Criminals aren't necessarily brave. You've noticed that yourself. Half the men Jason and Whit surrounded themselves with were cowards. They only went through with their deeds out of pressure from their friends, and isn't that the greatest of cowardice?

"Oh, how I've missed your philosophical musings. So what do you think will happen next? Will the foolish kidnappers negotiate with the old duffer a bit more quickly now that they know my beloved is hot on their trail?"

I wouldn't be so sure. They aren't all as frightened as your Rufus. Some of them may actually be looking forward to Jason and Whit showing up.

"Ah, I insulted you. I'm so sorry."

Why would I be insulted?

"Because you're one of them, for heaven's sake, and you know, quite well, as Rufus said, that having *them* on your trail is quite a bit different from some incompetent police dusting ransom notes for prints."

But I'm inside you. Not something you see. Like indigestion, or a stuttering problem, or alcoholism. Or the death of a loved one. Something you have to live with. The sooner you accept that, the easier it will be when the end comes.

" 'The end.' How cinematic. Am I supposed to be shivering now?"

Footsteps returning to the room. "Who are you talking to?" Rufus asked.

She had no idea how to respond.

XIX.

A fter an all-day drive in which Whit posited various theories for why they were still alive and Jason shook his head at every last one, they reached Dubuque. Flipping through a pay-phone directory outside a shuttered filling station, Jason found the address for Brickbat Sanders's mother. Ten minutes later, with the help of a map that Jason tore from the directory, they found her house, a small clapboard A-frame. They drove by the house twice before stopping.

His clothes nearly bursting with concealed weapons, Jason knocked on the front door as Whit waited four paces behind. It was dark and deathly silent, as if even the cicadas were out of work.

An old troll opened the door, wrapped in something green. "Hullo?"

"Hello, Mrs. Sanders, my name's Mr. Johnson. I'm the parole officer for your son and I was hoping to ask a few quick questions about him."

He looked past her and scanned what he could of the house. No big angry men, no sign of liquor or guns. No Darcy. Tellingly, the crone wasn't holding the door half closed or trying to block his view, not that she'd pose much of an obstacle.

"My son don't have a parole officer—he busted out a while ago. I ain't that dumb, sonny. And I ain't that blind, neither—you're Jason Fireson."

All those normal folks who looked at him and didn't make the connection, and this old bat took barely two sentences.

"Jason Fireson's dead, ma'am."

"So they say. But you look all right to me."

"People say I look like him, I know, but my name's Theo Johnson and I'm your son's—"

"I said I ain't dumb enough to fall for whatever you're trying to pull."

"Okay, I'm Jason's ghost, I admit it. Are you dumb enough to believe in ghosts?"

"Who isn't?" Though he hadn't seen any bottles, he was close enough to smell spirits on her breath.

"All right, then. I'm Jason's ghost, and Jason owes Brick—er, Bernard, a favor, so I'd like to find him." In the background, radio voices were dramatically accusing each other of adultery, assorted misdeeds, and a general failure to love. "Any idea where he might be?"

"Up to no good, probably. And it's all your fault. He was a good boy until he fell in with the wrong crowd. Serves you right to get killed." Jason didn't believe Brickbat had ever been a good boy. He'd no doubt tortured puppies and abused his siblings when he was still in short pants.

"And you ain't no ghost," she added.

"You got me again. I'm alive and well, which I'm admitting only because I'm sure no one will believe you."

"It ain't very nice, you pretending to be dead when you ain't."

"Don't worry, ma'am, I'm sure I'll be dead soon enough."

After another minute, he learned that her other son was back in jail. The guy's wife and kid had tried to hold on to their farm in Sedalia, Missouri, but were having trouble, the old lady said.

Jason said he was sorry to hear that, thanked her for her time, and walked off with his brother shadowing him.

An empty farmhouse tied up in probate would be a perfect place to wait out a ransom. Back in the car, they took out their maps and plotted the drive south.

Wherever they looked, things were crumbling. The bricks in old factory walls exhaled a fine powder of mortar. Abandoned porches sagged beneath invisible weight. Grass didn't see much point in growing. Dirt sneezed itself from one side of the road to the next. Street signs had trouble maintaining appropriate posture, their arrows pointing to heaven or hell.

As they passed another empty factory, Whit found himself remembering his time as a Lincoln City tire worker. While Jason had been out bootlegging, and then doing time, and back and forth again, Whit had played by the rules, but after more than two years he'd had nothing to show for it. Eventually he'd moved into a small apartment with some radically minded co-workers. They lent him their treatises and missives, the material so dangerous he was told to pass on whatever he read as soon as he finished it. As with so many of his fellow Americans, he wasn't sure whether it was socialism or communism or anarchism that made the most sense. Maybe the best answer was simply to admit that the current way had failed and wipe it off the face of the earth, then step back to see what would rise up to take its place. When his roommates told him they wanted to blow up the factory, he readily signed on.

His father was dead. He thought of that later, how perhaps he had used Pop's death as an excuse to get involved in something so dangerous. And, of course, there was the situation with Veronica. She'd told him her news a few weeks earlier, and he had been alternately bitter, terrified, and overwhelmed. He'd first met her when visiting recently laid-off friends who'd landed at the Hooverville, and, despite the squalor, he'd courted her in his unorthodox way, taking her for walks out of the destroyed park, buying her dinner, talking politics, and making irrational promises to one day help her family. He had been lonely, and confused, and desperately needed something to hold on to, something to make him forget and feel less fatalistic about this life, something positive and pure. And now he'd fouled it.

Planning the factory bombing was something new to cling to. The night before he and his roommates were to enact their plot, Whit had held one of the bombs in his hand, turning it over, marveling at the power contained in that small, awkwardly sized package. He laughed—not in happiness, not yet, but surely that would come. He would be so happy, tomorrow, to see the factory's roof drop to the earth.

But there was no tomorrow. How stupid of him to have expected one, to have believed in such a thing. Whit and his buddies were supposed to blow the place the next night—his job was to be one of the lookouts as they planted the devices—but by noon that day the others had been arrested.

He'd been out running errands that morning, and on the streetcar home he saw the cops all down the block. His heart doing double time, he rode the car past his stop. Where to go? Not to the apartment, and not to his job on Monday. Surely his name would be on lists. Surely the other guys—whichever of them hadn't been police plants to begin with—were coughing up his identity between bloody mouthfuls of teeth. He put up at a few friends', then slept in a few alleys, and eventually laid his head at the Hooverville, where the cops would soon come for him.

So although he never did get the satisfaction of blowing up the factory, he told himself that robbing banks served the same purpose. Jason could shake his head at Whit's insistence on finding meaning in their strange existence, but that wouldn't stop his search. There *had* to be meaning, didn't there? Otherwise it was just pain, as pointless as it was ceaseless. Whit had seen too many men who did not dare look for meaning for fear that such a search would only reveal a great absence, a void swallowing them and their families. Yet people need their lives to have meaning, need their stories to make sense. People tell their stories to place themselves somewhere solid in this great swirl that they can't otherwise understand. The stories define what is possible, what the tellers yearn for, what they believe they deserve. The self-made man, the American dream. Capitalism, socialism, religion—all those narratives that try to contain everyone's desires and fears within their neat lines. Different tales, different obstacles, but the hero is always *us,* and the ending has us attaining what we've always wished for.

We believe that we shall succeed where others have failed, thought Whit. The odds are against us, of course, but we will be the exceptions to the litany of misery that surrounds us. Surely we are not on this earth to suffer the same fates as those others.

Whit therefore did not share his brother's ambivalence at the many legends their adventures had spawned; he loved them. Reporters seized upon the occasional comments Whit made during their endeavors, chastising the bankers for their foreclosures and their interest rates. Jason was always telling him to stop with the goddamned lectures while they were on the clock. But it gave meaning to this madness; it made them better than mere thieves. And the people loved it! For every anti-Fireson screed penned by some starched-shirt columnist, the newspapers grudgingly printed half a dozen letters from the oppressed, praising the brothers' efforts.

Whit had been the only member of the gang to grant an interview, with a persuasive and relentless female reporter from Chicago. Whit had called her from a pay phone one day when he and Jason were in St. Paul, a moment before they were planning to bolt for an endeavor.

"It's a new world now," she had quoted him. "The old rules don't apply. How could all that's happened have happened? But it did, and we need to survive the best we can. I don't see us as villains or crooks or heroes or saviors or any of that," he'd added, even though the latter part was a lie. "Those are the old definitions. I see us as survivors."

Whit even talked to the reporter about their father, which enraged Jason. *Pop's no business of theirs,* Jason said, *and he's got nothing to do with this.* But how could he possibly think that?

The interview made the front page of the *Chicago Tribune.* They were in Peoria that morning, hiding out after another successful endeavor. It was a respectable neighborhood, yet an ominous rally of the unemployed was marching down the street that day, taking a circuitous route to City Hall. They didn't look angry, and they didn't carry signs, and they didn't make much noise other than the tired shuffling of feet. The brothers were sitting in their rented parlor watching the marchers trudge by, an endless caterpillar of voiceless need.

"Thousands will read this article," Whit had argued after Jason shook his head at the story. "We've given them hope, some pride. A story they can tell and hear told."

"What good are stories," Jason asked, staring at the march, "if people are still suffering?"

From the beginning, Whit had voiced his objections to his brother's choice of mate. The spawn of some wealthy auto baron? And Windham Automotive was a particularly awful corporation. It had violently cracked down on strikers back in '28, and over the past few years its workers had been suspiciously docile, apparently owing to Mob boss Frank Nitti's takeover of the Chicago unions. How could Jason cavort with the daughter of such people? Even if Darcy wasn't exactly on the board of directors, her entire life had been lived beneath the shadows cast by her father's vast greed and wrongdoing.

Even beyond the politics, Darcy just wasn't Whit's type. She would never outright insult Whit or anyone in the gang, but her tone, and the shape of her eyes when she pretended to smile, was enough. Whenever the gang was holed up together, Darcy seemed perfectly happy to let Veronica do all the cooking and the dishes, as if she was the matron of the estate. Ronny was too decent to object, but Whit seethed at Darcy's sense of entitlement.

"She thinks she's better than everyone," Whit told Jason one night the previous winter.

"Maybe she *is* better than everyone. Maybe that's exactly why I like her."

"You know what I mean. She's using you, Jason. You're just her little foray onto the wild side, and after she's had her fun she'll move back into her mansion and marry a nice banker."

Whit's objections went unheeded, so eventually he stopped voicing them, preferring to ignore Darcy as much as possible. They seldom had private conversations, but there was one that stuck in Whit's mind for a very long time.

It was in late April; the Firefly Gang had recently pulled endeavors in Ann Arbor and in southwestern Iowa and, after a time apart, the two couples had convened at a rented house in Fond du Lac, where Jason had begun planning what they hoped would be their final, masterful score, the Federal Reserve in Milwaukee. Patrick was ten months old and had woken in the middle of the night to nurse, and as Ronny did her maternal duty Whit had stumbled into the kitchen for a glass of water. He saw Darcy sitting at the table in the dining room, her right hand cradling a glass. She wore a black silk robe, the kind of thing Whit was always telling himself he should buy for Veronica. He hated how good she looked.

"Trouble sleeping?" he asked. The lamp above her wasn't on; the only light came from the kitchen and the window behind her, through which stars and their reflections in Lake Winnebago coldly shimmered.

"A bit of insomnia, yes. I didn't want to wake Jason."

He poured himself some water from the kitchen sink and walked to the dining room, sitting opposite her. "Mind the company? I can't sleep while she's up with the baby anyway."

Maybe it was the hour, and his defenses were lowered, or maybe he figured it was time he extended an olive branch. Maybe it was because there seemed something sad about her then, as if he'd stumbled upon an uncharacteristically vulnerable moment. He wondered why she was having trouble sleeping, what her nightmares were, but he didn't ask. They chatted for a bit, and, at some point in a story Whit was telling, he'd mentioned offhand something about Pop's being in jail, and Darcy started.

"Your father was in jail?"

"Yeah, of course. You didn't know that?"

She shook her head.

"Pop was in jail when he died," Whit said.

If Darcy had looked fuzzy from sleep deprivation, she was completely alert now. "He had a heart attack, right?"

"Yes."

"Jason told me that, but not that he was in jail at the time. What was he there for?"

Whit found himself reassessing his brother's relationship with Darcy. Maybe Jason was the one using her after all, and he'd never seen the reason to share such personal information with her. Still, they'd been together for months, and often seemed more like a married couple than Whit and Veronica did.

Answering Darcy's question was more complicated a task than he normally would attempt at that hour. But, regardless of the circumstances, Whit still never knew how to tell the story. *Should I start with a protestation of Pop's innocence, or by telling her about the crooked judges and fat-cat bankers who went after him?*

He told her about Pop's heated argument with his partner Garrett Jones, which ended with Pop storming out of Jones's house. The following night, the Firesons—minus Jason, who was off bootlegging then— had visited June and Joe for one of the boys' birthday. The cake had barely been cut when Pop excused himself, saying he needed to visit one of his stores. It was a Sunday, Whit remembered, so the store was closed, but Pop's departure wasn't so unusual then; he'd been spending countless, desperate hours at work, as if he could devise a solution to this disaster. As if the clockwork devices bent on destroying him had not already been set in motion.

When Whit, Weston, and Ma returned home, Pop still wasn't in. Everyone went to bed, waking the next morning to find Pop and Jason drinking coffee downstairs. Apparently Jason had driven to town for a surprise visit the night before, arriving just as Pop had returned from the store. Jason didn't often visit home, and, seeing that Pop was blue, he had taken him to catch some boxing matches downtown. Jason said that Pop had begged off, claiming he had too much work to do, but Jason had insisted the old man join him for a few fights. They wound up watching the full card, and weren't home until midnight.

The following afternoon the Firesons heard, through mutual friends, that Jones was dead, an apparent suicide the night before. Jason stayed in Lincoln City less than twenty-four hours before heading back to his "delivery work." He was gone when, late that night, the police arrived to arrest Pop.

Whit didn't go into much detail about that night or the subsequent trial, in which several prominent businessmen—all friends of the wealthy Jones—had clearly wanted to railroad Pop. All those bankers and speculators who would benefit from Pop's finances collapsing like this, all those vultures attacking at last. Jason had been Pop's alibi, as they'd been watching a local welterweight trounce a rival when Jones took his own life. But by the time of the trial, Jason was in jail again, on his second bootlegging rap, so he was shuttled under guard to the Lincoln City courthouse to give his testimony. Several character witnesses vouched for Pop, saying he was the most levelheaded guy around—a proud member of the local Boosters Club, a regular at weekly Mass, and quite simply the type of person who was constitutionally unable to raise a hand in anger.

Mrs. Jones took the stand and told her story of the second-to-last night of her husband's life, when Pop had pleaded for a loan and allegedly had threatened Jones when rebuffed. But she had no evidence, nor did she have any evidence that Pop had returned the following night—and why would he have? The only "evidence" at all was that Jones hadn't left his prints on the gun he'd shot himself with, but the defense attorney even got an expert to admit that fingerprinting was hardly an exact science.

The Firesons had been stunned when the jury voted to convict. Had the jurors even been listening? Had they been paid off? What kind of court was this? Pop's lawyer had vowed to file an appeal. But with what money?

Patrick Fireson's sentence had barely started when his heart gave up.

"It all just . . . made no sense. Like the whole world had been turned upside down. Crooked bankers are running around with people's life savings in their pockets, and here a decent, hardworking guy like Pop gets pinned for something he didn't do."

Darcy was staring at her hands.

"I suppose I can see why Jason didn't tell you," Whit said, though he felt differently. "It's not the sunniest subject to bring up."

"I'm sorry I made you tell me. Now you'll be the one having trouble sleeping."

"It's given me trouble for a while now. Telling it one more time doesn't make it any worse."

Whit could hear Veronica humming a lullaby. He told Darcy he should be getting back to bed. He could have asked Jason, the next day, why he'd never told Darcy. But instead, that became just one more thing the brothers never talked about.

The more time passed, the more Whit began to wonder what Jason's reasons might be for keeping so silent about Pop. And as the legends of the Firefly Brothers spread, and different stories were passed around, there was one that caught Whit's attention. He read it in a newspaper, not long after his talk with Darcy. With Jason allegedly responsible for so many murders during his bank robberies, the columnist wondered if it was possible that Jason's killing ways had actually begun a few years earlier. The reporter then told the story of Garrett Jones's death and posed a question. What if young Jason Fireson, at the time only a bootlegger, had taken it upon himself to come to his family's aid by forcing Mr. Jones to pay up? What if *Jason* had been the one who sneaked into the banker's house that night, maybe not with murderous intent but with some equally strong-armed, ill-conceived plan, and one thing had led to another, and tempers had been stoked, and then, and then . . . Whit's mind reeled as he read the story. He had never conceived of such an idea before, and he tore the newspaper into shreds as if he could so easily erase such suspicions from the world.

Or from his own mind. The more Whit thought about that awful story—and the more variations of it he heard spoken aloud, sometimes by awestruck accomplices, sometimes by men on the street—the easier it was to imagine Jason in that situation. To daringly swoop by Jones's house like that, to think that he was helping the family, to think he could play the role of hero so easily—it certainly sounded like Jason's style. It also would explain Jason's anger and evasiveness whenever someone talked about Pop or the trial. But if that was indeed how it happened, then surely Jason would have stood tall and admitted it, surely he never would have let Pop take the fall for him.

It made Whit sick to think of it. He only wanted to hear from Jason that it wasn't true. But every time he thought of asking his brother a coldness descended upon him, a whitening fear of what the answer might be, of what truth might be hiding behind that story.

The brothers traded shifts through the night and reached Sedalia, Missouri, the morning after talking to Brickbat's mother. Lies to a kind and trusting man at the post office won them the former address of the incarcerated Sanders brother. It was a large two-story house, set a good hundred yards from the road. A semicircular gravel driveway extended like a frown to its front porch. The front lawn was untended, the farmland yellow and desiccated. No cars were visible, but the barn doors were closed and the gravel in the drive appeared to be furrowed by recent passage.

Whit was at the wheel of their most recently stolen vehicle, a black Terraplane not unlike the one they'd driven before their first death. After crossing the Missouri border the previous night, they'd traded cars on the off chance the old bat had called the cops and recorded their tag numbers.

Whit drove by the farmhouse as slowly as he could without seeming suspicious. Jason scanned the empty acreage behind the buildings, half a mile of fallow farmland before some woods cropped up in the distance.

"Curtains are drawn on a hot day," he noted. "And the windows are open."

The country road was a long spoke off the local thruway that led to a distant hamlet and the few farms between. After driving on for two minutes, Whit turned around and made a second pass. This time Jason saw a lone figure standing behind the house, with his back to it, and close enough to the building that he was shielded from the road—unless a passerby was very persistently studying the area. The figure, standing in a bored smoker's pose, wore dark pants and an undershirt crisscrossed with the leather slashes of what appeared to be a shoulder holster.

The brothers drove past the next town and stopped for lunch ten miles later at the one after that. They had hours before nightfall to form a plan, as if all that time would allow them to come up with any better options than the very simple one they were already considering.

XX.

It was hot that night and the mosquitoes were ravenous. The droning of crickets was occasionally interrupted by what might have been coyotes or lost dogs crying for their masters.

The grass was too dry for Jason and Whit to walk silently, but they did the best they could. They were in a small grove of elms that extended a few hundred yards, ending at what was likely the Sanders property line. They stood there and saw the building's faint outline in the escaping twilight, as well as a few hints of illumination from where drawn curtains didn't quite meet. There was a light breeze and they smelled tobacco and a coal stove.

They waited among the trees, sometimes hearing raised voices, though none female. Supposedly a woman and her daughter lived here, but there were no sounds of children, nor any of their playthings in the front yard. Jason wondered if Brickbat's sister-in-law and niece had already fled the place, or if the thugs had shooed them away or worse.

The brothers decided it would be best to corner one of the kidnappers coming or going rather than storming the building when at full capacity. It would need to happen far enough away so as not to be overheard at the house. They turned and walked back to the Terraplane, which they had parked unseen from the road.

They armored themselves with bulletproof vests once again, though not without a sense of foreboding irony. Each had an automatic pistol in a shoulder holster; each held a Thompson across his chest with two hands. Their pockets were stuffed with extra clips for the pistols, but they would have to be sparing with the submachine guns. They had hidden the briefcase of cash under the driver's seat.

They took turns on watch, one resting at the base of the tree while the other stood to guard against sleep. The sky was starless and Jason didn't have enough light to check the pocket watch he'd forgotten to return to Marriner. He could have used a smoke but he didn't want to risk being spotted.

Jason figured it was past midnight when he heard the car suddenly near them. He was startled—he hadn't heard the driver's doors shut, hadn't heard or seen the car approaching. One moment the world was empty but for the two of them, and suddenly headlights were hurtling toward them.

Jason kicked Whit awake and rushed into the road, aiming his Thompson an inch above the headlights. After so much silence, it was hard to tell if the car's braking sounded loud only to him or if someone in the house might have been able to hear it, too.

The car, a Chrysler coupe, had barely stopped when a bleary-eyed Whit stepped forward, aiming his Thompson at the open passenger window. Two men sat in front. Jason told them to kill the lights, put the car in park, and step out without shutting the doors.

The men wore work clothes, denim pants and gray cotton shirts unbuttoned at the collars. Either they had little money or they were trying to disguise themselves as working stiffs as they drove into Chicago to post their latest instructions to Jasper Windham. One of them looked like a Norwegian just off the boat, blond hair and angular jawbones and ropy limbs. The other was heavier and had a face that reminded Jason that men are descended from apes.

Jason frisked them. Each carried a gat in his pants pocket, one a Luger and the other a revolver. Jason checked that they were loaded, added them to his own arsenal, then opened the glove box and made sure there were no hidden compartments beneath the floorboards. There were, but all he found was a stack of license plates. In the trunk was a sack of clothing.

"How many more men in the house?"

"Five," the primate said.

Then the blond rushed in with, "She ain't in there anymore—we let her go."

"Sure you did. I'll bet you're driving to the papers now to tell them the good news."

"I swear, she's just—"

Jason flipped the Thompson in his hands and smashed at the man's mouth with the handle. The guy crumpled. After a few seconds he sat up, leaning against the car and collecting teeth with his hands. Jason knelt down and pressed the Thompson's butt against the man's chest.

"The only reason I'm not pumping you now is because your buddies would hear the shots. Open your mouth again and I might as well do it anyway."

Then Jason stood, telling them to do the same. Whit got into the coupe, softly shutting its doors, and guided it into the woods where they'd stashed their other stolen car. Jason marched the captive kidnappers alongside the coupe, and when Whit shut off the engine he had one man lie down on the front seat and the other in back. Jason found some socks in the trunk and stuffed them into the men's mouths. With rope he'd bought that day, he tied makeshift gags and hog-tied the men's feet to their wrists.

Before gagging the primate, Jason asked, "Anybody keeping watch at night?"

"Not tonight."

"Guys sleep upstairs or down?"

"Three in the bedrooms upstairs, two more in the parlor."

"You keep Darcy on the second floor?"

The man seemed to consider this. "Yeah. Back bedroom, top of the stairs."

The guy in the backseat moaned something.

"I bet your boys have a lot of guns in there."

"They do."

"Bet they'll be awful ticked at you if we shoot some of 'em up. If me and my brother don't live to see morning, they'll come out here and plug you for messing their works."

The guy didn't say anything. Jason fastened the gag.

"So you'd better hope we come out of this alive and in no mood for more shooting. Then you might live to see prison."

The brothers rolled the windows up, then closed the doors. Jason handed Whit the Luger he'd procured from their captives, keeping the revolver in his pocket. A rift in the clouds like a celestial quake revealed a thin line of stars, that tiny amount of light helpful as the brothers crossed through the woods.

"So," Whit said in a whisper, "the worst that can happen to us is what's already happened, right?"

"Let's hope so."

"And we walked away from that just fine. Twice. So, really, there's nothing to worry about, huh?"

"Are you trying to talk yourself into this, or out of it?"

But even Jason was sweating beneath his heavy vest. He hadn't been nervous before an endeavor in quite some time, but this was something different. They should have made Marriner come with them, or Owney. They were two against five, if the ape was telling the truth. Apart from this strange magic they seemed to be carrying inside them, their only allies would be the element of surprise and their adversaries' midnight grogginess. Jason was accustomed to being on the side of superior man- and firepower, and even then he'd raided only banks whose floor plans he had memorized. He knew that he had killed people, but he preferred to think of those events as accidents, or as awful decisions that were necessary for his survival. Tonight, however, they would need to be quick and shoot anything that moved. Unless it was Darcy. Hopefully she was alone in her room. Hopefully the kidnappers would be too busy scrambling to think of using her as a human shield or a bargaining chip. Hopefully this wasn't a very bad idea.

They emerged from the trees and the farmhouse was before them, no lights in the windows, no sound but the crickets.

Jason stepped onto the old wooden porch first, trying to will his body into lightness. He hadn't yet put his hand on the screen door when whichever plank Whit was standing on groaned. Jason pulled at the screen door's handle, held the screen open with his back, then tried the knob of the wooden door. Unlocked. Thank you, boys.

It was the kind of door that liked to announce it was being opened.

Jason tried it slowly, but that only made it worse, so he swung it the rest of the way. His night vision was sharp enough now to tell him this was the kitchen. It smelled like things unwashed. That probably confirmed Darcy as the only woman in the place. Jason could hear snoring from close by.

Floorboards groaned again, but this wasn't Whit. Someone was moving upstairs. Ahead of Jason and to his left, a sliver of light fell from above, down a stairway. Forms slowly took shape.

"What the hell!" A man upstairs, screaming. "What the *hell!*" A man who sounded like Brickbat Sanders.

Then rustling from the shadows and the room exploded with light from a lamp. The guy who'd pulled the cord was sprawled on a couch six feet in front of Jason. Without thinking, Jason offered an explosion of sound to match the light.

The figure danced and threw violent new colors on the dull palette before him, and then the lamp shattered. Now the only light was that coming from Jason's barrel, and he spied more motion to the left. Before he could turn that way, Whit fired, too.

More light fell down the stairway. Feet were pounding upstairs.

Jason remembered how few Thompson rounds he had and stopped firing at the man on the couch. Stuffing was floating in the air like clouds.

Whit fired another burst at the corner around which a second man had disappeared. Plaster spat onto the floor.

Two flashes of light sneaked around that wall. Jason didn't hear the pistol shots until he felt them. Invisible nails hammered his back to the wall behind him.

Whit fired again and the kidnapper's hand and pistol disappeared.

Jason stayed nailed to the wall for an extra second, then slid down. His collapsed lungs tried to expand and he doubled over in a coughing fit. It felt as if the nails were still inside him, but he told himself they couldn't be. The day someone invented a bulletproof vest that didn't still hurt like hell when you took rounds in the chest would be a very good day indeed. He forced himself to sit up and made sure the Thompson was still in his hands.

A squat body and a submachine gun appeared at the top of the stairs. Jason remembered how to move just in time. Wood slivers dug into his hair as he fell forward and rolled out of the shooter's range.

Whit hurried to the corner that the other downstairs sleeper had raced behind. His Thompson had nearly torn all the plaster from the wall, revealing the ancient wood studs and the metal piping. Blood on the far wall told him his bullets had worked through the corner and found their target. He heard panting and fired through the corner wall again. The body that had been hiding there lost its fight with gravity. It fell facefirst, long limbs and jet-black hair that Whit figured for Elton Roberts. One of his hands held an automatic pistol, but Whit didn't have any extra pockets so he let the corpse keep it.

Whit's ears were ringing and cordite burned his nostrils. The shattered walls seemed to be releasing the scent of the building's past inhabitants, generations of roasts and firewood and hard labor escaping into the humid air. Around the corner was a large dining room, but it was empty of anything but a collapsible table, three chairs, and some playing cards.

In the living room, Jason stood up and trained his weapon at the topmost stair, where the other shooter had been. He sprayed a few rounds to keep the guy off guard. Where the hell was Whit? He heard a cry of pain and the staircase shooter's feet appeared again. One of them wasn't really a foot anymore but a pulpy mess. Jason fired at it and the screams weren't loud enough to be heard above the bucking Thompson. The rest of the man's body slipped down the stairs, presenting larger targets. It finally landed in a heap at the bottom of the stairs, a dead man who had liked to sleep in the nude.

Was that two, or three? Motion again and Jason swung around, nearly pulling the trigger on his brother. They stared at each other, both of them lowering their weapons, and stepped closer. They listened. Floorboards creaked upstairs. Whit pointed his Thompson at the ceiling. A very old ceiling. Cracks of light appearing through weak spots in the wood. Jason read his mind and grabbed Whit's barrel and pulled it down, scalding his hand.

Whit looked at him as if he was crazy.

"You might hit her, too," Jason whispered. Then he shouted into the silence: "Darcy!"

Nothing in return. Not her voice or anyone else's.

Then came shots from the kitchen, an automatic pistol. The brothers ducked. Jesus, maybe there was a second stairwell leading down to the kitchen. They hadn't thought to look for one. From behind a couch Whit poked his Thompson's barrel and fired toward the kitchen until the massive gun clicked. After that instant of silence, the kitchen shooter filled it again. Cushions exploded and Whit flattened himself to the floor.

Jason pressed himself against the wall and silently inched toward the entrance to the kitchen. Then he stepped away and was about to fire when the hand of something very large slapped his back and slammed his chest to the floor. Glass shattering all around him, cutting his neck and ears. After an instant of numbness, his back throbbed.

No.

Someone had leaped outside and gotten him through the windows. With a Thompson. The rounds had pierced his vest and burrowed into his flesh. But how deeply? He tried to inhale. He coughed. He rolled to his side. From across the room, Whit was staring at him with wide eyes. Jason coughed and something came out. A different window exploded this time and Whit blindly returned fire with his requisitioned Luger.

No shots for a moment, nothing but ringing ears and the occasional whisper of glass shavings falling from the jamb. Jason couldn't move his right arm. With his left he rolled himself onto his back. It felt as if he'd been impaled; it was as though parts of his insides were fixed in place and wouldn't budge even if the rest of him did. When he tried to move, they sent enraged messages that his brain could only begin to comprehend. Just concentrate on breathing, he thought. He could breathe, but not deeply.

"*Jason,*" Whit whispered. Jason thought about answering but decided it wasn't worth the effort. He sucked his neck into his body so he could stare at the windows through which he'd been shot.

Jason reminded himself that this didn't matter. He would walk away from this. He would be whole tomorrow. He repeated this in his mind, an endless mantra, while his body, unconvinced, did what it could to get the hell out of there.

He'd dropped the Thompson, so he took the stolen revolver from his left pants pocket and pointed it at the shattered windows. The automatic in his shoulder holster would have been better, but with his dead right arm it was unreachable. Compared with the Thompson, the revolver felt so light, as if his arm were floating upward, which was when he started wondering if he was about to pass out.

He dared to turn his head to the left, away from the kitchen and toward his brother. It was as if he had known what was coming, because as soon as he saw Whit—sitting there with his back against the wall, behind the ravaged couch and beside the stripped corner wall—someone stepped around that corner. Jason opened his mouth to warn Whit but only blood came out. He also aimed with his revolver. Whit saw his brother's gun pointed at him and his eyes scrunched in confused terror, but before he could respond Brickbat Sanders was in front of him. In Brickbat's right hand a Thompson was pointed at the ceiling. In his left was an automatic pistol. Brickbat reached toward Whit's head, and when Whit finally felt his presence and turned to face him Brickbat pressed the barrel of his pistol into Whit's forehead and killed him.

Jason's finger finally understood that it should be squeezing. His mouth opened weakly and his pistol screamed twice as loud to compensate. Brickbat leaped behind the corner again, too quickly for Jason to know if he'd been hit.

Somehow Jason sat up. He kept firing the revolver until its little merry-go-round was horseless. He tried to walk to the stairs but his legs didn't work. He dragged himself with his one good arm. He dared to look at Whit, but all he saw was a body, like the others. Sitting against the wall, the shoulders erect but the head leaning forward at such a sharp angle that at first it looked as if he'd been decapitated. There was a large circle of blood on the wall at what should have been eye level.

Jason again reminded himself that this didn't matter. What he had just seen happen to his brother didn't matter. His own pain and imminent death didn't matter. They would both wake up again tomorrow, surely. He was losing his mind.

He made it to the stairs. He crawled past the naked corpse. Still no sounds from the kitchen, so either that guy, too, was dead or he'd lammed off.

Jason tried to scream Darcy's name again but he had no voice. His voice was dead. So was most of his body.

He looked behind him to see if Brickbat was following. He didn't see anything or anyone alive. At the other end of the room was a pool of blood from his own mauled back.

He was so, so thirsty. He was sweating as if the building were on fire, and he was pretty sure he'd soiled his pants.

It actually got easier to crawl up the stairs once he managed some momentum.

So much brighter up there, a naked bulb dangling in the second-floor hallway, tracing an arc in the air as if the gunfire had shaken the whole house. Jason paused for a few labored breaths, then crawled toward the nearest door. He told himself again that this was not a problem. Death was not a problem. It was life that was so damn confusing.

His left palm was slick with sweat and it was difficult to pull the rest of him after it. The hand seemed the only part of him that was working correctly. He admired its tirelessness. Maybe the rest of him had been like that, too, once. Up until only a few minutes ago. Now the left hand seemed ashamed of the rest of Jason Fireson and was trying to get as far away from all this dead weight as it could. Yet the dead weight followed, as it always did.

He was in a small bedroom containing an old chaise in place of a bed. There was an end table in the corner and upon it sat an unshaded lamp that provided the room with its meager light. A thick chain lay in the center of the room, coiled around a two-foot metal base pinned down by what looked like barbells. His left hand reached forward again to pull, but it landed on something. The hand grabbed the something and wandered back to Jason's face, opening up to present its finding. It was gold and thin, with a red stone hanging from it. It was an earring. Jason had bought it himself.

The stairs groaned. Jason's left hand closed to a fist around the earring. He turned his head. The light from the lamp illuminated the imposing figure of Brickbat Sanders, a big gun in one hand and a small one in the other, a homicidal fiddler crab.

Brickbat grunted as he lowered himself, sitting on the floor a few feet from Jason. He rested the Thompson on his lap but held on to the automatic. Either he'd been sleeping in his dark slacks and shoes or he had found the time to put them on during the attack. Apart from that, Brickbat wore only a sleeveless undershirt. Pomade and a pillow had sculpted his blond hair into a violent wave. One of his shoulders was bleeding, but so little that Jason was envious.

"Well, you got me with one, Jason," his voice hoarse, his breath labored. "But I got you a lot worse."

Brickbat's automatic was so silver you could melt it into bars and make a fortune. It gleamed in the light.

"I was thinking I'd give you one more, right between the eyes like that idiot brother of yours. But you know what? I think it'll be more fun to just watch it happen, real slow."

He was no more than five feet away. Jason wanted to drive his foot through that ugly mug, but no single part of his body was obeying his commands. Even the left hand had turned mutinous. He was still breathing, and his heart was still beating, but that had nothing to do with him anymore.

"Take your time," Brickbat said, smiling. And Jason did.

THE THIRD DEATH
OF THE
FIREFLY BROTHERS

As more time passed and the official line on the Firefly Brothers became less believable, an equally absurd list of deeds and misdeeds were attributed to the outlaws, dead or not. The brothers had been endowed with supernatural powers, people told me, divine abilities. Calls came in from parents claiming the Firesons had visited them at night and cured their sick children. Formerly dry cows were producing milk again on farms where the Firefly Brothers had allegedly hid. A family in Kansas claimed that an elderly relative had died one night but that the Firesons had stopped by for dinner, and after their departure the old-timer had risen from his deathbed demanding steak and potatoes. Destitute families found bricks of hundred-dollar bills stashed beneath rocks at the periphery of their property lines, or hidden in decaying fences, or sitting beneath their bedframes, the mornings after they'd had vivid dreams about the brothers.

Across the country, newspaper editors debated the merits of sensationalism versus missing the story of a lifetime. Police officers didn't know whether to doubt their panicked constituents' stories, or their superiors' rational explanations, or their own eyes.

In Kansas City, three municipal employees who had been pilfering from a food bank were found shot to death; hungry witnesses claimed the Firefly Brothers had avenged them. The city of Toledo suffered an all-night power outage that began only moments after a telephone-line repairman had seen the Firesons driving into town. *Several reports out of Lincoln City claimed that mysterious fires had been lit on the surrounding hilltops, a spectacle beheld by thousands, but by the time firefighters reached those outposts there were neither flames nor ashes nor embers to welcome them. Rallies and marches had turned violent in Akron, Grand Rapids, Pittsburgh, and Omaha after the Firefly Brothers, rumored to be appearing, were no-shows. Governors' mansions in Ohio, Indiana, and Illinois were being patrolled by the National Guard after the chief executives received death threats allegedly signed by the Firefly Brothers, and citizens' militias were patrolling the streets outside dozens of the Midwest's largest banks.*

There was already so much in the world to be overwhelmed by, to be confused about. I used to think—or hope—that no sane person truly bought those stories but simply had fun telling them. It was a parlor game, a communal experiment in storytelling, something to pass the time. The whole country was sitting on a rocking chair, spinning a ridiculous yarn. The only true believers, I figured, were the pathetic, the depressed. Those unfortunate souls who were already unhinged by mental illness or who had become so by the hard times—the ones who had lost sight of anything else to believe in.

I would soon learn otherwise.

XXI.

Darcy had been woken by a voice whispering in her ear, so close the lips grazed the earring that had been hanging from her lobe for longer than she could remember. She'd been dreaming of lips, but not these.

"Wake up, miss. Don't say a word. Time to go."

She could feel and hear Rufus fumbling with the chain that connected her handcuffs to the mystery anchor in the center of the room. She felt a sudden slackening and inhaled deeply.

She whispered, "What about the handcuffs?"

"I don't have the key, and the guy that does won't be interested in handing 'em over."

"My eyes—"

"The goggles stay on for now. No more talking or I'll change my mind."

A large hand gripping both of hers. The crickets told her it was night. The lack of other sounds told her they were the only two awake.

He pulled her behind him. The floorboards were silent beneath his feet but piano keys beneath hers; he seemed to know the lucky spots, but in her blindness she was missing them. Twice her feet struck low notes and Rufus stopped, tensing to hear if anyone might stir at the sound. Then onward. It felt so strange to move forward, this linear trajectory so unlike the circles she had orbited around her anchor these many days. Her heels seemed curved from her detention, her body stubbornly listing fore and aft.

"Stairs," he warned in a whisper. She was disconcerted at how off balance she felt. Blind and bound, she could feel the universe shifting and spinning, gravity pulling at more directions than made sense, and she feared she was on the verge of falling. She thought of all the things Jason had escaped from and told herself that surely some of his magic had rubbed off on her.

Once they reached the first floor, Rufus seemed to feel a surge of confidence, or perhaps desperation. Her hands were yanked farther from her body and she raced to catch up. She heard the muted sifting of air through a screen door and suddenly she was outside. The creaking of a porch, but this time he didn't stiffen or stop, and instead forgot to warn her of more stairs. Her right foot swung up into the void, the heel landing too hard on a lower step. Rufus! She wanted to yell at him but her jaw snapped shut when it hit against something, his shoulder perhaps, and before she could fall to the ground she felt hands clamping at her sides. The palms and fingertips seemed to linger at her waist as he righted her.

Rufus hadn't told her freedom was coming, though she, of course, had hoped for it. Confused and half-asleep, she was responding to it as best she could.

She heard an engine purr to life. A door quietly announced itself as the driver emerged, the molars of a gravel driveway grinding against one another as he walked toward them.

"All right," Rufus's nameless conspirator said. "Point her and let's go."

Rufus's hands were on her shoulders now, and they rotated her to the right.

"When I let go, miss, you start walking forward. Once you hear us driving away, you can take off the goggles."

"But not before then," Nameless reiterated in a more threatening tone.

"Rufus, you can't expect me to—"

"Lady," Nameless interrupted, "we've put ourselves out for you far enough. Any lip and we'll tie you to the porch for the other guys to find."

"You'll be okay, miss," Rufus said, seemingly regretting his partner's tone. "We're going one way, and you're going another. You just have to walk a few hundred yards to the road."

Darcy breathed for a moment. After days of yearning for freedom, the idea of being separated from Rufus and his calm, sweetly stupid voice was, of all things, terrifying.

"And, uh, I'd appreciate you putting in a good word for me with Jason and Whit."

"I don't even know your name." She almost laughed.

He gently squeezed one of her hands in lieu of a farewell. Then the gravel munching again, and two car doors closing so quietly it seemed the vehicle itself was holding its breath.

Darcy felt paralyzed, the removal of one cage leading only to the imposition of a more psychological one. The sudden availability of options befuddled her.

The car pulled away. *Go,* she told herself. Hesitantly she stepped one foot forward, then the next. The sky did not collapse upon her. Alarms did not sound. She did not wake on the chaise bathed in sweat. So, more steps, and faster. The dizziness she'd felt on the stairway was magnified, the frightening emptiness around her combining with her blindness. She let the fear power her forward, and soon she was running.

She had never been terribly agile, and days of inactivity had turned her leg muscles to tar. She was breathing heavily and already her chest burned—so many insufficient meals had left her half-starved and listless. She wanted to lie down. The earth felt so soft beneath her feet.

No—run, faster. Her gait was awkward with her cuffed hands, not to mention her narrow dress. Thank God she'd worn flat shoes, though they were nearly slipping from her heels. Mosquitoes pinched at her ankles and calves, a swarm of them. Or was that dry grass?

The car was gone now—she could remove the goggles. Hallelujah. The width of her handcuffs was less than that of her skull, so she needed to attend to one side of the goggles at a time. She slid her fingers beneath the elastic on the left and pulled up, pain flooding the softness above her ear as the vise was released. She did the same with the other side, dropped the goggles and blinked.

Nothing. Why couldn't she see? Darkness, nighttime, or perhaps only fuzziness, residual loss of sight that would take hours to blink away. She rubbed at her eyes, which hurt. But it seemed to help, a little. Was she crying? *For God's sake, not now, not until you're safe.*

She walked quickly. Her knees twitched and her fingers shook. The palsy of freedom, the terror of choices. Then she fell. She stayed on the ground for a moment, feeling the dryness around her. She seemed to be in a furrow, where once the earth had produced something other than this spiny scrub grass. Mosquitoes continued to have their way with her.

A sound, jarring her. How long had she been lying here? Had she fallen asleep? She realized the sound had been a gunshot only when she heard more of them. Too many to be counted, that crazed rat-a-tat-tat of so much violence in so little time. Finally, she saw light.

So loud and so bright, yet so tiny. Her mind was having trouble decoding messages. Bursts of brightness from a house in the distance, like lightning, as if that one building contained its own weather system, powerful and angry yet dwarfed by the vastness of the dark sky above.

Could they see her from here? Were the shots flares to snuff her out? No, they were too chaotic. They had found Rufus and his friend, perhaps, and were doling our punishment. Or, Lord, they were fighting with one another; they had discovered her absence and were distributing blame. Which meant they soon would be searching for her. The shots ceased.

Darcy stood up and ran, almost wishing the shots would return to illuminate her path. Rufus had said there was a road not far from here, hadn't he? Had she veered off the intended trail? She ran until her body was shaking again. She would have sprinted for hours, she would have flown into the air, if only such things were possible. How deathly simple the world was. How uninspired. She was going to pass out again.

But first a form before her. Scraps and slivers of the darkness seemed to thicken and solidify into three dimensions. She walked forward and the darkness shifted before her, but that thing was still there in the middle. She touched it: an automobile. Cold in the thick air. Darcy circumnavigated the car but found no road. The car had been abandoned in the middle of the field, as lost and forlorn as herself.

She tried to control her breathing and listened. No sounds of pursuers.

And if she had possessed the capacity for rational thought—Lord, that had passed days ago—perhaps she would not have opened the car door and slumped inside. Perhaps she would not have closed the door as loudly as she did. Perhaps she would have kept running. But she could feel wakefulness fleeing her. She needed only to lie down, just for a moment, on the cool upholstery, and feel the way it crumpled beneath the awesome weight of her heavy, heavy head.

They had come so close to escaping from this life, she and Jason. Surely every thief or shyster or flimflam man entertained notions of escape or retirement or living the good life. Such ideas were likely half-baked and ridiculous, but surely Jason was different. She'd always figured he had some master plan.

He had hid in Darcy's apartment for two weeks back in April, staying inside all day and most nights. They passed hours reading the papers as they lay in bed. They read about Dillinger's and Baby Face Nelson's miraculous escape from a surrounded lodge up in Wisconsin, Clyde Barrow being riddled by bullets from a former Texas Ranger in Louisiana, and of course the miscellaneous villainy attributed to Jason and Whit. As a result of all the attention, the gang had temporarily split up, Jason told her, and he was weighing his options.

"Maybe it's time to stop," she said.

"Stop what?"

"This, everything. The banks and the accomplices and the *endeavors.*"

"Stop us, too?"

She jolted as if slapped. "Darling, no. Everything but *that.*" She slid an arm through his, put her hand on his waist. "The point of stopping all the rest is so we can hold on to each other."

"What would you do?" he asked her.

"What do you mean, what would I do? I would be with you."

"Just like that? You're used to a certain lifestyle, Darcy, and if—"

"I've told you I don't care about money. I *left* money, and happily so. Why do you have so much trouble understanding that?"

"Okay. But you've always seen me as the guy calling the shots. If I were to leave the one thing I know, it'd be different."

"Jason, it was never your being a thief or ringleader that won me."

"But imagine me digging ditches or turning screws. Would you still see this great unnameable *something* in me if I was following someone else's orders, coming home angry every night?"

"Yes. You'd be a good deal sweatier, of course, but yes. Emphatically yes."

She kissed him. It was a good kiss. It meant what it said. Why didn't he seem to believe her?

Then she tilted her eyes at him and pinched his side. "So, Mr. Fireson, what would *you* do if you settled down? Do you have a plan?"

"Move to California, open a restaurant. Plant a vineyard. Watch the sunset."

"It would be *wonderful* to be a restaurant owner's wife." She hugged him tighter. "I would greet the guests at the door, and pour the wine. . . . But who would cook?"

"I'd hire someone eventually, but at first it'd be me."

She was unable to suppress a laugh.

"What?"

"Nothing, I'm just . . . surprised."

"Does it seem too . . . *common* a career option after robbing banks?"

"I've never said I'm against being common."

"Can *you* be common?"

"Never." She laughed. "A common career sounds wonderful. A common wife, however—that would be dreadful. You wouldn't want that."

"No."

"Jason Fireson, you are"—and she kissed him—"*exceptional.*"

———

This time it was coughing that woke her. She had been dreaming about Jason; they had just lain down in one of their many bedrooms. But he hadn't really been there, for this was a car seat she was waking on, not a bed.

She opened her eyes. They seemed to be working better. Sunlight was glowing against the top of the seat, so much brilliance that the excess spilled down, illuminating the steering wheel by her head and the floorboards below. Almost blinding, yet barely dawn.

More coughs. She sat up and squinted, staring through the windshield and straight into a sunrise that could not possibly be that bright. As if the sun were no farther away than the next state, melting its way through the

Midwest. In minutes she would be consumed. She shielded her eyes and saw a silhouette stumbling toward her, a stencil of blackness carved from the night and accidentally abandoned to the dawn, its movements frantic. Then he was opening the passenger door.

He was hatless, which was a shame, because this was a face best kept in shadow. The nose as fat and scalloped as a cocktail glass. The green eyes sinking into his shiny cheeks, which seemed to inflate with each inhalation. Though his dark jacket matched his trousers, he wore only an undershirt beneath it. The undershirt was white in places and red in others. He was holding a silver automatic in his right hand.

"Hello there, kitten." He sat beside her, panting. "Sorry to disturb you."

Darcy accepted the fact that her dream had vanished. She accepted the world that was presented to her, currently starring Brickbat Sanders as the man in shotgun.

"I wouldn't call you *disturbing*, exactly. More annoying, irritating."

"Well, I hope to graduate to disturbing one day."

"It would be your first graduation, no doubt."

He looked exhausted and he breathed in impatient gulps, as if the world could not satiate him. "Got any keys?"

"I wouldn't be sitting here if I did." She wondered if he was tired or injured enough for her to wrest the gun from his grip. Brickbat's hands were freakishly large—thick mitts with wide, stubby fingers, barely prehensile. She once had found herself staring at them, wondering how the man tied his shoes. "I'm not surprised to see you're behind this."

"I wouldn't say I'm *behind* it. You'd get a real kick out of it if you found out who is."

This was one of the longest conversations she'd had with him. He had been an unfortunate part of Jason's gang for two months, perhaps three. He had ogled her with craven obviousness since the day they met. He seemed rather disinterested in her rank, unshowered body at this moment, however.

"You seem a bit worse for wear," she observed. "Did you have a fight with your gentlemen friends?"

"Not mine. Yours."

"I'm sorry?"

Still panting, he managed to purse his lips enough to grin. "You know, I didn't believe those stories myself, but turns out they were true. Don't know how Jason and Whit pulled it off, but there they were last night, very much alive. And now they're very much dead."

"What . . . what are you talking about?"

"Don't go all Niagara on me, kitten. You should be over that by now."

She straightened up. She hadn't had enough sleep or food to generate panic. She repeated herself, but much more quietly this time. "What are you talking about?"

"They came for you last night. Raised a fair amount of hell doing it. Let's just say I'll be getting a much bigger percentage of the ransom money now." He chuckled, but it seemed to pain him and he recoiled. "I told that son of a bitch Whit that one day I'd put one between his eyes, and I did. Jason took a little longer to go, though."

She turned from him and looked out the driver's window. The sun was just the slightest bit higher now and she could see the world before her, the fields tan and dry and helpless.

"They aren't the ones who freed me last night. Your own cohorts did, and—"

"Yeah, I've figured that much out by now, thanks." He inspected the glove box. "But then your boys came in. They shot the place up, but I rubbed them myself. Watched your boy sputter and moan right in front of me. For maybe an hour, until he was done. That was time I shoulda been spending looking for you, kitten, but I couldn't help myself. Just had to see it with my own eyes. And it turns out I found you after all."

"I don't believe you."

"Fine. I don't care." Then he reached into his jacket pocket and removed a flask. He took a snort and put it back. "People die terribly, kitten. They cough out all this stuff that's supposed to be inside them, like they're being turned inside out. They move and twitch in ways you'd never imagine. Couldn't imitate it if I tried."

"You will one day."

He chuckled again. "Yeah, guess I will. But not as soon as you'd like. Brickbat ain't as bad off as he looks, and he knows a doc in these parts can help him out." He opened his door. "Gonna fiddle with the engine. Try to run and I'll shoot your knees."

Darcy hugged herself. Surely Brickbat was only taunting her, trying to level her into shock, keep her docile. Surely Rufus hadn't released her only moments before Jason and Whit arrived for her. She was so tired and sore, her neck stiff, her ankles aching from myriad scrapes and insect bites, the skin of her wrists torn by the cuffs. She wasn't thinking straight. She needed only to be free of this man, and then in a real bed, and she would make sense of this.

The light on her world turned less harsh as Brickbat raised the hood. A minute later the engine kicked into life, and she jumped. With the engine on, all she needed to do was floor the gas and run her captor over. But before she'd completed this thought the hood fell with a *whoosh* and a slam and there was Brickbat aiming his automatic at her through the windshield.

"I'd hate to mess that pretty face, kitten." He grinned at her and she was, regrettably, motionless as he walked to the side of the Ford and got back in shotgun. He moved gingerly, or what passed for gingerly in a man of his size. His jacket concealed the source of all that blood; it bore no bullet holes, but it was possible he'd been shot before putting it on. Unless it was someone else's blood and he was only grunting from exhaustion.

"The road's straight ahead a ways," he told her. "Drive."

"I can't shift in handcuffs."

"Good point. Stick 'em out." She hesitantly held her hands up in front of her. He unholstered his pistol, and she was too stunned to say anything or even move her hands as he reached, the gun perfectly level, until the barrel touched the chain between the cuffs. Then he fired. It was the loudest thing she'd ever heard. The bullet escaped through the open window and the casing ricocheted off the ceiling, landing in her lap. Her hands fell there, too, and they flicked away the casing as if it could still hurt her. Brickbat chuckled.

Darcy tried to gather herself as she gripped the wheel, her fingers shaking, the chains dangling musically from her wrists.

The Ford had been sitting there God knows how long and the sounds it emitted were a warning that its resurrection would be brief. She and Brickbat bounced as she drove through the uneven field.

Finally, she could see the road. Brickbat told her to make a right onto it, and once she had he told her to go faster. To his chagrin, the Ford's maximum speed was barely a jog.

"I think you'd best look after yourself alone, Bernard," she said after gathering the composure to speak again. "You might as well admit that your little kidnapping ploy is a failure and run along before things get worse."

"That's so sweet of you to be thinking after my best interests. I appreciate it. But I happen to think it'd be best if I held on to you until I get that ransom from your old man."

"How are you going to do that if you're a one-man operation now?"

He didn't answer. Jason had told her that endeavors turned deadly only when steered by incompetents or by undermanned crews. Brickbat qualified as both.

"About this ransom money, Bernard. My old man isn't that flush. If you think you can siphon two hundred thousand off him, you're bound for disappointment."

He chuckled again. She'd never heard a more odious sound. "Don't worry, kitten."

"I'm quite serious. He's going through hard times as well—relatively speaking, of course, but still, your negotiations will drag on rather longer than either of us would like if—"

"I said not to worry. It's all taken care of. You'll see. Or then again, maybe you won't."

As the sun rose, the sky took on the same scoured, yellowish hue as the earth beneath it. The horizon was blurred, the difference between the two realms invisible or at least meaningless. The farms here looked inactive; she hoped they were, for she would have felt pity for anyone attempting to grow something from such desiccated soil. Already she had passed two abandoned cars and the splayed bodies of three horses. It occurred to her that she hadn't passed anything living.

Jason was still alive. She repeated this to herself, a silent mantra. No matter what false evidence might be presented to her, she would not believe in Jason's death. There were many things you could believe in these days, like all those practitioners of communism and anarchism, the Ouija board enthusiasts and palmists and other bedeviled members of various cults. They sought to impose their bizarre narratives on a world turned even more bizarre, sought to contain the madness with their stories. Here is your villain, here is the obstacle, here is how to be transformed from victim to hero. Everyone frantically searching for a new meaning of life, because only then could you create a meaning for death. Jason was all the meaning she needed, and, she told herself again, he *had* to be alive.

The Ford's pace slowed to more of a canter. Also, it was rather low on gasoline.

"I ain't falling for it, kitten. Speed up."

She tried to accelerate but the Ford refused. Her disbelieving passenger moved toward her, pressing his foot on hers. Hard. Her toes were crushed, but the Ford was only going slower. Despite the pain, she realized Brickbat's gun was closer now; he was holding it with his left hand, which was leaning against the steering wheel as he focused his attention on the accelerator. My, those fingers were large. But they were distracted, and surely he was weak from blood loss, and perhaps . . .

She released the wheel and grabbed the pistol with both hands. Its barrel was pointed out the window and when she tugged the automatic slid from his grasp, but not fully. She couldn't wrench it free. With his other hand he struck her right forearm. He leaned into her with his massive body and the wheel was spun counterclockwise. The Ford veered off the road with an emphatic burst of energy that surely consumed whatever it had left. The tires slid into a ditch, and had the Ford been capable of greater speed its passengers would have been flung through the windshield. Instead they were merely jolted, and the gun was back in Brickbat's mighty hands. It snapped forward and struck her.

Her eyes watered and her hands formed a steeple over her nose. The pain made her inhale sharply and not want to let the air out.

"That wasn't even very hard. The next time will be. In your mouth, taking out some of those pretty white teeth. And then I'll get really mean, understand?"

She nodded, closing her eyes. She heard his door open, and he told her he would flag a ride. She finally let herself breathe. She would not cry. She would not complain. She would see Jason again. And she would certainly get that gun.

They had taken her wristwatch the first night, so she didn't know how long she sat there while Brickbat stood a few feet away, hands in his pockets. Eventually she heard a car approaching. She turned her head to see it, coming from the direction they'd been heading. A maroon DeSoto sedan.

Driving on such a long, straight road, it seemed she heard it for minutes before it finally reached them.

Brickbat moved into the center of the road and as the DeSoto slowed he held out a palm. His other hand was in his pants pocket, where he'd hidden the gun. Darcy thought about honking the horn as a warning to the oblivious driver, but she didn't see how this would help her.

Brickbat strolled to the DeSoto and she could hear him talking to the old man at the wheel. Then Brickbat's pistol introduced itself, silently, the driver raising his hands.

"C'mon out, kitten." She paused a moment, wondering if she had any options, but could find none. Out she went.

Brickbat glanced inside the DeSoto, then checked the glove box and the trunk. "Take shotgun," he told her. "You can drive, old man."

The DeSoto's owner was gaunt but in a regal sort of way. His white hair was carefully parted on the right side and he had intelligent, forceful eyes, like a Civil War general. He wore a tan suit over a white shirt and a blue patterned tie. Detracting somewhat from his formal bearing was the fact that he needed a shave and, from the look of those eyes, a good night's sleep.

Brickbat sat in back, behind Darcy. He told the old man which direction to head and to drive at exactly the speed limit.

Darcy was just noticing something else about the driver's appearance when Brickbat asked, "What happened to your neck, old-timer?"

The skin of the man's face and hands, like Darcy's, was the pale white of one who hires others for their labor, but his neck was red and lashed with abrasions.

"I was hung two days ago. I was killed."

Darcy didn't stir. Brickbat chuckled, then said, "Seems I keep running into dead people. How about that."

Darcy's nose throbbed and she searched the long horizon for evidence of anything in this scorched world that might still be alive.

XXII.

Many things vanished from Agent Cary Delaney's memory the moment Chief Mackinaw hit him with the news: the long drive out to Points North; the clouds of locusts along the horizon; the conversation or lack thereof offered by Buzz Gunnison, the burly agent with him; the nagging fear that he was wasting his time.

All that disappeared when Mackinaw confessed, "The Firefly Brothers were dead when we found them."

Cary sat up. "What?"

Mackinaw rapped his chest twice, pursing his lips to conceal a belch. Points North was farm country, yet the chief had the type of gut one didn't often see on farmers. His head was equally round, and the thin gray hair atop it looked displeased by the heat and by the repeated application and removal of his hat. The small room smelled of tobacco and spit, a map of the county adorning one of the paneled walls.

"I know this looks bad. Things got a bit out of hand, and we just didn't see how—"

"Wait, wait, go back." Cary shook his head. "What happened that night?"

"We received an anonymous call from somebody claiming to've spotted Jason driving into town. It was almost midnight, but the caller said they'd stopped opposite each other at an intersection and his headlights shined right at Jason, said he was sure it was him. When we asked the caller who *he* was, he hung up. So we didn't put much stock in that. A little while later, we got another call from a trusted fellow saying he'd just driven past the abandoned Reston farmhouse and heard something suspicious, like fireworks or tinder popping, maybe squatters starting a fire to cook over. So I sent two officers to check it out." Chest whack, muted burp. "The house is set back a couple hundred yards from a small road. The officers drove up partway, didn't see any auto parked by the house, though they did see fresh tracks in the driveway. Checked out the house through their binoculars, saw that some lights were on in one room. Curtains were parted just enough for the officers to see what looked like a submachine gun lying on top of a table."

"So you sent in the cavalry," Cary said.

"I surrounded the place with eight officers and five volunteer deputies. Called out to the felons on the bullhorn to come out and surrender, but didn't get a reply. No one ever redrew the curtains on that one window, and we never saw movement anywhere. We searched the barn and found a '32 Terraplane, hood still warm, but then it was a hot night, so they could have driven in an hour or two earlier. We honestly weren't sure if they were in the house or not, and we started thinking about how Jason had escaped from that federal ambush in Toledo." Cops loved to bring that up when feds were in the room, Cary had noticed. "Still, we had officers who knew the property and knew there were no secret trails or tunnels. The light that was on never went out, and no others ever went on."

"And eventually you got impatient," Gunnison said. Gunnison was one of Hoover's cowboys, a longtime Tulsa cop the Director had recently lured to the Bureau. A virile forty-three, he had arms that could have snapped the neck of a bull. Cary had nothing in common with him, but he knew that a rural police chief would have laughed at his own, schoolboy attempts at questioning. Gunnison's mere presence in a room was usually enough to conjure information.

"Yes, we got impatient. I'd decided that we'd storm the place within an hour if it came to that, and it did. We fired tear gas at some windows, though, honestly, most of the canisters just bounced off the screens, so we had a big ol' gas cloud funneling at the base of the house. There was no breeze that night, so it kinder just hung there. Fired through the windows with our two submachine guns, and again, no response. Then a team of six went in, followed by another four. We finally found the Firesons in a back room. Whit had taken the one shot to the heart and Jason was riddled pretty good all over the chest."

Surely Cary had misunderstood. "Shot by your men, right?"

"No, it couldn't have been us—we hadn't fired on that room. They'd been dead the whole time."

"So . . . everything in the report, about a gunfight, about your men shooting them . . ."

Mackinaw folded his hands on his desk and looked down at them. "I know this does not reflect well on me or my office. All I can say is, things kinder spiraled out of control there. Everyone was so excited that we'd caught 'em, and they *had* been shot up, and we *were* all carrying guns, and we really did feel like the public deserved some sort of . . . triumph to end the Firefly Brothers story, so—"

"So you lied," Gunnison said in a bored tone. "Lied to the press, lied to police in other towns, lied to the Bureau of Investigation."

"When you put it that way, I know it sounds—"

"Wait, wait," Cary suddenly remembered. "I thought the Firefly Brothers killed one of your officers that night?"

Eyes again on his meaty hands. "Officer Fenton was accidentally struck by a fellow officer's bullet. Like I said, the boys were awful excited, and the lights in the house didn't work, and the layout was different from what our officers had remembered, and all that tear gas, my God. . . ."

"I can't believe this."

"I really don't see any reason why we would need to go public here. Losing their bodies was embarrassing enough."

"It certainly was," Gunnison agreed.

"How long had the brothers been dead when you found them?" Cary asked.

"Maybe a few hours. Could have been right about when the second caller said he'd heard something when he drove by the house. Or maybe a few hours earlier."

"There's no chance that they, I don't know, shot themselves when they realized you'd surrounded them? A suicide pact?"

"No. We never heard a shot."

Suicide would not have been the brothers' style; they would have come out firing even if they were surrounded by a hundred marines. "And the bodies—they were definitely the Firefly Brothers?"

"Of course."

"Chief Mackinaw, I'm sure you've heard some stories circulating that the Firefly Brothers themselves are still circulating out there. Now that you've admitted to . . . all this, I'm wondering why we should believe that you ever had the Firefly Brothers in your custody."

"You can't be serious." This time Mackinaw was the one who seemed shocked. "Look, I know we made some mistakes here, but we had the bodies. We let press come into the morgue and take pictures, for God's sake. Just what are you accusing me of?"

"We certainly wouldn't accuse you of incompetence," Gunnison said.

"Look, it was a madhouse once we made the announcement. Not only were we overrun by reporters from the entire Midwest, but every Tom, Dick, and Harry came by to take their own pictures, snip a locket of hair, shake the dead hands. They call people like that *morbids,* and, God as my witness, I never realized how many morbids we had in this country. We had 'em showing up at the farmhouse so they could dab handkerchiefs in the brothers' blood, tearing the walls apart to fetch bullets. Never seen anything like it."

"It sounds like you did an excellent job of maintaining order," Gunnison said.

"I have thirteen officers under my command, Agent Gunnison, some of 'em part-time. Easily five hundred people came to the morgue in less'n twenty-four hours, and almost that many to the crime scene."

"Well, maybe if you'd involved the Bureau from the beginning we could have been helpful." Cary gave him an icy smile. "Now, let's get back to when you and your officers were heroically storming the building. You find the bodies already dead. Please tell me you at least determined cause of death."

"Shooting, like I said." Mackinaw gave him a look like Cary was the moron here. "Bullets."

"No, I mean who and how, caliber . . ."

"Might have been an accomplice. Or the perpetrators could have gotten there first, laid an ambush. Could have been a prearranged meeting and one side decided to pull a double cross. Whoever shot them was likely a trusted person, given the close-range nature of it all, the perfect shot on Whit. But it's impossible to say."

"So . . . the anonymous caller who said he saw Jason drive into town. You're thinking that was the killer?"

"Probably."

"Surely that wasn't the extent of your investigation."

"Like I said, they'd been dead maybe a few hours. Bodies still warm, but then it was a hell of a hot night. Blood patterns showed they hadn't been moved."

"What kind of weapons had been used?" Gunnison asked. "Had the Firesons drawn their weapons, or did they seem taken by surprise?"

Mackinaw glanced out one of his windows, as if he would much rather be rocking on a porch and complaining to his wife about the needling existence of federal dicks. "The room was filled with firearms, though it's unclear whether the brothers had been holding any when we got there. Again, it was chaotic, and if there *had* been, say, a pistol by one of their hands, one of my men would have moved it."

Cary shook his head—so even before the crime scene had been vandalized by fanatics the police themselves had rendered it useless.

"And we're not entirely sure what kind of bullets killed them."

"Don't tell me you didn't perform an autopsy."

"We did, but the bullets that we removed—"

"They disappeared, too." Cary finished the thought for him, almost laughing. "Of course. The morbids again."

Mackinaw nodded.

"Your report says the bullets taken from the bodies matched your officers' automatic pistols and Thompsons," Cary said. "But at this point I'm assuming that, too, was fiction."

"Is this farmhouse even there anymore," Gunnison asked, "or did a twister take it up the next morning?"

"I acknowledge the fact that we in Points North did not do our jobs as professionally as we could have," Mackinaw said. "No world-famous outlaws had ever visited upon us before."

"Okay, let's talk about money," Cary said.

"Be happy to. Last I checked, you boys still hadn't sent us that reward check."

Cary dead-eyed him. "I meant the Firefly Brothers' money. Your report says they were found with sixty-eight thousand nine hundred two dollars on them?"

"Correct."

"We expected them to have considerably more, judging from their last bank job, so—"

"So this means they laundered the Federal Reserve money and paid a big chunk of it as a launderer's fee."

"That's what we figured, and once you send the money to our headquarters we can confirm it by checking the numbers on the bills. If it's been laundered, maybe we can determine where it came from." Though he knew the odds of such a determination were minuscule. "The way you've been keeping it after all this time, Chief Mackinaw, it's almost like you're holding it hostage."

"I don't care for your putting it that way, son."

"He's not your son," Gunnison snapped. "He's a federal agent, and he, like myself, is tired of spending his time investigating lazy and incompetent cops instead of smart and enterprising criminals."

With that, Cary and Gunnison stood.

"I guess we'll be in touch, Chief Mackinaw," Cary said. "Once we can make sense of all this. In the meantime, try to keep your men from committing any major felonies." They left without shaking the lawman's hand.

XXIII.

Jason opened his eyes and stared into the lidless gaze of an animal almost too ugly to be real. Its bald head lurched to the side, stunned by the sight of moving carrion.

"Beat it." Jason waved at the vulture. He slowly rolled onto his back, then touched his neck and face, glancing at his chest to make sure the vulture hadn't torn off any chunks. The bird paced the room, staying a few feet from Jason but not yet admitting defeat. It squawked in outrage.

It had happened again. He wasn't dead—at least, not anymore.

Jason looked at his left hand and saw that Darcy's earring was impaled in his palm. He pulled the metal hook from his flesh. "Ouch." A prick of fresh blood welled.

He had smelled her when he crawled into this room. Her perfume had been faint, and now he couldn't smell anything but the foulness of death.

He was disgusting. His skin felt like a rubber suit, old sweat congealed and cooled and reheated again. A window was open, and desperate avian hunger had gnawed through the screen, but still the room was hot. It looked midday, the sun too high to be seen, the surroundings bleached and dry. He stood. He had indeed soiled his pants.

Unholstering the automatic he'd been unable to use the night before—at least, it *felt* like it had been only one night—he explored the upstairs. In the other two bedrooms he found some clothes, as well as a

Thompson inexplicably left behind. Some of the clothes were short and squat, undoubtedly belonging to the bastard who'd killed him. But others would fit him well enough.

He heard movement from below. Slowly he walked downstairs, his pistol leading the way. Flies everywhere. The naked dead man at the foot of the stairs was still naked and still dead. Jason stepped around him, carefully avoiding the many puddles and trails of blood, some his own. Through a doorway he peered into the kitchen, where another body lay beneath the table. The house smelled very bad indeed.

The movement had come from dogs. There were three of them, surrounding the man on the couch whom Jason had gunned down first. Jason couldn't see their snouts, but he knew what they were doing. He yelled at them to git. They didn't listen. Looking to his left, he saw Whit's slumped body—head still down, for which Jason was thankful. At least the dogs hadn't gotten to Whit yet. Jason fired into the ceiling and the dogs craned their heads at him, startled but still unmoved. Yelling and stomping like a madman, he chased them from the building. Two of them leaped through the windows Brickbat had shattered, and the third escaped out the kitchen door. Jason took the quickest of glances at the body on the couch, enough to see that the dogs had already done quite a job.

He turned back to his brother and said his name. No reply. He decided he didn't want to look at the face. He crouched before Whit and lifted his body over his shoulder. It didn't feel as stiff as it probably should have, but Jason was no expert. Carefully he carried Whit to a powder room, knocking the toilet seat down with his foot, then leaning forward and lowering Whit onto it. Whit's head flipped back and smacked against the wall. Jason didn't look away fast enough. His brother had been shot in the forehead. The hole was small and round and black, burned by the mouth of Brickbat's gun, and no blood seemed to have escaped from it. It had all come out the back. Jason looked down, then stepped out and carefully closed the door so no hounds or vultures or jackals would be able to nose in and disfigure his brother.

There was a bathroom upstairs. Taking a shower might not have been the wisest use of his time, but he felt too foul not to. And Jason Fireson always did his best thinking when he looked good.

His chest was unmarked, so the vest must have stopped the bullets from exiting his body. But they'd certainly done their damage. He looked over his shoulder to the small mirror and saw the wounds in his back, at least seven of them. They were gaping and strangely black, not just holes but omissions, erasures of his self. He twisted an arm behind his back and touched one, fingering the hardened roll of skin puckering around it.

He dressed in borrowed clothes, keeping only his shoes, the keys to the Terraplane, and his shoulder holster and automatic. Downstairs, the scavengers had not returned, and Whit was still inanimate.

"Hurry the hell up, Whit. I don't want to deal with this by myself."

There appeared to be no logic to their plight: at the Hudson Heights fiasco, Jason had died first, yet Whit had woken first. Now, the opposite. And still he couldn't remember what had killed them the first time. He tried not to think of the possibility that Whit might not awaken, that he might be left to wander these nonsensical badlands alone.

He should have tied Whit to Veronica's bed to prevent his brother from following him this far. Even when Jason tried to do the right thing, to protect those he loved, things only came out wrong. The right thing was confusing, and difficult, and sometimes Jason wondered if it was in fact a nonexistent ideal, like heaven or the American dream. There was no right thing. You did what you did for whatever reasons occurred to you at the time, depending on whichever emotion was running thickest in your blood. Your desire and fear and adrenaline and longing. You made your choice and came up with the reasons later.

———

Not that Jason had much experience trying to do the right thing. He had worked at the family store after his first jail stint, but that hadn't lasted. By the time he left again, he and Pop had achieved an awkward truce; Pop seemed resigned to the fact that Jason was fraternizing with the old troublemakers and returning to past behavior, walking a path that would lead inexorably back to jail.

Still, Jason had been confident he wouldn't get caught again. He was bootlegging, yes, but he was spending more time in the speakeasies and restaurants and less time behind the wheel, all with an eye to learning the restaurant business. Repeal would happen eventually, he figured, and then with the money he'd saved he could open his own, legitimate place.

One night, more than a year later, Jason was between rum runs and had stopped at home for dinner, as he tried to do about once a month. He was struck by how preoccupied Pop had become with the hard times and their impact on his business. The old man had always been consumed by his work, of course, but what before had seemed a healthy, if annoying obsession now looked more like demonic possession or mental illness, the old man frequently muttering to himself during dinner or scribbling notes that he stuffed into his pocket. That night Jason asked if he was all right, and Pop said, Sure, fine.

After dinner Jason and Pop listened to more terrible news on the radio, sipping scotch in the parlor. Pop poured a second, which Jason had never seen him do before, when he turned off the radio. His eyes had turned glassy, and Jason asked again if he was okay.

"Things have gotten . . . a bit out of hand," Pop admitted. "I'm still try-ing to figure it all out myself, to be honest with you." He shook his head.

Finally, he explained how the troubles in Lincoln City were affecting the store. He'd gone in on some real-estate deals just before the crash, but now the construction teams that were supposed to build new housing were pulling out. He was paying steep mortgages for empty land that no one would build on anytime soon, because who could afford to buy or even rent new homes? The new supermarkets were eating into his busi-ness, and, worst of all, the tire factories were so cash-poor they'd started paying their workers in scrip—Pop's registers at the stores were filled with the useless paper, each slip a tiny wish. It was as if his entire life, a series of carefully configured financial transactions, were in fact a set of dominoes ready to tip.

Jason wasn't sure what he was supposed to say. Pop had never been one to unburden himself like this.

"If you need some money, Pop, I've saved a good amount and—"

Pop shook his head, slashed at the air. "Oh, no, Jason, I'm not asking you for money." An awkward laugh.

"I just meant, um, I'd like to help somehow if I can."

"It would be great to have you back at the store."

Jason shifted in his seat. "Ah, Pop, you know I'm no good at that. I'd only make things worse somehow. Better to have Weston and Whit there."

He talked in circles, telling Pop he was sure things would work out.

Ma and his brothers came into the room and they talked about other things. The fear that Pop briefly had revealed now seemed tucked away, and Jason relaxed a bit. Only later would he realize he'd said all the wrong things. Then it was late and Jason was off once more, off to his own life.

Jason would often think about that night, about how things might have turned out if he'd played it differently. Had he really believed that Pop would just figure out a way? Hell, it only made sense that Jason pursue his living the best way he knew how; booze was a far better source of income than helping at the store. Or was Jason so full of pride in his own success that he refused to let himself be tainted by someone else's struggles, even if it was his own family?

Weeks passed, and Jason was too busy to make it back home. He spoke to Ma on the telephone a few times and could hear how concerned she sounded over the family's finances. Pop wasn't telling her everything, he gathered, but she had picked up on enough.

Then one night Jason's own career came close to disaster when a partner drove into a stray cow on a country road outside Dayton. Jason helped the driver load his crates onto his own truck, and they removed the tags from the disabled vehicle, but the farmer who'd emerged from a nearby farmhouse was irate over the loss of his property and further incensed by the smell of booze coming from a busted crate. He'd been running to fetch his shotgun when the bootleggers finally got back on the road.

The thought of returning to jail haunted Jason. He knew the farmer hadn't owned a telephone—he had chosen that road partly because it lacked telephone lines—but he found himself wondering what if this had happened somewhere else. Jason would have been tempted to shoot the man, and that realization haunted him as much as the prospect of jail itself.

Maybe working for Pop again wouldn't be so terrible. He could do it temporarily, share some of his savings with Pop, and put the rest under a mattress. Work just long enough to help Pop get his house in order. Maybe this had been Jason's destiny all along, his blood, and he'd been stubborn to run from it. Maybe he could come home one last time, stay awhile, take Whit and Weston to a few ball games, try to take their minds off their troubles without allowing himself to be dragged into them permanently.

But is that exactly what wound up happening? Had he allowed himself to be dragged back in? The night of his return turned out so very differ-

ently from what he'd imagined. Jesus, all that blood—at the time, he'd
never seen so much. Jason closed his eyes, but the images lingered.

———————————
———————————

He opened his eyes. No sense pondering past problems when new ones
surrounded him.

And so Jason stepped forward and dared to inspect the bodies of the
kidnappers. The one who had tried to hide behind the corner wall was
Elton Roberts. Jason didn't know the naked guy at the foot of the stairs,
but he recognized him from somewhere. The face was white and waxy, the
lips curling into his mouth. The sleeping man on the sofa had lost too
much of his face to be identified. The guy in the kitchen was a stranger.
Jason rifled through pockets and drawers but found no identification or
receipts or letters, nothing with a name.

The two men who'd been leaving the farmhouse in the Chrysler—one
of them had claimed they'd freed Darcy. Had he actually been telling the
truth? That would explain why they had driven off the property so quietly, with their headlights off.

He walked into the kitchen and found the phone; it even had a dial
tone. He dialed Jasper Windham at his office.

The secretary was as excited as ever to be answering the old man's
calls. She put him through to her boss without argument.

"Have you heard from her? Is she okay?" Jason hadn't meant to sound
so panicked.

"Ah, Gabriel. I was beginning to think I'd only imagined your first
call."

Jason exhaled, the hope draining from him. "I lied about my name.
I'm not the archangel Gabriel. I'm Lucifer, and I'm having a very bad day."

"Forgive me if I don't sound sympathetic."

"Has anyone contacted you in the last twenty-four hours?"

"I don't understand who you really are or what games you're trying to
play here, sir. I am doing all that has been asked of me. Funds are being
procured, and unfortunately that takes a bit longer than the mere snapping of my fingers. I would—"

"Shut up a minute. I know the cops have your line wired, so, Hello, boys. Do yourselves a favor and trace this call. You'll find a hell of a scene when you get here. But at least one of them got away, and he must have taken Darcy with him. The guy you want is Brickbat Sanders. It might take him a while to regroup, and he's likely to be very, very angry. I wouldn't be surprised if he winds up asking for more dough, Windham, so brace yourself."

"Ah. So this is just another ploy to get more out of me, is that it? I've told you, sir, that no matter—"

"Damn it, I'm not in on this! You know who I am. And I'm surprised a guy like you would have so much trouble with a few low-life kidnappers—Nitti and his Syndicate pals should be happy to bail you out."

"I'm afraid I don't know what you're trying to hint at, sir, but—"

"I know you haven't had any troubles with the union lately—Mr. Nitti's done a swell job keeping the stiffs in line for you. But I wonder why he isn't helping you track down your daughter?"

"I have nothing to do with Frank Nitti, and I resent the accusation."

"Oh, that's right, this is a party line. I forgot. Wink, wink. Gotta go, you crooked bastard."

He placed the receiver on the table rather than hanging up, assuming this would help the cops run the trace. He wandered onto the porch to escape the old man's voice.

Windham hadn't admitted anything, but his hemming and hawing was enough. With Capone in jail, Frank Nitti controlled the unions and had also involved himself in some of Windham's shadier financial dealings. Brickbat Sanders had once worked for Nitti's chief rival, Tommy O'Neill, before supposedly running afoul of the big man and bolting from Chicago. Some of Nitti's boys had visited Jason in Chicago the previous winter, requesting assurances that Jason wasn't involved with O'Neill's mob and warning him to stay away from Brickbat, whom the Syndicate had targeted for a painful demise. It was that warning, more than Brickbat's penchant for turning endeavors into shootouts, that had been the true impetus for Jason's decision to part ways with him and his pal Roberts. Jason hadn't told anyone about his meeting with Nitti's boys, as he didn't like admitting how terrified he'd been. He scrupulously avoided Chicago bank jobs from then on.

But maybe they had come down on him anyway. A couple of months ago, Chance McGill had warned Jason of rumors that the high price on his head was beginning to entice gangland assassins.

So either Brickbat and Roberts had masterminded Darcy's kidnapping themselves—getting a few lackeys to help snatch Darcy from the very controlled streets of Chicago, at an exact location that few people knew of—or they had received aid from the Mob, likely O'Neill's mob. Was O'Neill using them and Windham as proxies in his war against Nitti? Thinking about all this made Jason's head hurt.

Okay, he told himself, forget the Mob angle for now. Just find Darcy, which meant: find Brickbat. Who had been shot in the shoulder.

Jason walked back inside, hung up the phone, then picked it up again to make another call. It rang and rang. Either the good doctor wasn't in or he was rather busy.

He hung up and checked on Whit again, finding him unchanged. A slab of flesh awaiting a spirit, Frankenstein's monster sans lightning.

Walking through the house, he collected every firearm he could fit into a large canvas case he'd found on the living-room floor. There was little extra ammunition, though—he found only two clips for an automatic and no extra Thompson drums.

Jason stepped outside into another searing day. He'd left his fedora in the Terraplane and he squinted in the sun. He was wearing a white shirt and tan slacks, both of which fit too loosely, but in this weather that wasn't so bad. His black shoes really didn't look right with the slacks.

The empty space behind the farmhouse had nothing in the way of a hiding place except for the barn, so he trudged toward it and opened the side door. Enough light fell through the ceiling cracks and wall slats for him to see a busted old tractor, but little else. He called Darcy's name. Even in desperate times, it was hard to imagine her choosing to hide in a hayloft. It didn't even smell of hay, the contents having been used up long ago.

He left the barn and called her name a few more times.

Jason might not see her again. Brickbat might conclude that the ransom was a lost cause and that killing her was the only way to tie the loose ends. Jason tried not to think about this.

He retrieved the heavy case of guns from the porch and carried it carefully into the grove of trees he and Whit had skulked through. Eventually he came upon the Terraplane. The kidnappers' Chrysler was gone. Brickbat must have untied the men and driven off, unless they'd somehow freed themselves. Either way, they were gone.

And then, the latest miracle: the briefcase was still under the driver's seat, still full of cash. However the men had escaped, they'd been in too much of a hurry or were too plain stupid to search the brothers' car.

Jason put the case of guns in the back, picked his fedora off the seat and put it on, then sat behind the wheel. The first death was still a black void in his mind, and the second had happened too suddenly to remember or even be aware of. But this latest had left plenty to ponder.

Brickbat had just sat there, smiling. He'd even laughed a few times. But he hadn't said anything after his initial taunting, as if he hadn't wanted to interfere with the purity of the act. Jason had been a spectacle. The passing of life, the turning of the earth, the changing of the seasons. It had hurt more than he could possibly describe.

He heard the sound of an approaching car. Multiple cars. Seconds later he saw them, black and slow, a funereal procession of law enforcement. Three Fords and a truck, windowless down its long sides. Something for transporting bodies. Neither Chicago cops nor the feds could have traced his call and relayed the information so quickly; maybe a neighbor had heard the shots, or had stumbled upon the house this morning.

Jason cursed himself for leaving Whit in the house. He crouched outside the Terraplane and slid the briefcase of money and the bag of guns beneath it. Then he closed the door gently and crawled beside the bags. The chassis was low and the grass tall, so the cops wouldn't spot him. Hopefully they would not be thorough—experience showed that cops weren't. Through the woods he could see the house, see the police parade up the long drive. Seven cops emerged from the vehicles, six of them in uniform and one in a tan suit and a cowboy hat.

He could just barely hear the cowboy yelling something to the corpses inside as the other cops hesitantly took positions around the building. The cowboy used binoculars to look in from the distance, then hollered again. More time passed, and they drew automatic pistols and revolvers. Two unlucky souls were nominated for the honor of approaching the windows to get a peek inside. Jason could see the terror in their jerky movements.

It was hot as hell under the Terraplane and none too comfortable as

Jason lay there, running various scenarios through his head. He wasn't sure whether he should be hoping Whit was awake now or still out.

Then the two cops gazing into the windows Brickbat had shot Jason through waved their colleagues forward. One by one, they entered the house.

Eventually two cops came outside again and seemed to spot the Terraplane. One of them reached into his pocket for binoculars. Jason rolled himself flat and prayed that the grass and the low chassis were as concealing as he'd hoped. He dared to look up a few seconds later and saw that the cops were walking toward him. Their sidearms were still holstered.

The Terraplane's keys were in his pocket. He double-checked that his automatic was loaded and released the safety and cocked it, then slowly unzipped the gun case.

He could hear them chatting in amazement as they slowly made their way. Finding a dead Firefly Brother in their own municipality—even though the brothers were supposed to have died days ago, in another state—was clearly the greatest thing that had ever happened to them.

"This is weird. Why would they leave it out here?" The cop sounded young.

"For a getaway, stupid." Equally young, equally excited. "Smart to scatter them like this."

Jason had used plenty of soap in the shower, and he feared they would smell it. He wished the air weren't so dry and dusty, and he breathed as shallowly and quietly as possible. He heard them open doors on both sides, felt the chassis sag as they climbed in. Each of them left a foot dangling, their ankles bobbing like bait. Shooting a guy's foot off would be a hell of a thing, but if he had no other option he could squeeze off the rounds before the second guy had a chance to jump.

"I still ain't making heads or tails of this."

"They faked their death in Indiana, dummy. They're like Houdini, with guns—remember the time Cincinnati police raided a place they were holed up in, but the brothers shot their way out? Or the time they vanished during that stakeout in Toledo?"

"But how do you fake a death?"

"Hell, it's been done for years. Like in *Romeo and Juliet*, right?"

"That's a play, Scooter. It ain't real."

"It's based on a true story, though."

Jason aimed his gun at the ankle on the passenger side, fearing that this inane banter might be a smoke screen as the two exchanged signals about the man beneath them.

"Then how do we know the ones in there are really dead and ain't faking it?"

"We don't, I guess. Shoot. We should get back in there in case the sheriff needs our help."

The chassis lifted a few inches and Jason saw their ankles and then their legs, the officers seeming to grow from the earth up as they walked back to the farmhouse.

He'd been hiding under the Terraplane for what felt like an hour and was desperate for some water by the time the cops started carrying bodies wrapped in bedsheets from the building. He groaned as he counted four of them; he'd been hoping maybe Whit had woken up and slipped out back, but apparently not.

More time passed as the cops deliberated. Jason did the same: his girlfriend had likely been taken hostage by a wounded Brickbat Sanders, and his brother was in the custody of the Sedalia police. The thought of choosing which to rescue seemed unnatural. Instead, he went with logic: he'd have better luck finding Darcy if he had Whit's help, but only if he was damn quick about it—and only if Whit woke up.

Two cops climbed into the loaded truck while the cowboy and some subordinates got into two of the Fords. If Jason had his math right, one cop was still in the building, presumably left behind to guard the crime scene. Then the sound of engines starting and clouds of dust down the long driveway.

Jason crawled out from under the Terraplane and loaded the money and the guns. By the time he'd driven through the woods and pulled onto the road, the police truck was the tiniest of specks in the distance. He floored the gas and watched the speck grow.

XXIV.

The woman at the unemployment office listened to Weston's story. She actually seemed to sympathize. She really wanted to help him. She just couldn't.

"I'm very sorry, Mr. Fireson. Your employer won't allow it."

"I don't have an employer. That's why I'm here."

"I meant your *former* employer, of course." A pursed smile, perfectly erect posture. "Employers need to file the appropriate forms for their former employees to be allowed to collect unemployment payments. To verify you've been laid off as opposed to quitting. Yours has not yet been filed."

The Lincoln City Social Services office was a large room on the second floor of a downtown building only five blocks from Mr. Douglasson's office. Gray buns bobbed as the clerks carefully typed, the hammers mashing government forms in triplicate. The place smelled of old ladies' perfume and sorrow.

"My former employer can deliberately prevent me from getting unemployment checks from the government?" Weston had been fired a month earlier.

"That would be the net result, yes."

"So I don't *work* there anymore, but I'm technically not *unemployed*, either?" Only later would Weston realize that this meant the feds were still pressuring Douglasson to make things difficult for him.

"I have to ask you to keep your voice down, Mr. Fireson." She hadn't shown any reaction when he'd given his name, but everyone knew it. "Perhaps you could file for state aid."

He nodded, smiling bitterly. He had heard stories about state aid—it took forever to apply, and they made the experience as unpleasant as possible. They asked about family, friends, and past associates, hoping to discover someone else who might be expected to provide you with funds so the state wouldn't have to. As if you wouldn't already have asked them yourself. Weston was a young, healthy man who, since he was single, technically had no dependents—his name would not shoot to the top of the list. And times were as bad as they'd ever been: he'd read in the *Sun* a few days back that the Lincoln City unemployment rate, now that two more tire plants had closed, had risen above fifty percent.

Weston thanked her and took his leave. He could hear the next guy beginning his story as he walked out the door.

How to spend all this time? Time overflowing, spilling out of his empty pockets. Time flooding the ground before him, washing him away. There was a surplus of time. If only he could have traded it for money, or for something he could hammer, weld, shape, smelt, or otherwise transmute into money. He was a magician staring at a hat, trying to remember the magic words for conjuring bunnies. And all down the street were other failed magicians, dressed in rags, everyone looking at one another with vacant eyes, silently asking if they remembered how to cast any spells.

Weston had applied for countless jobs. Anything he could think of. Legal and other white-collar positions at which his experience at Douglasson's might have proved beneficial, but such offices had no need of applicants, thank you. So, manual labor, at a lumberyard outside town, at a sugar-refining plant where the unionized workers turned him away before he could find the office, at a tool-and-die maker's shop, a movie theater, a trucking company, a furniture upholsterer. At hotels where he offered to carry luggage for nothing but tips. At restaurants that might need a cook or busboy or janitor. He had passed afternoons standing outside construction sites, just in case one of the men fell injured and the foreman needed a replacement. He had sat there hoping for some disaster, offering immoral prayers that a crane cord might snap, a scaffolding collapse.

He had even wandered into the local supermarket and asked if they needed help, argued his qualifications—his adolescence spent stocking shelves and calling suppliers and counting orders. His voice had cracked. He had been politely refused.

The day after his visit to the unemployment office, Weston spent money he shouldn't have at the cinema. But even though he carefully avoided gangster films, he still couldn't escape his brothers, who were featured in a newsreel before the picture started. This was in late May, two months before their death in Points North; J. Edgar Hoover sat at his desk and promised the American people that the Firesons would be captured, but his officious voice was drowned out by the audience's cheers at the sight of Jason and Whit's confident faces. Was it hometown loyalty, or did people everywhere love them like this?

He spared himself the streetcar fare by walking home. It was an hour's walk, and he took breaks on park benches and at bus stops. At least the springtime weather was agreeable, warm but still a couple of weeks before the humid air began suffocating the city.

He was tired, hungry, and a bit dizzy; he'd been cutting back on meals, which made the stomach pains more severe. It was dark when he approached his building. A young man standing on the corner called his name.

Weston recognized the voice from the phone, and he remembered the face from the confrontation at his mother's door.

"Agent Cary Delaney," the Justice agent said, extending his hand. He was Weston's height, and though he stood with confidence, he looked nothing like a cop. "Good to finally meet you in person."

Surely Jason or Whit would know how to respond, but Weston had no idea how to play this game. Say something witty, or does that mark you for a criminal? Act respectfully, or does that mark you for a heel? So he said nothing.

"Working late?"

"I'm ... I'm out of work at the moment." Surely that was not the right thing to say.

"That's too bad."

It took Weston a second to realize Delaney had known that.

"What do you want, Agent Delaney?"

"I want to find your brothers before they cause any more trouble."

"Why would I want to help you?"

"Because one of these days some country cops are going to shoot them up just so they can hang their heads on a wall. But if you can give me some information on your brothers the Bureau can at least try to bring them in alive."

"So they can be executed a few months later?"

"Not all the states in which they're wanted have the death penalty. Maybe I can pull some strings, get them put to trial in states that would only give them life sentences."

" 'Only life sentences.' You make it sound so agreeable. You think I want to see my brothers spend the rest of their lives behind bars?"

"I'm afraid that's their best option at this point."

"Prison killed my father awfully fast."

"I understand. I know your mother's been through a lot. Do you want her to see their faces all shot up on the front page of the *Sun*? Because that's where they're headed. I'll bet most papers already have the death stories written up; they've just left a few blanks for the where and the when. That way, when it happens they can go to press like *that*"—he snapped his fingers. "I'm offering you a chance to save them."

Weston laughed despairingly. That seemed to be the only way he laughed anymore. "Save my brothers. You make it seem like I'd be a hero to them."

"I know they wouldn't thank you for it. But that's how family is sometimes—we do things for the good of the people we love, even if they don't always see it that way. And you'd be saving other people, too. That's the thing none of these hero-worshippers like to talk about. Correct me if I'm wrong, but your brothers have killed people. Maybe they're naïve enough to think they didn't mean it, but fellows who steal at gunpoint can't blame anyone but themselves for what happens. So, yes, I'm interested in saving your brothers' lives, but I'm also interested in saving the lives that they're going to take with them. Some bank clerk trying not to lose his house. Some sad sack in to cash his CCA check. Some farmer hoping—"

"Enough," Weston waved his hand.

"Yes, of course—who cares about those other people? Empathy only carries us so far, huh?"

"You're talking about my *brothers*. You seem to be forgetting that."

"I think *you're* forgetting who they are—who they've become—and you're buying those stories and myths. That they go into Hoovervilles and carry the sick and injured to the hospital and pay their medical bills. That they tear up banks' new mortgages before they can be recorded. That they spread their money around to help folks keep up with the bills. You're letting the myths displace the reality.

"Here's who your brothers really are, Mr. Fireson: they're men who couldn't handle the pressures everyone else is facing, so they decided to just take from decent people, even if it means killing along the way. Whit gunned down an old bank clerk who was about to faint from fear. And one day he shot a fifty-year-old bank guard who'd only taken that job because he'd been laid off from a machine-parts factory. An old librarian in Louisiana took a ricochet to the head from a gunfight between your brothers and the police—I'm sure your brothers blame the police for that one. They killed two cops, and Jason shot a federal agent who I personally knew. His name was Mike. He was a Reds fan, had a son—"

"I said, *enough.*"

"I haven't even mentioned the reward money. We could get it to you secretly, so no one would know you were involved. Don't tell me you don't need it. Don't tell me your mother and your aunt and her kids don't need it. I know your mother's paid off most of her mortgage and your father's debts with money from bank jobs. But she won't be getting any more from Jason, not with all the heat on him. Her bills are going to be awfully hard to meet each year, what with feeding and clothing the little ones. Your brothers could have stayed home and supported your family the way everyone else is doing, but they made other choices."

"Yeah, it's been going so well for everyone else these days."

"Maybe they would have had dry spells, I'm not fooling myself. But they could have done it, just like you're doing it, just like I'm doing it. They chose to abandon your mother, abandon you."

Weston didn't contradict him.

The agent reached into his pants pocket and took out a crinkled Hershey's wrapper.

"Got a little hungry waiting for you to show up, so I stepped into the place around the corner and bought a little snack. First candy bar I've had in a long while. Want to hear why?"

"I'm sure it's a fascinating story, but—"

"I lived off the things for months at a time. In college and law school. I was there on scholarship—my family couldn't have afforded it otherwise. One time, I was evicted from my apartment and had to live in an old Model T. I moved it around different nights so I wouldn't get spotted by the campus cops. Living off the candy bars that had been passed out as promotions to all the students. Anyway, we hear that Jason and Whit have taken to living in automobiles lately, too. Funny coincidence."

"You know, I was wrong. That wasn't fascinating."

Delaney looked insulted as he stuffed the wrapper back into his pocket. "What I'm trying to say is that I know what it's like to be down on your luck. I know how it feels to be surrounded by people who could help you but won't. They just don't care. They're too concerned with themselves, and maybe if the shoe was on the other foot you would be, too. Look, the Bureau could have sent some thug to yell and threaten charges at you like they tried with your mother, but I understand the pressures you're under. You're the one stuck in the thankless position of having to keep everyone else going. Hell, I send most of my paycheck to my mother, too. But I also know there are right ways of dealing with this, and wrong ways."

"*Fuck you.*" Weston had never said that before. "Fuck you for even *thinking* you know what my family's going through."

Delaney stood there and took it.

"For God's sake, you're asking me to pass a death sentence on my brothers!"

"No, Mr. Fireson. I'm telling you that your brothers are already dead."

He reached forward and stuffed a business card into Weston's shirt pocket. "You can add that to your collection. Call me when you've made the right decision." He walked off.

Weston's anger was so vast, so all-encompassing, that it filled his body, pinned him in place. He lost track of how long he stood there. Other people entered or exited the building, all of them eyeing him queerly.

The anger he'd felt at his brothers was redirected at the Justice agent. Now he almost felt sorry for them, to be pursued like this. Were they really living in a car, or had Delaney made that up? Jason always tried to defuse the myths about them, but he also had implied he was having a grand time. Maybe it wasn't all booze and cheap women after all.

A man was sleeping in the first-floor corridor again. Weston stepped around the body and trudged up the stairs. At his door, he turned the key and walked into his apartment. He shed his shoes and sat on the bed to strip his socks. It was hot—he'd closed the windows in case of rain. He let some air in, then sat back on the bed and thought of his father.

Pop had always preached the importance of hard work, thrift, honesty. What would he think of his famous desperado sons? And what would he think of his unemployed, hapless middle son?

Weston had been there when they came for him. A Monday evening, late, the family woken by loud knocks at the door. Weston's room was closest to the stairs, and he made it to the door first. Police officers, two of them on the landing and two more a few steps behind. Was this a nightmare? But Weston had never had nightmares about cops before—he'd never had reason to. That would change.

They asked for his father, and he told them Pop was asleep. They told him to wake the old man up and followed Weston upstairs.

"... the heck's going on?" Whit's nineteen-year-old voice warbled into the hallway.

Pop opened the door in his nightshirt. The light from downstairs barely outlined his cheekbones, but his eyes shone.

"What's going on? It's the middle of the night."

"Patrick Fireson, you're under arrest for the murder of Garrett Jones."

Murder? Pop? Nothing was less imaginable to Weston. The family had learned of Mr. Jones's death the previous afternoon but had been told it was suicide. *Murder?*

Pop was asking could he please get dressed. He told them not to look at his wife in her nightdress, asked to close the bedroom door. They told him okay but no funny stuff.

Whit was beside Weston. "What the hell's going on?"

"Easy, son," one of the cops told Whit. "Just relax."

"I'll relax when you get the hell out of our house!"

One of the cops let his hand dangle on a club, or maybe the handle of a gun—Weston couldn't quite see. The motion was warning enough.

"I said, take it easy."

Then the police were walking a hurriedly dressed Pop down the stairs and out to one of their squad cars. Somehow this all happened without

Weston's meeting his father's eyes. He stood just outside the front door as Whit charged outside, yelling and grabbing one of the cops by the shoulder. Another cop had to pull him away and threaten him again as he thrashed about, eyes wild, mouth open. Pop told him to stop it and then told Ma to call Mr. Jeffers, his attorney. The doors slammed shut and the cops drove him away. The Firesons followed the taillights until they vanished.

The three of them were standing on the front lawn. It was summer and mosquitoes were beginning to notice their presence. The grass was wet. It was quiet.

"Ma!" Whit shouted, demanding that someone reimpose order on his world. Weston told him to stop making so much noise.

"I should just stand there and do nothing like you?" Whit stepped toward him. "You just *watched* that goddamn cop push me around?"

Ma collapsed onto the front steps. The brothers ran to her and asked if she was all right. Her face was the most frightening thing Weston had ever seen. But he would see that face again, and often. He would learn to accept it.

Weston sat there on his bed and thought of his outlaw brothers. He hated them and loved them all the same, loved them perhaps especially because of the end he knew awaited them. Agent Delaney was right: it was inescapable.

It was at times like these, when he was feeling generous toward his doomed brothers, when he allowed his anger at them to subside and instead focused on their shared past, that Weston would imagine some impossible scenario for them: that even if his brothers were killed they would come back to life somehow. They would spite the authorities—not only the police and the prosecutors and the bankers but also God, or whatever invisible, sinister forces had conspired to put them in such an untenable position. The brothers would refute them all, by dying but refusing to stay dead. The only thing that would truly kill them was old age, the passage of time, the grudging acceptance of life's limitations. But no one—no cop and no judge and no politician—would get to impose those limitations on Weston's brothers. No one would wield that power over them.

Let my brothers escape somehow, Weston found himself pleading. *Let my brothers escape.*

XXV.

$\mathbf{B}$rickbat's breathing became increasingly loud during the otherwise quiet drive to the North St. Louis physician he claimed would treat him. It was midday when the elderly driver steered them into the city, past an old brewery that had been reincarnated as a pop manufacturer during Prohibition but was now off the wagon again, as ecstatic billboards praising Repeal were plastered on top of unconvincing ads for ginger ale. Next was a working-class neighborhood of three-story houses carved into apartments, where bored members of the brewery's target audience stood at street corners, looking as if they very much wanted to partake of the local product if only they had a buck.

Darcy had pondered possible means for escape, but the best she could think of was simply to throw open her door and run. Which was not encouraging—she remembered Brickbat's entirely believable threat to shoot her knees. She stared out the window, haunted by her proximity to a safety she could not attain. The tension grew less bearable as she knew her time outside was nearing its end. She frantically tried to make eye contact with every pedestrian or driver they passed, but no one seemed to care about her plight. Her fingers twitched nervously; she constantly folded and unfolded her arms until Brickbat chided her to stop fussing.

The old man, who had not spoken a word since informing his passengers that he had been killed (had she really heard him right?), steered his

DeSoto into a narrow driveway that slunk like an excuse between two dark-blue buildings. The wide sedan barely fit, but behind the building was a parking area big enough for two cars. One was already parked there. Brickbat told him to pull alongside it, kill the engine, and hand over the keys.

"Sit tight and don't move," he told them. "Try anything and I'll maim you."

He slipped his silver automatic into his pants pocket and stepped out of the DeSoto, hobbling up a stairway to the back door.

"Do you have a gun?" she asked the old man in a tiny whisper, barely moving her lips.

"No." His patrician voice wasn't as quiet as hers.

"A knife, anything?"

This time he didn't even answer. She watched Brickbat, though from this angle she could see only his dirty shoes pointed in her direction. She tried to calculate how quickly she could open the door and sprint through the driveway to the street, but she was weak from hunger and desperately thirsty, her head had been pounding the past few hours, and her sprint the previous evening had left her with sore calves and blistered feet.

The door opened. Brickbat's feet shifted the slightest amount and she could hear the almost comic sound of two deep-voiced men trying to whisper. She couldn't make out a word, but Brickbat's host did not seem pleased by the visit. Then Brickbat was descending the steps. Glistening lines of sweat seemed to be eroding his limestone face, which was whiter than before. He gritted his teeth as he opened the driver's door.

"Out," he told them, his hand fondling his pocketed gun. He marched them up the steps and into a small, unclean kitchenette. Tiny shadows scurried from Darcy's peripheral vision. Beyond the narrow oven and stove stood a stout man with uncombed gray hair, dizzy eyes, and alcoholic breath.

After Darcy was allowed a quick visit to the bathroom—the door left ajar, Brickbat standing behind it with his gun drawn—she and the old man were led back into the kitchenette, where the doctor opened what Darcy had mistakenly assumed was a closet door.

"Down the stairs," Brickbat told them.

The drunk man, who wore an unseasonable wool houndstooth suit, walked down first, leaning heavily on the railing. He flicked a switch that cast a sad amount of light into the catacombs. Stairs creaked and sagged as Darcy descended behind her fellow hostage, with Brickbat the caboose of this slave train. The basement was dank and cool.

A small circle of emptiness was surrounded by a maelstrom of boxes, old furniture, wheel-less bicycles, and, Lord, maybe even dead bodies and whatever else the tangential characters of the underworld chose to hide beneath their stairs. The drunk man vanished into the mess and re-appeared a few seconds later with two wooden chairs. Brickbat told the hostages to sit.

With a thick coil of rope he tied the old man's hands behind his back, and tied his feet to the chair legs. Then Brickbat moved on to Darcy, un-locking her detached handcuffs. *The bastard had a key the whole time.* He dropped the cuffs to the floor, and before she could have the pleasure of stretching her arms he pulled her wrists behind her chair, retying her hands the way he'd done the old man's, and then her feet.

With Brickbat behind her, she looked at their new host, trying to plead with him silently. *Whoever you are, you can't possibly be as sadistic as this man. Please free us after Brickbat's surgery, when his brain is pickled in ether. Or, better still, give him too much ether. He will not be missed. Please.*

But the man's eyes, not entirely visible behind dirty, thick-rimmed spectacles, were unresponsive. He stood calmly, as if this were a daily oc-currence. She had seen blankness like this in some of Jason's associates, and it had chilled her even then.

"You ain't gonna gag 'em?" he asked Brickbat.

"That won't be necessary." Brickbat brandished his silver gun again, waving it before Darcy and the old man. "I think we understand one an-other."

He holstered it and was about to turn for the stairs when Darcy dared to say, "Some food or water would be appreciated."

"Save it. Easy life is over for you, kitten. After the doc finishes, we'll see what kind of mood I'm in. For now, be thankful I'm leaving the light on down here."

Then Brickbat motioned for the dizzy man to ascend the stairs, and he followed, shutting the basement door behind them.

"That man is a doctor?" The older captive's voice was slow and flat, phonemes tiredly walking across Nebraska.

"A pin artist, most likely." Darcy tried to scoot her chair, but it wobbled dangerously forward, nearly pitching her onto the cement floor. "Men like Brickbat take their girls to him when they're in a jam. Probably was a real doctor once, until he had his license revoked for it, or for doing his work while drunk, or for accidentally killing a few immigrants who couldn't afford a sober physician."

"You seem well acquainted with this subculture."

"He's probably shaved the fingerprints off a few gunmen, dug bullets out of shoulders, stitched up some knifings. I heard Dillinger paid a quack to do plastic surgery once. Maybe Mr. Sanders will pay for a new face? It would be an improvement."

The old man's head hung a bit, a momentary glimmer of despair breaking the granite stoicism.

"We need to get out of here," Darcy said. "Can you free your hands? Mine are tied too tight."

"Mine as well."

She looked at the massive piles surrounding them. Auto tires and gardening equipment and buckets of old paint. The doctor likely moved every few years to stay ahead of the law, so either he was quite the pack rat or these were the worthless possessions of prior tenants. "There must be something in there, a knife or a piece of metal we could use."

"It's fruitless. We can't move, and we can't hold anything. We will have to wait."

She stared at him. Wait for what? He didn't sound hopeless so much as unbothered, as if they were killing time in the doctor's waiting room.

"What's your name?"

"The Honorable Thrace Underhill."

She raised her eyebrows.

"I used to be a judge," he explained. "Until I was hung."

"Ah. I've been meaning to ask you about that." Looking into his eyes, which were neither guarded nor aggressive, was almost as uncomfortable as staring at the drunk surgeon's had been. In truth, she hadn't really *wanted* to ask this man what he had meant, but she felt compelled to. She'd had enough of hearing and thinking about people who had been killed but not killed. She still didn't know what to think of Brickbat's explanation for the gunshots at the farmhouse—she had to believe Jason was still out there, had to focus on that during this hellish internment.

The appearance of yet another person who claimed to have transcended death was an annoyance to her. "Surely I misunderstood you, but—"

"You did not misunderstand me. It is hard to comprehend, I grant that, but it happened. I was killed four days ago, by a mob. Men not so much bloodthirsty as unmoored by the events around them."

"What . . . what exactly happened?"

"Over the past few months," he began, "I have presided over many foreclosure hearings. I take no pleasure in dictating that the state or a bank foreclose on land that represents the livelihood of so many families, but it is my duty. There are laws, and I must uphold them. I did not write the laws. I did not tell the farmers to mortgage their homes. I did not set the price of grain. The farmers sometimes yell at me, accuse me of destroying their lives, destroying the state of Iowa. Beneath all their contempt is flattery—that they dream I have such power, that I am a mighty force leveling all that they consider good about America. I am just a man. I am neither divine nor malevolent. There are cases before me, two sides are argued. There are statutes and contracts.

"Deficiency judgments have been taking up a larger and larger percentage of my docket this summer. The farmers grew angrier. There was a time, last year, even last spring, when the farmers would stand there with acceptance. They would answer my questions with no extra guff. That has changed. They've organized, they've made plans, they've assigned blame. My court has grown more crowded, not just with defendants but with friends of defendants, or people who had heard of them and rallied to their cause. As if thinking that a show of support could alter the laws I must rule upon. People started shouting, calling me a toady of the bankers, a fascist. I had no recourse but to tell the bailiffs to remove them. I could have had them arrested. Perhaps a true fascist would have done so. But I understood that these were desperate people, confused people. I represent the government of the United States, and these people have grown to hate their government."

Upstairs, Darcy heard footsteps but no voices. She had a feeling where this story was going, had read about this sort of thing in Iowa and elsewhere across the cursed Plains.

"Every person knows that he is not the center of the universe," the judge continued. "Yet this basic understanding—of the randomness of fate, of the insignificance of our own lives—does not stop us from endowing certain events in our lives with added meaning. *I lost the job because I am not worthy, my wife took ill because I thought unclean thoughts, my children were harmed because I did wrong. I can't provide for my loved ones because I'm a failure.* At the exact moment that you're learning just how unimportant you are, you still believe that the flotsam of the earth is circling *you,* that the decisions of powerful men are made with *you* in mind. You are tiny and insignificant, but still you are the center of everything you perceive.

"Four days ago, the courthouse was overflowing as I took my chair. I could sense something, see the look in people's eyes, the firmness of their jaws. The first hearing regarded a man who had defaulted on his mortgage of eleven thousand dollars. He had not made a payment in months. He did not deny anything that the bank stated. I ruled that the bank could initiate a foreclosure sale on the property, and he screamed at me. He said his farm was worth eighty thousand and that I was being unfair. That *I* was cheating *him.* As if my whole reason for being, and every law written before me, revolved around the desire to bring him harm. Then everyone was shouting. I broke the handle of my gavel. I shouted at the bailiffs to restore order. The crowd swarmed. The bailiffs left the room. The attorneys from the bank must have done the same. The crowd rushed toward me as if the room had been lifted by a giant's hand and tipped backward. They struck me down. So many hands were grabbing me, pulling my hair, nails scratching my face. They took turns kicking me. Someone tried to gouge my eyes out with a stick. I clamped them shut and screamed but could not hear my voice above the rolling din. The terror of one cannot equal the rage of so many. Then I was outside. So many feet trampling the earth, dust everywhere. They threw a rope over the branch of a dead maple and tied a noose. Hands held my shoulders down as one of them dangled the noose before me. So many people, so much anger that they were jumping up and down, deranged. Dust in my nose and eyes. I couldn't see. I thought of my departed wife and my children and grandchildren. They fastened the noose around my neck and pulled it tight. Then, silence.

"When I opened my eyes, I was lying on the ground covered in dirt. The maple above me was still dead and its branches swayed in the wind—

another dust storm was coming. I sat up and the noose was gone, but still my neck burned. I had soiled my pants. Forgive the vulgarity, miss, but the details are important. I see that now. I see only the details, the two crows bouncing among the tree branches above me when I woke, the fact that someone had left a matchbook behind, the way one of my laces had become unthreaded through the top hole. It has been my job to master the details and understand their relation to the whole, their role in the bigger story. But now I see how wrong I was. There are only details, and there is no whole. The threads at the cuff of a young boy's pants as I walked along the dirt road, the bleeding paint on a handmade FOR SALE sign. I see only these details now, and they overwhelm me."

"I'm sorry that happened," Darcy said after what she figured was a suitable silence. The man was clearly unhinged by his near-death experience. She would have touched his shoulder if her hands weren't bound. "I don't mean to sound disbelieving, but, that is, isn't it obvious that they took pity on you at the end? That you . . . fainted before they could hang you, so they decided they'd done enough?"

"They had no pity. I did not faint. Everything was different. Usually, empathy for others only carries us so far. It's how we survive—it's *why* we survive. But I understood them now. I should have hated them, but I didn't.

"I made it back to my house just before the storm hit. I took off my clothes and bathed as the windows creaked at the pressure from outside. The bathwater was black with the dust and soil within minutes. Then the storm passed and I left the filthy tub and shook the dust from my clothes, and dressed. I got into my car and drove away."

He was mad, she decided. He could believe what he wanted. "Where are you going?"

He didn't answer for a long while. The footsteps upstairs were now intermittent. She heard the sink turn on and off.

"I don't know. I don't know why I'm still here. I don't know why this life has been granted to me. I can think of only one reason, though it makes little sense."

Silence again. Darcy asked him what the reason was.

"Ultimately, how can a person imagine his own death? We may not be the center of the universe, but we are the center of our own consciousness.

And to imagine an end to that consciousness? This is not possible. We die, but we do not die. No one can imagine it. And so it cannot happen. They tried to kill me, yet I live."

What egocentric grandness, she thought. "You do look rather alive to me. If it's any consolation."

"You can mock me if you wish, young lady. I have been mocked before. I have suffered worse than whatever that man and his gun have planned. I do not fear his plans."

"Well, I'm not ashamed to say that I *do* fear them. There has to be some way for us to get out of here."

Then he closed his eyes and hung his head, as if sleeping.

"Excuse me? Judge Underhill, excuse me? Those of us who aren't immortal would like a hand devising our escape, Your Honor."

He opened his eyes but would not look at her. "I've been driving for days. I only want to sleep." He closed his eyes and the shallow rise and fall of his chest was the only evidence that he was indeed alive.

Darcy heard the flush of a toilet. She prayed that Brickbat's procedure would be an unsuccessful one. She begged for the onset of gangrene, she implored the aid of invisible bacteria. Or perhaps the drunk surgeon would snip an artery by mistake.

It was dank and her head throbbed and within minutes the old man was snoring.

Then the light burned out.

XXVI.

Whit opened his eyes and was blind once again. He tried to move his arms, yet the world narrowly bent around him, a malleable prison confining him. His nails made odd sounds as they tried to claw through, his fingers slick with sweat. The air was scant and he tried to inhale with dry gulps.

Jesus, had they buried him? Was he underground? Terror seized him as he thrashed about. He screamed for someone to dig him out, let him out, help him. He called his brother's name. Memories of the night in the farmhouse flashed before him. He didn't remember being shot himself, but he did remember seeing Jason fall. Again.

He finally realized he was in an automobile as it pulled to a stop. Voices that had seemed like tiny, mostly forgotten memories scurrying in the furthest corners of his mind were louder now, not memories at all but persons close by. Muffled by this death shroud and maybe by something else, a wall. He needed to break through.

"Let me out of this! I can't breathe!"

On and on for nearly a minute and then he stopped. He was panting but he tried to listen to the voices from the cabin.

"Don't tell me you didn't hear that," one of them said.

"What in the goddamn hell . . . ?"

The first voice came in louder now: "Who's back there? I said, who's back there?"

"Get me out of this!" Whit screamed. "I can't breathe!"

The voices were quieter again, conspiratorial or maybe terrified. Seconds later, the sound of two doors opening. Footsteps on dry earth. A metallic yawn and its echo. Then silence.

"Let me out!" He kicked and thrashed, but all he did was roll onto his side. His entire body was wet with sweat. "I can't breathe!"

"Says he can't breathe."

"He's not *supposed* to breathe!"

"God almighty."

"How in the goddamn hell—"

"Which one you think it is?"

"Let me out, goddamn you!"

Finally, he heard them walking toward him, tinny footsteps light with fear.

"All right, hold still." An unseen hand pulled at the covering over Whit's face. There was a sudden burst of light along with the whisper of a blade being pulled against cotton, and then a gasp, and a face Whit saw too briefly to be sure was really there.

With his elbows pressed into his chest, Whit managed to poke his two hands through the opening and tear it wider. Air like shovelfuls of snow fell on him. It was divine. He gasped, burning his lungs with it. The world he was staring at was the corrugated roof of a truck, but he focused on the wonderful texture of the air and the feeling coursing through his limbs. The truck's engine was still on, the world beneath him purring with life.

After he had regained his breath, he sat up and saw two cops staring at him from the far corner of the truck, by the open back doors. The cop was able to meet Whit's stare for only a moment before conceding defeat and turning white. His fall was cushioned by one of the other bodies on the floor.

His partner stood frozen, unsure whether he should rally to his colleague's aid. He made the sign of the cross. Whit wasn't yet sure what to do, so he echoed the man's gesture.

"Man, it was hot in there."

"You're . . . you're not . . ."

A wood railing ran the length of the interior, and Whit used it to pull himself up. He could stand in the truck, but he needed to duck his head. "Your buddy okay?"

"Um . . ." The conscious cop was middle-aged, with a round, cheerful face and the unimposing physique of a man who spent most of his time at a desk. He hesitantly knelt down to inspect his partner. As he did so, Whit reached forward and grabbed the handle of the cop's sidearm. He pulled, but it was latched, the gun nestled in there pretty good, and the cop's head turned while Whit was tugging at it. The officer didn't think to fight back, just knelt there staring in amazement. Finally, the revolver came free and Whit backed up a step, pointing it at him.

"Just stay down there a minute. I'm not going to hurt you. Which of these is my brother?"

The cop's eyes were blank, and it took him a moment. "Your brother ain't here. We found you and three other fellas, but none of 'em was him."

"You aren't lying to me?"

The cop shook his head. The poor man did seem incapable of dishonesty at the moment. More important, Whit didn't want to unwrap three bodies on the off chance that one of them was his brother's. Had Jason abandoned him? Had his brother survived the shots and escaped?

"Where are we?"

"Sedalia. Just a few miles from the house where we found you." The cop touched his own forehead, staring at Whit's. "So that ain't really a—?"

Whit asked what day it was, and learned that only hours had passed since his passing. He felt neither the confusion of his first resurrection nor the sense of encroaching dread and dismay of the second; this time he mainly was relieved to realize that he'd survived that hellish scene at the farmhouse. Or perhaps *survived* wasn't the right word. But, hell, here he was.

The other cop began to stir, so Whit pointed his gun at the first to warn him off, then reached down and relieved the awakening officer of his revolver. He stuffed it into his pants pocket. The officer looked up at him, then clamped his eyes shut again.

"Cuff yourselves to that railing," Whit told them. "And hand me the cuffs' keys." As the cops obeyed, Whit asked where their colleagues were.

"We were behind some squad cars, but they pulled away. Must not've seen us pull over."

He asked them again if there was anyone else outside and the cops shook their heads. Still, the others would realize eventually that their caravan had diminished.

And with that Whit heard another engine approaching. Both cops were sitting now, their right hands up and attached to the railing, and behind them the back doors stood just slightly open. Whit glimpsed a car coming toward them. It looked familiar, but Whit had been in many cars during the past year. The engine grew loud as it approached and then came the sound of tires skidding to a stop behind the truck. Sunlight glared off its windshield.

His brother's fedora-topped head emerged from the driver's side of the Terraplane, and submachine-gun fire rang out as Jason shot at the van's tires. The truck sagged and the cops flinched beside Whit, who kicked open one of the doors. He raised his empty hand where his brother could see it.

"Come out real slow!" Jason commanded.

"Jason, it's me!"

A two-second pause. "Finally decided to wake up, huh?"

Whit jumped out of the back and Jason was walking toward him, a Thompson smoking in his arms. He looked bathed and very put-together, though his shirt was dirty and wrinkled.

"You let 'em put me in a goddamn hearse?"

"Sorry. There were seven of them and one of me. I made the best play available." Jason peeked in at the captives. "Howdy, boys." One of the cops waved back with his uncuffed hand.

"They say there were some squad cars," Whit said.

"Yeah, just in front. Probably going to turn around any minute now. In fact"—he stepped back and gazed down the long highway—"that might be them. Let's go."

Jason hurried behind the wheel of the Terraplane as Whit got into the backseat. Jason reached back and handed Whit the Thompson. "Plenty more guns in that case," he said. "But that's the only tommy, and we don't have any extra drums."

Whit rolled down the rear windows and faced backward as Jason pulled the car around, clouds of dirt obscuring Whit's view of the squad cars, which were only a few hundred yards away now. Jason pressed the gas to the floor.

"They're stopping at the truck," Whit said.

"Good. That buys us about thirty seconds or so, depending on how stupid they are."

The Terraplane's speedometer was topping out at eighty. It was a fine ride; the shocks were strong and the brothers didn't much feel it when Jason drove over rocks or clumps of earth that had blown onto the road. Jason had filled the tank just before they staked out the farmhouse. Still, given their past automotive luck, they easily could blow out a tire or overheat the radiator. Normally on getaways they had spare tires and extra cans of gasoline and boxes of tools, not to mention roofing nails and tacks to throw on the road behind them, and multiple gunmen. Worst was the lack of a git detailing all the side roads and cat roads, listing the landmarks, distances, and average travel times. They knew where the nearest highway was, yes, but still it was like walking into a bank that they'd cased only from the outside. This was how thieves got caught.

Jason hadn't been impressed by the look of the police Fords, but at least one was keeping up with them fairly well. He couldn't tell if the other two cops were still behind it or if the drivers had taken side routes to head them off.

"Where's Darcy?" Whit asked.

"Gone. I woke up and it was just me and four dead bodies, including yours."

"What about Brickbat?"

"Gone, too."

"Did he . . . ?"

"Yes. Both of us."

"I don't remember being hit." Whit had taken his eyes off the Ford and was scanning his own body, confused by the lack of bullet holes or gaping wounds. He didn't even see any blood. "Maybe I was just unconscious."

"Afraid not. He got you square in the forehead."

Whit leaned forward to get a look at himself in Jason's rearview. "Oh, Jesus!" He gingerly touched the hole, then pulled his finger away. He was still leaning forward, obscuring Jason's view of the trailing Ford, when Jason saw something straight ahead.

"Oh, hell. Sit down!" Jason hit the brakes, hard.

A police Ford raced out of the Sanders farmhouse driveway and pulled into the middle of the road, right in front of them. Off the two-lane road were narrow dirt skidways, and between those and the farmland on either side were ditches that Jason would never clear. He pulled left of the cop onto a skidway, the speedometer's needle swinging back to thirty, the fastest he could go while navigating such a tiny channel. Yet it was so slow that he and the cop made eye contact as the cop's head was raised above the Ford's roofline. Jason could see the old smallpox scars on the man's face. The cop fired.

The front passenger window spat itself at Jason, his fedora knocked at a slant. He ducked down and the Terraplane sped along, gravel and dirt scraping beneath the wheels. By the time Jason lifted his head and saw that he was still aimed straight and not headed into a ditch, Whit was leaning through the back right window and firing with the Thompson. Jason edged back onto the asphalt.

"Were we hit?" he yelled once they were away. He straightened his fedora and glass shards spilled from the brim. He glanced down and the seat glittered at him; if he so much as shifted, they'd embed themselves in his skin.

Whit leaned his head out the window. "Yes. Two in the body, but I don't think they got anything important. Wheels are okay. I got his radiator, and his wheels."

"We'll be on the highway in a minute." Hopefully they had already encountered every police officer in this county. "I say we stick to that till we get closer to Jefferson City—I know the side roads there, and we can get off the highway and switch cars."

"How far is that?"

"Half hour, maybe."

"That's a very risky half hour," Whit said. Surely the cops would get word out to the neighboring jurisdictions; the question was how quickly the wire would hum.

"I'm willing to consider any alternative strategies."

Whit offered none, instead taking stock of his arsenal and deciding which weapon he'd use once the Thompson was empty. The Firefly Brothers maintained their barely tolerable distance from the two police Fords for the five minutes it took to reach the highway interchange. Jason saw that the short connecting road on his right had been laid at a harsh angle. He waited as long as he could before he started braking for the turn.

Then the cops pulled a quality maneuver he hadn't been expecting. While one Ford pulled onto the entry path for the highway, the other continued straight on the country road, fast as ever. Which meant that as Jason carefully took the hard turn the second Ford pulled alongside on his left, closing the gap enough to fire a few shots. The Terraplane's roof seemed to shudder, and what Jason hoped was only a headlight exploded in front. More shots, but then the Ford had made its pass and Jason was on the highway.

Two lanes in each direction, separated by a grass median. One Ford was still tailing them, but the other would be farther behind now, once he turned around.

Whit leaned out the window and inspected the damage again, pronouncing it minimal. There were no holes in the hood, no gaseous clouds escaping from the radiator. The Terraplane was zipping along.

The Ford behind them was no closer than before. Because this stretch of highway was vacant, the cops fired some desperation shots. With the air rushing past at eighty miles an hour, the gunfire sounded farther away than it was. After maybe ten missed shots, the cops stopped firing. Then they remembered to turn on their siren.

In another minute, Jason came upon a few other cars. Drivers gave him dirty looks as Jason veered between lanes, and some of them seemed to notice the bullet holes in the Terraplane. At least the cops wouldn't fire with civilians around. Jason pulled the brim of his fedora lower and told Whit to avoid displaying his bullet wound if possible; the last thing they needed was for some old codger to pass out at the wheel and sideswipe them.

Twenty minutes passed this way, long stretches of empty highway in which the police would assert their relevance by firing a few helpless shots, broken up by brief maneuvers through pockets of traffic. They were nearing Jefferson City when Jason noticed a horizontal line in the distance. It was black, though it glowed red and blue.

"They've got the highway blocked."

Half a dozen squad cars were parked across the two lanes and the skidways. The cops had set up just past a right-hand exit so other traffic could get off, but if Jason tried to do the same he'd waltz into a shooting gallery.

He told Whit to hang on and he started braking, then swung the Terraplane hard to the left. They drove onto the grass median and now the car's shocks didn't seem so impressive. But the axle managed to remain intact and the tires did not burst. Jason turned again and hit the gas, and they were on the opposite side of the highway. He narrowly avoided being clipped by a long touring car, whose owner leaned on his horn in outrage. There was another car on Jason's right, hemming him in on the left lane. One of his pursuers was pulling a U and was almost behind him again, but the other Sedalia squad car had instead stopped on the median a few hundred yards back. As Jason sped in the direction from which he'd come, he was about to pass that cop at a distance of barely twenty feet. He saw this too late.

Whit had started to yell something when the windshield exploded. Glass stung like wasps at Jason's cheeks and neck and fingers. He blinked instinctively but when he tried to reopen his eyes the right one didn't feel like obeying.

Whit was firing at the police car, which had been stationary on the median and therefore nothing but a memory within seconds. Most of the other automobiles on this side of the highway were getting the message that continued travel on this road was not recommended for anyone without firearms, and they were pulling over. But soon Jason's speed caught him up to the next pocket of oblivious travelers. A police car was still trailing them, but so far behind they could barely hear its siren.

"You all right?!" Whit had to scream to be heard above the hot wind blowing through the open front.

"I think so!" Jason's right eye was still shut and still angry but at least it felt as if it was intact. That and the wind in his face forced him to squint the other eye.

Whit brushed the glass shards from the passenger seat and climbed up beside Jason. "You gotta take the next exit before they put up another roadblock!"

Jason replied that he goddamn knew that, but they hadn't reached an exit yet. A minute later, hallelujah, he came upon one. He missed Jake Dimes, his old wheelman, more than ever. From his bootlegging days, Jason had a number of chases to his credit, but speeding past firing officers while avoiding terrified civilians was hardly easy.

Jason had the distinct thought that he would not survive another death. He didn't understand his new existence, but surely there was a limit. More important, surely his adversaries would devise some counter-measures. If they shot him down again, maybe they'd skip the press conference and drop his body in a cast of wet cement, and he would spend eternity trapped inside a commemorative statue of himself. Or the coroner would saw the brothers' bodies into a thousand pieces, to be distributed as trophies to police stations across the country. Or they'd just burn the corpses. Whether the brothers were enjoying an unfathomable stretch of good luck or heavenly beneficence, Jason knew it couldn't last forever.

He flashed his headlights—which might not have been working any-more—at a meandering Studebaker that was insisting on the left lane. Finally, Jason angled to pass it on the right, but he was doomed by the Studebaker's belated decision to acquiesce. They didn't hit hard, but at eighty miles an hour it was enough. The Terraplane's front wheels skittered and one of the tires lost its tether to the ground. Jason tried to straighten the car but that only made it worse. It swerved to the right, onto the skidway. A roadster was already pulled over there, the hood raised as someone peered inside. Whit was screaming at Jason to brake and he thought he was but the car skidded back into the left lane. The Terraplane nosed into the side of the Studebaker and the steering wheel seemed to leap forward and whack Jason's chest, hard. His knees hit against the steering column even harder. Then Jason lost track of what was happening. Dozens of separate events seemed to occur every second.

Finally, they were motionless. The stasis was surreal. The Terraplane was pointed backward, facing oncoming traffic. Not that there was much to face: the few moving automobiles were like a barely trickling river, slowly winding their way past the many wrecked or stalled cars that sat like rocks jutting from a creek bed. Doors were opening and people were emerging, shaking their heads, rubbing their necks, yelling. Two bodies were facedown on the road twenty feet in front of a car with no windshield. Women were screaming, children were wailing. A uniformed milkman was limping and holding his right arm at an unnatural angle. Someone else's arm dangled through the open window of a smashed flivver, his head slumped on the dash. Traffic on the other side of the highway slowed in morbid curiosity.

Jason's right eye was working again. Every other part of his body hurt. "You okay?"

"I'm stuck," Whit said. "My legs are trapped."

The front of the Terraplane was crumpled, the hood misaligned by a few feet, and the dashboard was compressed and knocked down. The interior of the car reminded Jason of something he'd seen at some terrible art exhibit Darcy had once taken him to—all the angles wrong, nothing but vanishing points and no center. Jason looked for Whit's legs but couldn't find them.

"Jesus. Can you move them at all?"

"Little bit. I don't think they're broke, they're just stuck." Whit was leaning forward, his hands underneath, blindly trying to feel his way out. "Something's pressed into my knees. Something that feels hot."

Jason smelled gasoline. He offered Whit his hands and started to pull.

"Stop, stop!" Whit winced after the first tug. "It's not going to work."

Jason could just see smoke emanating from the torn hood, the wispy trail fading into the sky. A police siren was getting louder, and multiplying.

Jason tried to think of something to do other than yank harder and ignore Whit's cries. Suddenly a breathless young man appeared at Whit's window.

"You fellas all right?"

The man looked about twenty, with a broad chest and thick arms. Jason couldn't have thought up a better Good Samaritan if he'd tried.

"What's your name, friend?" Jason asked as he scooted closer to his brother.

"Eddie."

"Eddie, I'm going try to lift the dash with my feet. Grab my buddy's hands here." He turned to Whit. "Once you feel your legs have more space, tell Eddie to pull. Got it?"

Jason could see that Whit was not enamored of the plan. "Got any better ideas?" Jason asked him. Whit shook his head.

"That's smoke, ain't it?" Eddie asked. Then for the first time he seemed to notice something funny about Whit's forehead. Eddie's eyes grew wider, and then he saw the very large gun draped across Whit's lap. "Oh, goodness."

Eddie began to backpedal, and Jason quickly unholstered an automatic and pointed it at him. "Don't you walk away, Eddie. You do what I told you to do and we're square, got it?"

Eddie nodded and stepped closer to Whit, hesitantly reaching for his hands. Still holding his pistol, Jason pressed his knees into his chest and placed his feet against the dash. He counted to three and pushed out with his legs, slowly exhaling as he tried to muscle the dash off his brother. It refused to budge. He stopped for breath and the sirens were louder, singing their castrati chorus.

Then the front of the car glowed, and flames rose from beneath the hood.

"Try it again!" Whit yelled. "Hurry, goddamnit!"

Jason kicked against the dash. In that one inhalation he smelled smoke and melting rubber and what he hoped was not singed cotton. The force of his kick broke the seat from the floor and he and Whit fell back, heads snapping.

Whit screamed as his legs were released. Eddie let go of Whit's hands and backed up as Whit lunged out of his open window. The Thompson had slipped onto the seat, and Jason grabbed it with his free hand as he, too, jumped free of the burning car.

When Jason got to his feet, he saw Whit thrashing on the road in a cloud of smoke. One of his legs was on fire. Eddie was trying to kick dirt and pebbles at him, but there wasn't enough debris to smother it. Jason placed his two guns on the road and tore at the buttons of his shirt and pulled it off. He used it to whip at his brother's leg as Whit screamed and rolled and kicked. Finally he just fell on Whit, smothering him. He felt a strange heat at his chest but it faded almost immediately. Whit lay beneath him, gasping for breath. Jason rolled off, leaning on his hands and staring at his brother. Whit was on his back, wide-eyed. Dirt and dust hovered in the air; as most of it settled, more rose into the sky. Jason realized it wasn't dust at all but smoke from Whit's pants.

Superheated metal popped like a gunshot and Jason winced as if struck. The front of the Terraplane was engulfed now and he felt the heat on his face. He scrambled to his feet, opened the back door, and grabbed the bag of guns and the briefcase.

Eddie was still standing by Whit, not realizing he'd just missed his golden escape opportunity. Jason picked up the automatic pistol and the Thompson.

Despite the screams and the fire, Whit and Jason had attracted little attention from the people standing on the road and on the embankment; they were all immersed in their own private dramas. Cars were no longer winding their way through the disaster but had pulled up just behind it, creating their own roadblock that the cops would have to navigate.

Whit was gritting his teeth. His right pant leg had been burned black and was still smoking.

"Are you okay?"

"I don't know." Whit's voice was a thin rasp between quick breaths. "Hurts like hell."

Eddie broke from his stupor and pointed to someone. "There's some other fellas look like they need help," he said, meekly, and made as if to assist them.

"Hold on—you're not done helping us yet." Jason asked where Eddie's car was, and if it was still working.

Eddie pointed to a two-toned, black-and-red four-door Dodge that was pulled onto the skidway, twenty yards away. Jason couldn't see any signs of damage. And Eddie had taste. Still holding the Thompson with one hand, Jason handed Eddie the briefcase with the other and told him to put it on the floor of the backseat and be quick about it. Then he had him do the same with the heavy bag of guns. As Eddie obeyed, Jason fished the fedora out of the not yet burning backseat and put it on.

"You'll be okay, Whit," Jason told his brother, handing him the Thompson. "Hold this and I'll drag you to the backseat."

Jason threaded his arms beneath Whit's armpits, pinned his own forearms together, and pulled his brother up. Only now did he realize that Whit wasn't the only one who'd got banged up. His own chest ached and he limped on tender knees.

He could see the lights of a police car flashing, its sirens and horns berating the parked cars that blocked its path. There didn't seem to be any cops on foot yet, but surely they'd shoot before making themselves visible. Hopefully the cops would decide there were too many civilians around for them to open fire. Most of the drivers and passengers had run to the embankment beyond the highway, but Jason could see some of them sitting shocked in their cars, and a few were still standing in the road. A young boy in a Cardinals cap stood a few feet away from two facedown bodies, staring.

Jason remembered the chaotic Milwaukee job and realized that any number of people had gotten good looks at the Firefly Brothers. If one of them had a gun, he could step forward and try to claim the reward money. Unless it had already been paid to whoever had plugged them the first time.

He slid Whit into the backseat. Whit, breathing heavily, drool on his chin, sat up and smashed at the back window with the barrel of the tommy. Eddie didn't seem to mind—he was too busy staring at Whit's forehead.

"That ain't . . ." He didn't want to complete his sentence. "That can't be, um . . . ?"

"It's not as bad as it looks," Jason told him. He unzipped the bag of guns and pulled out a Browning rifle. He told Eddie to get behind the wheel and drive as fast as he could to the next exit.

Before they could move, Jason felt something whiz past his head. Then multiple shots, and people were screaming again. Whit let loose with a volley from the Thompson and Jason told Eddie to drive.

Eddie started the engine and Jason took shotgun.

"A hostage means they're not supposed to shoot at us," Jason said. "You're not a very good hostage, Eddie."

Jason faced backward and leaned out his window as Eddie apologized. Flashes timed with the gunshots came from behind a wrecked Reo convertible. A dark streak of smoke from the burning Terraplane blocked Jason's view but he fired anyway. Holes popped out of the Reo's sides as if it were inflatable and bursting with air. Windows on other cars exploded from ricochets. Bits of asphalt geysered ten feet high.

Eddie pressed the accelerator and they lurched forward. Whit's gun started to click and he dropped it onto the road, pulling an automatic pistol from his pocket and firing. Within seconds, they had pulled away from the scattered wreckage, and from that vantage point Jason could see the squad cars from the roadblock losing ground as they wove their way through the crashed cars.

Eddie took the first exit and Jason told him to head east on the country road. They sped past farms and then the sparse shops of a tiny main street, then farms again. Jason had hoped to stumble upon terrain he knew, but he hadn't yet. In the backseat, Whit had closed his eyes and was sweating badly, though he still seemed to be conscious. At a country intersection Jason told Eddie to turn south, hoping to put more distance between them and the highway. It was still midafternoon and they had many hours of sunlight to go.

XXVII.

Do you believe now? Have you accepted it?

It was pitch-black in the basement. Darcy wasn't sure if her eyes were open, wasn't even sure if she was awake.

"Leave me alone."

But you are alone. Unless you count the crazy old man sleeping on the chair beside you. And don't worry—he can't hear me.

She hadn't wanted to believe that there were voices in her head, that she was losing her grip on reality, but she no longer had the strength for such denials. This was her world, after all. Voices in her head, Jason supposedly dying but now alive, an old judge not dying but insisting that he had. She told herself her sanity would return one day. She hoped she would know what to do with it when she found it.

"What do you want?"

Brickbat's upstairs and he'll be awake soon—you know that. You have to accept Jason's death and understand that you can only count on yourself to escape this place. You can't afford self-pity or mourning. You need to be thinking, thinking of how you're going to get out of here.

"I seem to be tied up rather well. You are not being helpful. Unless you'd care to untie me."

Voices lack fingers, unfortunately. But be ready. He'll be drugged when he comes down the stairs. There will be an opportunity, somehow.

"Why don't I just wait for the ransom to be paid? It's taken so long already—"

Because you know your old man can't pay it. He can't save you—you'll need to save yourself. No one knows you're here. No one really cares. People are reading about your story, they're following it in the papers, but do you think it matters to them whether you're set free or your decomposed body is found in the woods next fall? You're a story, and that's all you are to them. Just like your precious Jason.

"Jason was not a story."

He was. He hated being one, of course, and he fought against it, but he knew. He was a story people could tell themselves, a way for people to believe that the world wouldn't always conquer them, that there were ways of fighting back. All those myths and legends—that he could escape any ambush, that he couldn't be killed. They said angels watched over the brothers, deflecting policemen's bullets. He was a prophet, an Old Testament judge let loose to save his people. Those stories gave people hope. Whit understood that, but Jason didn't care. He was only out for himself.

"He wasn't that selfish." She was crying again.

Wasn't he? He cared about you, of course. But only because you were his. He was selfish. He was the embodiment of selfishness. What else can a thief be? Jason was who he was. And you admired him for it.

"I *do* admire him. And I *despise* you."

We hate so much about ourselves. He did, too, but he tried not to let you see it.

"He showed me everything."

Not everything. You notice a lot, but you don't notice everything.

"Leave me alone. Let me sleep."

And what would you like to dream about?

"Jason. And escaping."

That can be arranged.

She had always known how ambivalent Jason felt about the Firefly legends. One night the previous spring, while the gang was planning the

Federal Reserve job, she had asked him why he didn't get the same kick out of it that his brother did.

"Because it's all bunk." He shook his head, then told her again about the time he'd saved Whit at the Hooverville. "I let them put a bunch of other sick folks in my car, too, so the story gets twisted that I'm this saint ferrying the poor to the hospital, like I run my own ambulance service for the needy. And, yeah, whenever we've needed to hide out on someone's farm because we had a busted tire or a breakdown, we've paid 'em for it, paid handsomely. But it's not like we were redistributing the nation's wealth. We were just trying to make sure they wouldn't think bad of us and rat us out." He shook his head. "And once, during an endeavor, Marriner happens to put out his cigar on some banker's papers and they catch fire, and next thing I know, people are talking about how we burn up mortgages for them, erase their debts." He laughed. "And people believe it!"

"Maybe it helps to have something to believe in."

"Well, they shouldn't."

"Jason." She was surprised by his bitterness.

"They're getting their hopes up for something that isn't there. I don't want to be blamed when it all comes crashing down on them."

She put a hand on his shoulder. He was overreacting. "I can't tell if you're saying you don't deserve to be loved or that they don't deserve to love you."

"Maybe both. I just hate them thinking I'm their hero. It was never about that. Maybe I only do this because I'm good at it, and it was the only way I could help Ma save the house, or maybe it's because I'm lazy and shiftless and I don't like to work eight hours a day. Maybe I should've stayed at Pop's store and none of this ever would have happened. Maybe I just like fine clothes too much, and I like showing off, and I'm vain and selfish and Pop was right."

She kissed his cheek. "Is it so terrible to be loved?"

His eyes softened. "We're not as bad as some people say we are. But we sure as hell aren't as good."

"I think you're plenty good."

"Whit talks a great game, about fighting back and helping the people. He spread some money around to some factory pals in Lincoln City, yeah, and I know he brought food to Hoovervilles a few times, but that was a while ago. I haven't seen him donating his share of the last few bank jobs to the Salvation Army or anything."

"Well, he does have a family to take care of."

"And that's what I'm doing. That's all I've been trying to do. People can take those silly ideas about heroes and—"

"It's not your fault what people say."

He was silent for a while. "We're just goddamn thieves. That's all we are."

"You don't have to feel guilty for not living up to—"

"Who said I felt guilty?" he snapped.

"Darling, I didn't—" He always acted so comfortable in his skin, so strong in his suit of armor, that she was startled by how easily he could be hurt.

He turned around and walked toward the door. "I need to get some air, sweetness."

"No, Jason, don't. Where are you going?"

"I'll be fine. I just need to walk a bit."

She stood there as Jason escaped into the darkness outside the apartment, whichever one it was then—Gary? Fond du Lac? Springfield? The nights of so many different cities had borne silent witness to the anger he so carefully held inside.

———

Darcy woke to the sound of someone descending the stairs. A narrow beam of light shone on the bottom of the stairway. Seconds later, the room brightened to the meager level it had attained earlier, and she saw the doctor screwing a new lightbulb into the fixture dangling from the ceiling.

"Please help us," Darcy said to him, so quickly it was pure reflex. Then she heard the stairs creaking again.

Brickbat reached the bottom, turned, and smiled at her. He had removed his jacket and wore only a shoulder holster over his sleeveless undershirt and slacks. A large white bandage covered only part of his massive shoulder; it would have taken a dressing the size of a bedsheet to cover the whole thing. He had shaved and was apparently enjoying the painkillers; he held a white pillow as if he still wanted to cuddle with it.

"Sorry, kitten. Ride's not quite over yet."

"I don't want them down here much longer," the doctor said. He was looking around at his vast piles as if hoping to find a box large enough to stuff them in. Jesus, she hoped that wasn't what he was looking for.

"And what's with the pillow?" the doctor asked.

"It's gonna help us get rid of them. Here, hold it. I'll show ya."

He handed the pillow to the doctor, who looked as if he hadn't had a drink in a while now and sorely missed it. He seemed more annoyed than confused as he held the pillow to his chest. Then Brickbat unholstered his gun, pressed it deep into the pillow, and fired.

Darcy was too startled to shout. She didn't so much hear the muted shot as feel it. The doctor was on his back now and the pillow had landed beside him. Feathers hung in the air and the basement smelled of burned laundry.

Brickbat picked up the pillow, torn on both sides, stained red on one and black on the other. "Worked pretty well," he said to himself. Darcy looked down at her feet. She felt him take a step toward the silent judge but was unable to look up. He was putting the pillow on the judge's lap. A blackened feather landed on her knee.

"No need to rush with a guy who's tied up," Brickbat said. "Any last words, old man?"

"That won't work on me."

Brickbat chuckled. "That so?"

"Yes."

"Why not?"

"I cannot die. I cannot imagine it."

Brickbat laughed harder this time. "Ain't that a riot. Imagination's got nothing to do with it, old man. Sweet dreams." Then a metallic crunch, gears straining against each other. "What the hell?"

From the corner of her eye she thought she saw Brickbat move the gun closer to his own face. He shook the gun, then extended his arm so that it was pressed into the pillow once more. Again the failed sounds of un-yielding metal.

"Damn thing's jammed," he muttered.

Darcy finally dared to watch. Brickbat was fiddling with his gun. She had never touched one of Jason's, so she wasn't sure what was wrong. Finally, he shook his head.

"Your lucky day, old-timer. But not so lucky." He swung the gun into the judge's face. Darcy didn't look away quickly enough. The force of the blow against the judge's head toppled him in his chair. There was no moan or cry of pain, just the dry crunch of wood snapping, and maybe bone. Finally, she was able to look at the heap on the floor—the chair legs pointing up at her like an inept lion tamer's stool, unable to prevent the mauling.

"Just you and me, kitten."

"Please." Her voice was not usually so small. "Please don't do this."

"I'm not going to—the show must go on." Brickbat holstered the problematic gun. "Sorry you had to see all that, but I don't like to leave messes."

"Please, just let me go and you can disappear. Isn't that what people like you want?"

"Disappearing broke is what plenty other saps been doing, so no thanks. Disappearing with loads of cash, though—that sounds nice. Speaking of which, I gotta go back up and make some calls."

He took something from his pocket. "You too good to look at me? Then I guess you don't want any hooch."

She looked up. He was holding a bottle of rye. He tipped the open mouth in her direction. She hated him, but she lifted her chin.

He lowered the bottle to her lips and she drank. She could have spat in his face, of course, and she did consider it. But that wouldn't gain her anything, and drinking this surely would. She gulped, and he made an admiring sound.

"Some food would be nice, too," she said when he let her breathe. But goddamn that had tasted good. She inclined her chin again as he was moving to pocket the bottle. He laughed and gave her another snort. She swallowed and felt the burn in her throat. When she closed her eyes, she felt lighter. She willed her feet to be lifted into the air, willed her body to float away.

She heard him pocket the bottle and she opened her eyes. They looked at each other silently. Then she asked if he had really killed him.

"Which one?"

"Jason."

"Yeah, kitten. I really did. Hopefully this'll all end soon and you can make it to his funeral."

Then Brickbat gagged her with a dishrag. As he stuffed it into her mouth, she tried to bite him. She thought she was successful until she saw his fingers move, and then he was tying the ends behind her head. She had only bitten the rag. The bastard hadn't even bothered to find a clean one—it was damp and tasted of grease and old dishwater. She felt her stomach turn, but she closed her eyes to control her insides. She needed to stay calm. There would be a way. There had to be a way.

"Sorry, kitten. Can't trust you to keep quiet while I run a little errand. Say a prayer and maybe you'll be a free woman before long." He walked up the stairs and closed the door.

Darcy saw that the judge's chest was rising and falling, so the old man had managed to escape death once again, though he likely wouldn't be moving anytime soon. She tried to call out to him, to wake him up, but she could barely make a sound, and when she tried to move her tongue she nearly choked.

She wondered again how long she would be down here. The bulb did not burn out, and the bodies on the floor did not stir.

XXVIII.

——————————————
——————————————

"People are saying you can't be killed." Eddie's voice quavered as he drove his commandeered Dodge. They'd been off the highway for half an hour, and apart from a few driving instructions not a word had been spoken. "Dillinger was the crook who couldn't be caught, and you're the crooks who can't—"

"They caught Dillinger eventually," Jason noted.

"But what about you two?" He peered at Whit in the rearview. "That bullet hole real?"

"Let's drop him off here," Whit rasped. His eyes had been shut for the past ten minutes.

They were on a country road and hadn't passed an inhabited building for a few minutes. More important, Jason hadn't spied any telephone lines in a while. He told Eddie to pull over when they reached an intersection with a narrow, badly rutted road.

Once Eddie was out of the car and Jason had slid into the driver's seat, Jason told him to step a few paces off the road, close his eyes, and spin in a circle for ten seconds. Then he ordered the dizzy hostage to lie facedown in the field and to stay that way, with his eyes shut, for two minutes.

"You do that," Jason said, "and I promise you the police will find this fine automobile not far from here and in good condition."

After another twenty minutes, Jason was driving them through a particularly barren stretch of farms when he pulled over to the side of the road. The engine still running, he stepped out of the Dodge and opened the back door to get a better look at his brother. Whit's right pant leg had been burned black. It was warm to the touch as Jason tore it open. Whit winced, his eyes still shut. The skin of his leg was lobster red, like a very bad sunburn. It wasn't white or blistering, at least not yet.

"Think you'll be okay. Lucky we got it put out so fast."

"You crashed and I got burned. Doesn't feel so goddamn lucky."

Back behind the wheel, Jason soon came upon a small town with a block-long commercial district; fortunately, it boasted a pharmacy but not a police station. Jason parked the Dodge at the far end and told Whit to stay the hell awake. Whit nodded unconvincingly, one hand gripping the pistol in his pocket. Jason put the fedora on Whit's head, slanting it low over the bullet hole.

Jason had no glasses or disguise of any kind, but hopefully he was disheveled enough to be unrecognizable. Still, he was self-conscious at his mangy appearance, hatless and wearing only an undershirt, with highway-blown hair and various cuts across his filthy face. His right hand rested in his pocket to conceal the barrel of an automatic pistol as he bought dressings and burn ointment from the pharmacist, telling the young man that his wife had burned her hand something awful at the stove. He also bought an eighth of rye, some painkillers, a *Post-Dispatch*, a state map, and a quart bottle of pop. No radios were on, and he hoped that word of their misadventure had not yet spread. If the pharmacist noticed that Jason wasn't wearing a wedding ring, he didn't say anything.

He was back at the Dodge in less than five minutes. Half a mile later, he found a filling station that was closed on account of its being the Lord's Day. He pulled over and emptied the bottle of pop, then refilled the bottle and wet the dressings at a spigot. Whit opened the bottle of ointment and poured a good amount into his right hand, impatient to begin the healing, but then he stared at his throbbing legs as if realizing for the first time that he'd actually have to touch them to apply it. He sucked in his breath as he began. Jason wished Whit would hurry but he understood, so he held his tongue as Whit slowly slathered himself. Whit was panting by the time he finished, then Jason laid the wet dressings on his brother's legs. Finally it was over, and Whit washed down four painkillers with a healthy swig of rye. He added a much longer pull for good luck.

"I'd like you to stay conscious," Jason told him.

"Too late," Whit said, drinking again. "Just drive. If you need to wake me up later, try shooting me in the head."

Jason kept his word to Eddie; the kid would surely tell the police the make and model of his car, so the Dodge needed to go. Jason stopped at a farmhouse whose driveway was cluttered with automobiles; either some kind of party or a farm auction was in full swing. Crouching all the while, Jason transferred their possessions to the backseat of a new but otherwise nondescript black Nash. Hot-wiring the engine took less than a minute; waking and then moving his injured brother took considerably longer. But no one seemed to notice, or, if they did, no one dared interfere, and Jason backed onto the road and pulled away.

The Firefly Brothers' many getaways were usually conducted in less harried a fashion, but not always. Once Jason had been shot in the forearm when exiting a bank, and of course there was the time Jake Dimes was killed before Jason could even get into the car. Other allies had suffered broken bones and bullet ricochets, so the stress of traveling with a grievously injured companion was not entirely foreign. Still, it complicated their already long-shot plan to find Darcy.

Jason drove south for another hour. Because the cops had chased them east on the highway, they likely would assume the brothers were headed for the state line and would set up more roadblocks around Jefferson City and along the border to Illinois. This suited Jason fine—the doctor he suspected Brickbat was visiting lived on the Missouri side of St. Louis. Their brief detour would allow them to drive into the city from the southwest, bypassing Jefferson City and the main highways. The foothills of the Ozarks rose calm and dark on the horizon as Jason followed signs for a park and a campground to hide in until sunset.

"This is a punishment." Whit startled him by speaking suddenly, his eyelids still clamped shut. Jason had assumed that his brother was asleep or unconscious. Even now he wasn't sure.

"What, your leg?"

"No, *this*. Waking up after dying, haunting each other. It's a punishment."

Still Whit insisted on finding some grand narrative within which to place them. "Okay, fine. It's punishment. But for what? Robbing banks? For not being nicer to each other as kids? For shooting folks that got in our way? What, exactly, do you think we're being punished for?"

But Whit was silent, and a moment later he answered Jason's question with a snore.

After hiding in the park for a few hours, Jason drove to a filling station to get more water for his brother, who had finally woken up to a terrible thirst. Jason again risked being identified by purchasing four dollars of gasoline from the old-lady proprietor, and, since he didn't have a car key, he risked annoying her by explaining that he couldn't turn off the engine during the transaction because the starter had been giving him trouble.

"Looks like a new car," she said.

"Lemons come in all shapes and sizes these days."

Whit was feigning sleep in the backseat, the fedora crooked over his eyes, and he'd delicately laid the pages of the *Post-Dispatch* over his legs to hide his injury. Jason idly asked the lady how far they were from Jefferson City, receiving an answer he paid no attention to, then asked if she knew of a place where they could get some supper. She told them the pastor's family tended to barbecue in their front yard and sell to neighbors and whoever should pass by on Sunday evenings, and she gave him directions. She advised against the chicken, which the pastor's wife tended to overcook.

The sun was setting and the gathering at the pastor's was breaking up, but judging from the output of the smoker there still seemed to be some fixings left. A dozen adults and that many children were spread out on blankets or the well-watered lawn of a three-story white house surrounded by elms. Packs of kids were running around with sparklers. None of the men looked like trouble. He removed the automatic from his pocket, replacing it with a smaller revolver that could nestle there without being noticed.

Adrenaline had done much to mask the initial toll of the crash, but now he was suffering his injuries' delayed wrath. His neck was stiff, he felt a stabbing pain in his left shoulder if he lifted his arm more than ninety degrees, and the center of his breastbone was tender from its multiple impacts with the steering wheel. He tried his damnedest not to limp despite his throbbing knees, and he hoped that the cuts on his face didn't look so bad in the dimming light.

Jason smiled at the middle-aged man working the grill and asked if a traveling salesman could buy some dinner for himself and his dozing partner. The cook, who Jason figured for the minister, speared two chunks of brisket and piled them on a paper plate beside a heap of potato salad, and only now did Jason realize how hungry he was. He sat on a bench near the grill and tried to eat as quickly as he could without appearing frantic about it.

When asked, he told the minister that he and his partner were salesmen for a growing line of men's wear out of Chicago. He joked that he normally would look more dapper but they'd had auto trouble and he'd spent half the weekend lying beneath their company's supposedly new car. His partner was sleeping their troubles off. The guy in the plaid shirt pointed out that Jason had left his engine on and Jason repeated his line about the starter. They chatted about the Cardinals, and Jason tried not to appear nervous as two boys strayed toward the Nash, pointing at the fine scalloped lines above the front wheels.

The minister asked Jason for the salesman's opinion of the hard times. Jason tried to plagiarize the nonsense that the jellybean at the diner had told him a few days ago, but he himself didn't believe it. *It's a cruel, awful world,* he wanted to say to the minister. *They take it from you if you don't take it first. They'll ignore your pain, or laugh at it.* But instead he smiled and said he was sure things would turn around by Christmas, God willing.

Then one of the boys screamed.

Jason leaped off the bench and ran toward the car, along with a couple of parents. One of the kids said there was a dead man in the car's backseat.

Jason saw that Whit had passed out again, and the fedora had slipped off his head. It was growing dark, but Whit's gunshot wound was still plenty visible.

"My partner's just dead tired," Jason clarified with an awkward smile.

"There's a hole in his head!"

Jason realized that the kid didn't sound so much frightened as enthralled; he was pointing into the Nash with one hand and eagerly tugging his father's sleeve with the other.

"He got some oil on his forehead when we were tinkering with the engine," Jason said.

The other boy was hesitantly walking toward the Nash again, but Jason told him not to come any closer.

"Don't you talk to my son that way," said the overall-clad father, who was tall but a weight class below Jason. "What's going on here?"

The adults were exchanging whispers, pulling at the boys' shoulders. The minister left the grill to come closer, and soon the scattered picnickers became more of a pack.

A woman gasped. Some of the whispers weren't quiet enough anymore and Jason heard his name spoken, then repeated, carefully handed from adult to adult as if it were a cursed, unholy relic.

He couldn't be sure none of the men had guns of their own, so he took out his. More gasps, and people backed away. Keeping his gun pointed at the ground, Jason apologetically told the minister that he needed to be leaving now, and how much did he owe?

"Just take the food. I don't want your blood money."

"It's not blood money."

"Radio says you killed five people today." The minister was standing closest to Jason; he'd held his ground as the others had backed off. "One was a young mother. Two were police officers."

"You got your news wrong." Jason had tried not to dwell on the myriad results of the shootout. "Don't believe everything you hear."

"Do not tell me what to believe." The minister held his gaze.

Whit started snoring. The congregation gasped again. Hands were raised to mouths or made the sign of the cross.

"Keep those hands where I can see them," Jason said, more nervously than he'd meant to.

"It's true," a woman said.

"Yeah, it's true," Jason echoed. "Whatever else it is, it's certainly true."

"So even Hell rejects you," the minister said.

Jason had had enough of the preacher. He walked backward to the driver's side of the Nash, his eyes keeping watch over the five men of the group, none of whom appeared eager to intervene. Jason apologized for disturbing their cookout and got into the car, leaving Whit's share of the food behind. He turned on the headlights and pulled onto the road.

Ten minutes later, Whit stirred when Jason hit a pothole. So far Jason hadn't seen any cops, and he wondered how quickly the picnickers would spread the alarm.

"Where's supper?" Whit asked.

"They said they only feed Seventh-day Adventists."

"Really?"

"Yeah. Minister was a real jerk about it."

Jason saw Whit's foggy eyes in the rearview. Whit took another sip from the half-empty eighth. "Why do you smell like barbecue?"

Jason dodged the question. "You missed your chance to ask a man of God all your deep questions."

"I have a feeling I'll have other opportunities."

Jason thought of the minister's claim that hell had rejected them. As if he and his brothers were bad checks no bank would cash, left to wander a devalued limbo.

"Yeah," he said as he stared out at the dark road. "Welcome to the land of opportunity."

XXIX.

The number of reporters in the hallway had increased. Cary needed to employ much patience as well as elbow work to force his way through the packed hallway to the Bureau's office door.

He exhaled deeply as he shut the door behind him. It was eight at night but the bullpen was frenetic. Cary had been getting ready for dinner when he received a call from Gunnison telling him to hurry back to the office and to bring a suitcase with a couple days' clothes.

"The Firefly Brothers are alive," Gunnison had said. "We think."

That was all he would say over the phone. As Cary hurried into the bullpen, Gunnison stomped toward him in a shirt stained with coffee.

"What's happened?" Cary asked.

It was only that morning that they'd driven out to Points North and heard Chief Mackinaw's admissions. Then they had driven back to Chicago and Cary had filed a carefully worded report for Washington. He didn't want to sound hysterical by hypothesizing that the Firesons might somehow be alive, but the last thing he wanted to sign his name to was a statement that the Firesons were indeed dead only to find out later that the outlaws were still at large. And here was Gunnison telling him they were larger than ever.

"They were in a gunfight with police in Missouri this afternoon. Started in Sedalia, continued on to Route 50 west of Jefferson City. Two officers and three civilians were killed on the highway, and a few folks in the hospital might get added to the list."

"Who says it was the Firesons?"

"Numerous witnesses."

"Why are we believing them?"

"We're not entirely sure we do. But the Sedalia cops swear to it; they say they got prints from a car the brothers abandoned, and from the scene of another shooting. They're sending the prints to the Washington lab for final comparisons."

Cary had dropped his suitcase somewhere. He sank into the chair of whomever was behind him. "What other shooting?"

Gunnison sat on the desk. "Sedalia police got a call from a probate attorney who said he'd stopped by what was supposed to be an abandoned property and saw some dead bodies. Cops find four corpses, one of which they identify as Whit Fireson, and a lot of shell casings but only a few guns. During the drive to the morgue"—and Gunnison chuckled—"the cops claim that Whit started yelling from inside his hearse. They pull over, unwrap him, he jumps up and accosts the officers, who were rather stunned. Then, from out of nowhere, Jason drives up and takes him away. A chase ensues."

Cary had to take a few seconds. What Gunnison was saying was impossible, yet he relayed the data in the matter-of-fact tone of a bleacher bum recapping a one-two-three inning for a friend returning from the john.

"Whit was only *pretending* to be dead?"

"St. Louis agents are interrogating the two cops who claim Whit came back to life. The cops are reportedly being unhelpful and have been quoting Bible verses."

All around Cary, agents were shouting into phones, running in and out of the bullpen, into the SAC's office, into the interrogation room. The mood was more panicked than usual.

"I know Mackinaw seemed like a dolt, but still, how can you fake a death and trick the police—twice?"

"We're rustling every underworld doc we can think of—one of them has to be involved in this. Maybe someone's come up with a kind of sedative that can knock a fella out so bad it'll convince an incompetent coroner he's dead, only to wake up a few hours later. Who knows, I ain't a scientist. All I know is, when we do find these fellas we need to blow their damned heads off to be sure the job's done."

Cary asked about the scene at the farmhouse.

"One of the other bodies was ID'd as Elton Roberts. Apparently the house used to belong to a relative of Brickbat Sanders, though it looks like Brickbat, if he was ever there, made it out alive. Cops found some women's items and two drafts of notes that are almost verbatim to the ones that had been delivered to one Jasper Windham the last few days."

"They're the ones who kidnapped Darcy Windham?"

"Or pretended to. 'Cause it gets even more interesting. We've been talking to a limey insurance investigator from Lloyd's of London. It seems Windham had taken out a kidnap insurance policy on himself and his lovely daughter a couple years back—it's the thing to do among the moneyed and paranoid, I guess. Policy offers to cover ransoms up to two hundred thousand. But the fine print says that all is null and void if any of the insureds have 'criminal or unsavory' associations."

"So the policy was voided because Darcy ran with the Firesons."

"One would think. I guess Lloyd's has been slow about mailing its cancellation notices, 'cause Windham was under the impression the policy still stood. He's been on the phone all week hollering at the adjusters, saying they need to cover the ransom for him. It seems the finances at Windham Automotive aren't what they used to be. Windham's also been receiving some suspicious calls lately from someone who sounds, according to one of our agents, a lot like Jason Fireson. One of the calls was traced to the Sedalia farmhouse."

"Jesus Christ. They faked their deaths thinking that if Darcy had no underworld associates, at least no *living* underworld associates, the policy would be good. Then they kidnapped her, or pretended to, thinking they'd collect the ransom either from Windham or the insurer."

"Give the college boy an A."

"Is Windham in on it?"

"He's under questioning at his estate. Started yelling at our agents and saying they were putting his daughter's life in jeopardy. Then our agents started yelling back, and he asked for his lawyer."

Some things were clicking, but just as many things seemed unconnected.

"So the Firesons faked their second death at this Sanders family farm-house, but the other bodies really were dead?"

"Allegedly. We told the Sedalia cops to lock 'em up in the morgue and put 'em under armed guard just in case. Once they stink, we'll know for sure."

Cary exhaled. "If this is all an elaborate ruse for a kidnapping, why would the Firesons kill all their partners?"

"So they could get a bigger slice of the pie? Who knows. Windham had agreed to let us tape his calls, so we got Jason on tape—sounds like he was speaking in code or something, talking about angels. And he name-dropped Nitti. We're trying to figure it all out. I say Windham breaks by the end of the day."

Cary shook his head and looked around. Every agent at least tangen-tially involved in the Fireson case or the Windham kidnapping was in the bullpen. Men on the phone held their receivers with white knuckles, as if trying to strangle out confessions.

"Good God. Please tell me Dillinger is still dead."

"Last we checked. And his old man had him buried under six feet of concrete and scrap iron to keep out grave robbers. So I think we're safe."

The Bureau chartered a flight into Jefferson City, piloted by a chatty old man who claimed to have been part of the crew that had shot down the Red Baron in the Great War. He also bragged that he was the only Amer-ican military pilot to crash seven times and live. He was very good at crashing, he explained. Cary noticed that the plane lacked seat belts.

Cary and Gunnison were traveling with ten other agents, one of whom, Norris, had arrived only two days ago from the Oklahoma City field office. There had been no official announcement, but word was that Norris was going to be installed as the new Chicago SAC, and as such he was taking charge of the newly re-formed Fireson Squad. He was as pow-erfully built as Gunnison but taller. He was bald, and even his scalp looked muscular. He spoke in a dry voice that Cary couldn't always hear above the sounds of the engine.

"Mr. Hoover has made clear what he expects of us," Norris said once they were airborne. "People are telling all kinds of wild stories about the Firesons, all because of the mishaps in Points North and now Sedalia. We are being sent to correct those mishaps." The agents discussed various locations where the Firesons—if this really was the Firesons—might be trying to hide: safe houses they or other Public Enemies had used in the past, nearby addresses of past associates or ex-girlfriends or stepsisters. The nearest mechanics of ill repute, in case they had car trouble, and the nearest underworld physicians, in case they were injured. It wasn't a long list, and the possibility existed that the Firesons could be attempting to flee to Lincoln City, but the Missouri police claimed to have sealed off the eastern border.

Norris detailed the weaponry he had arranged to have loaded onto the plane: submachine guns, automatic rifles, grenades, and a few things Cary hadn't heard of and would have to ask Gunnison about later. Now Cary felt even less safe on the plane. More weapons were waiting for them at the St. Louis office, Norris explained.

The plane shook during its descent and Cary glanced out the window. They were already low enough, and the moonlight bright enough, for him to see the patchwork of farms and country roads neatly laid out like the chess set of a bored midwestern God.

"People like to say the Firefly Brothers are bulletproof," Norris continued. "We're going to give the brothers an opportunity to demonstrate that ability. The Director wants the Firesons—or whoever these people are—eliminated, dramatically. That was his choice of words. *Dramatically.* We leave nothing to chance. If we trace them to a building, we blow the building up and burn the rubble. If we see them in a vehicle, we shoot the gas tank and strafe it to ribbons. We let the American people see there is no way these crooks can possibly escape this time. Justice and order prevail. The Director holds a press conference and you-all get to catch up on sleep."

And then, Cary thought, *I return to a safe routine of phone calls and paperwork, and I send my résumé to every law firm I can think of.*

XXX.

———————————

Darcy woke to the judge standing before her, whispering insistently. The dim bulb was behind him, yet she could see the welt rising from the left side of his face. His hard fall had snapped his chair, and he must have slid his bound wrists through the breaks in the wood to free them, although they were still behind his back. He had wriggled his feet from their bindings as well; loops of rope hung loosely around his ankles.

"I'm going to look for a blade or some glass," he told her, and she nodded. The gag had pinned her tongue to the bottom of her mouth. The insides of her cheeks felt moldy.

After his beating, the judge finally seemed to have accepted that he was mortal, after all, and had to get out of here. Darcy tried to keep calm, but she could feel herself trembling. Was Brickbat still upstairs? He had mentioned something about an errand—was he still gone?

Something landed on the cement floor, and seconds later the judge emerged from the mess. He stopped in front of the bloodstained pillow and bent down as far as his aged knees would allow, an awkward position with his hands bound behind him. Then he dropped the something onto the pillow: it was a small window frame with four panes of glass. With his feet, he carefully slid the window off the pillow and onto the floor, then nudged the pillow on top of it. He stamped and the pillow crunched.

The judge kicked off the pillow and bent down to pick up a piece of glass. His stiff old body made this a complicated task indeed. Darcy silently, desperately, cheered him on. It was like watching a starving, toothless man bob for apples. Finally, he stood again. His expression as was vacant as before, and sweat ran down his temples.

"I'm holding a small piece of glass," he said as he walked behind her. "When I tell you to, saw your hands back and forth."

He gave her the cue and she obeyed. She felt a stabbing at her wrist, so she stopped. He adjusted the way he was holding the glass and they started again. She moved her hands slowly, cautiously, her muscles warm as they moved in that awkward position, torsion numbing them. She felt bits of frayed rope tickling her palms, and a surge of excitement caused her to move too fast. Stabbing again, but now she didn't care. She was so close! Then her hands lunged and she felt an even more painful scrape— but her hands were free.

She pulled them in front of her face. She had seen so little of her hands these many days of blindness and bondage. Ten long fingers, white knuckles, bloody wrists and palms. They were beautiful.

Darcy wrenched the gag down her jaw and moaned with relief. She opened her mouth, unclenching the muscles as she got to work on the judge's ropes.

She sawed him loose in seconds. Then she leaned over and cut at the bindings on her ankles. It felt *so* good to stand. She took a few steps to remind the blood that it could flow.

"There are no windows," the judge whispered. "No exterior door. We'll need to go up the stairs."

They stared at the ceiling. Suddenly they could hear Brickbat's voice, a low murmuring. Had it been there before and they hadn't noticed? Who was he talking to?

Darcy looked down at the dead body of the doctor. His chest was damp, a stain darkening his gray shirt but not quite reaching his open collar. She wondered what he had in his pants pockets.

She bent down and dared to check. She would not have had the stomach to frisk his jacket pockets—they were likely soaked with blood—but she didn't need to, because in his right pants pocket she found what she was looking for: a small revolver, nestled there quite unobtrusively.

Then the basement door opened.

Their eyes met in panic. Already Brickbat was walking down the stairs, albeit slowly. *Give me the gun,* the old man motioned. She didn't have time to deliberate, only a moment to think that, yes, she probably was not the best one to wield a firearm. She handed him the gun, which he promptly opened.

"No bullets." She could barely hear his whisper. Then he lay down on the floor, in more or less the same position he'd fallen in before.

Why was he just lying there? Surely he could at least bluff Brickbat into disarming. The footsteps getting lower and closer. She barely had time to find a weapon of her own: there, on the ground in front of her, part of the destroyed window, a five-inch-long sliver of wood with a triangular piece of glass protruding from it. Yes, maybe she could hold the wood and drive it into . . . Her dazzled mind would go no further. The footsteps louder now.

She sat in her chair and pulled the gag back up to her mouth. She had to bite hard to prevent it from falling off. Then she bent over, picked up her makeshift dagger, and pulled her hands behind her back as if she were still bound.

The judge had moved the pillow back on top of the other pieces of glass, concealing evidence of their movements.

Then a thought: her feet. She had cut her bindings. Brickbat would notice if he looked.

And there he was, standing ten feet away. Watching her. Looking at her ankles? She wasn't sure. The cocky smile he'd worn before was gone. He seemed ashen. Or determined. He was holding something large and flat.

"Nice nap, kitten?" He stepped a few feet in front of her, bending over and pulling out the legs of a card table he'd carried down. At least now he couldn't see her feet. He placed upon it a small black sack; whatever was inside it sounded heavy and metallic. Then Brickbat wandered over to her right, deeper into the basement. Darcy looked down at the judge, who was still playing dead. Her fingers were shaking and she wondered if that meant her shoulders were, too.

Brickbat emerged from the catacombs and placed another rickety chair at the table, opposite Darcy. Before sitting on it, he leaned forward and pulled her gag down. If he noticed that it hadn't been very tight, he didn't show it.

"Might as well give you a chance for some last words."

She swallowed. Her throat ached. She wanted to ask what he meant, but she feared her voice would break. He unholstered his silver gun and placed it on the table before him. Then he reached into the sack and pulled out a long, thin metal rod, a small can of oil, two soiled rags, and a coarse brush. Her mind reeled at the possibilities.

"Things haven't turned out well, kitten. This has been a goddamn catastrophe." He seemed to be addressing his gun, which he was slowly disassembling. He laid the pieces on the table, then used the scouring brush to clean the barrel. His fat fingers moved with surprising dexterity, performing this ritual with a calmness approaching reverence. "I never planned on killing you. I don't like to kill dames."

"You don't . . . you don't have to."

He looked at her. "But I do." He returned his attention to his quartered and beloved device. "That's the sad thing. No other way out for ol' Brickbat. And no payoff. All this work, all this goddamn waiting. Elton dead, the other guys." He shook his head. "This is why I never tried yaffling before, and I shoulda remembered that. It's a lesson for me."

He was essentially unarmed while the gun was in pieces. If she was going to strike him, she had to do it now. Instead, feeling like a failure, she asked, "Why?"

He poured oil onto one of the rags, then rubbed it on the various pieces of disassembled weaponry.

"Because your old man messed up is why. He got himself arrested, you believe that? S'what I get for working with an amateur. Because that's what he is, kitten: an amateur. He had some connections and I let that make me think he knew things, but he doesn't."

"What are you talking about?"

He looked at her again. She saw, from the corner of her eye, that she had smeared blood on her sweater. Not much, but it was certainly there, almost glowing on the white cotton. He hadn't seemed to notice it yet. She had to keep him talking. She had to act.

"It was all his idea, kitten. An insurance scam. But the dumb suit didn't read the fine print on his policy, and the company ain't gonna ante up. On account of you being a known accomplice of the Firefly Brothers. Ain't that just the kicker? You being Jason's twist is what's gonna get you killed. If you'd been just another rich girl, the insurer would be paying the ransom and this'd've gone off without a hitch. But because you were slut to a bank robber you're uninsurable. You're worthless." He began reassembling the gun.

It took even more time for Darcy to reassemble the facts he had laid out. They did not yet assume the shape of a coherent whole.

"My *father* arranged this?" She had long hated him, but something like this she hadn't thought possible. The world slowly came together, in a sickening way, an even darker place than she had imagined but, alas, one that made its own cruel sense. She willed herself to concentrate, to ignore what Brickbat was saying. She tightened her grip on her weapon.

"Yeah. Badly, too. Last time I work with a goddamn carmaker. And you know his cars are junk? I've stolen a few, and they always die on me. Everything dies on me."

Where was she supposed to aim? His neck? The soft spot of his temple? If she leaned forward, she could reach him. But she would need to stretch. And her hands were so very far away. He would see it coming.

Brickbat peered through the barrel of the gun, assessing his work. He blew into it, then looked again. The gun was nearly whole now, everything but the magazine lying beside it. Pointing the gun to his right— away from Darcy as well as from the two bodies on the floor—he pulled the trigger and it snapped ruthlessly.

"Don't move."

Brickbat managed to show little emotion at hearing the judge's voice. She saw Brickbat's eyes narrow, a tightening of the skin, and his large head slowly rolled toward his left. The judge had sat up and was aiming the revolver at Brickbat's chest.

"Didn't hit you hard enough, I guess." The unloaded pistol was still in Brickbat's hand, the magazine within easy reach. The fingertips of Darcy's right hand were slick with blood. His neck would be too hard to hit; he barely even had one. The face, then. The right temple. What would happen? How would it sound, feel? Could she do this?

Brickbat was reaching for the clip.

"I said, don't move."

"I heard you, old man. Go ahead and shoot me with that empty gun." He snapped the magazine into place. Then he stood up and kicked the judge in the face. The old man's body lifted into the air, his bent legs straightening until he was stretched to almost his full height before gravity regained control. Then his body folded up again and collapsed into itself, a puddle on the floor.

Brickbat snapped the clip into his gun. The sound of readiness, of inevitability. He was standing a good five feet away from her. She had missed her chance.

"Stupid bastard. You think I hadn't frisked the doc?" He shook his head at the old man. Darcy didn't know if the judge was breathing this time. She didn't care. She herself was breathing twice as fast.

She let her head sag for a moment. She heard Brickbat lightly kick the judge to see if he needed a bullet. Then she stood up and stepped forward and swung.

She realized she was shouting only when she stopped. And she stopped because her blow had found its mark. Not its intended mark, but something. Jesus, had she closed her eyes? She had. She opened them. Her arm was stiff, energy surging through it. Paralyzed with power. Her fingers throbbed from the impact. They were clenched around the wood handle and the glass had vanished inside Brickbat's raised left forearm. For such a big man, he was fast. They were motionless for a moment, joined together in that violent embrace, and then she saw the blood seep out of his wound. Now he was the one screaming.

He yanked his arm away from hers but the weapon was still embedded there. He reached for the wood with his right hand, but he was holding his gun with it, so he couldn't pull the blade out. He looked blind with rage and pain. He bit down on his bottom lip as he straightened his right arm and pulled the trigger.

The gun jammed again. He yelled at it: *Goddamn gun, fucking jamming, goddamnit.* He was staggering in a semicircle, keeping his distance while he shook his gun hand and tried again. Nothing. He looked at the gun, shook it, peered into the barrel, and screamed at it. He shot himself in the head.

Brickbat was staring at her but not seeing her. There was a hole in his forehead, and she looked away. Then she heard him land.

She was breathing even faster now, hugging herself. She spun in a circle. What had happened? She smelled an industrial smoke. The gun had jammed, and then it hadn't. This wasn't possible. He had shot himself in the face. He was dead. She looked up and saw the soles of his shoes, the toes pointing up at angles. Near them the judge's eyes were open and lifeless. Nothing was moving but her.

She ran up the stairs.

There was a small table in the kitchenette and on it a set of keys. She ran out the door and into the night—a deep, quiet darkness. The doctor's car was an old Chevrolet, and one of the keys worked in the ignition. The engine started and she drove in reverse, too fast, scraping shingles from the side of the house as she pulled out.

Brickbat was dead, yet still she felt pursued. Surely there was someone else. She needed to be free. Was this freedom? Where was she going? She backed into the street and realized the Chevy's lights weren't on. She turned them on but nothing happened. *Fine, fine, just go.* She could see well enough. There were arc lights, a moon. She pressed on the gas. Every movement was more than she meant it to be. The car lunged and her head snapped back. She took a corner too hard, tires squealing. There was a car approaching. Brickbat's confederates coming to his aid? Whoever they were, they were in her way. Or she was in theirs. Yes, this was the wrong side of the road. The other car honked its horn and she twisted the wheel and the Chevy leaped a sidewalk. She didn't brake in time.

She was breathing fast but it seemed she was only exhaling. Nothing was reaching her lungs, let alone her brain. She hated herself. She was stronger than this. God, she was hungry. She lifted her head and wondered if she'd been knocked out. Perhaps she was dead. Yes, of course. Why would Brickbat have shot himself? He must have shot *her*. She was in the land of the dead now. And that's why he was knocking on her window.

"Darcy? *Darcy!*"

The door opened and she screamed. Her hands were still bleeding and she held them before her to ward him off, her fingers were blades, she would shred him. This could not be. If only reality shredded so easily.

At first she couldn't even say his name. She could only look at him as he bent down before her. She lowered her fingers slowly, cautiously, as if they really were blades and she feared cutting him. Cutting that beautiful face. His cheeks were silver in the moonlight and she didn't remember his eyes being this round. As if *he* was the one who should be shocked at this discovery.

"Sweetness," he said, and her fingers dared to alight on his shoulders, and they did not pass through him, because he was not a ghost. When he reached for her she did not wake up in an empty car or in a field or tied up in a basement. Her eyes were not blindfolded but the tears were doing the same job.

"Jason." She squeezed him as they held each other. This was real, if only for a moment. *God, please, let this moment last. I'll take the rest later. But for now, please, just this moment.*

She tightened her grip as he rubbed her back. She said his name again, her voice choked. Then his fingers were on hers, carefully prying them loose as if disarming a bomb. He didn't know that she had already exploded, too many times. She was shrapnel.

He looked at her bloody wrists and fingers, back into her eyes. "Are you all right?"

How could he ask her that? Her cry mutated into a laugh.

His thumbs beneath her eyes now, tracing a path for the tears. She opened them and saw him watching her. "Darcy, we need to go. Come on."

"I never should have believed him. I can't believe I did. Of course." She kissed him with lips pursed hard. An ecstatic but defensive kiss. Then he was kissing her cheeks and eyes and forehead and chin.

"I'm so sorry for all this. I've been trying my damnedest to find you."

Slowly she was containing herself. His face was cut in several places, red scratches on his cheeks and across his forehead, but it was him.

"Your former associates leave something to be desired."

"Are they chasing you? You were driving like wildfire."

"No one's chasing me."

"Wish I could say the same."

"Jason," said another voice, Whit's. "People are turning their lights on. Let's go."

Jason coaxed her to her feet. Whit was sitting up in the backseat of an idling Ford, a rifle in his lap and a fedora pulled unusually low on his head.

"Good to see ya, Darcy." Whit sounded drunk. "Glad ya hit the light pole instead of us. Jason's already gotten into enough accidents today."

She didn't remember getting into the passenger seat but here she was, Jason at the wheel, the car speedily moving through town. She was sitting sideways, staring at his profile. He smiled at her through that side of his mouth.

"It's okay, Darcy. I'm here. We can explain. It'll take a while, but we'll have a while."

When? Always there was promised time, in the future. Still, she nodded. He put an arm around her shoulder and she sank into him.

"Don't let me fall asleep," she said, her lips pressed into his shoulder and barely moving. "Don't let me. Don't."

XXXI.

That summer Weston walked countless hours through Lincoln City. He wasn't looking for anything, though at times he irrationally hoped he might somehow stumble upon some money. A briefcase of money, like the kind his brothers often ran off with. Or maybe he'd bump into a man desperate to hire someone. Yes, of course—that happened all the time, didn't it? In this mad, chaotic world, where timing was everything and luck appeared when least expected. So Weston tried not to expect it. Hell, the walks were just something to do. To get him out of the house, to see the world and remind himself that he was better off than some. But funny how we only notice those who are better off than we are. He did not linger on the people sleeping in broken-down flivvers, and instead fixated on the shiny Packards driving by. Rich folks were wise enough to refrain from flaunting their wealth these days, but still, the faintest glimpse was blinding.

It was early August, six days before his brothers would be put on their cooling boards in Points North.

Weston hadn't worked a regular job in three months. He had picked up a few handyman tasks here and there, and in June had managed to land a disappointingly brief stint with the CCC carrying water to firemen fighting a blaze across the Kentucky border. He had been fed three squares a day and lived in a tent for a week, each night praying that the fire would continue. It didn't.

One night he told himself that the next day he would visit a breadline, that he couldn't wait any longer. His money was all but gone and his digestive pains were exacerbated by the hunger, stomach acid burning the walls of his insides. Yet the next day he avoided the breadline once again, instead buying a loaf with his few remaining coins, eating a couple of pieces, and telling himself good news would come. By evening he was telling himself to go to the breadline the next day, but again he couldn't bring himself to do it. Finally, after four days, he went.

The breadline operated out of a formerly abandoned restaurant—a collection of local churches had pooled together to supply food and volunteers. The restaurant was on the edge of downtown, uncomfortably close to where Weston had once worked. Everyone in line was well aware of all the passing businessmen on lunch breaks and workers shuttling by on their various errands and deliveries, all the people who were lucky enough to have a paycheck. The people in motion barely glanced at the unfortunates; when they did, they looked away immediately. Even the people in line refrained from looking at one another, heads bowed. Weston saw only the heels of shoes, tattered pant legs. He got a sunburn on the back of his neck.

After an hour of this, he was given some stew that even had a few chunks of meat in it. He didn't talk to anyone as he ate, hurriedly. He'd been going every day for the past week, and neither the food nor the experience had improved.

Weston had been threatened with eviction, and each time he returned from his walks he was surprised to see that his meager furniture was not yet on the curb. He wondered if the local Unemployed Councils were still active or if they'd disbanded or been arrested. Maybe the only reason he hadn't been evicted yet was that the landlord feared his Fireson connections. That would be nice, to actually benefit from what had cost him so much. No, the landlord had probably held off only because he knew he wouldn't find anyone else to let the room to. The papers said nearly two-thirds of the men in Lincoln City were unemployed, which was all the more staggering given how many of the jobless had left town. At his worst moments Weston wondered if he, too, should leave, but he knew he couldn't abandon Ma and June, even if he had so little to offer.

It would have made financial sense to move in with Ma, but her place was crowded enough with June and her kids. He didn't want to add to their troubles, but he hadn't been able to buy them groceries in weeks, and he knew that Ma would soon run out of the money that Jason and Whit had provided before they went into hiding this summer.

Men on street corners were trading job tips and talking about Dillinger. Two weeks ago, the Man No Jail Could Hold had been gunned down by federal agents while leaving a movie theater with his girlfriend. Weston wondered if Agent Delaney had been one of the shooters. He heard the nighthawks debating whether Dillinger was still alive—maybe it was a government plot, all public relations, or maybe they'd just got the wrong guy, because hadn't Dillinger been seen robbing a bank in Bloomington last week? The gossips noted that, with Dillinger (officially) dead, J. Edgar Hoover had now jointly designated the Firefly Brothers Public Enemy Number One. Their voices glowed with hometown pride, some of them tossing predictions of when the Firesons would reach their inevitable demise, others insisting they would never be killed.

Weston didn't know what time it was when he made it home—he had hocked his pocket watch—but he figured it was past midnight. He was wearing thin cotton pants and a short-sleeved shirt, but still he was sweating from the heat and humidity—the only things Lincoln City seemed to be producing these days. It was surprising that people chose to sleep in the building's entrance and hallways, given that the motionless air was more oppressive here than outdoors, but apparently the knowledge of a roof over their heads was comforting. Weston had to step past a snoring man as he used his key to open the inner door.

Upstairs, another derelict slept a few feet from Weston's door. Weston's key was in the lock when the waking man slurred, "Spare a dime, brother?"

"Sorry," Weston muttered. He was turning the knob when the man rose to his knees and clamped a hand on his wrist.

"Goddamnit, I said no!" And with a ferocity that surprised him, Weston pulled his hand free, compressed it into a fist, and swung to knock the man away.

His punch sounded more like a slap as it was enfolded by one of the man's quick hands, inches before it would have struck his nose.

"Nice punch, Wes. Didn't know you had it in you."

Jason released Weston's hand, then shook his own to lose the sting.

"Jesus Christ." He hadn't seen his brother in months, and Jason's disguise was remarkable. He had a full beard, and in the dim hallway his clothes looked filthy. A thin sheet had been draped over him, but it had fallen off when he sat up. Weston took his eyes off his brother's face long enough to see a rifle barrel poking from beneath the twisted covering.

Jason put a finger to his lips, then pointed to the door. Weston opened it and was about to flick the light switch when Jason again intercepted his hand. "Draw the curtains first." Weston obeyed.

Jason had looked better in the hallway. His normally well-coiffed hair was disheveled, shining with dried sweat. He had gray bags under his eyes and the rest of his skin wasn't much better, his neck pocked with either mosquito bites or some terrible rash. His eyes were veined red. He wore a loose-fitting cotton shirt untucked over gray pantaloons that were fraying at the bottom. He didn't smell very good.

Jason dropped the sheet by the door and laid a long, thick rifle on Weston's table. Weston noticed from the way Jason's shirt hung over his hips that he was also wearing a sidearm. He didn't seem to be carrying a briefcase of money, but maybe a bag was strapped to his back.

"Sorry to scare you, Wes. How've you been?"

"Fine." Weston knew he himself looked bad, but he was reeling from this twisted incarnation of his brother. "Fine."

Jason checked the space behind Weston's small wardrobe, then the closet.

"Are you all right?" Weston asked.

"Haven't been sleeping much. But I'm alive."

"Where's Whit?"

"We split up for a bit. I needed to swing by town real quick. He's okay, though."

Weston wondered how much worse Whit, who had never taken as much care with his appearance as Jason did, could possibly look.

"It's good to see you, Jason. But it's pretty risky you dropping by."

"You aren't being watched," Jason said. That was news to Weston; though he hadn't seen Agent Delaney since their confrontation, he had assumed the agent was still keeping tabs on him. They'd finally decided Weston wouldn't bend to them. Or maybe he'd simply bored them. "Only person watching you the last two days has been me."

Weston stiffened. He tried to remember what he'd done for the past two days.

"Had to do it. Just to be sure. Ma's place is being watched, I figured, but wasn't sure about you. Sure now, which works out. Works out great."

Who was this person? He was speaking more quickly than Jason Fireson ever had, with a quieter voice, spitting out the words half formed, the sentences incomplete. Where was Jason's grandness, his calmness and confidence?

Weston told him to sit down, but Jason shook his head and said he'd done plenty of sitting. Weston offered to get him a glass of water, but Jason told him to stay there.

"How's the job?"

"They're still paying me." If he had been following Weston for the past two days, he should have known that Weston wasn't working. Then again, Jason had never worked a straight job apart from his brief time at Pop's store, so he probably didn't know what a working man's routine was. For all Jason knew, Weston had been given a couple of days off. "Why are you here?"

"Need a favor. It's a simple one, won't be any trouble. And there's money in it for you, after the fact."

Something in Weston's gut dropped a few inches. "Do you have any now?"

"No." Jason looked insulted for a moment, then he explained that he and Whit had knocked over a bank in Wisconsin—the Federal Reserve, Weston knew from the papers—and had quite a lot to show for it, but the money was marked. He rambled a moment about money laundering, whatever that was, and said that in five days he was to meet with a man who would exchange the money for spendable bills. *Jesus*, Weston thought, *I would settle for marked money right now. I would settle for crinkled, torn bills, dripping with blood.* He barely followed Jason's story and could think only of how hungry he felt after his walk—a stupid waste of time and precious calories. His daily trip to the breadline was keeping him alive, but the past few mornings he had spat up blood. Even after washing his mouth out, it was all he could taste.

"Look, Jason, I'm in a bad spot—me and the whole family. You don't know how hard it's been. If you could just get us s—"

"Were you listening to me? I passed it all to the washer. I meet him in five days, and then I'll have it. Until then, I have nothing. This is where you come in."

He explained that one of his confederates, Owney Davis, was due a cut of the money, but that he didn't know where Owney was. He did know a guy who could get in touch with Owney, but he didn't dare go to him because that guy, too, was probably being watched.

Weston shook his head, overwhelmed and confused.

"There's a place up in Karpis called Last Best Chance. Guy that runs it is Chance McGill. I trust him, but it's too risky for me to show myself there. Chance will know how to get a message to Owney for me. I need you to go there and pass the message."

"Why me?"

"Because you aren't being watched. Because everybody I used to trust is either in jail or dead or talking out the other side of their mouths to the brass buttons."

"Just because I wasn't watched *today* doesn't mean—"

"It's a gamble, but a good one. I'm not going to lam off without paying Owney his share. I've done you plenty of favors, so it shouldn't be too much to ask for one in return."

"That's one way of looking at it."

"The hell's that mean?"

"Nothing. Never mind."

"Christ, Wes. I'm sorry I don't have anything for you now, but if this works out me and Whit'll be flush. We'll get some to you and Ma. I'm asking you a simple favor, and it isn't even illegal."

Just talking to Jason Fireson was illegal now. A cop or Agent Delaney could break down the door and Weston would be locked up for aiding and abetting; he'd read about the mother or aunt of one of Dillinger's associates being jailed for no more than this.

"Okay. Let me get a pen and—"

"You don't write any of this down, Wes—for Christ's sake."

"Then tell me again."

Jason did, in a slower tone of voice this time, not out of consideration for his brother but because he seemed to be tiring with each syllable.

"I'll need to borrow Ma's car to get there."

"No. They'll see you at her place and might get suspicious enough to follow. There's a train that'll get you there."

Trains cost money, but Weston didn't say anything.

After Jason was satisfied that Weston understood the message—for Owney to meet Jason six days later, at a certain restaurant in Detroit, at five in the afternoon—Jason seemed to relax, but only slightly.

"Do you want to spend the night?" Weston asked.

Jason seemed to ponder this, or maybe he was falling asleep with his eyes open, standing up. After a moment, he stirred and said yes.

"Can I get you that water now? I'd like some myself."

Jason finally sat in one of the wooden chairs. Weston fetched two glasses of water from the bathroom, and the brothers sat at the table in such an arrangement that the rifle wasn't pointed at either of them.

"Are you sure you're all right?"

"We've been sleeping in cars and empty houses for weeks. Sometimes barns." The shadows cast by Jason's nose and brows, combined with his bedraggled hair, made him look like something out of a haunted house. "You don't sleep too well when there are people looking for you."

"I guess I assumed it had always been like that, but it never seemed to bother you before."

Jason explained that it had all changed a few months ago, that he never would have set this complicated chain of events into motion if he'd realized that the feds would be cracking down like this. Weston wasn't sure he believed him.

"Where's Darcy?"

"Darcy's fine. She's waiting for us to get that money. I can't be with her now because she might be watched, too. They'd probably have arrested her by now just to lean on me if her daddy wasn't a big shot. That's how the law works. He doesn't care a damn for her, but he still wouldn't be happy if the cops locked her up. Bad for business."

"Doesn't she have money?"

"No, she doesn't. And her old man's not inclined to leave her any in his will, either. I'm not with her for the money, Wes."

"I didn't say that."

Weston asked Jason if he wanted to shower—almost for his own sake, as his brother was stinking up the room—but he shook his head. "I just want to sleep."

They both stood and Weston took one of the pillows from his bed, then searched the closet for a blanket. "You can have the bed; I'll sleep on the floor."

"Nah, I'm used to floors," Jason said. "How's Ma?"

"She's worried about you two. Real worried."

"But how is she otherwise?"

"There *is* no otherwise, Jason. She's afraid her sons are going to be killed."

"Do you think she's still torn up over Pop?"

It was as if he'd asked if she still breathed oxygen. "We all are."

"I'd like to think I'm getting past it."

Jason had removed a pistol from his pocket and was crouching down to place it under his borrowed pillow as Weston stood there, stunned. He couldn't believe what Jason had said. Or how he'd said it—just an offhand line, tossed to the side as he lay down on Weston's floor, folding his arms on his chest. As if Pop had never mattered to him at all.

Weston's feet felt mortared to the floor as he watched his brother close his eyes and seem to fall asleep in seconds. Who was this man? Did he even care about his family, or were the other Firesons just a bunch of suckers to pay off now and then so they'd leave him alone?

Jason's breaths were heavy by the time Weston managed to crawl into bed.

Jason had vanished like a ghost by the time Weston woke up. When Weston hesitantly looked under Jason's pillow, the gun was gone, too. He walked into the kitchenette and saw a note scribbled on the back of a used envelope: DON'T FORGET. GO TODAY OR TOMORROW. THANKS.

Beside the envelope was a single match in a matchbook. Weston shook his head. But he obeyed, lighting the match and setting fire to the message, which caught surprisingly quickly and singed his fingertips before he could blow it out.

The sad truth was, he had nothing better to do that day.

After killing time in his apartment, then waiting in the long breadline for lunch, he walked another twenty minutes to the train station. He winced at the cost of the local to Karpis; he had planned to ask Jason for a dollar that morning but had never had the chance.

He couldn't stop thinking of what Jason had said about Pop. The two had always fought, Pop scolding Jason for his laziness, Jason wise-mouthing back. Pop the moralist, Jason the contrarian. Pop the avatar of hard work, persistence, and decency—all the things that the Firefly Brothers seemed to be against. Maybe Pop's death just hadn't hurt Jason the way it had hurt Weston. Maybe those two prison stints had done something to the eldest brother, leeched out his compassion and left only survival instincts. Surely Whit missed Pop as Weston did—Whit had seemed especially close to the old man—but then again maybe a year of running with Jason had hardened Whit's personality as well. Maybe Weston didn't know his brothers anymore. Maybe his brothers—the good part of them, at least—had already died, as Delaney had said. All that was left was their petty anger and vengefulness, like poltergeists stripped of everything that had made them human.

The longer he sat on the train, the angrier he became. Why was he doing this? What did he owe his brothers anymore? What had they ever done for him, other than cost him his job?

Last stop, Last Best Chance. He tried not to ponder the symbolism. Instead, when he arrived he took in the odd sight, an enormous and amorphous gray building, ugly as a boil and clearly not intended to be viewed by daylight. It was as if a twister had hit a red-light district and deposited the pieces in this otherwise unassuming neighborhood.

Weston had checked, but no one was following him. He just wasn't that interesting to anyone.

He expected some sort of guard or henchman at the door, but it was unattended and unlocked. He took a breath and entered his brothers' world.

Photographs of boxers, soldiers, and pilots stood sentry in a long hallway of dark-oak walls, which led into a vast ballroom fronted by a serpentine bar encrusted with hammered tin. Off this central area snaked rooms that receded so far into the dim light that he couldn't see the end in most directions. Hatted men were scattered at the bar and at the tables in the farther reaches. It was quiet at this hour; Weston could hear a phonograph playing jazz coming from one direction and a radio broadcast of the Reds game from another. Outside of nickelodeons and theaters, it was the biggest windowless indoor space he'd ever seen.

He smelled steak, and his stomach lurched inside him; he'd still been hungry the moment he finished his watery stew, ninety minutes ago. But that animalistic response was nothing compared with what he felt when the woman in the black strapless dress approached.

She had curly red hair that was almost brown in the darkness, and her shoulders were so white they looked as if they'd bruise if a man touched them. Jesus, to be that man. Weston felt overpoweringly self-conscious as she walked up to him, heels tapping, dark lips smiling but not too much. Maybe she was just the hostess; he knew that prostitutes weren't supposed to be good-looking, that this woman couldn't possibly be what he'd first assumed. He told himself not to glance at her chest, but she caught him doing it anyway.

"And what can I help you with?" She looked a few years older than him and was all the more intimidating for it.

"I'm, I'm looking for Chance McGill."

"Mr. McGill is a busy man. I don't even know if he's here. What can *I* help you with?"

It felt as if everyone in the place was watching, but maybe they were just catatonic with drink.

"He'll want to talk to me." He spoke quietly. "I have a message for him."

She still had that look, as if she was entertaining and assessing him all at once. "What kind of message?"

"Please, I'm . . ." Could he just say it out loud at a place like this? He lowered his voice even more. "I'm Jason and Whit Fireson's brother."

He had expected the name to change something in her expression, but it didn't. "You have Jason's eyes." She raised her right hand to his face, her fingertips gliding against his cheekbone. "I've always liked Jason's eyes."

He wondered what else of Jason's she had liked.

"Sit at the bar." She turned and walked away, and he watched her walk. Then he sat at the bar, self-conscious as ever. He stared at the many bottles arrayed before him, the browns and ochers and clears. The bartender, a young man who looked fifty pounds fitter than Weston, soon came his way, but Weston waved him off.

He took another look at the place. Even in its near-emptiness the joint was impressive. The depression didn't seem to exist here. People who walked through that door had money, ill-gotten or otherwise. As Weston sat there studying the mahogany molding and the glittering chandeliers, and imagining the clientele who would traipse in once the sun had set, the waves of envy nearly knocked him from his stool.

He turned back around and saw that an impeccably groomed, silver-haired man had appeared behind the bar. He was thin and short but didn't seem to know it, moving as if he owned the place, which Weston figured he did. His white oxford shirt was pressed, his cuffs linked with gold, the buttons of his tan vest tiny pieces of ivory. The man motioned for Weston to move to the far end of the bar.

"You wanted to see me?" McGill's calm voice betrayed nothing.

"My brother Jason wanted me to give you a message. For Owney Davis?"

McGill watched him for a moment. "Didn't know there was a third brother."

"Yeah, well, I'm not really, um, in*volved* in what they do."

"No kidding." McGill smirked, giving Weston the up-and-down. Weston just sat there and let himself be eyeballed.

"What makes you think I know anything about an Owney Davis?" McGill asked.

"Nothing. I don't . . . Jason just asked me if I could—"

"What makes you think I know anything about Jason Fireson?"

Weston was sick of smelling food he couldn't eat and staring at booze he couldn't drink. And the redhead had returned, standing just far enough away for her to see but not quite hear the conversation.

"Look," Weston said, "I don't know what the rules are here, okay? I don't know your secret passwords or etiquette or . . . whatever it is you judge people by, all right? My brother asked me to do him a favor, so I'm spending half my day—"

"All right, all right." A cigar was between McGill's teeth, though Weston had somehow missed its introduction. McGill lit it and was at least decent enough to exhale to the side.

"No one followed me here, if that's what you're worried about."

"I know you weren't followed. What's the message?"

Weston passed on Jason's instructions. He still barely understood them, and McGill neither nodded nor shook his head.

"How'd he look?" McGill asked.

"Like he'd turned into someone else."

McGill was so stonily calm and motionless that he reminded Weston of the lady at the unemployment office. It was as if everyone, when confronted by Weston's palpable misery, could only hold still and wait patiently for him to drag his sorrows elsewhere.

"What are you drinking?"

"I don't, um, I don't really have enough on me for anything."

McGill smirked again. "What are you drinking?"

Weston asked for a whiskey and McGill turned, selected a bottle of something Weston had never heard of, and gracefully poured a few fingers, more like a fist, into an octagonal glass.

"You need this pretty badly, I'd say."

It felt like charity and condescension but tasted much better. McGill poured himself a smaller version and offered a toast: "To your brothers' health. And to yours."

Weston was so sick of pity. But it was one of the few things he had left.

He took another sip. Even on a full stomach it would have been a lot of booze for Weston, and he felt a formerly tight space inside his brain opening up. Emboldened, he dared to ask, "I don't suppose you need any help around here? Even busing tables or something like that?"

The skin around McGill's eyes seemed to soften, but not his lips. "I can't have any more Firesons crawling around my place, kid. Sorry. Nothing personal."

Thanks again, brothers. His sips had become gulps and his head was swimming. He glanced at the redhead, still out of earshot, leaning over the bar to share a story with the bartender.

"So, out of curiosity," Weston ventured, his eyes still on the redhead.

McGill said a number far higher than Weston had imagined.

And because he'd already lost face in front of this man, as well as his own self-esteem, Weston said, "I don't suppose . . . I don't suppose you owe my brother a favor?"

"Getting a message to Owney is one *hell* of a favor. Jason and I are more than square after that. You want a girl to lay her frame down for you, you'll goddamn pay her for it."

Then his eyes gave Weston the up-and-down again and he shook his head.

McGill walked away, toward the bartender and the redhead. He whispered something to them. Two smiling faces turned his way and Weston averted his eyes, staring straight ahead, at the glass he was two sips from finishing. But he could hear them laughing. He hated them all. His face burned as he downed the glass. It might have been more fitting—a nice *and the hell with you, too*—to have left that last bit of booze before he walked away, before he hurriedly fled the building, but he just couldn't bear to leave it behind.

He was still drunk and still angry more than an hour later when he made it back to Lincoln City. He walked out of the train station and crossed the street to a telephone booth, closing the doors behind him.

He dropped his coin and told the operator long distance, Chicago. The number, he realized with shame, he had memorized after staring at it for so many nights. He looked out the windows on both sides to see if anyone was watching. The world was swirling.

The secretary who answered the phone was coldly professional, as if she knew why he was calling. As if she were holding the receiver with black gloves.

"I'd like to speak to Cary Delaney, please."

Weston slept for the rest of the afternoon. He had feared that making that call would be like tying a noose around his own neck, but instead it was the opposite, as if a heavy burden had been lifted from his shoulders and he could breathe again. He felt weightless, drifting up and into sleep. But when he woke it was dark and his head was throbbing.

He opened his door to fetch some water from the bathroom and again a man was sleeping in the hallway. The man hadn't been there that afternoon, had he? Weston tried to remember, but the day was fuzzy. He felt a surge of fear and he wondered if he could be hungover and still drunk at the same time, because he was being irrational. Surely this couldn't be—

It was. Jason looked up at him and motioned his head to the door. Weston nearly dropped the empty glass. He turned and his hand was already shaking as he twisted the knob. He swallowed and thought for a moment he might vomit.

Weston took two steps into the room, then stood still as Jason again shut and locked the door, again checked behind furniture and under the bed, again laid his natty sheet and long powerful firearm on the kitchenette table.

Jesus, did Jason know? Had this all been some elaborate test of Weston's loyalty?

Jason was in the same clothes as the day before. Apparently his night's sleep on Weston's floor hadn't been a good one, because his eyes remained red and baggy.

"Didn't think you were home," Jason said, his voice unreadable but tense, like the night before. "I knocked a while back and you didn't answer."

"I was . . . pretty tired." Weston tried to act naturally. "What happened this morning?"

"Nothing. Just didn't think I should stick around by day. So. Did you do it?"

He swallowed. His voice was tiny. "Did I do what?"

Jason stared as Weston just stood there, stunned. Weston had done it. And if this had been a test that he had failed, he would stand here and take his punishment. He would not back down. This was not his brother anymore.

"Jesus, Wes." Jason shook his head. "Did you go to Karpis or not?"

Weston exhaled. *Calm down.* "Yes. I saw McGill, gave him your message. He, um, I don't remember him ever explicitly saying that he'd tell Owney, but—"

"He wouldn't say that," Jason interrupted with the first smile Weston had seen on his face in the past two days. "He'll just do it. Perfect. Thanks, Wes."

The fear began to subside, and Weston felt all the smaller for having been so scared of his own brother. And angrier. He kept replaying Jason's words from the night before: *I'd like to think I'm getting past it.*

"Are you spending the night again?"

Jason shrugged. "Sure, why not?"

Weston seemed to be gaining control of his insides, but his stomach felt even worse than usual, scoured by alcohol and otherwise empty. He told Jason that McGill had fed him some whiskey and he desperately needed to get some water.

He walked to the bathroom and filled two glasses, standing there for a minute while he drank and refilled and tried to calm down. He hated how meek he'd been around Jason. Last night he'd wanted to say something but hadn't possessed the nerve. He needed to act this time.

Back in the room, he handed a glass to Jason, who twitched at the slightest sound from the hallway or the street.

"There's something I've been meaning to ask you," Weston said.

Jason waited.

"Have you ever wondered," Weston asked, "how differently things might have turned out if it had been me Pop had gone out with that night?"

Jason didn't move, but his red eyes were much colder. "How's that?"

"Maybe the jury . . . maybe they would have believed me more than you."

"Why?" Jason's voice was quick now, nearly interrupting his brother.

"C'mon, Jason," Weston said, softening already. "I mean, no offense, but—"

"None taken. Get it out. Why?"

"You were on the stand in a prisoner's outfit, for God's sake. I'm not blaming you, I'm just saying that maybe if it had been me, then—"

"You're not blaming me."

"I only mean—"

"You're not blaming me."

He would not cower. He would not shake his head or let this subject go undiscussed one moment longer. "I'm just saying I wish Pop's alibi hadn't been a guy in a prisoner's uniform. A guy with two arrests."

Jason sucked in his bottom lip and nodded to himself, as if Weston had confirmed something he'd always known. "They didn't not believe me because I had a record, Wes. They—"

"It certainly made it easier."

"—didn't believe me because I was his *son.* Any son would have lied for his father, and they knew that. The alibi was all Pop had. Any son would have lied. The only difference between you and me is I can lie better."

"What does that mean?"

Jason waved his hand at Weston. "I am so sick of carrying this with me. No, Wes, I *don't* think of how it might've been different. Because it would have been *worse* if you'd been the one up there perjuring himself."

Weston's tongue still worked, but his chest had trouble forcing the air out. "What are you saying?"

"Do you have any goddamn idea how difficult that performance was? The prosecutor tried to poke his fingers into every hole he could think of, but I had an answer for him each time. And you had the goddamn nerve to be angry at *me* for not being with you all during the trial. Not being able to 'support' you and the family." He shook his head. "Support you? I was the one shuttling back and forth from a prison cell to the courthouse, I was the one turning that prosecutor back with every answer and not breaking a sweat. I never stuttered. I didn't blink. You think you could have done that? You think you have that in you?"

Weston didn't remember stepping backward, but he was now leaning against the wall. The world had moved around him.

"Pop was *lucky* I was the one."

"Do you mean—?"

"I knew Whit bought it, but you, too?" Jason laughed in derision or disbelief. They felt the same to Weston. "I figured you were smarter than that. I figured that, at the very least, you were smart, Wes. Jesus Christ." Jason shook his head. "Fine. Believe what you want. If it had been you, Pop would've been acquitted. If it had been you, all would be well. A big, happy family. I didn't mean to stomp on your beliefs, Wes."

Jason reached into his back pocket and put on a grimy brown cap, pulling it low over his forehead. Then he picked up his rifle, wrapping it in the filthy bedsheet and cradling it in his left arm.

Things were happening too quickly for Weston. He didn't understand. No, he did understand—he just didn't want to.

"You're, you're sure? Pop . . . told you?"

Without answering, Jason walked to the door and had his hand on the knob before Weston could ask, "Wait, what are you doing?"

"Leaving. Don't worry, Wes, I'll find a way to pass you some of the money once I get it washed, no problem. And then you can forget about me. You'll never have to look at me again, and you can blame your no-good brother for all your life's problems."

"Wait, Jason, please. I didn't know, I never thought he, I mean, how—"

"*Shut up!*" Jason spoke through gritted teeth. He pulled at the knob and realized he had forgotten to unlock it. "Just stop talking, Wes, before you make it even worse."

The images still hadn't finished forming in Weston's head—Jason's story, this new awareness of things.

Good God, what had Weston done?

"No, please, don't go to Detroit."

Jason was unlocking the door. Weston had to tell him.

"Jason, you can't go there. You don't un—"

But instead of turning the knob Jason put his hand in his pocket, and when it came out there was a pistol in it.

"I swear to God, Wes, you say one more goddamn word and I'll snap." He was pointing it at his brother and his eyes were wet. Weston had never seen Jason look so unhinged. "*Stop talking. Just stop.*"

He had to tell him. But the gun was pointed at his chest, and Weston's mouth was too dry to say a thing.

Then Jason opened the door and stepped out. Weston expected a slam, but his ever-wary brother shut the door quietly.

Weston didn't remember sitting down but here he was on the floor. Had he fallen? The world had moved up three feet and knocked him down. Had he passed out?

He had to warn Jason. His legs were shaking but he managed to stand, pulling himself up alongside the table. He could chase after Jason, but would his brother really shoot him? Was he that angry, that deranged?

Weston ran to his bed, pulling open the curtains and lifting the window.

"Jason!" He didn't see his brother out there but he screamed all the same. "Don't go to Detroit! They know you're coming! The feds know about it!"

Two pedestrians looked up at him, this madman screaming into the night. Jason should have reached the bottom of the stairs by now, should have made it outside. Tears were running down Weston's cheeks.

He screamed his warning again. He screamed that he was sorry. Someone yelled for him to shut the hell up. Weston screamed and screamed and finally collapsed, his head on the windowsill, hoping his brother had heard him.

XXXII.

Heading north from St. Louis, Jason had driven as long as Whit could tolerate. Whit's scorched leg was hurting more with each passing hour; he needed rest, and not in the backseat of the car. Jason drove past the bedroom communities and into quieter country, stopping at a tourist camp just off the Mississippi. He figured everyone in the state would be hearing radio updates about the Firefly Brothers and he hated the idea of letting rooms from a suspicious proprietor, but the only alternative was to pull into a park and sleep in their latest vehicle, a stolen Ford. He'd spied signs for the camp on the country road he'd been driving, and had followed its cursory directions here, off an even smaller road. He surveyed the area—a dozen small cabins scattered about the property, connected by walking trails. The branches of oaks and hickories hung heavy with leaves; the camp would be hidden in shadows even by day.

The manager was indeed listening to the radio, bluegrass twanging in the moonlight, but he was elderly and probably had bad eyesight. Jason gave a false name and paid for three nights in advance, asking about fishing conditions as if he gave a damn.

The cabin was in the back, with an obstructed view of the road. The gentle shushing of the river in the distance was the only sound. He roused Darcy and guided her into one of the bedrooms. Whit so reeked of booze that Jason feared being vomited on as he helped him hop his way into the second bedroom. When Whit lay down, Jason checked his leg again: it looked worse than before, and he wondered if they'd misjudged the severity of the injury. He gave Whit two more painkillers and downed a few himself.

Next he carried the money and the guns into the cabin and locked the door.

With wet towels he cleaned Darcy's wounds and dressed them with the bandages and some towels. Lying on the bed, she bit her lip as he did this, but she didn't seem to be in as much pain as he thought she would be. He would need to buy more dressings, and some antiseptic, but this was good enough for now.

"Did they hurt you?"

"No. I did that to myself, cutting my ropes loose."

He leaned over and kissed her on the lips.

He hadn't slept since his last death, if you could call that sleep. Given their all-night watch outside the kidnappers' lair, that meant he hadn't slept in two days—days that had covered hundreds of miles and many gunshots. And the car crash: various muscles he'd never even felt before ached with each motion.

"What happened to you?" she asked.

"Let's talk about it in the morning. We should sleep while we can. It'll make more sense then."

"I don't want this to make sense."

"That's good, because, honestly, it won't. But I'm tired, and you look exhausted."

"My father did this."

"Did what?"

She told him her father had been arrested earlier that day for masterminding the kidnapping. Jason told her he would buy the morning papers and see if it was true. But already he knew that it was. Windham had somehow arranged for the brothers to be killed, likely through his Mob connections, and then he was free to kidnap his own flesh and blood. As if sending his grieving daughter to a sanatorium those many years ago hadn't been enough, now he'd gone this extra mile. Jason wished he had figured this out before the cops had, just so he could have had the pleasure of sparing the old bastard from life in prison. Windham deserved a different fate indeed.

Jason lay beside her, both of them fully clothed on top of the sheets.

She half rolled onto him, one arm across his chest. He winced but didn't let on how sore he was. He carefully clasped her bandaged hand, and even though the light was still on he closed his eyes and fell asleep.

In the morning, Darcy was still out cold when Jason left her a note and drove to the nearest town.

His various injuries had worsened overnight. He shuffled cautiously, and again he had to hope that because he looked so bad off no one would possibly think he could be the great Jason Fireson.

At a clothing store he bought pants and shirts for himself and Whit, as well as two dresses, undergarments, some bandannas, and a yellow tam for Darcy. He slanted a new boater atop his head and donned a pair of dark-amber sunglasses as soon as he was out of the store. Next he bought some groceries, more ointment and bandages, another bottle of rye, and the *Post-Dispatch*, which he read in the car. Stories about the Firefly Brothers took up the entire top half of the front page, and many other pages besides. Police in Sedalia as well as state cops from the highway shootout had identified them, despite their alleged death twelve days ago. This had spurred J. Edgar Hoover into admitting he was no longer convinced that the brothers had been killed or even arrested in Points North. But at the same time Hoover warned people not to get carried away with far-fetched stories of miraculous escapes, reminding citizens that his very capable agents would rectify any mistakes made by less competent local police squads.

Jason read the stories twice. Reporters invariably got most of their facts wrong when writing about the brothers, and today the conjecture was intensified, as the impossible events of the past two weeks had left the poor hacks with vast holes to fill. The Firesons were also blamed for a bank robbery in Jefferson City, as well as a shootout in Liberty and the burning of a library in Macon. There were no updates on Darcy's kidnapping or any hints of her father's involvement, and there didn't seem to be anything about Brickbat or the doc.

Ten minutes later, Jason was back at the cabin and Darcy was still asleep.

Whit had certainly been in better moods. He woke up either drunk or hungover or some vicious combination of the two. Jason handed him a doughnut and a bottle of orange juice when he finished applying a new coat of ointment. They talked about what was in the paper and what it meant for them. Normally, Jason's strategy would be to drive as far from a police presence as possible, but Whit's leg and Darcy's exhaustion required a different strategy. The cops probably thought they were trying to get somewhere in Jefferson City, or maybe even back home, so hopefully they were relatively safe here.

"Let's stay the night," Jason said. "Maybe the next one, too. Then we can head up and get Veronica and Patrick."

He still had his California restaurant plan, but he hadn't the faintest idea what Whit was considering as his next step. He had a feeling Whit didn't, either.

After the short-term plan was settled, Jason folded a piece of gauze in half, affixed some medical tape to it, and reached down to stick it on Whit's forehead.

"What's the idea?"

"You have a bullet hole there, remember? Darcy didn't see it in the dark, luckily, and I don't want to have to explain it to her later."

"So how do I explain a bandage on my forehead?"

"You grew a wart. Real nasty one. I'm sure she'll believe that."

Whit popped another doughnut into his mouth, and a cloud of powdered sugar was all that Jason heard of Whit's curse before he walked into the other bedroom.

Darcy woke with a start. She was on a bed. Praise be, an actual *bed*. She had been dreaming of a bed for so long. Her body had not been perfectly horizontal like this in, what, a week? More? The events of the previous evening returned to her. Had she really seen Jason? But the bed was empty. Where was she? Wait, a note. Running an errand, food and medicine. His handwriting. Proof.

She walked out of the bedroom. The chintzy cabin smelled of mildewed freshwater from previous occupants' forays into the river. The curtains in the living room were drawn, but Darcy cracked open the windows for some air. She kept thinking of Brickbat Sanders walking down the stairs. She would never enter a basement again.

What time was it? Ten o'clock, and Jason's note had been written nearly an hour ago. Should she be worried? She hoped he was buying her some clothes. She wanted to burn these. She checked the bathroom and saw that there were some thin towels and a slightly used bar of soap. A marble tub would have been nice, a lavender bubble bath with floating rose petals, three bars of Parisian soap, and a plush bathrobe, but an old bar of lard in a sportsman's cottage was good enough for today. She turned on the water and waited for it to be almost scalding. There was much she needed to burn off. She undressed and climbed in.

In the shower, the bandages fell from her hands and the soap stung at the raw wounds, but she didn't mind the pain. She washed until the soap was a mere sliver, falling from her hands again and again until there was nothing for her to drop; it was just vapor, she was just vapor, and even on that hot day the air was so full of steam that she needed to breathe through her mouth.

Not until the hot water was fading did she turn it off. One towel attempted to contain her unruly hair—its time was up; she would go flapper as soon as she found a blade—and another she wrapped around her torso, though it was immodestly small. Hopefully Whit wasn't prowling about. She opened the door and as the moisture escaped in a cloud so did she, floating to her room, closing the door, and lying on the bed. She stared at the ceiling and closed her eyes and didn't wake until Jason walked in.

"Hungry, beautiful?" He looked smashing. Wearing the same dirty clothes as yesterday, the ones he had slept in.

"I could eat a farm."

She sat up and he walked over to kiss her. Then he laid out the Sports section of his newspaper like a picnic blanket on the bed and opened a bag of pastries. An acceptable snack, but after dispatching her share (and most of his), she was ready for bacon, ham, chicken, steak.

He asked about the days she'd been held, but there was nothing she wanted to do less than relive that. She wanted to drive with him, lie with him, laugh with him, do whatever they could to expunge the memory of those hellish days. Whether this was a healthy or a pathological response to her situation she didn't care. She was alive and so was he and they were going to *live*, goddamn it.

"I bought you some new clothes." He motioned to a bag he'd left by the bedroom door.

She kissed him. "I don't feel like wearing clothes. I've been wearing them for days."

They kissed again, and he lowered himself onto her. He tasted like pecans and chocolate. It hurt when she ran her cut palms over his chest, but she ignored the pain, or told it she didn't care. Pain would always be there, after all. Many people spent much time and even more money trying to run from pain, but she had learned you could never escape it. You just needed to tell it that it could not master you. She grabbed one of his hands with hers and interlocked their fingers and squeezed, so tightly she felt a wound reopen, the work of millions of white blood cells undone in one motion. She squeezed again and when he came up for air she laughed with him.

They were lying beside each other, the sheets and her towel and most of his clothes somewhere on the floor, although he'd strangely insisted on leaving his undershirt on. Sunlight glowed on the drawn curtains.

"This may sound a bit odd," Jason said, "but, should I ever die, promise me that you'll have them wait awhile before they put me in a coffin. A long, long while. Maybe a week."

"That *does* sound odd, Jason. Please. I don't want to think of you as a corpse."

"I've been thinking of myself as one for a while now."

"Jason! Enough! It's not like you to be so . . . macabre."

"I know it's strange, but I need you to promise me. At least a week before I'm put in a coffin and buried."

"*Jason*—"

"Just promise me, Darcy."

"Very well. I promise I won't let anyone bury you until an inordinate amount of time has passed, and I've been consigned to a home for wayward necrophiliacs. Thank you for painting such a bright future for me. But *you* have to promise *me* you won't die."

"Hmm. I definitely can't promise you that—"

"Jason!"

"But I *can* promise I won't stay dead very long. I can very confidently promise that."

"I'm falling asleep again, Jason. You're not making sense. You're babbling, and I'm falling into the babble. Your words are cushions. They comfort me regardless of what they say."

"Then I'll throw words all around you."

"*Mmm.* Bury me in them."

"I look forward to digging you out when you wake up." He kissed her forehead. "Just promise you'll do the same for me when the time comes."

They woke after noon, hungry again. Jason donned one of his new outfits, a simple white oxford and light-gray slacks, dispensing with a jacket. Darcy had pronounced the two dresses he bought for her "rather drab," and he'd told her that was the point. She chose the yellow one, which hung shapelessly around her. Darcy was not accustomed to being un-memorable, but she seemed to understand the situation.

She pulled her hair back and tied it with a matching yellow bandanna. She looked as un-urban and un-Darcy as he'd ever seen her, but it worked.

"Maybe I should forget the restaurant idea and buy a farm instead," he teased. "Think you'd like milking cows?"

"Oh, it sounds divine. And milking goats, and milking horses, and milking chickens . . ."

"Never mind."

Before leaving, Jason went to check on Whit. He could hear his brother snoring before he even opened the door. Whit was sprawled on his back, the new bottle of rye unopened on his nightstand. Jason was about to skulk off again but he backed into the doorjamb, his heel loud against the wood.

Whit's reflexes would have impressed Jason under other circum-stances. Whit hadn't even stopped snoring yet when he opened his eyes, reached behind his pillow, and pulled out an automatic.

Jason held out his palms. The fuzziness in Whit's eyes faded with star-tling quickness and he frowned, a force more powerful than sleepiness or wakefulness or regret pulling at him. Finally, he put the gun down on the bed. They stared at each other for an awkward moment.

Jason asked Whit if he wanted anything. Whit closed his eyes as he said no. His leg still didn't look good, and Jason said so, but Whit said he was confident he'd live.

Jason left the room and tried to smile at Darcy, wondering why he felt so shaken.

They drove into town, he in his boater and sunglasses and she in her bandanna. She told him that maybe she wouldn't cut her hair after all, and instead would gather a bandanna collection. They bought sandwiches and a sack of fruit and some pop, and Darcy chose a pair of sunglasses so unstylish that she laughed.

Even with the windows down, the afternoon heat felt aggressive, the humidity surly.

"We should have bought swimsuits," Darcy said. "We should soak in the river all day."

"We don't need suits for that."

"I thought you didn't want to be attention-getting, Mr. Smith."

He told her the plan to drive up to the U.P. and gather Whit's family as soon as Whit was ready.

"Is it safe to go there?"

"Hopefully. Either way, I owe Whit for helping me find you. Plus, you know darn well he'd get into trouble without me there to bail him out."

"You always have been your brother's keeper."

"I just need to watch out for him, is all. He has too much anger in him. Makes him do stupid things."

"You're funny. You always say that about him, as if he's the only one."

"What does that mean?"

She smiled at him to defuse the sting. "You're as angry as he is, Jason. You just show it differently."

They drove in silence for a short while, on a long street that cut through woods shading them from the sun. Then she asked him to pull over.

"What's wrong?"

"Nothing's wrong. Just pull over."

He was grinning at her, probably misinterpreting. Once the car was motionless, she opened her door and got out. Closing it, she bent down and smiled back at him through the window, then stood on the running boards. "Continue, driver."

"What?"

"Keep going. Drive. But *faster,* please." She couldn't see him from here. Maybe he was shaking his head, maybe he was rolling his eyes. "Pretend someone's chasing you."

"Someone's always chasing me."

"Well, pretend they're right behind you. And gaining."

For a moment she feared he was going to refuse, but here they were on a secluded street, in the woods, all the weight of summer pressing down on them. The Ford's engine roared. She laughed as it picked up speed. Her dress ruffled most immodestly, and her bandanna was gone, a memory— not even a memory but whatever you call a memory that you forget instantly. Something that didn't happen. But *this* was happening—yes, definitely, the wind in her hair and the almost painful glinting of the sun off the Ford's roof and the familiar tension against her finger bones. She remembered this. Along the tops of her ears, where the kidnappers' goggles had once chafed, she could feel the desperate grip of her sunglasses, barely holding on as the Ford raced faster still. Pebbles biting into her ankles, the unexpected lurch of a pothole. She thought she heard Jason yell something. Calling her crazy, most likely. Or saying he loved her. She yelled, gleefully, triumphantly, her reckless voice reclaiming her place in the world.

The Ford coasted for a moment, then began to slow. She laughed again, patting the hot roof of the car as if congratulating her prized stallion.

When it stopped, she bent over and peeked inside.

"Still there?" she asked.

He smiled. He seemed to know what she was asking. "Yeah, sweetness, I'm still here."

XXXIII.

It wasn't a sound that woke Jason that night but the memory of a sound.

Beside him Darcy was breathing heavily. A sick feeling was emanating from his stomach to his fingers, a helpless sort of terror. He hadn't woken up from something, he'd woken up *to* something.

He got up and quietly put on his pants. He was already wearing his undershirt, of course, as he couldn't let Darcy see the fading bullet wounds in his back. He opened the door and walked into the hallway, then into Whit's room. His eyes were used to the dark and he saw Whit on the bed, sprawled on his back. For once he wasn't snoring.

"Whit," Jason said, just above a whisper. No response, so he repeated it. By the door was a small table with a lamp, and he pulled its cord.

Whit didn't pull his gat on Jason this time. Once had been more than enough. He opened his eyes and sat up, calmly, as if he'd been expecting Jason.

"I remember," Jason said.

Whit leaned against the wall. He wore only boxer shorts, and he looked so pathetic with the one red leg and the other dark, hairy one. "Yeah. Me, too."

Jason closed the door behind him. "When did you—?"

"Just this morning," Whit said. "Or maybe I've known for a while, too, and just didn't want to believe it. Or didn't really understand."

Jason sat on the edge of the bed. They were talking around it without talking about it, he knew, the way brothers talk about what's important. All brothers, or just his?

He stared at the wall, the memories unspooling no matter how badly he wanted them to disappear. *God, let it not have happened that way.*

———

This is what they remembered:

Two weeks earlier, one day before they would be killed in Points North, they had received their clean money from the launderer. The euphoria of their score had registered immediately, as they realized that the hellish summer of living destitute was finally over. They were still notorious, Public Enemy Number One, but the irrefutable fact of the money was like a surge of adrenaline. Finally they could escape someplace, start over, live well, all those warm phrases whose full meaning they didn't entirely understand but were quite ready to learn. They checked into one of Detroit's finest hotels, paying in advance for two extra nights they wouldn't need, confident that in their beards they were unrecognizable. In their rooms they showered and scrubbed for thirty minutes each, then splurged at a barbershop, buying the shave and hot towels and haircut and shampoo—usually a weekly ritual for Jason but one he hadn't dared enjoy since the Federal Reserve job. They had their money now, and with it invincibility. Then, on to the haberdasher's. Even Whit was drunk with freedom, and despite never much caring for clothes he bought duds nearly as expensive as Jason's. They ate at a French restaurant and drank expensive wine and slept late the next morning.

They stayed in their hotel room all that day, ordering room service and waiting out the hours until their meeting with Owney. Finally, as five o'clock approached, they left the hotel, clean-shaven, wearing new suits, and carrying one briefcase full of weapons and one full of dollars. But as they drove to the restaurant where they were supposed to meet Owney something felt wrong. Maybe Jason was paranoid after so many past near-arrests, but maybe not: too many men were chatting on the sidewalk or waiting for a bus or sitting in parked cars. The brothers drove past the restaurant twice, Thompsons on their laps and pistols in their shoulder holsters. Whit agreed—this was all wrong. Their secret meeting with Owney had become a widely advertised event.

Jason headed for the highway, and for three blocks they were followed by a pair of blue Packards, until Jason pulled a U and ran a red. Then sirens were placed atop the Packards and all pretense was lost. Jason made a few more maneuvers that would have made old Jake Dimes proud, and after five frantic minutes that felt like fifty the brothers lost their tails and got on the highway.

"You think somebody recognized us?" Whit had asked as they drove west. "Maybe we shouldn't have cleaned up after all."

"No, the cops were there before we were. They knew we were coming."

"So Owney ratted us."

"Maybe. I don't know yet."

"Then who else? Who else knew we were meeting him?"

As usual, Jason had been the one handling the advance planning. He made the connection but couldn't bring himself to say it. *Jesus Christ.* He hadn't even considered the possibility when he'd gone out to Weston's apartment. Never. He felt sick to his stomach and he tightened his hands on the wheel, taking a deep breath to control himself. He didn't want Whit to notice or ask what was wrong. He couldn't say it out loud. He swallowed and took another breath.

"I don't know," he said.

Once they were out of town, he stuck to the speed limit and Whit strained his neck facing backward for the next half hour, anxiously keeping watch. The Firefly Brothers were in a car that the Detroit cops—or had it been feds?—had surely spotted, so that needed to be changed. They took an exit and traded cars, swiping a red Terraplane from a train depot and affixing to it one of the many tags they were carrying.

They drove back roads through Michigan and into the Indiana countryside, headed toward the designated meeting place with the girls, hoping that rendezvous wasn't blown as well. Whit removed a flask from his pocket and took a few healthy pulls.

At a small joint off the highway the Firefly Brothers bought two chicken dinners, eating in the car as they continued west. The steering wheel was slick with grease beneath Jason's fingers and he drove with the windows down, yet still the car managed to stink of fried buttermilk and dark meat.

They were less than ten miles from the pickup point when Jason passed a motel and saw a police car parked across the street. A few miles later, another motel and another police watchman. A third cop passed them going the other way.

"We're getting damn close and there are too many cops around," Jason said.

"You're just worried. It doesn't mean anything." Whit took another snort from his flask.

"I say it does. I say the girls are being watched, or at least the cops know enough to be near every motel in this county."

"Jason, we're so close—"

"Which is why I don't want to ruin it here." He was exhausted—the panic from the chase in Detroit had long faded, and his brain and his body were numbed by the long hours on the road. He wished he could think more clearly. But all he could think about was Weston. "We're not picking them up tonight."

"Jason—"

"Not till we've had a chance to think it through. And you'll be thinking better when you aren't drunk."

"I'm not drunk. You're just worried, and—"

"Of course I'm worried. You should be, too."

"So what do we do, pick another barn to sleep in?"

Jason told his brother to hide out of view. Whit, cursing, slumped in his seat.

Jason headed south, away from the motel. After thirty minutes without seeing cops, he pulled to a stop in front of a foreclosure sign. It sat at the edge of a long, untended yard on the other side of which was a secluded farmhouse. He could barely make out its silhouette in the night, so he pulled into the drive and let the headlights bring it out. White paint was flaking from the front of the building. No lamps were on, and all the windows were shut despite the heat. No other structures were in view.

"Looks vacant," Jason said.

"It better be. Or an angry farmer's going to come out with a shotgun thinking we're here to repossess."

They had made such a mistake once before, a couple of months ago, so Jason cautiously scanned the property as he inched up the drive, looking for signs of habitation. He didn't see any as he stopped in front of a small barn. Whit, stretching his neck after hiding so long beneath the dash, got out of the car, leaving the Thompson on his seat but holding his right hand in his jacket. He opened the barn door, stuck his head in, then emerged to give his brother a thumbs-up. Jason parked in the barn and they took out their briefcases of money and weapons, shutting the door.

Jason shined a flashlight into the kitchen, seeing enough dust and cobwebs to make him conclude, "We're safe."

They broke in easily, the place moldy and dank. The electricity was off, as was the water. The previous owners had employed newspapers as wallpaper in the first-floor hallway and in some of the rooms. Summer humidity had caused the ink on many of the pages to blur and run, rendering photographs ghostlike. Faces like skulls stared eyelessly at Jason. He found himself reading some headlines and was startled by the words "Firefly Brothers" in one of them, smudged but legible. He followed Whit into a small room whose window afforded a view of the road. Jason watched it for a solid minute and saw not a single vehicle pass—even by day it probably saw little traffic.

"Okay," Whit said. "Now what?"

Jason rested one of the Thompsons on a small table and lowered the satchel of guns to the floor beside it. There was nothing to sit on, so he leaned against the wall, too bothered to realize he was getting ink on his new suit. Whit had placed two lanterns on the floor and the light was orange and flickering, the flames refracted through the dirty glass.

"I just need to think," Jason said.

Whit paced the room and took another snort from his flask. Apparently he had decided that if he wouldn't be celebrating with Veronica tonight, he'd still do some goddamn celebrating. It grated on Jason to see Whit making himself sloppy.

Jason was motionless as he thought about what had happened. He tried to tell himself that it had been Chance, or maybe Owney, who had ratted them out to the cops. *Please,* he thought, *let it have been one of those two.* But he knew in his heart it was neither of them. He still felt sick, and when Whit proposed finding a telephone to call the girls' motel he snapped.

"Could you just give me a minute to think? Do I always have to do the thinking for this family? Jesus. I have to cover the angles and keep you out of trouble all at once. Could I at least have some quiet to figure this out?"

"That's out of line."

The elder brother sighed and leaned his palms onto the table, staring at the floor.

"I've pulled my weight, Jason. Don't take it out on me just because things aren't going right."

"You're supposed to be keeping your eye on the road."

Whit bent down to take another Thompson out of the satchel. Then he walked back to the windows, using the gun barrel to part the curtains.

The ceiling creaked. They both looked at it, but then relaxed, figuring it was just an old floor's sigh. They hadn't actually checked the upstairs, but surely no one was there.

After a long pause, Whit spoke in a quieter tone. "There's something I've been meaning to ask you."

"Go ahead."

Whit paused. "How come you never told Darcy about Pop?"

"Never told her what about Pop?"

"About him doing time. About him being in prison when he died."

"Who says I didn't?"

"I mentioned it to her in Fond du Lac and it was the first she'd heard of it. We both thought that was kind of strange."

Jason felt both perplexed and annoyed that Whit was bringing this up. "We never happened upon the subject."

"How could you not?"

"I guess I'm not inclined to wear every past injury like a badge of honor the way you do."

"It's almost like you were trying to hide something."

"Maybe I was. Can we leave it at that?"

Whit was watching him coolly, and Jason could feel his every word and gesture being analyzed.

"No, we can't. Every time Pop comes up, you get this way. You got so damned angry when I mentioned him to that journalist. For a while I couldn't understand why, but now I think I get it."

"Get what?"

Whit smiled emptily, then looked out the dark window. "You like to say most of the stories about us aren't true. Okay, maybe so. I can vouch for a lot of them being wrong. And then there's a few about you that I assume are lies, too, but sometimes I get to wondering." Eyes back to Jason. "You've heard the story about you and Garrett Jones, right?"

Jason was still leaning forward, but now he gripped the table tightly. "What are you getting at?"

Whit waited a beat. "Did you do it, Jason? Did Pop get pinned for something *you* did?"

Jason raised himself to his full height. "Thinking's never been your strong suit, but I want you to think very, very hard about what you're—"

"I've been thinking about it for *weeks*." Whit stepped forward. "I didn't want to admit it, but your story never quite added up, and *that's* why the jury convicted. I guess I was too much the little brother, following after you and wagging my tail like an idiot. Wasting all my energy blaming the wrong people for what happened."

"Well, congratulations, Whit. You're half right. You half figured something out. Because, yes, something about that story didn't add up, and yes, Jones wasn't a suicide like you always hoped he was—he was a murder. Cold-blooded murder."

They stared at each other, motionless.

"You can't blame me or anyone else for what Pop did," Jason said. "Because I was there. I was at home, sitting in the dining room, eating some pie, when he walked in all covered in blood."

Whit looked so helpless in that one instant, Jason almost wanted to hug him. What was it like to go through life with such illusions? Jason was tired of the effort he'd expended to help Whit believe in them, setting up all those mirrors and conjuring the smoke. It was amazing what people could believe.

"You're lying," Whit said.

"I'm the one who told him to take off his clothes and give them to me so I could burn them at the dump. I'm the one who made up the alibi for him and told him what to say. Pop was just stunned. I've never seen anything like it. And after all we've done together, Whit, I've still never seen anything like it."

Pop's clothes had been wet with the stuff, soaked through to his undershirt. The hair on his arms. Jason had coaxed him into the shower—all this without waking anyone—then had taken Pop's clothes and gloves. At least he'd been wearing gloves. But he didn't have the gun. Where was the gun? Pop said he'd left it there. Where, on the desk, on the floor? Could it look like a suicide? How close had he been standing? Had anyone else been at Jones's house? The gun wasn't registered, was it? Jason's experience at averting disasters on his bootlegging routes lent him a strange calmness. Only later, alone in his car, would he break down at the enormity of it all. Pop, though, was a man sliced in half, his sentences dropping in pieces, disjointed verbs and nouns and long stretches of silence, or sobbing. He had only partial answers, fragments of memories. He'd been standing close to Jones, he said. The gun might be on the desk, but maybe the stairs. No one else had been home. It had been quiet. No, the gun was on the desk, definitely. Pop reeked of booze.

"You're lying," Whit said again. His eyes were wet.

"I wish I was. It's so much easier, believe me."

Jason had stuffed Pop's clothes into a bag. Then he saw that his own hands had become streaked with blood, so he washed them in the kitchen sink, dried them on a dishrag. There was blood on the rag now, too, and some on his own shirt, a new one. And so he had added them to the bag of things to be burned.

Pop's car was filthy—blood on the steering wheel and the gearshift, blood even on the seat. Had he really shot Jones only once? Jason cleaned the car as quickly and quietly as he could, cursing the fact that Pop's garage was full of junk and he had to do this in the driveway. Then he had driven to the dump with matches and some gasoline.

"He never had the heart to tell you all the truth. I assumed he would eventually, and I think he might have, but he didn't realize how little time he had. So then I figured it wasn't my place to do it, just let Whit and Wes and Ma think what they want. But now I'm realizing I was wrong."

Whit was pacing again, the Thompson heavy in his arms. He was like a wildcat carrying something dead and trying to figure out where to stash it. "You can't—"

"He was guilty as sin, Whit. I guess you can still blame the bank for putting him in that position, sure, or blame his other partners, or blame dead Garrett Jones for pushing Pop till he snapped. Blame them all. I'm just tired of lying about the rest of it."

After the disposal and the cleanup he had driven through Lincoln City for hours, thinking, too distraught to go back home. Even if the gun couldn't be traced to Pop, the fact that there were no prints on it would only rule out suicide—surely Garrett Jones would have left his own prints on the gun he'd supposedly killed himself with. It would still look like murder. And had Pop left any bloody marks while exiting the crime scene? Maybe Jason could sneak into the Joneses' house, wrap the dead man's fingers around the gun handle, clean up any mess? But Mrs. Jones would have discovered him by now, surely. Maybe Jason should try anyway. He circled Lincoln City for hours, even driving to the Joneses' neighborhood, but that was as close as he came. He would always wonder what would have happened if he'd tried.

Instead, he crawled into his old bed, tried to sleep, and rose early, when he heard his shell-shocked father doing the same. They bought the *Sun* and memorized the results and highlights of the boxing matches they had supposedly attended.

Jason would leave town that afternoon. He never got around to telling Pop his reason for coming home that night, his intention to help out at the store again. Now he just needed to get away.

Pop would go to work that morning one last time, and eat supper at home with his family one last time, and go to bed, and be arrested in the middle of the night. One week later, Jason would lose his cool while some Indiana cops shook him down, and he would wind up with an assault rap added to a bootlegging charge the cops never would have been able to prove otherwise. The only time he would ever see Pop again was while taking the stand to perjure himself at Pop's trial.

"*No!*" Whit said, still refusing to accept it. "Pop would never have—"

"Why is this so hard for you to believe? Don't tell me that in all this time you didn't at least think it might be true. He was out of his head with worry and panic and he got drunk on top of it, and there you go. Jesus, Whit, *you've* pulled the trigger on enough people. Why can't you see that Pop did it once, too?"

"Because he was different! He was . . . better than us!"

"No, he goddamn wasn't. He was not better."

"Don't talk that way!"

Jason tried very hard to stay calm. "Fine, he was a saint. He was a saint who got pushed too far. I tried to save him on the stand, but it didn't work. He was past saving."

"Don't say that!" The light glinted off Whit's wet eyes.

"He made stupid mistakes with his money and his partners, and then he made the biggest possible mistake. Clarence Darrow couldn't have saved him in that courthouse. All he had was me—"

"Shut up!"

"And I guess I wasn't enough. I'm goddamn tired of you and Wes thinking I wasn't enough. He made his grave, Whit, and that's why he's lying in it."

"Don't talk about him that way!"

"It's the only way I know him! I used to be glad I was the one who saw it, so you and Ma and Wes wouldn't have to, but now I wish everyone had been awake when he walked in! I wish everyone could have seen how—"

"Stop it!"

Light and sound, and Jason was thrown back into the wall. He was standing, but not really standing. It was more like gravity had turned sideways, pinning him against the wall as his brother loomed above him, the Thompson smoking in Whit's arms. Beyond Whit in the dark window, headlights appeared and vanished. Jason tried to say something or breathe, but he couldn't. Then gravity began returning to its senses and his body slowly slumped downward.

"Oh, Jesus," Whit whispered.

Jason coughed and his mouth was warm and wet.

Whit took a step forward, his eyes large, terrified, the Thompson nearly falling from his hands as if it had tripled in weight. Jason was sitting up against the wall now, blood not seeping from his chest but pumping out of it, spigots full, a flood. He couldn't form words and he could barely think, but his right hand moved so fluidly, so naturally, as if his mental powers had been transferred there and now his hand was in charge. It was powerful and angry. It had been unfairly attacked so many times, but now in the worst imaginable way. And so it reached into his jacket and pulled out his gun and fired a single, perfect shot.

The bodies lay there and the lanterns flickered from the force of their falls, but they soon calmed in the still air. The blood ran without sound, the pools mixing on the wood floor. Fingers of smoke crept along the ceiling, blindly searching for some way to escape.

———

"I'm not sure what to say," Whit told him as they sat on opposite ends of the bed at the cottage in Missouri. It was two weeks after that awful night, two weeks of madness and death and resurrection. "Other than I'm sorry."

"Yeah. I'm sorry, too."

"For what?"

Jason tried to talk but his throat seized up on itself, as if rejecting what he was trying to say. Or as if overwhelmed by how true it was. "For everything."

He wondered if he would always carry this pain at how his family had suffered, no matter how much he tried to ignore it, or even if now he dared to confront it. Maybe if he hadn't run with bootleggers, he would have been home to hold the family together. He hated this guilt that he didn't think he deserved, yet he felt it tremendously. It is so hard to absolve yourself when you're surrounded by the sordid evidence. Pop in jail and then dead, Ma bereft of almost everything she'd ever had, Whit turned into a spiteful killer, Weston's betrayal. The people they'd murdered. The people *he'd* murdered. He liked to blame all the dead on Whit, on Brickbat, on Owney; he liked to say the papers always got it wrong when they said Jason Fireson had gunned down another man. But the papers weren't as wrong as he wanted them to be. Jesus, how many had he killed? He didn't even remember anymore. He thought of all these things that might not have been, but were. When such terrible events so encircle you that they're all you can see—you are the center, and this is what you have wrought—how can you not blame yourself? By trying to run away, or hide, or by making yourself into something new.

"I guess I didn't handle the news very well that night," Whit confessed.

"I didn't deliver it very well, either."

We believe there are things that are possible and things that are not, actions we can imagine doing and others that are beyond the pale. But then doors are swung and what once was impossible, unthinkable, is there before us, happening to us. Sometimes we throw open the doors ourselves, sometimes someone else pushes them open and points at what lies beyond. Sometimes we don't even want to look. But we never have a choice.

Was it Pop's murder of Jones that had made Jason and Whit's robbing and killing possible? Or was it Jason's early crimes and lawlessness that had made Pop's violence possible? Who had swung that door open? How had this all happened?

"He wasn't as bad as you think," Whit said. "He wasn't a failure. You can't reduce him to one night, or even to the last few months."

Jason sat there, remembering.

"He worked every day of his life for us," Whit continued. "What happened wasn't right or fair, but it also isn't right for you to . . . reduce him the way you do. I know you hate him for making you feel shame about who you are—"

"I never said that."

"—but you need to remember everything. Not one night or a few months. Not the end, but everything in the middle."

Jason nodded. "You're probably right."

"And just because . . . he made mistakes, or he was a hypocrite, that doesn't doom us to the same thing. It doesn't mean you have to hate him for it, or run away from him. It doesn't mean that's all we are."

"Yeah. But we've made plenty of our own mistakes, haven't we?"

They sat there for a while. Then Whit pulled the bandage from his forehead, the gauze tape slurping as it lost its hold. "Is it still there?"

"Yeah. Looks a little smaller now, but it's still pretty ugly. Guess that means I can't let Darcy see my back yet."

"I had to leave my T-shirt on with Veronica the other night, too. Felt strange."

They both laughed, which, of the many things they could have done at that moment, seemed the least painful.

Jason stood to leave. He had never wanted his life to be reduced to a story, to be summed up that way, but apparently it had happened: he and his brother were trapped in their own ghost tale, haunting each other for their unspeakable crime.

Whit asked Jason if he thought this would keep happening, or if maybe this was the last time. How much longer would they haunt each other like this. Or would they both vanish, to each other and to the world, the moment they forgave each other, the moment they released themselves from the anger of their shared past, the moment Jason walked out of the room.

"I really don't know. I guess I could stay in here awhile longer, just in case."

"Yeah. Maybe you should."

Jason sat at the foot of the bed again. They talked about Pop and their childhood, growing up, when the world was so normal but so full of wonder. They sat there and breathed their past—their family, their selves—back to life.

XXXIV.

Darcy woke alone the next morning, shaking from a nightmare.
In her dream, too, she had woken alone, but she had heard the shower running. So she had walked through the hallway of the cabin, which in the dream felt more like a honeymoon suite. She had thought to herself that perhaps she and Jason should call a justice of the peace to make it official, and had laughed at the thought, at how impossible it was.

Still dreaming, she had slipped inside the bathroom where he was showering, warm mist enveloping her. The shower curtain was an opaque white, so Jason couldn't see her as she slipped out of her dress and kicked off her underwear. She had gently pulled at the far edge of the curtain, just enough to lean her head in and get a good look at Jason before pouncing. He had been facing away, his head beneath the spigot. She had always loved that backside and marveled at his powerful calves, but her eyes were drawn elsewhere.

His back was covered in welts. Not really welts, as those would have been three-dimensional and these were the opposite: ghastly concavities in that precious flesh. Her first instinct was not pity but a revulsion she could neither suppress nor deny. These were no mere wounds.

Finally, Jason had noticed the draft and turned around. Her eyes inspected his unblemished chest and legs and the rest of him, but then she finally saw his eyes, which were wide with surprise and with what she figured—for she'd never seen it there before—was guilt.

"Sweetness." He had sounded calm, almost apologetic. His eyes were red, as if he'd been crying.

"Jason, what . . . what happened?"

"I had a vest on, Darcy." He had looked so absurd trying to explain. "I got hit, but they didn't go deep. I know they look pretty bad, but they're just flesh wounds."

She had backed away. The sight of her wounded lover was again covered by the curtain, a flimsy death shroud. Then he had turned off the water and yanked the curtain open, snatching a towel and wrapping it around his waist.

"Darcy, I'm fine, really."

Water beaded on his clavicle and ran down his chest. The scrapes on his cheeks and forehead were less noticeable now with his face red from the heat.

And then she had woken up.

In the same bedroom now, the same loneliness. Where was Jason? He'd woken earlier than she, perhaps. Or had he ever been here at all? Fragments of the dream echoed in her head. She heard a sort of fuzziness— was that the shower running, or only the memory of sound from her nightmare? She needed air.

She could almost hear the Voice clearing his throat.

She hurriedly put her dress on and walked into the hallway, her mind reeling, and stopped at the small dining table. A stack of napkins sat beside some car keys, which she picked up. Get outside, walk, breathe a bit. *It will all make sense then,* she wanted to tell herself. But hadn't he warned her that it wouldn't?

Outside, the grass was wet with humidity, dirt sticking to her bare soles as she staggered to the Ford. She put the keys in the ignition and pulled away from the cottage, unsure where she was going, knowing only that it needed to be *away,* that she needed to be alone. This last day and a half had been so divine, hadn't it? To not be alone. But she hadn't really been alone before, either—there had always been others. Maybe she only needed some air and a country road and, God, perhaps a drink.

She was mad. This couldn't be happening.

She navigated the labyrinth of cottages, and after pulling onto the road she noticed all the autos pulled over in the far-side ditch. Some of them police cars, others dark sedans. Reality had begun to register when three men strode into the middle of the road, only a few feet before her. Their left hands clasped badges at their breasts and their right hands were held high.

She stopped the car. Another man was walking up to her open window. She could smell honeysuckle from the trees drooping around her, and on the man's breath jerky and cigarettes.

"Darcy Windham? We'd like you to step out of the car, please. Keep those pretty hands where we can see them."

Since landing in St. Louis, Cary and the other agents had dispersed across a dozen locations each time a new discovery revealed itself, demanding analysis, the taking of notes and photographs, the lifting of prints and the moving of more bodies. At least three so far: Brickbat Sanders, at long last; Chet Wasserman, an underworld physician who had been living in North St. Louis under an assumed name; and an old Iowan judge who had disappeared days ago after nearly being lynched outside his courthouse by a mob of angry farmers. The judge had died in Wasserman's squalid basement, of a crushed skull. The other two bodies had been shot at close range, and someone had sunk half of a shattered window into Sanders's left forearm. The local police had received a tip from a neighbor who'd heard a shot late at night. Cut ropes beside wooden chairs indicated that two people had been held captive there. The house was rife with prints, so the Bureau would have answers soon enough.

Cary had little direct experience with corpses and had hung in the back while the city cops did their guesswork as to what, exactly, had transpired. Sanders had a recently treated shoulder injury and apparently had sought the doctor's aid, but something had gone wrong. And how was the judge involved?

Word out of Chicago was that Jasper Windham had finally confessed to hiring Sanders (the muscle) and Elton Roberts (the brains) to kidnap his daughter. But he claimed to have nothing to do with the Firesons, and he said his daughter wasn't in on it. No one could figure why he would implicate himself but lie to protect the two outlaws, who clearly were involved. Maybe Windham was scared of them—everyone seemed to be either scared of the Firefly Brothers or in awe of them.

The aggrieved police chief in Sedalia, meanwhile, had checked in to say that the other bodies from the farmhouse shootout were still dead and were smelling very bad indeed.

And then came the kind of rare tip the Bureau always hoped for. It was routed to Cary, sitting in the Bureau's St. Louis field office after leaving the local police to their chemistry kits in Wasserman's basement. He found himself speaking to the manager of a tourist camp in the riverside town of Ferris, Missouri. The manager said a suspicious character had shown up at his establishment very late on the night of the Firesons' last known appearance. A man who might have been Jason had paid for three nights and had requested the most remote cabin. This man had since been seen running errands in town with an attractive young brunette. There had been a second man in the car that first night, but he hadn't shown himself since.

The information was no more striking than the hundreds of other useless tips that had washed in. The manager had sounded sincere, but so did most people who were wrong. To be professional, Cary had asked him for the number of the town's pharmacist before thanking him and hanging up. Remembering reports of the previous day's fiery wreck, Cary dialed the number and asked if by any chance someone had purchased burn ointment that day. Why yes, he was told. The purchaser—a tourist, no doubt—had worn his sunglasses inside the pharmacy, which the old druggist found rather uppity. People around here aren't like that.

It was probably nothing. Still, Cary called the cabin manager back and told him to keep watch but not to do anything. Then he contacted the Ferris police and found a car.

Again Darcy was surrounded by men who knew her but whom she did not know. First it had been goons on a Chicago sidewalk ferrying her into a car, and now it was police on a wooded street hurrying her out of one. So at least there was a certain symmetry. At least madness had a sense of humor.

Hands again on her forearms, circulation cut off once more. No blindfold this time, unless you counted the morning sun piercing its way through the woods. She demanded explanations and was told they were police officers, or federal agents, or Pinkertons. Then arguments broke out, various parties insisting on primacy here, jurisdictional disputes. She told the man on her right to release her arms unless he wanted to be walking funny the rest of the week.

An authoritative voice told someone named Buzz to obey the lady. Her arms were freed and she was able to employ a hand as a visor against the sun's glare. She saw a tall, thick, bald man stride up to her. He had a long nose and looked like some hairless anteater, the cigar in his mouth an extension of his tongue.

"Miss Windham, I'm Special Agent Guy Norris with the Department of Justice. Are the Firefly Brothers in that cottage?"

"The Firefly Brothers?" She tried to laugh. Or she laughed without trying to. Which had it been? Moments skipped by, her mind fixated on what she'd seen in the shower. But hadn't that been a dream? "The Firefly Brothers are dead."

He smiled, a man patiently enduring the repetition of a joke he hadn't found funny the first time.

"We haven't frisked her yet, boss," one of the cops said.

"She's fine." Norris's hands were fists on his hips. "You do look awfully good for a lady who's supposedly been kidnapped. Maybe someone should kidnap my wife sometime. I can't wait to hear your story, but first there's some things I need to know, like who else, if anyone, is in there with them."

More than a dozen men had materialized. Some were uniformed officers and others wore plain suits. She had never seen so many guns at one time, which was saying a lot. Behind the row of parked cars were two green trucks containing God knew what kind of freight. Heels tapped on the asphalt and birds called confused responses to the clicking and snapping of magazines.

She turned and saw that other men were stationed behind some of the cottages, heavily armed. The last cottage was out of view from here, but its thick woods doubtless concealed more invaders.

"Your long ride is over, Miss Windham. Your father's fessed up and your pals in there are surrounded. Why don't you just tell me who else is in that cabin before the local police drive you off to their nice jail."

"No one's in there. No one." Her own voice sounded foreign, a recording played back at the wrong speed. "I'm alone."

"I'm sure. We're all just wasting our time out here, aren't we?"

"I haven't done anything wrong." She finally regained control of her facial muscles and pulled their strings like the expert she was. "I was *kidnapped*, for God's sake, and I escaped and I needed some time alone to get my head right and thank *God* you're here, it's been so terrible and—"

"Then I guess there's no reason we can't shoot up the building, just to be on the safe side." Darcy Windham was capable of eliciting male sympathy from even the most heartless of sadists, but Norris only seemed entertained. "Look around you, miss. They've made some great escapes before, but not today. Either you tell me the truth, and there's a chance we can get them out of there alive, or you can keep acting, and I'll have no choice but to protect my men by blowing that cottage sky-high."

"I'm telling you the truth. The Firefly Brothers are dead."

He watched her for a moment. Then he turned to one of the men at his side. "Delaney, cuff her and put her in your car. If she has a change of heart, let me know."

With cuffs he had borrowed that very morning, Cary shackled Darcy Windham's wrists and guided her to his car. She looked as if she had just woken up, her hair a mess and her face unpainted, but still she was the most beautiful woman he'd ever touched. Her eyes were large from sleep, fogged almost, but he found himself staring at them so long that when she broke from her spell and looked back at him he dropped his glance as if scolded.

His hand on her shoulder, he guided her into the back of the Ford, then closed the door. The windows were down and he stood beside the car, keeping her in sight but trying not to stare.

"There are so many of you. It seems rather an overreaction, wouldn't you say?"

"I don't think I would say that, Miss Windham. Your friends are dangerous men."

"I've heard." She sounded as if she were in a trance. Maybe she was always like this, carefully parceling herself in small amounts, aware of her power.

"I'm sure they've shown you a different side, miss. I know they have a way of winning over the people around them. But they aren't so kind to the people who get in their way."

"They're two men. You have dozens. And so many guns."

He'd heard the criticism before—that the Bureau was inflating the threat of bank robbers to justify an increase in government power, that Hoover was nothing but a PR man puffing up the exploits of a few country thieves, all the better to frighten a cowering nation into handing a big stick and a blank check to its self-appointed protectors.

Its sleep-deprived protectors. Cary and Gunnison had been the first ones here, just after sunset. They had shown the manager their best photos of Jason and Darcy, and the old man swore they were the couple staying in cottage No. 12. Local cops canvassed shops in the town's tiny business district, and a number of store owners had looked at the photos and nodded, marveling at the enormity of what they had missed. More agents soon arrived, and by ten o'clock Norris had even phoned Mr. Hoover in Washington to receive marching orders.

As silently as they could, the agents and cops had emptied the other cottages, one by one. Some of the agents had wanted to storm the Firesons' cottage immediately, but Norris had held off. The Bureau had received plenty of flack for the perceived recklessness of the Dillinger shooting, which had taken place in a crowd. Mr. Hoover wanted the Firesons dead, yes, but he wanted a perfectly executed execution—a spectacle, but a reassuring one. After civilians from the other cabins were quietly removed to safety, Norris had mapped out his strategy and assigned positions, and Cary wondered whether he should have felt insulted or relieved that he was not one of the men Norris wanted to surround the cottage.

Eventually the birds had awoken, and the sky had brightened, and fears began to spread that locals or the press would learn about the stakeout if this took much longer. But Norris was patient. Just another hour, he had advised, and the time was nearly up when the cottage door opened and out came a very flustered Darcy Windham.

"Miss Windham, I know a lot of the men out there holding those guns," Cary said. "I'd rather not see them get shot today just because your friends want to be dramatic about this. Why don't you tell me exactly who's in there and what kind of weapons they have, and we can end this peacefully?"

All she did was smile and echo the word, "Dramatic."

"I've spoken to their mother, you know. I've spoken to their brother. I know how much they mean to the people who love them. We don't need this to get out of hand. Maybe we could even let you use the bullhorn and talk them into surrendering."

He dared to look at her again and this time when her eyes focused on his he didn't break the stare.

"They're dead," she said. "They're not really in there."

"We know you aren't alone."

"Fine. They are in there. But they're dead. It doesn't matter."

"It doesn't matter to you?"

"That's not what I mean."

He had read about her, had imagined the type of woman she might be. This was not who he had expected, this coldness, so detached.

"If you don't help us, they're going to die. For real this time."

Something in her turned, and it was as if she were there for the first time. Then she laughed, freely and happily. Like she had just figured something out. Or like she was completely mad.

She was so loud about it that other agents were giving Cary looks. He opened her door and hastily rolled up the window, then closed it. She was still laughing in there. He drummed the hot roof of the car with the fingers of his left hand. Jason Fireson had been a lucky man, for a while at least.

Darcy leaned forward and held her head in her hands. The young agent asked through the window if she was all right, but she didn't answer. She was tired of him. She was tired of *this,* whatever this was. She had never been one for routine, of course, but she craved her bed in Chicago right then. Her memories, at least the few good ones. She wanted to hide in those memories, wrap their warmth around herself.

The agent tried to talk to her again, but she ignored him. Later she heard a man's voice over a bullhorn. He was calling out to Jason and Whit, telling them that they had Darcy, ordering them to come out. She pressed her fingers into her ears, but the voice was too loud.

There were always voices that you didn't want to hear.

We will have no choice but to use deadly force.

Did you really believe they could be alive? After all I've tried to explain to you?

Come out with your hands up.

You're as bad as the rest of them. Clinging to the impossible, drunk on belief and faith. Staggering with it. Time to stagger home, or to what's left of it. You leave us no choice.

And then gunfire. She ducked, even though surely they had put her someplace safe. She had to be safe, didn't she? Was she ever safe? Gunshots upon gunshots, exponentially increasing as if each time a gun fired it was replaced by five larger weapons. Now it wasn't gunshots but explosions, fists rapping on her skull. She couldn't push her fingers into her ears deeply enough. She felt the concussions on her chest, her stomach. She tried to press her fingers in through her ears, press on her brain and tell it to stop working, press on her heart to make it stop beating. The car was shaking, the roof rattling above. She could feel the shuddering beneath her damp feet, the dirt crumbling from her toes.

It stopped.

The silence was so wonderful, but then so frightening. Slowly she had the courage to pull her fingers out. She heard voices. Men were running. She looked out the window and the young agent was many feet away, his back to her. A plume of smoke curled in the air like a finger beckoning her forward. She reached with her cuffed hands—she'd grown quite accustomed to maneuvering her hands while bound, and the agent had foolishly cuffed them in front of her—and opened the door. She took a few steps until she was nearly beside the agent. She could see where the cottage was supposed to be but wasn't. There was, instead, only a heap of rubble—wood and plaster and dust and dirt rising up and falling again—several snapped branches, and a downed tree. In the midst of it all, the shower inexplicably stood intact. She could hear men talking about guns; she heard the word *grenades*. Why was the shower still there? Did its tiles look wet?

Agent Delaney turned, finally seeming to notice her.

"I'm sorry, Miss Windham. They're dead."

Men with long guns cradled in their arms were hesitantly walking into the rubble, kicking at the largest pieces and turning them over. Archaeologists of the present, sifting through the many layers of now.

"I tried to tell you," she said. Holding herself with shaking arms. "But no one would believe me."

I often think of that morning, when I seemed as close as I would come to solving so many mysteries that instead would elude my grasp. Like that beautiful, haunted woman, who was standing right beside me but might as well have been in another world.

They never even let me get close to the rubble. As a member of the now disgraced Fireson Squad, I was one of the many agents whom Norris viewed as scrub brush that needed to be cleared away. Other agents were given the task of looking through the wreckage and making sense of the brothers' recent movements—if there really had been any—while I was sent back to Chicago and assigned casework on various New Deal frauds. The white-collar nature of that suited me just fine, at first, but as time passed I began to wonder about what I might have missed that morning. Had the brothers even been in the cabin, or had I been a pawn in an elaborate ruse? Had they really managed to escape death so many times only to reach their final end that day? Why had we blown up the building without knowing exactly who was inside?

The Bureau's secrecy surrounding the event only intrigued me further. Most of us weren't allowed to view the reports of that morning or the reports detailing the strange days between the Points North "shootout" and the final detonations. Fingerprint records from the Points North and Sedalia incidents vanished, as did the coroner's report from Points North. Even memos I myself had written were now classified, like a dangerous part of my personality that was sequestered from the rest of me. Mr. Hoover wanted everything stage-managed for public consumption: the federal apprehension, the inescapable ambush, the victorious government, the thankful people. But the Bureau refused to offer many details about what exactly the Firesons had done during those intervening two weeks, and even Mr. Hoover's subsequent book about the War on Crime was vague on the Firesons' final days, dedicating more ink to simpler tales like the shooting of Pretty Boy Floyd or the ambush of the Barker Gang. Still, rumors persisted. When the brothers were buried after their much delayed funeral, what exactly was put in those coffins? According to what little information I was able to get out of Norris's foot soldiers, all that was left of the Firefly Brothers were a few shards of bone and scraps of charred clothing, but those remnants could well have been squirrel parts and bedsheets for all anyone knew. So what was in those coffins? The fragment of a hip bone, the sole of a shoe? Or nothing but broken glass and crumbled brick, mortar, and ash?

Even after the very well-publicized burial, people continued to see the Firesons in various cities, at state fairs and traveling carnivals, in bank heists and lesser crimes, in subway cars, in speeding Packards, in storm clouds. But no one could produce evidence confirming such visions, so they were ignored by the Bureau and even the newspapers, both of which had moved on to the hunt for Baby Face Nelson. Either the Firefly Brothers did, indeed, blow up that morning or, if they escaped somehow, they went on to lead quiet, lawful lives.

I know we can't rise from the dead, yet sometimes I wonder if I was surrounded by exactly such an event without wanting to admit it. The very stories that I had earlier dismissed soon began to make sense to me, albeit a sense that could have rung true only during the strange crucible of those times. After many years had passed and I'd moved on to a position at a Chicago law firm, I called Chief Mackinaw again, chatted with some of his men. I sweet-talked the Bureau's Chicago field-office secretary into showing me confidential files. I made the mistake of calling Weston Fireson, but he hung up as soon as I said my name.

I let myself wonder if the impossible could have occurred, and why. I tried to think of the Firefly Brothers the way their legions of loyal fans had, but still I couldn't see it.

Finally, I tried to see the brothers the way they themselves did. Then I understood.

I still wonder about Darcy. Her disappearance was equally mysterious, not to mention illegal, as she skipped bail days after that morning by the Mississippi. I let my imagination run with her sometimes, because she seemed haunted by something I was unable to understand. Imagination. We tell ourselves to ignore it when times are tough, when we need to focus, concentrate on the facts. But facts make only so much sense on their own, when they're laid bare, like little corpses, with nothing to animate them.

XXXV.

Thousands had come for the funeral, but Darcy was not among them. She was out of jail by then, so imprisonment was not her reason for missing it. With what little money she could gain access to she had hired a lawyer, careful to choose one who was not a friend of her old man's. The authorities had quite a case against her father, yes, but little in the way of evidence against Darcy. Regardless of Mr. Windham's sinister machinations, the kidnapping had been quite real to *her*, and the prosecutor's attempts to make her seem complicit in it—or in the deaths of the various kidnappers at the farmhouse, or even in the deaths of Brickbat Sanders and the doctor and the judge—were flimsy indeed. At the hearing she had done her part to look the poor, distraught victim, and, despite the prosecutor's accusations, the judge was swayed by her performance. The charge of conspiracy to commit insurance fraud was dropped, the accessory-to-murder charges were expunged, and she was released, on bail, to await trial for aiding and abetting multiple bank robberies.

Dozens of photos had been snapped as she walked out of the courthouse and ducked into the stylish Windham Windster commanded by her father's faithful, distraught old driver. The codger just didn't know what to do with himself now that his employer was behind bars, so he had offered his services to Darcy. He had dutifully driven her back to her apartment, and she had smiled and shaken his hand afterward, then told him to park the Windster on the street, give her the keys, and take the streetcar home. She told him he would never see her again.

Her three days in jail had been awful, though no worse than being in her kidnappers' lair. At least she hadn't been blindfolded. They had kept her apart from the rabble, as she was considered something of a celebrity villain. A *gun moll*, a term she'd never understood. *Larger than life*, she'd heard someone say. What can be larger than life? Death, or is that smaller? People do tend to become larger in death, their finer qualities extending outward like an endlessly serialized tale, their flaws and foibles forgotten, their stories continually retold. *Larger than death.* She thought about that and smiled, here, late at night, in a graveyard.

Breaking in hadn't been nearly as difficult as she'd expected. If there was a night watchman, he wasn't on duty, or he had been watching something else when she'd steered the Windster into the cemetery. The two men she'd hired for the job had been silent all along, but their silence became almost reverential as she steered them through that land of the dead. She had no map but her memory to guide her—she had cased it earlier that day. The papers claimed that thousands had visited the brothers' graves, and the worn paths and trampled grass were evidence enough. The funeral had been in a local church, and the viewing—closed casket, of course—had lasted an entire day. The burial had been conducted in privacy, family only—she had been touched to receive an invitation from Mrs. Fireson, and had felt terrible about declining, making up some excuse about being prohibited from crossing state lines—but in the days since, the brothers' grave had been well visited. She had wanted to come sooner but had waited until no more reporters or private dicks were skulking outside her door.

Here she was, with these two young men she'd found on a street corner, broad shoulders and long arms and a willingness to take on a job regardless of how macabre it sounded. They with their shovels and she with her flashlight, and the earth was still fresh—surely this wouldn't take long. She saw the men's expressions in the light of the full moon, wordlessly asking if she was sure before they began. She was quite sure. They began.

They were large men—she had chosen wisely—and of course they might have considered simply *taking* her money. Here they were in a dark graveyard, no one around to save the damsel, at least not yet. But she knew enough of male desperation and low mores and therefore had allowed them to glimpse, during their short drive, the gun barrel poking out of her skirt. She was an employer, not a victim, and the men would act accordingly.

She had waited for him to contact her again. There was much she didn't understand, but she was trying. Would there be another coded telegram from the great beyond? Or would he show up at her door unannounced, or nearly drive into her one night? How would it be this time? Because surely this madness—whatever this madness was—could not end this way.

Then she had remembered one of the last conversations she'd had with him, the strange promise he'd extracted from her. And here she was.

The shovels seemed to whisper with each plunge. It was taking longer than she had hoped, but she told herself to be patient. She had waited this long. She had not been able to keep her promise to Jason—she hadn't understood it at the time—but she would make good tonight.

In the distance she could see stove fires lighting the southern hills of Lincoln City, the Hooverville that Whit and Veronica had once called home. To the west the office towers were dark, no one working on this late night. The tire factories weren't operating, either, yet she could smell the melting rubber, that burned-chemical odor she always found so noxious when she visited, leaving her bewildered as to how anyone could actually live here. A smell Jason and Whit had known for so long they claimed not to notice it; it was a part of themselves.

She had read a snide editorial commenting on the lunacy of a burial without bodies. The grenades had decimated the brothers' persons as well as their hideout, the columnist noted. What had been buried was not a pair of bodies—which no longer existed, he argued, and may he rot in hell for being so flippant about it—but misguided hopes for a sad and broken people.

So much death, and so contagious. She'd read that old Marriner Skelty had been found in a rented house in Gary, Indiana. One of the rooms he had turned into a makeshift laboratory, cluttered with vials and jars of bizarre solutions and notebooks filled with indecipherable chemical equations. He had consumed a number of these potions, as well as an entire bottle of whiskey. Suicide or an accident, the authorities weren't sure. And only two days later Owney and Bea Davis, chased by police in the woods of northern Michigan, had lost control of their car while crossing a bridge, plummeting to their doom. At least Veronica had disappeared with her son, as she had done so many times before.

"Miss," one of the men said. *Resurrection men,* that was the other term for grave robbers. A far more poetic description. She darted toward him, close enough to see how sweaty he and his partner had become. She could smell the rich loamy earth exhaling beneath them. He reached down with his shovel and gently tapped it on something.

"Clear it off, clear it off!"

She had told them to start with Jason's, of course. Whit would understand, though likely he would hold a grudge.

The two men looked at each other, as if afraid to continue, but she ordered them again and they set to their task. They threw dirt in both directions to clear the top of the casket. She grew impatient—hurry!—and wanted to yell for her lover, but she was afraid it would only tease him, as she didn't know how much longer this might take. More shoveling and the men grunted, and Lord only knew what they would say the next morning or whom they would tell, but, for God's sake, they were taking too long! Darcy fell to her knees and crawled into the gaping hole, reaching forward, tearing at the soil with her bare hands. Dirt beneath her nails, grit tearing the pads of her fingers, but she was so close, and breathing so fast, and the two resurrection men had backed off now, as if amazed, or frightened. And what was that sound? Again and again, a pounding. She tore and grasped at this earth that dared get in her way, and though she may have been hearing only the frantic beating of her heart, it sounded—could it be?—like barely muted fists inside a coffin, a plea to the heavens, a wish for the impossible.

ACKNOWLEDGMENTS

Anyone wishing to learn more about the real-life bank robbers of the Great Depression should read Bryan Burrough's definitive history, *Public Enemies: America's Greatest Crime Wave and the Birth of the FBI, 1933–34.* Also helpful to the author were *Pretty Boy* by Michael Wallis, *The Dillinger Days* by John Toland, *Hard Times* by Studs Terkel, *The Hungry Years* by T. H. Watkins, *The Case That Never Dies: The Lindbergh Kidnapping* by Lloyd C. Gardner, *Public Enemies: America's Criminal Past, 1919–1940,* by William Helmer with Rick Mattix, and *Daily Life in the United States, 1920–1940,* by David E. Kyvig. For a list of other works the author found inspiring during the research and writing of this book, please go to www.thomasmullen.net.

A tip of the fedora to my agent, Susan Golomb; my editors, Jennifer Hershey and Laura Ford; and everyone else at Random House for their hard work. Big thanks to Lloyd Gardner for his fine historical eye. A two-Tommy-gun salute goes to my family, and a wink and a smile to Jenny.

THOMAS MULLEN was born in 1974, raised in Rhode Island, and graduated from Oberlin College. His first novel, *The Last Town on Earth*, was named Best Debut Novel of 2006 by *USA Today*, was a *Chicago Tribune* Best Book of the Year, a *New York Times* Editor's Choice, and was awarded the James Fenimore Cooper Prize for excellence in historical fiction. He lives in Atlanta with his wife and son.

ABOUT THE TYPE

This book was set in Minion, a 1990 Adobe Originals typeface by Robert Slimbach. Minion is inspired by classical, Old Style typefaces of the late Renaissance, a period of elegant, beautiful, and highly readable type designs. Created primarily for text setting, Minion combines the aesthetic and functional qualities that make text type highly readable with the versatility of digital technology.